Robert Anton W  hea, of the *ILLUMINATU* ghized as a New Age classic. In addition, he is the author of more than fifteen other books, including *Sex and Drugs*, *The Schrodinger's Cat Trilogy*, and *Cosmic Trigger: The Final Secret of the Illuminati*. He is a former *Playboy* editor, a philosopher, and a well-known iconoclast.

The truth about the *Illuminatus!* trilogy:

"The ultimate conspiracy book, . . . the biggest sci-fi-cult novel to come along since *Dune* . . . hilariously raunchy!"
—*The Village Voice*

"An epic fantasy . . . a devilishly funny work . . . shimmers with illusion and paradox that provide delight after magical delight . . . a farcical black tragicomedy that turns out to have been written by you and me . . . it strips away illusion."
—John White, *New Age Journal*

"Funny, savagely sarcastic, definitely anarchistic . . . a marvelous amount of fact and inspired fiction . . . one of the most dizzying tales I've come across in years . . . !"
—Fred Pooj, *Limit*

"Devilish . . . I loved it!"
—Greil Marcus, *Rolling Stone*

Books by Robert Anton Wilson:

THE BOOK OF THE BREAST
COSMIC TRIGGER: THE FINAL SECRET OF THE
ILLUMINATI
THE EARTH WILL SHAKE: Volume I, the *Historical
Illuminatus Chronicles*
THE ILLUMINATI PAPERS
THE ILLUMINATUS! TRILOGY (with Robert J. Shea)
   The Eye in the Pyramid
   The Golden Apple
   Leviathan
MASKS OF THE ILLUMINATI
NEUROPOLITICS (with Timothy Leary and George
Koopman)
PLAYBOY'S BOOK OF FORBIDDEN WORDS
PROMETHEUS RISING
RIGHT WHERE YOU ARE SITTING NOW
SEX AND DRUGS: A JOURNEY BEYOND LIMITS
THE SCHRODINGER'S CAT TRILOGY
   The Universe Next Door
   The Trick Top Hat
   The Homing Pigeons

Forthcoming:
THE WIDOW'S SON: Volume II of the *Historical
Illuminatus Chronicles*

THE HISTORICAL
ILLUMINATUS
CHRONICLES · VOLUME I

THE EARTH
WILL SHAKE
ROBERT ANTON WILSON

LYNX BOOKS
New York

ILLUMINATUS VOLUME 1: THE EARTH WILL SHAKE

ISBN: 1-55802-176-0

First Printing/August 1984
Lynx Edition/July 1988

Published by special arrangement with Angel Entertainment,
Inc. and Bluejay Books, Inc. Previously published by Bluejay
Books, Inc.

This book is published by Lynx Books, a division of Lynx
Communications, Inc., 41 Madison Avenue, New York, New
York, 10010. The name "Lynx" together with the logotype
consisting of a stylized head of a lynx is a trademark of Lynx
Communications, Inc.

Printed in the United States of America

0 9 8 7 6 5 4 3 2 1

CONTENTS

THE HISTORICAL
ILLUMINATUS
CHRONICLES VOLUME I

THE EARTH
WILL SHAKE

PART ONE

THE FOOL

During their stay in France the [Jacobites] had been deeply involved in the dissemination of Freemasonry. [They] established more direct connections between Freemasonry and the various activities—alchemy, Cabalism, and Hermetic thought, for instance—that were regarded as Rosicrucian.

Michael Baigent, Richard Leigh, and Henry Lincoln, *Holy Blood, Holy Grail*

What strikes the stranger most about Naples is the common occurrence of assassination.

Johann Wolfgang von Goethe, *Letters from Italy*, 1792

Sigismundo Celine was lost in a dark forest with a Red Indian, seeking the supreme *wakan*. At the same time, with another part of his mind, he was very aware of everything going on around him in the Cathedral of San Francesco di Paola on this Easter Sunday morning.

The trick about getting up early for Mass, Uncle Pietro always said, was to enter into deep meditation, total empty-headedness, so that the mystery of the Sacrament could wash over you gently, but not to get so relaxed that the people in the adjoining pews could hear you snore.

In that deep passivity, Sigismundo was watching the priest prepare for the Holy Communion and still listening to the Indian talking about the *wakan* (whatever that was) and not letting his head sink forward to indicate he was half-dreaming and almost noticing the four strangers in black who were approaching the Malatesta pew.

"*For this is my Body,*" the priest intoned solemnly, in Latin.

The Latin was similar to the Italian that everybody spoke, and yet it wasn't Italian; but Italian had once been Latin. Somewhere back in time, maybe six or seven hundred years ago, Neapolitans had been speaking something that was half Latin and half Italian, an in-between language.

"*And this is my Blood . . .*"

Did they know, back then, that they were speaking a halfway language? And now that the bread and wine were the Body and Blood of Christ—the *Mystical Presence*—Sigismundo found himself wondering about the exact point in time, the instant *t* in the calculus, when it was half bread and half Christ the way language was once half Latin and half Italian, and then he saw that the four strangers had taken daggers out of their cloaks and were moving in much faster.

He, the boy Sigismundo, came fully awake thinking it was like one of the overly-detailed frescoes of Filippo Lippi: too much rapid action, too many moving characters, too much color and violence for the mind to comprehend. For the four dark men were all stabbing Uncle Leonardo Malatesta at once, and above them in perspective was the priest in his gold and blue robe, and there was he, Sigismundo Celine, off to the right corner of the Malatesta pew because the Celine pew was too crowded, and there in the new center of everybody's attention was Uncle Leonardo looking pop-eyed (like a cuckold in a *commedia*, the boy thought) as if he himself could not believe what was happening as the strangers plunged their daggers into his belly again and again.

And Aunt Gina was falling on top of Sigismundo, the prettiest woman in Napoli everybody said, screaming with red blood splotching her blue skirts. Then it all seemed to whirl around him for a moment—language changing from Latin to Italian, half-dream becoming awful reality, wheat changing into bread, bread changing into Christ, wheat then becoming flesh, the symbolic sacrifice of Christ becoming the real *handwritten top margin:* at what shame is there in seeing murder as ignoble and base? MURDER IS DISGUSTING; we have a more noble protagonist who feels 'retchèd' even is HE ADMIRES LOWER VALUES IN HIS NAIVETE

right margin: violence messiness anonymity sacriledge

sacrifice of Uncle Leonardo. He even thought in shame that he was about to retch, because the blood was on him now, too, and the priest had been calling for God's blood, the Sacrament had become a Devil's Sabbat, and instead of doing anything he was frozen, thinking that Father Ratti at school had explained that the bread was still Christ even if it fell to the floor and was covered with dust and dirt and muck (and blood? he wondered). Because all physical appearance was *accident* and the spiritual *essence* remained the same, it was still God, whatever the physicality of the *accident*. You had to understand those terms to pass the final examination in Religious Knowledge. So, in his vertigo, he thought crazily: We have come here to eat flesh and drink blood.

right vertical margin: AS COWARDLY AS THE ASSASSINS. POINT OF VIEW) — (THE SEMI-OMNISC. ACT, THE NARRATING PESCRIBES THEM IN TONES OF ATTITUDE OF ADMIRA-

But then he knew he would not retch. *I am a Celine and even a Malatesta.*

handwritten: Hide your humanity, your sympathy; do you now appear more, or less human? Are you now more or less human?

But everybody and his brother and a few of their cousins seemed to be pushing and running now, some trying to flee and some attempting to get to the scene of the atrocity, to help Uncle Leonardo; and the priest was still standing as if frozen, looking back over his shoulder absurdly (almost like a man who suspects a hole in the seat of his breeches), the Host high above his head, the Mystical Presence of God looking down on the way men butcher men in this year of Our Lord 1764. And there *he* was, the boy Sigismundo, trying to rise, trying to push past Mama and Aunt Gina to help Uncle Leonardo, but still seeing it as a fresco, a scene painted by Lippi or Angelico, unchanging, like the arrow in Zeno's paradox, not able to move—whispering, "I am not a coward," although nobody was listening to him, seeking perhaps to explain to himself why he was immobilized.

right margin: last rites! He is seeing it over & over comes by his humanity

And then the murderers retreated all at once, the four of them, like a staged tableau in an opera by Vivaldi, four swarthy

bottom handwritten: left w/ assassination being merely murder w/ no transcendant justification or purpose

Southerners in plain black wool moving outward toward the four corners of the church and leaving Uncle Leonardo suddenly alone in the gold-embroidered brocade of the Malatestas—even more like a painting: their black against his bright colors—and he was able to move then, Sigismundo, leaping the pew to charge at the nearest assassin and immediately getting a good grip on the weapon arm, the arm that could kill, trying to swing the swine around to land a punch in his face and surprised at how easy it was, the *Siciliano* spinning lightly, quickly, almost like a child's top, just the way Giancarlo Tennone, Master of Fencing, said a man should spin if you exerted a push and a pull in that way. But then it was not what the boy had planned because before he could land a punch he felt the stinging and the wetness and knew he had been stabbed himself. It was impossible: he was holding the dirty hound's dagger arm. And he was still trying to understand, still holding the dagger arm, when he felt the second stinging slash and realized the *Siciliano* had caught him with the oldest trick in the book: the filthy foul dog's get had a second dagger in his left hand, God curse him and plague the town he was born in.

And as he lost his grip, not knowing if he was slashed on an artery, the boy Sigismundo stared directly into the eyes of the assassin (eyes with a strange glint of violet swimming in the black) and saw that which he could not, would not, believe.

The *Siciliano* did not want to kill him.

No, more: the assassin (who was a youth, only a few years older than Sigismundo himself) was determined and *resolved* not to kill him, as if he had sworn it on his mother's grave at a full moon and perhaps even spit over his shoulder. Sigismundo was being preserved for something else. You could read that much in a man's eyes sometimes, Uncle Pietro claimed. It was the witch power, and it came to everybody, not just to *strege*, at special moments of excitement. If you were open to it, Uncle

Pietro said, it would tell you what your opponent in a fight was going to do next.

But then Sigismundo stumbled, the whole church spinning weirdly for a moment, because he was nauseated by so much of his own blood spurting from his arm, like life itself leaving him in a visible crimson rush, and the assassin tore loose and fled.

Sigismundo thought: They train them young in Sicily; and then: His face was familiar, but damn my eyes if I know where I ever saw him before; and then he allowed himself to think a wry joke: God Almighty, in the morning, maybe he allows himself only one murder on an Easter Sunday; it may be his kind of piety. Maybe he abstains from deflowering virgins on San Gennaro's feast day and doesn't rob the blind and halt during Lent.

Because being spared by such a creature—a fully trained professional killer—was like opening a door in your own house and finding yourself in Baghdad or Cathay. It was a violation of nature. The only explanation of such a monstrosity was grisly to contemplate: it could be that old, vicious Sicilian game, like sticking a dagger into your pillow at night, right next to your throat. The message was that you had been spared this time but you had to find out what they wanted or you would not be spared the next time.

But maybe he was letting his imagination run away with him. The assassin was young; maybe he, curse his violet eyes, just had a moment of panic. Or maybe "Cyrano" Maldonado (the only one who could be behind this) had paid for only one murder. Assassination must be like any other profession, Sigismundo thought: you don't get rich giving two for the price of one.

"Oh, my God, I detest all my sins," Uncle Leonardo was saying, gagging on his own blood, trying to make an Act of Contrition, but then he was falling at last, his eyes shiny and jewellike and empty, and then he hit the floor with a crash that made the boy realize what the phrase *dead weight* means.

There seemed to be blood everywhere, on everything. Sigismundo dry retched once and then started tearing his sleeve to make a tourniquet for his arm. He had always thought men died nobly, making heroic speeches. This had been as glorious and operatic as the time Sigismundo saw the cook pulling out the intestines as she cleaned a chicken.

But then what happened next was just ordinary life again, with time moving in a regular and normal manner without those jumps and freezes, and maybe he was still a little dizzy even though the slashes on his arm seemed superficial. And Uncle Pietro had taken command of everything, just as he always did: Sigismundo's father, Guido Celine, was sputtering and shouting, without anybody paying attention, while Pietro spoke quietly and firmly. At such times, Sigismundo knew, everybody did what Uncle Pietro expected, simply because he, Pietro Malatesta, could not imagine (or would not allow himself even to suspect) that anyone would have the brazen, unmitigated stupidity to contradict his orders.

So there he was, the boy Sigismundo Celine (who was the most brilliant young musician in all Italy since Antonio Vivaldi, in the estimation of the only two people whose opinions mattered, himself and Uncle Pietro), having learned in only a few minutes that people do not die in real life the way they do in operas, and it was off across the Via di Roma to the barber-surgeon's for him, Uncle Pietro dragging him as fast as they both could trot, and a trail of blood dripping from his arm behind them because the tourniquet was not properly made and was now starting to flap loose, sounding like a bat's wings in a dark room.

And then the church bells started, clanging from one end of Napoli to the other: communion services were over everywhere, except in San Francesco di Paola, where they were probably still mopping up the blood. They are commemorating the Resurrection, Sigismundo thought; they are not doing it to mock our grief. I must not let myself think the chimes are the sounds of a thousand demons pounding on the anvils of Hell to celebrate this latest atrocity against God and Man.

He was unable to believe, still, that the assassins (even if Sicilians and thus, by definition, children of the Devil) had actually struck at the very moment the Sacrament was being consecrated, when the Mystical Presence of Christ was entering the church, and on a high holy day when everybody was attending Mass to thank God for ending the recent typhus epidemic. It was as if they wanted to show Christ, to His very face, that they despised religion itself as well as human life—as if they were demons incarnate.

Dante put the murderers in different *bolge*, depending on the horribleness of the crime. At the very bottom of Hell, *Caina attende*, were those who treacherously killed their friends or relatives. There should be a deeper pit, Sigismundo thought, for those who kill in church on Easter, to mock the mercy of God.

But it was a surprise to learn that he was a hero already, the legend having preceded him across the Via di Roma to Portinari's shop here on Via Cristoforo Colombo, where all the boys in Napoli, it seemed, had gathered to watch in awe as the fresh bandage was professionally applied. They were all trying to tell each other what he had done and were asking him for more details, one beardless and pimply face shouting to be heard over another (Uncle Pietro and the barber-surgeon being the only adults there) and all so excited they could not even wait for the answers to their own questions and did not notice that Sigismundo was trying to ask a question of his own, until finally he had to roar above all of them to be heard:

"Did the fatherless ones get away?"

And when he received the bitter answer that he already

expected, he guarded his face very closely, because Uncle Pietro was there and he knew, although he had had the white sticky evidence of his manhood for over a year now, that he was still a boy to the family. A boy; a noisy nuisance; slightly better than a girl, of course, but not to be trusted with grown-up men's business.

"Professionals?" the barber-surgeon, Signor Portinari, who had lost two children to the typhus, asked.

"The one this young idiot wrestled with had another dagger in his left hand," Uncle Pietro replied, cold as a herring, holding it all in.

"Ah," Signor Portinari said. He repeated significantly, as if he had not expected it: "Professionals." He was always a bit slow and had about a half inch more forehead than a gorilla. Then he asked, abruptly tightening the bandage painfully, "*Siciliani?*"

"They looked it," Uncle Pietro said.

"Ah," old Portinari said thoughtfully, like a mathematician solving an equation. "Professionals."

And Sigismundo knew—everybody in Napoli knew—what *Siciliani professionals* meant. Uncle Pietro had said many times it was a known fact that the *Siciliani* were the oldest and most intractable people on earth, older than the Roman Empire and the Caesars, older even than the Etruscans or Minoans, so old that their ways and ideas were incomprehensible to anyone but the Devil himself. If a *Siciliano* was determined enough—everybody believed it—he would kill you even if it meant his own death, which was a species of honor Neapolitans could understand, but the mad Sicilians went further, much further: they would kill you if their whole family had to die for it, or their whole town, or even Sicily itself. It was as if, Uncle Pietro said, they had decided, knowing they were a minority on the earth, that the only way to survive was not to care about survival, to be so crazy-mean that nobody would challenge them—like the bee, Uncle Pietro said, who will die in order to sting you, just to be sure nobody ever lost respect for the testicles of bees.

That was why the Neapolitans had a joke that there were four kinds of sons of you-knows: the ordinary, everyday son of a you-know who was mean only if you came between him and his profits, and the revolving son of a you-know who was always a son of a you-know no matter when you encountered him, and the son of a you-know on wheels who devoured ordinary and revolving sons of you-knows for breakfast and chewed up a consecreated bishop for lunch, and finally the transcendental Sicilian son of a you-know who was like the Platonic ideal toward which all other sons of you-knows could only aspire. If you want to prove your bravery, Uncle Pietro said often, try taking food from a feeding tiger or kick a lion in the testes, but don't, if you want your grandchildren's grandchildren's second cousin's gardener to walk the streets without looking over his shoulder all the time, don't, for Jesus' sake, get into a feud with the fornicating *Siciliani*.

Because Sicily itself and every last Sicilian could be wiped off the face of the earth, extinguished, erased, and every Sicilian would agree to it, stubborn as a mule, if it were necessary to go that far just to make sure nobody anywhere ever lost respect for the Sicilians. Uncle Pietro said that a master swindler could cheat an Armenian rug merchant once in a million times, and a demon from Hell might frighten a Spaniard once in a million million times, but not even God Himself with the Twelve Apostles to help him could stop a fully resolved *Siciliano* without first killing him and then methodically killing his brothers, and then his cousins and uncles, and next his second cousins and great-uncles, and of course his women cousins, and any toddling infant old enough to throw a rock, and so on forever, but until God Himself killed the last Sicilian great-great-grandfather still able to totter weakly on his crutches and hawk to spit, they would keep coming against Him, ineluctable as He Himself, because that was the way Sicily had survived the Greeks and the Sullas and Belisarius and the Normans and the Hohenstaufens and everybody and everything thrown against them and Southern Italy in general since time itself began.

Nobody in Napoli ever lost respect for the Sicilians, and nobody in Roma either: even the pope, Uncle Pietro said, prayed every night that he hadn't inadvertently offended a Sicilian. Some claimed that people were afraid of Sicilians even as far away as Rimini or Firenze or even in Spain where the divine Scarlatti had gone, or far away over the Alps in Bavaria where the women were all you-knows and the men were heretics and wizards.

So it was back across Napoli, the bay gleaming like silver and tin and ruddy copper in the morning sun—the bay that people from Venezia and even England came thousands of miles to gawk pop-eyed at and, having gawked and popped their eyes, went home to tell their envious neighbors what a lucky thing it was to be a Neapolitan, Uncle Pietro said—and across the Palazzo Reale and past the splendid golden Teatro San Carlo where he, (the boy Sigismundo) had received the part of his education that mattered most, having encountered there Vivaldi and Jommelli and Pergolese (although it was on his own that he had discovered Scarlatti and Telemann). It, the golden *teatro*, was the only good thing that fat Bourbon hog Don Carlos had ever done for Napoli, Uncle Pietro once said—in a *very* low voice, of course—but what could you expect of a hell-spawned half-French Spaniard except that he would give the Neapolitans a golden wedding cake of an opera house named after his patron saint no less, to advertise his good taste to all posterity, and then bugger the Neapolitans every way a conniving half-Spanish Frenchman could think of?

The arm was hurting now, with sharp little throbs of pain like an aching tooth beginning to abscess.

"Those fatherless ones as you called them, and where does a boy your age learn such language," Uncle Pietro was chattering, ignoring the *teatro*, trying to shake off his own furies, "those *motherless and* fatherless things, those sons of poxy half-a-lira whores by goats and hounds and *Barbary apes*, to be precise, those bastards in black who murdered my brother, damn them to Hell fire for a million eternities, are probably out of Napoli by now. Real professionals, as old Portinari was saying, and very well trained, may their wives abort and their mothers go blind, and it might be a proud family tradition: their grandfather's grandfathers could have done similar work for the Borgias."

"But why—"

"Why?" Pietro stopped in his tracks on the street and glared at the boy. "What else is Napoli or for that matter Portici or Resina or this whole lower peninsula famous for if not for the high quality and superabundant quantity of our professional belly-stabbers and widow-makers? We are the ornament and envy and *ne plus ultra* of the world, lad. Let infidel Turks brag of their riches and hareems, or the French of their dramatists and philosophers; we have the most accomplished knife artists here. That we should live in this madhouse of Napoli and call ourselves men, it is, you see, Siggy, a joke. Human beings. God's own image. Rational animals, Aristotle says. Rational . . ."

And then he was weeping, Uncle Pietro, the most crafty and (some said) coldest man in Naples, weeping unashamedly on the public street.

"I teased him," he said, leaning on the boy's shoulder. "When we were children, I teased him, the little shrimp, and I bullied him. God forgive me, God forgive us all, we are such perfect fools," his whole body shaken with spasms for a moment.

"*Uncle*," the boy said, embarrassed and frightened.

"I know, I *know*. But it is all a joke, you see," Pietro Malatesta protested, more to God perhaps than to the boy. "That when the typhus goes away and all seems safe again, murder falls on us like a thunderbolt from the skies. An hour ago he was just one of my brothers, not the smartest one at all, the very last one in fact that I would trust with important financial matters, and then they kill him and I realize what I always should have honored in him—that he was the kindest of us, the best Christian! The best husband, the best father, the best man! I was too busy making money to notice little things like that. We are all *too busy*! Jesus, Jesus, *Jesus*!"

And then Pietro Malatesta was walking erect again, his face calm and closed once more except for dark suffering eyes, those Malatesta eyes that people said were like a falcon's: so cold that their cleverness was frightening, so clever that their coldness was itself a warning.

And when they got home everybody was there, all the Celines and Malatestas in Napoli, and Aunt Gina kept crying and crying. The men were talking very quietly to each other, always lowering their voices still further when Sigismundo came near, or any of the other children either, so it was obvious. He was, at fourteen, still a boy; they would not include him in on it. He would have to start a separate, private vendetta.

But what was insufferable was that not once, all through the afternoon of mourning and whispering and on into twilight, did anybody mention the name, until he wanted to shout it, scream it in their ears: Count Maldonado. "Cyrano" Maldonado, with his huge dork of a nose in every plot ever hatched against the Malatestas as far back as anyone could remember.

(But later, after his own attempt at assassination, Sigismundo was to think: It was the music, always the music. Because if he pursued a vision of the heroic, an eidolon of human perfectibility that was to seem insane to some and eventually farcical even to himself, it had been the music that had maddened and inflamed him—the music that was produced by human beings, by men who were not in all cases admirable or noble people at all, produced many times by men who were as petulant and prancing as a French *contessa*'s spoiled poodles, but still, in the music, there was that voice, that insistent cadence of something that was not human, something toward which humans only aspire and to which they only approximate, as any circle drawn with chalk approximates to a true Platonic circle, as every soul aspires toward God, as all sons of you-knows seek to attain the brilliant, blinding perfection of a Sicilian son of a you-know.)

So he, Sigismundo Celine, had an appointment with Count Maldonado, or anyway with the first spaniel-nosed Maldonado he met. Because it was *moira*, as the Greeks said: a destiny predestined, a knot woven by the Fates, all of the past coming together in one vortex, just like the morning over a year ago when he woke to discover the warm white evidence of his manhood, alive and sticky on the bed sheets (and he had been afraid at first that Mama would think he had done you-know with his hand, which was one of the most terrible sins); and now, another step toward manhood had occurred during the malign *pavane* in San Francesco di Paola—the Mystical Presence, not of Christ alone, but of Death also.

And he had failed. They could all treat him like a hero, but he knew he had been an oaf. He had been fencing for three years now, learning every *riposte*, feeling the knowledge sink below his mind into his muscles to function automatically, he was now at the top of the class. But that had all been a boy's playing, not adult reality: at his first real challenge, he had lost his wits, behaved as a boy against a man, easily fooled—and easily killed if the Sicilian had not had some mysterious reason to spare him.

He had been clownish and lamebrained. Giancarlo Tennone would have been blisteringly sarcastic if he had performed that way in class. Tennone called that kind of thing being a *brave fool* and repeated continually, like his own Pater Noster, "The brave fools die first." Tennone was a blond Northerner, from Milano originally, and knew more about fencing than the Devil's grandmother knew about you-knowing. He had taught in Firenze and Roma and even Paris before coming to Napoli to soothe his old bones in the Neapolitan sun.

As sunset came finally, they sent the children to their rooms. Sigismundo stood at his window, watching the sky turn tangerine and soft cinnamon, composing a variation on a Vivaldi theme in his head, making it come out the way the great, the ingenious Telemann might have done it, even though Aunt Gina was still bawling in the living room. He was perfectly serene, working on the music. He knew exactly what he was going to do.

He heard Uncle Antonio's voice: "I keep remembering when we were boys. He was afraid of the crocodiles in Africa that somebody told him about. Mama had to keep telling him the crocodiles never swim across the Mediterranean to Napoli."

"God forgive me," Uncle Pietro said. "I used to tease him, saying I heard crocodiles coming up the stairs in the dark . . ."

Sigismundo remembered his own fears as a child and thought how horrible it would be to lie in bed in the darkness and listen for slithering reptiles at the door.

When twilight turned to night, he lit a candle next to his bed and began writing down his new melody, adding more harmonics. He did not want to play the *clavicembalo* now; that would be sacrilege. But the tune had begun to take on forms so intricate that he had to capture it before it escaped: it was like *moira*, Fate, knitting and cackling, knitting and cackling, as She moved a million lives in a pattern none of them could see. With a crossover of the hands, the sonata would sound more like Scarlatti after the variation on the third bar, having it all planned: where he would do it, when he would do it, how he would do it. They would have to consider him a grown-up then, with the blood red on his dagger, the blood of the Maldonado dogs.

"God has a reason for everything," he heard his father's voice downstairs.

"Sometimes I don't believe in God." That was Aunt Gina, still hysterical.

"Gina! Not even at a time like this. The walls have ears." That was Uncle Pietro. He always called the Dominicans *dominicanis* when they were out of earshot: dogs of God. A very clever knot in language, and it was true that the Dominicans were houndlike. Everybody in Napoli was afraid of those wolf-eyed bureaucrats of the Holy Inquisition.

But you could say things in music that were knotted even more amusingly than saying *domini-canis*. In counterpoint you could say A and *not-A* and *both-A-and-not-A* all at once, making a monkey of Aristotle and interweaving the jokes so that nobody but another musician could understand them but everybody would be entertained without knowing why the sound was so merry and yet as inevitable as the multiplication table.

If I die tomorrow, he thought, I will never write the music I alone can hear. I will go to Heaven and people will never say Celine and Scarlatti and Vivaldi. They won't even say Scarlatti and Vivaldi and Celine. If they say Celine at all it will be to refer to the family's wine business.

"At last he was free of the damnable books of Romance."

The sentence drifted up from the abyss of memory, and then he saw Uncle Pietro's face laughing, laughing helplessly until tears shone in his eyes, and he remembered the whole scene then. It was years ago, when he was only nine, and Pietro had been coaching him in French and Spanish; they were working on the great *Don Quixote* by the wonderful Cervantes. It was a very sad scene, but that sentence seemed unbearably hilarious to Uncle Pietro, laughing and laughing the way Sigismundo had laughed the time he and some other boys had tied a cat to the bell rope in the cathedral and the clanging and meowing and howling had awakened the whole town. So Sigismundo asked nervously, "What is so funny there, then?" Don Quixote was brokenhearted, disillusioned, in despair.

And Uncle Pietro said, "You would have to be my age to understand."

Which was the kind of answer adults gave to nine-year-olds too often, especially if you tried to get any detailed information about you-know, and the reason Uncle Pietro was his favorite uncle was because he didn't talk to Sigismundo that way usually. And even on that occasion, sensing the boy's immediate resentment, Pietro added quickly, "I'm sorry. There are some jokes you cannot understand until you have been a fool many, many years and thought yourself finally cured and then found out that you had just become a different kind of fool."

And so, as he slipped between the covers and blew out the candle, Sigismundo wondered why Uncle Pietro, who was generally considered tricky enough to be able to steal Machiavelli's underwear without taking his blouse and breeches off, should consider himself a different kind of fool. And then he began to see Uncle Pietro much thinner and much taller, so that he looked like Don Quixote in the illustrations, and then Sancho Panza came in, but he didn't look like the illustrations at all, in fact there was something dark and teratological about him, and then Sigismundo realized it was not Sancho Panza at all but the violet-eyed assassin in the church. And then, no matter where he went, from house to house and from door to door, nobody was home, all Napoli seemed to have gone away, and as he trudged through the streets and alleys looking for help, the violet-eyed assassin was always behind him, never very close but never very far away either. And then he was in the villa of the damnable Count Maldonado and Maria was in the bathtub, stark naked, and he wanted to lean over and see her you-know, God forgive him, but a windmill came between them, concealing her, and then the assassin came in and it started all over again: going from house to house and nobody home, Napoli empty except for him and his inexorable pursuer. So he tried to hide in the Teatro San Carlo, but the musicians were all crocodiles and they came slithering and waddling toward him, mouths agape. And it was in the darkest middle of the night as he sat up in bed, coming out of the nightmare, but still possessed by the child's mind within him, wondering if there were crocodiles hiding in the corners.

"Our Father who art in heaven," he prayed, "hallowed be thy name. Thy kingdom come . . ."

He finished the prayer and followed it with an Ave Maria, and then his fears were gone.

He went down the backstairs to the jakes, ordering himself not to think about the crocodiles. As he urinated, he suddenly remembered a day perhaps a year and a half ago. Uncle Leonardo had arrived in the market just after the weekly entertainment—a discussion about whose sister was or was not a you-know—and he naturally asked what the excitement had been. "Just another murder," Sigismundo had answered. And Uncle Leonardo had stared at him in a melancholy way, repeating, " 'Just another murder.' My God, boy, is that what Napoli does to us? Twelve years old and you say, 'Just another murder.' At least say a prayer for the poor dead bastard, whoever he was."

And now Uncle Leonardo was the latest victim, the latest poor dead you-know. Things were not like that in the North. They had criminals and murderers too—every place did; that was the result of Original Sin, Father Ratti said—but no other kingdom could show a record of what Uncle Pietro called unneighborly use of cutting implements like that of the territory between Napoli and Sicily. For the first time in his life, Sigismundo wondered why it was like that. We have the greatest musicians and the best climate and Uncle Pietro who has been everywhere says nobody laughs as much as Neapolitans; why do we have so many assassins also?

Going back up the stairs he resolutely did not allow any of the lurking shadows to look like a scurrying crocodile. You could control your imagination, even if you were the temperamental, artistic one in the family. Even if it was dead midnight, when (they said) graves opened and Things walked that really should have crawled and witches rode in the skies. Even if some shadows did look suspiciously like crocodiles.

As he got back under the covers he began to hear his new sonata inside his head but just like it would sound on a real *clavicembalo*. He would meet his challenge tomorrow, as a man, fearlessly. Gradually the *clavicembalo* music became more complex, more Scarlatti-brilliant—he wasn't writing it anymore—and then he was in the Vatican with a gigantic chicken and then Scarlatti himself came in and Sigismundo had to go with the Red Indian again to find the golden waters of the *wakan* and they met crocodiles everywhere they turned in the dark forest . . .

And then he was awake again, the sun high on the horizon above the bedroom window, half-hidden by blushing clouds.

He thought for a moment that all the horrors had been one long nightmare—Uncle Leonardo being killed and trips to America to hunt crocodiles and assassins trailing him through Napoli—but now he was awake and it was all over.

His arm hurt. He really had been stabbed. Uncle Leonardo's death was not part of the dream.

He sat up and contemplated the challenge ahead. He would do it, execute the vendetta personally, and they would all have to treat him like a grown-up after that.

But after he dressed and went to the garden—where the Celines always had breakfast on sunny days—Mama's face shocked him. This is what grief looks like, he thought; there is nothing noble about it at all, it is merely ugly and pitiful. Because Mama was only thirty-three, but now she looked at least fifty or even older. He thought of the disease of the heart, which kills so many who have had sudden bereavements, and he prayed to God that it would not kill Mama.

Death is like the tides and seasons, Uncle Pietro once said: there is an inevitability about it, a regularity, that is almost a consolation. We may not like winter or old age, but we know they come to everybody, saints and sinners, noble Malatestas and raggedy peasants, just as the clock goes from noon to midnight for all people. But murder is not like that at all, Sigismundo thought bitterly: it's like being struck by lightning, by God's personal vindictiveness. Worse, for the survivors. Why pick on one of our family? they must ask. Does God have some special grudge against us? It is, Sigismundo thought, as if we of all the world have been selected to solve a dark riddle: we have to comprehend why, when a priest calls for God to enter the church, Death can come in answer.

Sigismundo said good morning to everybody without looking at anybody, embarrassed by his own pity and a guilt he could not understand.

All the Celine children were somber; even little Guido, at the age of four, understood enough to be subdued. Beatrice, at eight, was almost as haggard as Mama; probably, Sigismundo thought, Beatrice is just discovering that it isn't just old men like Grandpapa who die, that she herself might die at any time.

Bianca, at six, merely looked confused; if Uncle Leonardo is in heaven, she was probably thinking, why are the grown-ups so unhappy?

They silently ate figs and hard black bread dipped in olive oil and hot sausages. Papa Guido softened his bread in wine instead of olive oil, but that was not allowed to the children.

Sigismundo thought of his cousin Antonio, Uncle Leonardo's son. Antonio was considered, like Sigismundo himself, "sensitive," although not artistic; he was always mooning around, thinking very private thoughts. It was impossible to imagine what Antonio was feeling this morning. If it were Papa Guido instead of Uncle Leonardo, Sigismundo thought, what would my mind be like now? It was not something you could imagine, because what he was feeling now he could not have imagined before the assassination.

Papa Guido finally tried to break the mood of anguish that hung over the table. "Well," he said, "at least the weather is still bright and sunny." Mama looked at him as if he were feeble-minded, and he looked guilty again.

Sigismundo wished Uncle Pietro were there. Pietro always knew how to change the mood in a room, usually without the others even realizing he was doing it. Papa Guido said that "Pietro the Peddlar," as he called him, could pee on your boots and convince you it was rain. But Pietro was having breakfast with his own family, Aunt Violetta and their two daughters, high up the hill on Via Capodimonte, where the Malatestas had lived for more than a century. Uncle Pietro said it was good to live up there, because it gave you perspective: if you could see a whole city below you every time you looked out a window, you would become a philosopher because you would eventually realize that every time you laughed and celebrated somebody else was alone and weeping, and every time you wept somebody was dancing and getting drunk, and every time you passed wind some gentle nun was singing a hymn, and it all balanced out somehow.

Sigismundo looked at Mama again, then looked away quickly, guilty that he could not cure her pain. What was it the Southerners said? "Christ never got south of Eboli." They meant there was no mercy down there in the hot sun, with the cruelest landlords in the world. But the way we carry on around here, Sigismundo thought, you might as well say He never got south of Roma. No wonder Nero, the King of all Monsters, took his holidays here. We are his kind of people.

And then breakfast was finally over and Sigismundo was free to get his dagger from the closet and head for the market.

The streets that carried him downhill twisted continually, so that he was walking toward the bay one minute and away from it the next. They had been built that way to create a gentle slope for the ox carts, he knew; people must have figured that out when this was a Greek city—twenty-five centuries ago, when it was *neo-polis*, "new city," and the famous mermaid had just washed ashore, indicating good luck. Never trust a mermaid, Uncle Pietro said: we've had little but bad luck since then.

And then, as Sigismundo descended, past Via di Sapienzia and Via Tribunali, as he approached his rendezvous with the Maldonados, he kept thinking of the *Inferno* of Dante: down, down, down, twisting and turning, deeper and deeper into the heart of Hell. Via di Roma at last. There was the circle of the fornicators, blown about by endless winds (and Uncle Pietro said Napoli could supply that *bolgia* indefinitely, if the rest of the world turned celibate), and the circle of the Makers of War, with their heads torn off, and the circle of the violent against art (which reminded him of the Dominicans, hounds of God, always fuming and fulminating against some painter or writer), and the circle of the usurers, buried in you-know, and the heretics who were buried upside down, and the suicides who were turned into trees . . . but the farther down he went, the more he thought of the circles of the treacherous and homicidal. Still, he knew he was justified. He was doing this for Uncle Leonardo.

Sigismundo often wondered how he could describe the Neapolitan market to someone who had never seen it. It wasn't just the colors, so many and so vivid; there were the *improvvisatore*, the strolling musicians and acrobats, the endless clumping hooves of asses and oxen, the incessant whine of the beggars—one-third of the entire population of Napoli, Uncle Pietro precisely estimated—and the painted you-knows, almost as numerous as the oxen. Ten florin you-knows, young and beautiful; five florin you-knows, not so young anymore; even five lire you-knows, popularly known as "alley cats." Whores, Sigismundo thought angrily. They're called whores. If I'm going to murder a man, it's silly to worry about bad language.

The colors of the banners above every shop and stall—every merchant trying to catch your eye even before you were close enough for him to catch your ear—seemed brighter and more brilliant than ever. That's because of my excitement, Sigismundo thought; perhaps my pupils have dilated. Because the banners were like jewels: ruby red, emerald green, stripes of blood red and angelic white, a pyramid of black on a field of indigo. All for gold, for the god of this world, as Uncle Pietro said. It was as subtle as a poke in the eye with a pointed stick.

"How's your middle leg, fellow?" She had a soft voice with a clammy intimacy to it, like a dog's nose prodding your knee. "I can straighten it out for you."

"Fresh fruits, all kinds of fresh fruits, get your fresh fruits here . . ."

"Hottest spices this side of Constantinople . . ."

"Cloth, you've never seen cloth like this, look at these colors, *signora*, just look . . ."

And then Sigismundo saw the splendid brocade of Carlo Maldonado, who was not even his own age. That wasn't what he had planned; he wanted to carve up one of the Maldonado elders. And Carlo was the brother of the lovely, angelic Maria. But still . . . still *what*? He wasn't really arguing with himself. There was a pig-nosed Maldonado, it didn't matter which one, and Sigismundo was hot in the belly and moving in fast, even though murdering a younger boy was hardly the operatic gesture he had wished. The excitement was all through him, even hardening slightly his male organ, as if the dagger created an erotic intimacy.

But he was nauseated, too, at the thought of more blood. It is enemy blood this time, he told himself harshly, not family blood. He had the dagger out and was closing in.

"*Peaches, peaches, sweetest peaches you ever tasted . . .*"

And then Uncle Pietro was between him and Carlo with a most terrible expression.

There was a short, chopping blow—Pietro was skilled at many arts, including combat—and the dagger hit the cobbles, clanking. To Sigismundo it was the apocalyptic sound of a Christmas toy breaking and a boy's fantasy smashing with it.

"You seem to have dropped something," Uncle Pietro said stonily. "Pick it up before we attract a crowd."

Sigismundo picked up the dagger—his arm ached again as he stretched—and slid it inside his cloak, his anger mounting. Of course, he thought, Uncle Pietro watched everything, read every expression, knew every secret; he probably knew what I was planning as soon as we got to the barber-surgeon's yesterday.

But Pietro already had an arm linked to his and was walking him rapidly downhill, away from the market, toward the bay, and it was as obvious as a mule in a drawing room: Sigismundo was still being treated like a child.

"I haven't wet my pants in eleven years," Sigismundo said bitterly, when they were alone. "I go to the jakes all by myself. Mama doesn't have to hold the handkerchief when I blow my nose. I. Am. Not. A. Child." He enunciated slowly, as if speaking to a lackwit.

Because when you are fourteen, you know that you are not a boy anymore, but it is hard to make your family realize that. You may have the proof of your manhood twice a week even without committing the sin of doing you-know with your hand, so you know you could father a child already; if you were a king, they might even at this age force you to marry and *order* you to produce an heir, and if you failed, or produced only girls, you would have to hire a food taster because they might decide to replace you with your brother.

"I am not a child," Sigismundo repeated angrily. He had completed twelve sonatas, the last three of them really original, and had part of a *sinfonia* written. He could solve equations in conic sections, could recite stanza after stanza from Homer and Ovid without peeking at the crib, and over six months ago he had learned from an older boy just what it is that happens to girls at that time of month they don't tell boys about.

They were walking down by the docks, where the boats left twice a day for Capri.

"Enough," Uncle Pietro said, his dark eyes crinkling. "Regard the whole adult world as fools if you will—that is your prerogative, the natural conclusion of any bright fourteen-year-old. But give me some credit as an observer. I have always watched you with special love, because of your talent, because our ancestors, the princes of Rimini, once had interests that went beyond money grubbing and commerce, because I would like to think that one of us, even if he is only half Malatesta, might do something for the arts again. I watch; I notice many things. Your mother and father may still think of you as a child, but I know better."

"Then it is because you have no faith in me," Sigismundo cried. "Because I made a fool of myself yesterday, not checking both hands before I grappled with the assassin."

"No," Pietro said. "Tennone tells me you are his best pupil. You did miscalculate a bit yesterday, but they were the attackers and had surprise on their side."

"Then why did you stop me?" Sigismundo burst out, thoroughly exasperated.

Uncle Pietro took a silk handkerchief out of his cloak and blew his nose noisily. It was like the honk of a duck. Every sound mocks my ideals, Sigismundo thought. Nature quacks at me.

"Suppose young Maldonado is smarter and faster at twelve than he ever seemed to either of us," Pietro said finally. "Suppose *he* had killed *you*. How do you think your mother would take that, while she's still dazed with grief by a brother's death?"

Sigismundo felt his neck and face flushing. "It wouldn't happen," he said. "I am brave and trained beyond him."

"But just *suppose* . . ."

Sigismundo could not believe what he was hearing; it was as if Uncle Pietro had literally started quacking like a duck, or tried to persuade him that the Holy Ghost was dancing with the archbishop on the chimneys.

"You don't think 'just suppose,' " he exclaimed. "The man who thinks 'just suppose' is the man who gets bowel movements on his head. Are we to let the Maldonado dogs kill every Malatesta in Napoli because of 'just suppose'?"

"How well you understand the Neapolitan code," Uncle Pietro said gently. "Only fourteen, and you explain it as well as a man of sixty. 'You don't think "just suppose",' " he repeated with a cruel mimicry of Sigismundo's tone. "You don't *think*," he added. "Sigismundo, I am going to tell you something that you will find almost incredible, as if I asserted my donkey speaks Homeric Greek. You may not even believe me, but I will tell you anyway. In the North, they cannot distinguish us from the Sicilians. They think we are all murderous black-hearted bastards south of Roma. And it is because of this damned code of vendetta."

"Everybody knows Northerners are effeminate—"

"Like Giancarlo Tennone?"

"Well, but he's different." How did I get trapped into defending the masculinity of my fencing teacher?

"Sigismundo," Uncle Pietro asked, "who told you Count Maldonado hired those assassins yesterday?"

"Nobody had to tell me. The feud—"

"Ah, the feud. Yes." Pietro put his hand on Sigismundo's shoulder. "I do not expect to have Count Maldonado for dinner this year, or even next year, or even in 1780 if I live that long. But I have been working quietly and patiently to end that imbecile feud, and, after many years, I have evidence that the count wishes it to end also. The feud is dwindling away, after more than a hundred years. We all got excruciatingly tired of it, and it is bad for business."

Sigismundo felt something very familiar—something that came over him every time he played chess with Uncle Pietro. "The Maldonados had nothing to do with the murder?" he asked wretchedly.

"Nothing," Uncle Pietro said. "You were about to brutally kill a child younger than yourself for no damned reason at all. Because you are like all of Napoli after a thousand years of conquest: you believe it is honorable to be angry and violent and quick, and you don't wait to find out what the flaming hell is actually going on."

"So," Sigismundo said. He was no longer furious, because he was learning something, as he had learned something when he had finally figured out the Noah's Ark trap with which

Uncle Pietro had won so many chess games. "Tell me," he said. "I will listen."

"You are as philosophical as most men twice your age," Uncle Pietro said. "That is to say, you are willing to listen to reason after I have forcibly restrained you from running amok."

"Please, Uncle. I know I was a fool."

"The bright magnificent star of Sacred Heart College, Father Ratti," Uncle Pietro said. "He has spoken of our late philosopher, Dr. Giambattista Vico?"

"Yes. He also warned us that some say Dr. Vico was a heretic."

"That is often the name given to a man who is lucky enough to have an original idea. Do you recall what Vico said about the economic classes in society?"

"At certain times," Sigismundo said, "the classes turn upon each other, and there is war between them. It happens when the conditions are ripe, just as a Homer happens when people are ready for an *Odyssey* or a Nero happens when monsters are inevitable. There is an intelligence in the species that produces the appropriate men and women for each situation, just as the intelligence in my body produces hair and fingernails as I need them. That is what I remember."

"It is more complicated," Uncle Pietro said. "There are various depths in what Aristotle calls psychology. Those who dig very deep, who almost touch the bottom of the psyche, are poets or creators in the general sense. They bring up new metaphors that are new ways of seeing ourselves and our world. When these visions are spread among a people, they become myths and then harden into laws. This is a process that is always continuing. New metaphors and myths are being found by creative people all the time. It can be most violent and explosive."

"Do the musicians have any role in this?"

"All creators have a role, since all are poets in Vico's sense of the term. Newton is as much of a poet as Homer since he gives us a whole world, and your beloved Scarlatti is a poet in this sense also. That is why Plato banned original music in his Republic. He feared the violent changes a new myth can unleash; he knew, before Vico, that a myth can trigger a war between the classes. That is why every secret society has its own myth. You must have heard sermons denouncing such cults? The reason there are so many sermons about this is because there are so many of these clandestine societies in our kingdom." Pietro lowered his voice. "Such groups always flourish in conquered nations, when the government is a bunch of thieving foreigners." He lowered his voice further. "You have heard of M.A.F.I.A.?"

"Of course," Sigismundo said. "*Morte Alla Francia, Italia Anela.*" (Death to all the French, Italy cries.) "They're a bunch of sleazy *Siciliani* who think they can drive the Bourbons out of Napoli and Sicily."

"There is now a new group, who have separated themselves out from the M.A.F.I.A.," Uncle Pietro said. "They call themselves *Rossi*, after the red flag that was the emblem of the plebian regiments in the Roman army. They want to kill all of us who are rich, not just the Bourbons."

"The secret police know about this?" Sigismundo asked, shocked.

"Of course," Uncle Pietro said. "But the *Rossi* are very clever. They appear and disappear like the Devil in an opera, as if our whole world and not just the opera house was full of trapdoors. However! Have you heard of the *Carbonari?*"

Sigismundo nodded. Everybody knew of the mysterious "coal burners," who were famous for their anonymous charitable activities.

"This is where it gets Byzantine," Uncle Pietro said. "Now you will learn that political history is a kind of philosophical spaghetti.

"The coal burners," Uncle Pietro went on, "were originally

a band of mystics living in Scotland—at least according to legend. One day the king of France is said to have stumbled upon one of their retreats while he was lost. Some versions of the story say this was Francis I and that he had been out hunting one day, rode ahead of his party, and became hopelessly confused when darkness fell, wandering aimlessly until he found himself in Scotland."

"That is absurd," Sigismundo said. "I have heard that story and cannot believe it. Are we to think the good Francis I was so absentminded that he swam the English Channel, on horseback, without noticing all that water?" It was like being told the king was so dumb he couldn't find his you-know with both hands.

"The legend is a very simple allegory," Uncle Pietro said. "*Scotland* is a code word for a state of mind, not a physical place on the surface of the earth. The *Carbonari* have many names in many nations, but, like all other Masonic brotherhoods, they always say they have a secret inner group 'in Scotland.' This inner leadership is in a state of special mental focus called 'illumination.'

"*France*, in this code, means 'darkness.' When the king of France, or of darkness, met the coal burners of Scotland, he had been lost and hungry for days; this myth means that he was confused and aware of his spiritual ignorance, like Dante in the *selva oscura*. The coal burners fed him and cared for him; this means they gave him spiritual light, as Virgil did for Dante. The burning coal symbolizes this illumination. The king of darkness was then able to see beyond the phenomenal and contingent world to the eternal and noncontingent."

"But what does all this have to do with the *Rossi?*" Sigismundo was confused.

"Patience. You have heard of the *Alumbrados?*"

"Of course." Father Ratti had taught (and refuted) the doctrines of every heresy from Arianism onward: a Jesuit education did not scant.

"You will remember that the *Alumbrados*"—the name was Spanish for *illuminati*—"were condemned by the Inquisition in 1623. That was a long time ago, you might say. Nonetheless, they still exist."

"I know," Sigismundo said. "Father Ratti told us that every heresy changes its name when it is condemned and comes back in a new form."

"The *Alumbrados*," Uncle Pietro went on somberly, "believed, like the Gnostics, that Satan was literally the God of this world. He created matter, to hide the spiritual light from us with a filter, as it were, and he is the secret chief, these maniacs say, of all bishops and kings and nobles—all the rich and powerful and mighty. They believed original Christianity can be restored only when all men and women are equal and there is no hierarchy or structure anywhere."

"Yes. Father Ratti said they should be called *an-archicos*, those who deny all authority."

"They believed, and still believe, that when there are no pope and no king, no property and no marriage, no restrictions on anybody, we shall all have the same miraculous powers as Jesus and the first apostles—to heal the sick and blind, to walk on water, to raise the dead. Maybe they expect to multiply loaves and fishes, too."

"So, we still have *Alumbrados* among us today?" Sigismundo interrupted trying to get to the point.

"Yes. But they call themselves *Carbonari*."

"What?"

"The way to survive, when your movement has been condemned and outlawed, is to be very subtle. Pretending to be somebody else is a first step."

"This is all like *Don Quixote* rewritten by Machiavelli," Sigismundo protested. "Let me try to see if I follow. There are *Rossi*, who were part of M.A.F.I.A. but aren't anymore. There are *Carbonari*, who do charitable works and teach spiritual enlightenment. There are also *Alumbrados* who pretend to be *Carbonari* but are actually more like *Rossi*."

"You understand it so far," Pietro said calmly. "The *Alumbrados* and the *Rossi*, I believe, are actually allied at this point. But you have the general picture."

"*Ma che*," Sigismundo muttered. "If I were to go to join the *Carbonari*, to help them in their praiseworthy works of charity, I might be much the worse for my efforts, right? Because I wouldn't know if I had found the true *Carbonari* or just the maniacal *Alumbrados* posing as *Carbonari*."

"Exactly," Uncle Pietro said. "God makes many fools, but the world is so constructed that only the wise and lucky die of old age."

"I see what you mean about philosophical spaghetti," Sigismundo said. "It is spaghetti *alla marinara*, in fact. The cook threw in everything but his horse." He pondered a while. "And just how is it," he asked finally, "that you are so sure it was these *Rossi* or *Alumbrados* who murdered Uncle Leonardo?"

"I have my own sources of information," Uncle Pietro said in a tone that tried to close that subject. But he added vaguely, "A large business like ours—we control most of the wine in Southern Italy, I hope you realize—well, we cannot afford to be ignorant."

"Do you mean you have *your own* secret police, just like the court?" Sigismundo exclaimed.

"We have our sources," Pietro replied. "Let it go at that . . . Oh, of course, there is the matter of the black uniforms the assassins wore. That is an old trademark of the *Alumbrados*. It proves that they and the *Rossi* are now virtually one."

Sigismundo remembered that Uncle Pietro often met with

strange men from far places who seemed to have little or nothing to do with the wine business and that they often shook hands with him, in a peculiar way, when leaving. They usually muttered something about "squares" and "levels" during these strange handshakes.

Masonry. Of course, many honest men were Masons, but it smacked of heresy. It was a Machiavellian business: secret societies competing with secret societies, secret police spying on secret societies, a warfare in the darkness with few clues to distinguish friend from foe.

"The *Rossi*," Uncle Pietro resumed, "have been using assassination as a terror tactic for a long time. You know it is a hard life on the *latifondi* down there. The sun is too hot: the crops fail more often than in decent climates. The peasants work like donkeys, and still the sun burns up the crops too often. The landlords are merciless, because their own success is only marginal at best. What can you expect in such a situation? Banditry and murder are more common than horse turds if you get off the main roads. It has always been a powder keg waiting for somebody to strike the match. The *Rosso* ideology is that match."

Sigismundo was confused again. "But the Bible says we will always have the poor with us. Do the Reds think they can change the laws of God?"

"The Bible also says, 'Thou shalt not kill,'" Pietro replied, lowering his voice still more—a habit rather than a rational precaution, since they were far from anyone who could overhear. "Princes and prime ministers never seem to notice that passage. Siggy, let me tell you, everybody finds in the Bible what he wants and conveniently ignores the rest. Do the holy monks of the Inquisition remember 'Thou shalt not kill' when they set a man on the pyre?"

"Are you comparing the *Rossi* to the Inquisition?" Sigismundo cried. "That is worse than your *domini-canis* joke.

All those visits to England must have made you half-Protestant."

"I was carried away by my rhetoric," Pietro said quickly. "The Dominicans act directly under the infallible command of our Holy Father the Pope, who is the divine representative of God on earth. I meant no sarcasm. We are the luckiest people in Europe: where others flounder about in endless confusion and perpetual questioning, we have these good, holy men to tell us when we are thinking correctly and to correct us, with proper firmness, when we stray into error. Still, once you admit that God wants us to kill the bad people, it is a matter of some careful judgment, is it not, to decide whom the bad people are? The *Rossi* do not know it is heretics and Jews. They think it is anyone with a clean shirt on."

Sigismundo became angry again. "You are mocking me. You are not saying what you really think. I am not a boy, I keep telling you, and I recognize irony when I hear it."

Pietro sighed. "What I believe," he said, "is a matter between me and my Creator, and we will discuss it at length when we meet face to face, and if He disagrees with me, I will immediately defer to His judgment, since He has much more experience and vaster knowledge."

There was a silence. The bay was as tranquil as an old man saying his rosary. Then a pelican dove into the water and came up with a fish in its mouth, chewing it. "Just another murder," but part of nature, part of God's plan.

"The poor are all ignorant and lazy," Sigismundo said finally. "These *Rossi* or *Alumbrados* or whatever they call themselves these days must be great fools to think society can survive without the wellborn and educated to guide it."

"They are also great fools to think they can change this kingdom by adding more murders to its bloody history," Pietro said softly. "That is a matter of philosophy, however. Right now, we are discussing what a hot-blooded fourteen-year-old male should do with his energies. I assure you, my . . . contacts . . . are at work already, trying to find which of the mad dogs of the *Rossi* killed my brother. It is a deadly, dangerous business, and until you are a little older, you might trust it to my hands, I think."

"Yes," Sigismundo said. "Of course."

"Concentrate on your music," Uncle Pietro said sternly. "Develop your own style and stop imitating this Scarlatti nobody ever heard of but you. Leave murder to the professionals."

"I'm sorry," Sigismundo said lamely.

"You should be. Everybody is preparing for Leonardo's funeral—the second our family has had this year—and you rush about trying to create more murder and raise havoc. The undertakers are getting rich off us already. Must they earn enough from our family to start lending at interest and organize their own bank?"

"I was a fool," Sigismundo said.

"Of course, you say that now," Uncle Pietro said, "but do you understand, really? It frightens me. I didn't understand anything at your age, but I was sly enough to say what the adults expected of me. I hope you're not playing that game. A boy your age is almost an adult, but only to the extent that an iron tub falling downstairs is almost melody. Listen to me, Siggy. You may live a long time and write glorious music. And everybody will say: 'The noble Celine, our greatest composer since Vivaldi.' Or you can try to be a hero, with no real knowledge of the evil of this wicked world. And people will say: 'That Celine boy, he was a tough customer. He chewed up walls and chimneys and spat out the bricks; even the Sicilians crossed the street when they saw him coming. Too bad he died so young.'"

"I know, I *know*."

"God damn it, I hope you know." Pietro gazed upon the repentant face of the boy. "Sometimes," he added, "I think you play upon me, and upon the whole family, as you do upon the *clavicembalo*. I never know what you are really thinking."

"You knew this morning," Sigismundo said wretchedly.

"Yes, well, maybe you have learned a lesson. But you are a sly one. I will be watching you. Any man will listen to reason for a while, but when the passions rise, reason is as quickly forgotten as the graffiti in a shit house."

Pietro Malatesta was right. Two hours later, Sigismundo decided how to pursue his vendetta against the "illuminated" *Rossi* or *Alumbrados* or whatever they called themselves.

When Sigismundo went to the royal palace and explained his offer, the head of the guards laughed at him.

"But I am a *Malatesta*," Sigismundo told him hotly. "We are the oldest nobility in the kingdom. You cannot treat me like this."

"You are a beardless Malatesta and no more than sixteen," the guardsman said. "Go home before I spank you."

Sigismundo trudged away, thinking: Persistence; I will wear them down, and the Malatesta legend will finally penetrate.

Besides, it was cheerful news that he looked two years older than his actual age. It's the way I wear my sword and what Tennone taught me about carriage, he thought; it's obvious that I am a *dangerous character*.

But then in the night, in his dreams, the *Rossi* came back to him, wearing their plain black wool as a symbol of humility (or a Satanic caricature of a religious order), slashing, stabbing; murdering every Malatesta and Celine; turning crocodiles on Sigismundo in the worst of the nightmares. And his father, Papa Guido, was grim all that spring as Napoli bloomed more beautifully than ever, the fig trees and olive trees and the emerald green apple trees spreading their scents in the air, and the white Neapolitan sunlight everywhere (God's gift to

Napoli, Uncle Pietro once said, in a *very* low voice, to compensate us for the buggering Bourbons that inscrutable history had wished on us), but perpetual shadows, it seemed, hanging over all the Celines and Malatestas, Aunt Gina in particular a haggard figure in her black dress of mourning, no longer the prettiest woman in the city but a stark, brooding presence out of tragic opera. Sigismundo almost feared she would burst into a soprano *aria* at any moment and then stab herself during the final *arpeggio*.

So what else could he do but tell his soul: Be patient. Wait. The time will come; I have an appointment somewhere, in some green field with seconds and sabers or in some filthy alley with daggers. But now I must wait and learn what it is to be a man.

And meanwhile there was the music, the language of the angels themselves, which everybody was urging on him, Uncle Pietro especially, who kept saying, "Nobody remembers dead wine merchants. Everybody remembers Costanzo Festa, and he's been buried two hundred years now."

Which was the one thing wrong with Uncle Pietro: he was always going on about Festa and people like that, pretty tune makers but not at all comparable to a man like Domenico Scarlatti in Spain, who had found whole new dimensions in music that Uncle Pietro and Napoli as a whole refused to recognize. And, in fact, Uncle Pietro did not even approve of Scarlatti's "crossover" technique when Sigismundo showed it to him—how one hand crosses the other on the *clavicembalo* so that more complex harmony is possible. A whole new music would grow out of that, Sigismundo knew, a music even greater than that of Father Vivaldi, the "Red Priest," who was currently everybody's favorite. Because *bel canto*, at which Vivalidi, the priest with the rooster-red hair, excelled over all the world, was the heart and soul of music, everybody knew that, but harmony was its searching mind, and the mind of music was becoming mature in this century, struggling toward forms of counterpoint and intricacy that were tragic and comic at once and therefore beyond comedy or tragedy; beyond concept and beyond intellect; beyond what analysis knew or poetry imagined.

After a month and a half, Sigismundo had been to the court five times—always careful, always checking that the all-observant eye of Uncle Pietro was elsewhere occupied. Of course, they continued to laugh at him. Ferdinand IV, even at the age of thirteen—one year younger than Sigismundo—had the typical Bourbon attitude about ordinary Neapolitans trying to involve themselves in government.

The sixth time Sigismundo returned, the head of the guard was drily ironic instead of openly sarcastic and took Sigismundo inside. The name Malatesta had registered finally, the boy thought. Evidently, the Marchese Bernardo di Tanucci, who really ran the government, had told these clods who the mighty Malatestas were.

They went to a room where two men were waiting. The guardsman left at once. Sigismundo was alone, he knew, with "di Tanucci's boys"—agents of the secret police.

One of the men was a Neapolitan with a barbaric, Sicilian-looking face. He seemed to be breathing and awake but beyond that he was not doing any more than a chamber pot and was about equally attractive. This one is from Interrogation, Sigismundo thought uneasily.

The second man conducted the interview. He had a walrus mustache and white blond hair and as soon as he spoke Sigismundo knew he was an Englishman, but not the I-know-bloody-everything type of conceited-ass Englishman; his Italian was finicky, like that of the Roman rich.

"You are the musician who believes he has a talent for espionage," the Englishman said.

There were a lot of these mysterious Englishmen in Napoli.

They belonged to a strange group called the Jacobites of which Sigismundo knew little and cared less; but everybody knew they could not return to England under penalty of death.

"Casanova is a musician," Sigismundo replied boldly, in English. "And he has proved useful to more than one prince."

"And a royal pain in the bum to some," the Englishman said, registering Sigismundo's talent for language. "God's pajamas, lad, there are some of us who think a free-lance agent is worse than no agent at all. I would never hire a man who is for sale to the highest bidder."

"I am not for sale," Sigismundo said firmly. "I offer my complete loyalty to Ferdinand IV. He is *my* prince."

"He's a Bourbon—aunty's drawers, I am not so feeble-minded as to think you Neapolitans really adore being governed by foreigners."

The Neapolitan gorilla just stared. It was not an unfriendly stare, but emphatically nowhere near being a friendly one; it missed nothing.

"If you don't trust me, why are you talking to me at all?" Sigismundo asked sharply. "Why, for that matter, do *you* serve the Bourbons?"

The Englishman relaxed. "You have a debater's skills," he said. "I almost think I should be on the defensive now. Why don't you sit down and see if we can be of use to each other?"

Sigismundo took a chair, observing the Englishman more carefully, as Giancarlo Tennone had taught him to study an opposing fencer. This man was past fifty and had probably been involved in clandestine activities most of his life. You could never really trick him, because he would never trust you fully. The Jacobites had been exiled from England for trying to overthrow one king and install another; they were living all over Europe now, but Napoli had a particularly high concentration of them. If this man was working for the Spanish Bourbons, it was probably with only part of his devious English mind. A perfectly sane Englishman, Uncle Pietro said, could logically decide on monstrosities that would curl the hair of a Sicilian bandit.

"I am serving Ferdinand," the Englishman said, switching to Spanish, "because I am a Catholic. Increasing Catholic power is, to me, the only way Europe will ever come out of the age of wars and chaos that Protestantism has produced. Does that answer your question?"

Yes, Sigismundo thought; when there are enough strong Catholic monarchs again, they can combine and drive the Protestants off the throne of England. But why is he telling me this?

"You wonder why I am telling you this," the Englishman went on, shocking Sigismundo. (So: even the English may have the witch power sometimes.) "I want you to understand that there are wheels within wheels. I am watched day and night. Signor di Tanucci appreciates my special talents, but he wonders, always, when my interests and Bourbon interests might begin to diverge."

"If you use me," Sigismundo said, switching to French (I'll impress him yet), "you are telling me I will be watched also."

"God's hooks," the Englishman said in his own language again. "You have the kind of mind that can appreciate these games. But tell me: What is the most absurd feature of this whole interview?"

"My age," Sigismundo said quietly, waiting.

The Englishman grinned. "That is precisely why this might work," he said. "Not even the *Alumbrados* would suspect us of using a lad of your years. That is why I am talking to you. Do you think you are brave?" The question came suddenly.

"Yes. I have been fencing for four years."

"And you tackled an assassin bare-handed when your uncle was killed. Don't be startled; we know a great deal about you. As soon as you first came to the palace we started an investigation. But a spy must be intelligent as well as brave. Do you think you are intelligent?"

The gorilla was still staring; he seemed to have about as many nervous fidgets as a tombstone.

"I am intelligent enough to know that this is leading up to some sort of a test," Sigismundo said.

"That is extraordinary," the Englishman exclaimed. He opened a drawer in his desk, almost absentmindedly. "But to be a spy," he went on softly (too softly), "is to deal continually with intrigue, uncertainty, treachery . . . to, um, find surprises when you least expect them." He had taken a pistol out of the drawer.

Sigismundo hated guns. The sword was a weapon of elegance, of art, of honor; guns simply killed people, even at a distance, without giving them a chance to fight back. They were ugly, and he had refused to learn anything about them.

The Englishman casually pointed the pistol at Sigismundo and smiled. It was not a nice smile by any means: the Sabine women must have seen that kind of smile on the faces of the Roman soldiers. This is where he rams it into me all the way, Sigismundo thought.

"It is not the policy of the palace to encourage Neapolitans to meddle in affairs of the sort we are discussing," the Englishman said. "It is the policy to *dis*courage them."

There was a pulse beating in Sigismundo's temple. He ignored it and breathed as Tennone had taught him. "This is a test, as I said," he stated calmly.

"You are *quite* sure of that?"

"Yes." The pulse was beating faster. Sigismundo ruthlessly ignored it and watched the Englishman's eyes and mouth: those were the places where signals would show, telling you what to expect.

The Englishman put the gun back in the drawer. "One learns the most amazing things about people in moments like this," he said. "Of course, it was a minor little test, and of course you knew it. But you showed something to me. I like you, lad."

The Neapolitan gorilla grunted, as if he was disappointed that he hadn't had to hit Sigismundo with a lead pipe to keep him from wrestling for the gun. Maybe he doesn't talk or walk at all, Sigismundo thought. They might just keep him around to look like the Second Murderer in a revenge tragedy.

And so Sigismundo Celine found himself working for an Englishman who claimed to be called Mr. Drake (which probably meant his real name was Jones or Greenhill), allegedly to aid the secret police of Ferdinand IV in rooting out the *Rosso* assassins; and, of course, Sigismundo wondered to what extent he might also be helping the Jacobites to change English politics, about which he cared not at all.

(And "Drake," after Sigismundo left, wrote a brief note saying only, "The mouse has taken the cheese" and sent the Neapolitan agent to deliver it to the appropriate person; but Sigismundo did not know that.)

But Sigismundo was not yet a perfect fool; as Uncle Pietro said, perfection always takes a while. Sigismundo sought out Father Ratti, the most enlightened of his teachers at Sacred Heart College.

"All those Englishmen who live around Capodimonte," he asked, "why are they called Jacobites?"

They were walking in the college garden. Father Ratti was old enough to pass as Caesar's grandfather, so wrinkled was his face, but his eyes were lively and brightly curious. Like all Jesuits, he could argue the case against any Church dogma as well as the case for it; that was because of their training in dialectics.

"The Jacobites," he said quickly, ticking off the facts with no effort, "were followers of the late King Jacobus, or, as they say in their language, James II. You must remember the 'Bloodless

Revolution,' as it was called? The English nobles and Parliament wanted a Protestant monarch, so they deposed James and imported his son-in-law, William of Orange, from Holland. The Jacobites tried to restore James and now that James is dead, the Jacobites are allegedly trying to place his grandson, Charles, on the throne."

"The Jacobites are Catholics then?" Sigismundo asked, somewhat relieved.

"Most of them. But they have many Protestants among them, because the royal family of the Stuarts, to which James and Charles belong, is Scottish. Many of the Scots support the Jacobites, even though Charles is Catholic, because they would like a Scottish family back on the throne of England."

"You mean the Jacobites are an alliance of English Catholics and Scottish Protestants?" Sigismundo was astonished.

"They are said to be Freemasons, too," Father Ratti added calmly. "Some people say, in fact, that all Masonic lodges are just fronts for the Jacobite conspiracy."

The *Carbonari* . . . the secret "inner chiefs" in Scotland . . .

"Charles," the priest was going on, "or, as they call him in their language, Bonnie Prince Charlie, has about as much chance of gaining the English crown as I have of flapping my arms and flying off like a stork. The last Jacobite coup, or attempted coup, ended in total failure. They were terribly beaten at a place called Culloden Moor, in Scotland, in 1746. Bonnie Prince Charlie, I am told, is resolutely devoting his remaining energies to drinking himself to death in Roma."

I see, Sigismundo thought; they want to put a Catholic drunk on the throne of a Protestant country. They are indeed idealists.

"Is it true that the *Alumbrados* still survive?" he asked. He knew the answer; he just wanted the digressions that would come when Ratti started ransacking his memory.

"Well," Father Ratti said, "if one believes our good and pious friends, the Dominicans, every heresy since Adamitism still survives somewhere and if the Pope looked under his bed every night he'd eventually find a Manichaean hiding there . . . Do you think your uncle was murdered by these *Alumbrados?*"

The abrupt question was a shock. "Well," Sigismundo said, "I heard some men in my family talking; it was suggested."

"It might be true," old Ratti said somberly. "Do you know what the clue is? The timing of the murder, having it coincide with the blessing of the Host. That is deliberate, calculated blasphemy of exactly the flavor of the *Alumbrado* madness. do you recall from history class the murder of Guilliame de Medici in 1478?"

"Yes," Sigismundo said, suddenly seeing an impossible possibility.

"Guilliame was killed at the *moment* of the raising of the Host," the Jesuit said sorrowfully. "Just like your uncle. The *Alumbrados* may not be as recent as we think. It was an organized conspiracy that killed Julius Caesar. It was an Egyptian oracle—intoxicated on wine and strange drugs —who told Alexander the Great to invade India; and who knows what powers were behind that oracle? Any violent, emotional person can easily be converted into an oracle, a trance medium, a virtual automaton by those who know the techniques of mind control. Saint Paul says the Church must war, not against flesh and blood, but against Powers from elsewhere."

"But what is the purpose of such blasphemy as committing murder when God is called down into the church?" Sigismundo asked, beginning to feel a new sensation that was worse than physical fear. Strange drugs . . . mind control . . . Powers from elsewhere . . . conspiracies as old and evil and bloody as Moloch, the child-eating god of Carthage . . .

"Perhaps I will begin to sound like a Dominican," Father Ratti said as they turned into the main hall leading to the library. "According to the confessions obtained by the Inquisitors, no man may be admitted to the inner circle of these illuminated ones until he has committed three major sins: sodomy and murder and blasphemy. In that way they break all ties with the Christian community. All that the *Alumbrados* say about restoring original Christianity is just for the outer circles, the dupes. The inner rulers of the cult hate Christ as well as the Church; they despise morality as well as civil law; they aim, not just at anarchism, but at universal atheism."

Sigismundo made the Sign of the Cross, almost trembling.

"Yes," old Ratti went on, "you do well to fear such men." He turned to enter the library, then abruptly turned back. "Tell your Uncle Pietro that I answered all your questions," he said. "Tell him I did it for *the widow's son.*"

It was obviously a code phrase of some sort. Sigismundo felt that the wheels were turning faster than he could understand: wheels within wheels, as Drake said. Maybe the Freemasons were a front for some continent-wide Jacobite plot with Drake as a kingpin. Certainly Uncle Pietro knew the Masonic handgrips, and how much else? How old were the *Carbonari*, and was the secret group in Scotland only an allegory? And the opposition, the illuminated ones, of *Rossi*, who hated Christ and government, rich men and priests, with equal fervor, who killed in church to crown murder with blasphemy? Wheels within wheels, faster and faster. And he would be going down, down, down into this web of treachery, down to the blackest *bolgia* of all, where were found the avatars of Satan himself, the violent against God and Man.

▲

It was only a day later that "Mr. Drake" contacted Sigismundo —through a man who looked like but did not exactly talk like a peasant. The message was brief. They would meet at a villa high on Capodimonte that afternoon.

When Sigismundo arrived, he was overwhelmed: not even the Malatestas had such a pleasant home. The Jacobites must have gotten away with a lot of their money when they fled England. Uncle Pietro said that *traitor* was a word so unspeakably vile that in common courtesy it was applied only to losers; Sigismundo wondered how rich the winners in England might be.

There was a magnificent Venus in the garden; Sigismundo couldn't tell if it was a Roman original or one of the countless forgeries that proliferated these days.

"You like her?" Drake asked, noticing Sigismundo's glance.

"The priests say such art is dangerous. It can lead to sin."

"*Sin* is a term in theology," Drake said. "*Beauty* is a term in aesthetics. Mixing the two is like multiplying apples by altar boys."

"I thought you said you were a Catholic."

"I am," Drake said, "and, as my enemies in England will add, an unmitigated reactionary to boot. What I admire in Mother Church is her blatant pagan beauty. Catholicism has all the qualities of the greatest artworks: sublimity, mystery, grandeur, and a transcendental inner coherence to be found nowhere in the real world. By the way, the Vatican has an even better Venus. I've seen it. In fact, a certain famous Cardinal once autographed it, when he had, ahem, a bit too much wine aboard. Perhaps I had better not mention *where* the Cardinal put his autograph on her." Drake laughed coarsely, glancing with more than aesthetic appreciation at the naked goddess, patron of love and pleasure.

Sigismundo was uncomfortable. One did not discuss Popes and Cardinals that way, not in Napoli anyway.

Drake quickly got to business. A bundle of rags was produced; it took Sigismundo a moment to realize this filth was the clothing of a peasant.

"Get out of your silks and into these."

Sigismundo removed his clothes and donned the reeking uniform of poverty.

"Good enough," Drake said, looking him over. "But you don't smell rank enough. Twenty push-ups please."

Sigismundo exercised. Drake studied him afterward and rubbed some soil on his neck. "Tell me about how God made the world," he said then, "the way one of your servants would explain it."

Sigismundo got about three sentences out before Drake stopped him.

"You just bleeding said *entelechy*," he howled. "Do your servants read Aristotle?"

"Of course not. They can't read at all."

"Then, by the sacred chamber pot of the Holy Virgin, do you think the bleeding *peasants* read Aristotle?"

They went over the Creation three times before Sigismundo caught the knack of using only lower-class words.

"Ask me for the afternoon off, to visit your sick mother," Drake said then.

Sigismundo thought an instant. He carefully removed his straw peasant's hat, as a sign of respect, and began, "Pardon, *signor*—"

"Jesus Christ and his black brother Harry," Drake screamed. "You are looking *right at me!*"

Sigismundo lowered his eyes, as peasants must when addressing their superiors, and started again.

After an hour of this sort of practice, Drake was somewhat near satisfied.

"Do you know where the Osteria Allegro is?" he asked.

Sigismundo nodded dubiously. That was a bad neighborhood, one he had never entered.

"We have reason to believe the *Rossi* do some of their recruiting there," Drake said. "You are Antonio Mostra from

Marechiaro. Your landlord has raised the rent so high that your father cannot pay, understand? There is nothing left over after the rent is paid—*nothing*. Two of your sisters have come to town to work as harlots, but still there is not enough. Your father is terribly ashamed, but he does not forbid them. A man's conscience, ethics, and morals are luxuries, but food is a bleeding *necessity*. I was homeless for three years; I know about such things . . . But, as I was saying, your family is near starvation. You are going to drink and complain, drink and complain—understand? But be careful—don't drink so much that you really get drunk."

Sigismundo wondered if he was crazy to get himself into such a masquerade; but he remembered Uncle Leonardo's blood.

"I may be sending you to your death," Drake said at the gate. "But God is on the side of the damned fools and optimists, sometimes. Good luck, my brave musician."

And so it was again down, down, down through the curving Neapolitan hills, deeper and deeper, until he was going further down than ever before, past the market, into the pits of squalor. He thought of Dante again. The nobles high up on Capodimonte and other peaks were like the Thrones of the *Paradiso*, the merchants below them on the lower hills and in the center of town were like the souls in the *Purgatorio* struggling to achieve the golden grace to join the blessed souls above, and down at the very bottom were the monstrosities of that Hell on earth, poverty. The stink became intolerable: it was a mixture of sewage that never drained properly and stale sweat and raw fish and vomit and one wine house after another. Even animals were never this filthy; this was why the great Aristotle said the common people would never be capable of self-government. The sights were even worse than the odors: small children, half or completely naked, playing in the dirt; men, too drunk to walk, leaning against walls as they tried to urinate without splashing their boots; the blind, the legless, the armless—veterans of God knows what armies, paid once and then cast out, no longer useful for dismembering other men; people with unspeakable swellings and tumors; harlots too old or too ugly for the market, working here to cadge a few coins from men as poor as themselves—the "half-a-lira uprights" or "row boats" that drunken sailors would do you-know to standing up, leaning against an alley wall. And then on a fence he saw:

LA TERRA TREMA

Somebody down here can read and write, he thought; but then the meaning sank home. "The earth will shake." It was not necessarily scrawled by some religious fanatic, predicting apocalypse: it might be a *Rosso* warning to him and all his class. *La terra trema! La terra trema!* It was like a drumbeat entering the score of an opera, promising you that the stage would be thoroughly littered with corpses of tenors, baritones, basses, and sopranos at the final curtain.

So when he found the Osteria Allegro and began drinking, it did not require histrionic talent to express bitterness and melancholy. All he had to do was remember he was a peasant's son who hated his landlord; his wild emotions were real. He did not understand why the world was so vile, nor why an innocent bystander like Uncle Leonardo had been brutally murdered because the world was vile. Maybe he was too shaken by this new Napoli, this Napoli he had never known; maybe he forgot Drake's warning about not drinking too much.

The more wine he drank, the more he raged against all he had learned since Easter Sunday. A priest calls on God, and four murderers appear in answer. Uncle Leonardo is butchered like a hog in an abattoir because some madmen blame him for the accumulated injustices of thousands of years. Most people live in misery while a few wear silks and eat caviar imported from Constantinople. God has a reason for it all, Sigismundo reminded himself; God always has a reason. God is all-wise and all-good. To prove it, he will reward these wretched people with an eternity of bliss in heaven after they starve to death, and to show His transcendent perfection even further He will personally burn in hell every desperate girl who left a ruined *latifondi* to come to the city and intercourse men in alleys. And now God was making the bloody room spin around. Maybe you couldn't trust God after all.

But then he noticed the bartender had not warned him that his rambling diatribe was dangerous. He was in the right place, no doubt about it.

And so, when another peasant invited him to come along to a party where the drinks were free, he was only moderately surprised that it had been so easy. And when they were on the street and the peasant girl said that the party was actually, well, a kind of political meeting, Sigismundo carefully hid his exultation.

But when they arrived at the *baracca* or hut where the party or, "well, kind of political meeting" was being held, everybody already there was wearing hoods that hid their faces. Dante's *Caina attende*, Sigismundo thought: the bottom pit, *bolgia* of the violent traitors. On the walls were black candles, just like at a witch's sabbat. There was even a kind of altar with a huge black book and a red flag covering the wall behind it.

"Who comes here?" one hooded figure, who seemed to be in charge, asked suspiciously.

"One who seeks the light," replied Sigismundo's guide. That was probably ritualistic.

"El Eswad," said another voice, "I say that the stranger should be removed. We do not know him."

El Eswad was Arabic, Sigismundo knew. It meant "black man" and was a title of Satan.

"El Eswad," said Sigismundo's guide, "if we do not teach the stranger who comes to us, how will we spread the light?"

More ritual, obviously.

"We will examine the stranger later," said El Eswad. He ceremoniously removed a dagger from his belt and raised it to the north, east, south, and west. "I call up Orpheus," he intoned. "I call up Tana. I call up Lucifer. I call up Aradia." The dagger was placed upon the book, pointing south.

"Orpheus, Tana, Lucifer, Aradia," everybody repeated.

"What is the first duty of a Master Mason?" demanded El Eswad.

"To see that the *baracca* is secure," came the chorus.

"See to it," intoned El Eswad.

Guards moved to the two doors. They removed daggers from their belts and held them, point upward, at their breasts.

Now I am locked in with them, Sigismundo thought.

"What is the second duty of a Master Mason?" asked El Eswad.

"To fight to the death against the accursed Pope and all the damnable nobles," came the answer.

"What is the third duty of a Master Mason?"

"To journey to the East, to find the light."

The sun rises in the East, of course, but there seemed to be a double meaning there. Sicily had been under Moslem rule for a long time; El Eswad was an Arabic title. Could *baracca* be a pun on Arabic *baraka*, soul power? The first duty is to see that the *baraka*, the power, is in the circle.

"Who is the new candidate for illumination?" El Eswad asked suddenly. Sigismundo tried not to tense.

"He is a poor peasant's son. Their family is wretched, because of a cruel landlord," Sigismundo's guide said.

"How do we know he is not a police spy?" El Eswad demanded.

Sigismundo felt a belch coming on and deliberately let it out explosively. "Who, me?" he asked, exaggerating his drunkenness. "I don't know any police."

"Come here," El Eswad said sternly.

Sigismundo lurched forward, still playing the drunk.

"Let me see your hands," El Eswad ordered.

Sigismundo felt his heart begin to pound rapidly. With effort he kept his face impassive. You may be born male, he reminded himself, but you have to earn the right to be a Man.

He held out his hands and by sheer will he kept them from trembling.

"Those are not the hands of a peasant," El Eswad said. "Those are the hands of a goat-copulating aristocrat who has never worked a day in his worthless life."

Sigismundo was suddenly surrounded by hooded figures. His belly lurched in terror and he told himself: The coward is controlled by fear, the brave man ignores it. But his heart pounded louder.

"Who are you?" one of the hooded figures asked, holding a dagger to Sigismundo's throat.

"I am Antonio Mostra from Marechiaro."

He was slapped brutally across the face.

"You are an aristocrat, and you probably live on a hill right here in Napoli. *Who are you?*"

"It was a college initiation," Sigismundo improvised. "I had to prove I could pass as a peasant—"

"You are a police spy," El Eswad pronounced, "and a particularly stupid one. Does anybody think we should let this little defecation out of here alive?"

There was a long silence—at least it seemed long to Sigismundo—and then somebody said, "Hell, no," just to make it official, probably.

El Eswad held his dagger to Sigismundo's nose. "We will give you one minute to pray," he said.

I'm going to piss my pants, Sigismundo thought. They don't do that in opera: they just sing a brave *aria* and then die. Why didn't I listen to Uncle Pietro's warnings?

"Pray, you drunken imbecile," El Eswad said passionately, "you have only thirty seconds left!"

I am a Celine. And a Malatesta. I will not pee myself.

"I surrender my soul to the mercy of Our Lady," Sigismundo said tightly, not allowing his voice to quiver. "And I die a good servant of my God and our Holy Father the Pope."

Everybody laughed. It was like the funniest climax in the most hilarious *commedia* that ever played a theater: they couldn't control themselves. They were slapping their thighs and practically falling over with mirth. Sigismundo could hardly believe his ears; how could even atheists like these wretches laugh at a brave boy's dying prayer?

"Jesus, Jesus," El Eswad howled, bending over, gurgling. Then they started to take off their hoods, one by one. El Eswad was a silk merchant, a friend of Uncle Pietro's. And there was Father Ratti and Mr. Drake and Uncle Carlo and then other merchants, and the last was Uncle Pietro himself.

"You are a hard boy to frighten," Uncle Pietro said.

"Damn you!" Sigismundo cried, not caring that Father Ratti was there.

But Drake stepped between Uncle Pietro and Sigismundo. "It wasn't his idea," he said. "It was mine. As soon as the guards at the palace told me your madcap idea, I knew you'd get yourself killed if we didn't teach you a lesson in reality first."

"Damn you," Sigismundo repeated, meaning all of them.

"Listen," Drake said. "This is exactly what would have happened if you got anywhere near the *Rossi*, except that the hoods wouldn't have come off at the end and you wouldn't be alive. If it hadn't been your hands, it would have been something else. You have no idea how many ways they have of detecting infiltrators."

"He's about to damn us all again," Father Ratti said gently.

He was wrong. Sigismundo bolted for the door. He could no longer control his bowels; the relief of not dying was even more intense, physiologically, than the fear had been.

They found him coming out of the jakes, trying to walk with dignity.

"Forgive us," Father Ratti said. "There was no other way to stop you from getting yourself killed."

Sigismundo ignored him. He walked boldly to Uncle Pietro and stared him in the eye, unflinching. "Now I know why Cervantes seemed so funny to you," he said coldly, with icy dignity. And he added with quiet, restrained melancholy, "'At last he was free of the damnable books of Romance.'"

"Very touching," Uncle Pietro said with equal coldness. "You'd be more impressive, though, if you had remembered to button your fly."

▲

And Sigismundo did not sleep at all that night, but, once he was home, paced his room continually, thinking about the monstrous, monumental immensity of his own folly. Even though Voltaire was banned in Napoli, he knew one joke from the French cynic: "The only way to understand what mathematicians mean by infinity is to contemplate the extent of human stupidity."

Everything Father Ratti had ever said about humility was beginning to make sense. He had been a fool in San Francesco di Paola, attacking a frigging professional assassin without any awareness that the formalism of fencing class might not apply to men who really knew about murder. He had been a fool again the next day, almost killing an innocent child because he thought he knew everything when he actually knew nothing about the real situation. And he had been a fool for the third and most shameful time when he had imagined an agent of the secret police would actually send a flaming idiot like himself into a revolutionary meeting.

Father Ratti had often explained, in Religious Knowledge class, that true humility did not mean a sense of worthlessness or the kind of timidity that caused some people to be cheated and bullied all their lives. The virtue of humility, Ratti said, was merely the faculty of intelligence operating properly. "The man of wisdom," Ratti explained once, "fears only one man on earth. Do you know who that is?" And when everybody guessed wrong—some said the Pope, some said King Ferdinand—Ratti said, "The man of wisdom fears *himself*. He knows who it is who tells him the most plausible lies, the lies he wants to believe."

So Sigismundo, thrice a fool, was determined to acquire humility and to catch himself if he tried to tell himself a lie. This was by no means easy. It was much simpler, and very tempting, to put on elaborate airs of abasement, like some of the Franciscans, or to grovel in a sense of enormous sinfulness, like the penitents who whipped themselves in public (which could be a secret form of pride, Father Ratti said), or just to be slavishly submissive, like a peasant. Real humility was more complicated: it was like walking around two steps behind yourself watching everything you did.

He went to the great Cathedral of Naples on Via Duomo when the latest miracle was reported; he was sure some of God's grace would enter him that way. Of course, the miracle happened two or three times a year, and he had seen it before, but now, as he was seeking to "put away childish things," in the Apostle's words, it would have new meanings for him.

San Gennaro had been beheaded in A.D. 302, and the

Cathedral held two vials of his dried blood, which most marvelously would come alive—liquify again—whenever Napoli needed a reminder that their patron saint was still thinking of them. Next to the tomb of the great poet Virgil, the vials of the blood of San Gennaro were the most stupendous things in Napoli, as everyone agreed, even if some tourists were so ignorant they looked only at the bay and the paintings by Titian in San Domenico Maggiore and the terras cottas by Mazzoni in Santa Anna dei Lombardi that were so real they made you jump.

There were penitents at the Cathedral, of course—they always turned out for a miracle, beating themselves with their whips and howling about their unforgivable iniquities. There were also the usual peasants, kneeling for hours without moving—but they were probably not praying for enlightenment, Sigismundo thought; such was beyond their childish, illiterate minds. They were probably just asking for the recovery of some sick infant, or maybe for the landlord not to raise the rent again. Still, such immobile passion was awe-inspiring. It was almost as if their souls had left their bodies and gone directly to Heaven to plead with God in person while their fleshly parts remained here, frozen like statues.

And there were the usual gawking tourists. When the priests brought the vials from the *Restituta* (the old Basilica, dating from the fourth century) and carried them through the Cathedral so all could see the red miracle, Sigismundo heard a disturbing thing.

It was a Frenchman, among the tourists, and he spoke softly to his companion, and in German—probably he assumed nobody in Napoli would have the mental energy to learn a non-Latin tongue. "Isn't it incredible," the Frenchman whispered, "that they can still pull off this hocus-pocus and the arseholes believe in it?"

Sigismundo closed his eyes and prayed, to put down the sin

of rage. Why, if the miracle were a fraud, that would mean
that these devout, holy, and pious priests were *cheats and
charlatans*—and not just these priests, but all the priests
in the Cathedral, all the way back to the ancient times
when the miracle was first reported. Centuries of deliberate
deception that would be—a Machiavellian conspiracy to
delude men's minds and, worse yet, a *conspiracy that had succeeded for ages and ages*. That was a monstrous, frightening
thought.

Still, Sigismundo had always been fascinated by the tricks of
the *improvvisatore* in the market and had nagged Uncle Pietro
until some of the basic principles of conjuring were explained.
Only the principles; Uncle Pietro insisted that "telling too
much makes the intellect lazy," so Sigismundo had to apply
the principles anew to each trick he saw, figuring out for
himself how the magic was done. With guilty discomfort he
visualized how easy it would be to fake the miracle of the living
blood of San Gennaro. There would be no art to it at all: the
priests went alone to the *Restituta*. They could spill out the
dried blood, add fresh blood (from a stray cat even; who would
know?), and then march out with the vials to astonish everybody. The tricks of the *improvvisatore*, performed in public
with a thousand eyes watching, were much more difficult.

Of course, this terrible fantasy could not be true; why, if it
were true, then *anything* might be a trick or a lie. The world
would be a madhouse of intrigue and deception, no man ever
daring to trust another. Mother of God, if you couldn't trust
the Church, whom or what could you trust? Maybe San
Gennaro never lived, maybe this was a ritual of Janus disguised
as Christianity, maybe San Gennaro was never beheaded by
Diocletian, maybe Diocletian was a lovely fellow and a barrel
of laughs and never beheaded anyone, maybe the Roman
Empire never existed but was invented by storytellers. Maybe

for Jesus' sake there was no France and some *actors* were hired to visit Napoli occasionally speaking the alleged "French" language to keep up the pretense.

Such thoughts were madness. You could end up unable to decide anything. There was a peasant in Posillipo, a mad fellow who claimed a flaming rock had fallen out of the sky into his field one night. You could think that this cuckoo was right and that all the most learned theological and scientific minds in Europe were involved in a gigantic conspiracy to hide the fact that such rocks did fall, just because rocks from the sky did not fit into either the Bible or Newton's theories. That was where total skepticism landed you: in the *selva oscura* of Dante, the endless labyrinth or philosophical spaghetti (as Uncle Pietro would say) in which men have been wandering since the Unity of the Faith was shattered.

Some things are for sure and it is crazy to question them, Sigismundo reminded himself. Priests do not lie; flaming rocks do not fall out of the sky; Mama was never unfaithful to Papa; and I am Sigismundo Celine of Napoli, not the man in the moon.

Having come to this conclusion, Sigismundo decided to say a prayer for the misguided Frenchman, hoping that God would shed grace upon him and bring him back to the light.

▲

It was time to pay a condolence call on Aunt Gina. He knew it and had been postponing it for days, because at fourteen he simply did not know how to deal with the grief of an adult.

On a Wednesday in June, he forced himself to go.

When he arrived at the old house where the Via di Roma crosses the volcanic Posillipo ridge, he was still reminding himself not to think of it as "Uncle Leonardo's house"; it was "Aunt Gina's house" now, another sign that nothing would ever go back to the way it was before Easter.

When old Bianca, the chief housemaid with the bouncing bosoms, showed him into the living room, he was shocked by Aunt Gina's face. She had always been renowned, not just for her beauty, but for her taste: the room was decorated in pinks and cinnamons and siennas, rugs and drapes and divans and paintings all coordinated exquisitely, a loveliness as simple but splendid as the Parthenon by moonlight. It hurt the heart to see the ugly old woman (not yet forty!) in widow's black sitting amid so much beauty she had once created.

"Auntie," he said, "I want to say—" And then, in horror, he found that he was weeping, the dozen speeches he had rehearsed were all forgotten, and it wouldn't have mattered if all the boys in his fencing class were watching; he couldn't have controlled it even then, because it was an explosion from within. Even his nose was running, along with his eyes—he remembered that strange expression in Homer that Father Ratti said meant, literally, "Compassion exploded in his nose."

Don't snivel and whine, don't snivel and whine: that was what he had been learning from boyhood on, how to stop being just the artist in the family, how to become a Man. And now he was both sniveling and whining, whimpering even, and Aunt Gina was hugging him, and he was hugging her, and they wept together for what seemed a long time.

Finally, they stopped weeping and sat down. Old Bianca, who had probably expected the explosion of grief and had been listening for it to subside, entered unobtrusively and served tea.

"Those men will be caught and punished," Sigismundo said, remembering his speech. "Uncle Pietro has many contacts—"

"I know," Aunt Gina said wanly. "But that will not be the end of it. It will never end—never—as long as I remember Leonardo. And there is worse now."

But before she could explain that, Uncle Pietro himself

appeared, at the top of the stairs, with a Dominican monk. From where he sat, Sigismundo could see that they were arguing, but in very low voices. As they came down the stairs, their voices became more audible:

"I tell you, I know the signs," the Dominican was protesting in a sad, soulful whisper, like a waiter explaining how the dead mouse got into the *cioppino*.

"You have tried three times and failed," Uncle Pietro whispered back. "It is time to try an alternative."

But by now they were in the living room and Uncle Pietro was composing his face.

"Madame," he said formally to Aunt Gina, "Brother Eugenius has not yet succeeded. He wishes to summon a better-trained exorcist. In the meanwhile, I again propose that we see what medicine has to offer."

"Any doctor will tell you at once that this is outside his ken," the monk said sullenly.

"You may well be right," Uncle Pietro said smoothly. "Summon your demon-conquering exorcist from Roma. Meanwhile, no harm can be done by trying a simpler approach."

Sigismundo was thoroughly confused.

"He is my son," Aunt Gina said. "We will try both ways. All I want is for poor Tony to be himself again."

"You will just waste time and money," the monk said. "I recognize the signs from many similar cases. This is demonic possession, I tell you."

Sigismundo felt a wave of horror move up his spine.

When Brother Eugenius finally left, still warning that doctors do not understand such cases, Uncle Pietro sat down on the burnt-sienna divan with Aunt Gina and took her hand. "You know of my affection for you and your unfortunate son," he said. "I beg you to trust my judgment."

"Do you really think it is an illness?" Aunt Gina asked timidly, as if afraid to entertain hope again.

"I am convinced of it," Pietro said.

"Then take him to your wise doctor," Aunt Gina said. "Living with Tony the way he is now is worse than living with my grief."

When Antonio was called to the living room, Sigismundo was startled. His cousin looked paler than seemed possible for a Neapolitan, paler even than a Swede. And he smelled putrid.

"Uncle Pietro has come to take you to a doctor," Aunt Gina said.

Antonio looked at Uncle Pietro absently, as if a million more important things were distracting him. "My mother is a whore," he said, with no particular inflection. "Some noses are roses," he added thoughtfully.

"You are upset and confused," Uncle Pietro said.

"She became a whore to punish me," Antonio explained, reasonably. "Because I murdered my father. He had a funny nose, too. I am going to Hell, Jesus says, but so is everybody else."

"That is all nonsense," Pietro replied calmly. "You are frightened and confused, and that is all."

"Noses, noses, noses and pink roses!" Antonio screamed, suddenly losing his detachment. "You are another of the demons. Do you want to sodomize me, too?"

Sigismundo made the sign of the cross.

Aunt Gina sobbed again. "You see?" she said. "Can you imagine living with him, day after day?"

"It is just an excitement of the senses, caused by shock," Pietro said. "It can be cured."

"Nothing can be cured," Antonio said, suddenly drained of emotion again. "The Last Judgment is coming. They will chop off our noses. You have to go to Philadelphia," he added, turning abruptly to Sigismundo. "Everybody goes to Hell, but Siggy goes to Philadelphia. As there is a God of all things, my mind is a complete blank."

But Uncle Pietro was not buying that line of merchandise, and, despite a good deal more of it along the way, he remained calm as he led Antonio to his doctor friend. Sigismundo trailed along, perhaps for extra restraint if Tony got any wilder. Soon they were entering the Jewish ghetto.

"Are you sure you know what you're doing?" Sigismundo asked.

"I know his talk sounds like the language of Hell itself," Uncle Pietro said. "It is merely the language of dreams. It is happening to him when he is awake only because of shock."

They had arrived at the shop of a chemist called, according to the sign in the window, Abraham Orfali.

Pietro pushed open the door, and Sigismundo was overwhelmed by scents he could scarcely categorize. This Signor Orfali was better stocked than the average chemist.

Orfali came from behind a curtain as the bell over the door announced customers. He was white-bearded and almost dark enough to be a Moor: one of the Eastern Jews. Then Sigismundo noticed the old man's eyes. They were the eyes of one who penetrates everything he looks at, without surprise, without approval or contempt, with the detached absorption of a natural philosopher looking down a microscope.

"Pietro," Orfali said with genuine affection.

"Abraham, my friend," Uncle Pietro said. As they shook hands, Sigismundo noticed that their fingers curled in a strange way.

"You're another nose," Antonio remarked casually. "And a sodomite, too." He giggled childishly, but his eyes were like those of a family dog caught killing the chickens.

"So?" Orfali looked at Pietro inquiringly.

"This is Dr. Orfali," Pietro told Antonio sternly. "You will address him with respect. He does not practice medicine because of certain prejudices in this community, but he is the only one in Napoli who can help you."

"Nobody can help me," Antonio said dully. "I killed my father, and there are crocodiles behind that curtain."

"He's the one whose father was killed in the church?" Dr. Orfali asked Pietro. "I see. And this one?" pointing to Sigismundo.

"Another nephew, one you may know well some day," Pietro said. "Sigismundo Celine, Dr. Abraham Orfali."

"What are you going to do to me?" Antonio asked. "Brother Eugenius says they may need whips to drive the demons out. I'm afraid of whips."

"I do not think whips are what you need," Dr. Orfali said gently. "Come into the back room, and we will just talk a bit first."

"Very well," Antonio said. "I think the crocodiles have left. Except their noses."

They went into a tiny room that seemed to be crammed with books—in Hebrew, in Latin, in Spanish, in Arabic, even in Greek.

Dr. Orfali had brought an herb jar from the front of the shop, and he began mixing powder with water. "Why did you kill your father?" he asked. "Was he a very bad man?"

"Because I am a terrible sinner. Jesus says Napoli isn't bad enough for me and I must go to Hell."

"Oh, I see," Dr. Orfali said judiciously. "I suppose you've been committing these loathsome sins for about a year now?"

Antonio suddenly blushed. So did Sigismundo, vaguely understanding this.

Dr. Orfali was finished with his herbal mixture. "Please drink this," he said, as if it were a real favor to him. As Antonio obeyed the doctor said, "Thank you" very warmly. Then he added, "I'm not really sure you murdered your father. Maybe you just imagined that, because you have been excited and confused."

"But I have committed horrible sins," Antonio said vehemently. "I insult my mother and call her a whore. I don't know why. It is the devil inside me that takes over my nose . . . my nose."

He dropped the cup.

"You are getting tired," the doctor said. "I can understand that. You probably haven't slept well lately, yes?"

"I can hardly sleep at all," Antonio said. "At night the demons talk to me about Hell and sodomy and things that will happen in the future. Terrible things."

"What do the voices tell you about the future?" the doctor asked curiously.

"The Last Judgment is coming. Mobs will riot. Kings will die. Monasteries will be looted. Many will have their heads cut off in public. All Europe will be at war."

Pietro and Dr. Orfali exchanged glances.

"You are more tired," Abraham Orfali said, very softly now. "You can hardly keep your eyes open. Why don't you just rest for a while? The devils will not bother you here. I can see that your eyes are closing. You are safe here. With every word I speak and with every breath you take, the voices of the devils are going further away, fading away."

Antonio was now sound asleep.

"*Atoh Malkuth, ve-Geburah, ve-Gedullah, le-olahm,*" Abraham chanted, almost singing, looking upward passionately. Then he turned to Antonio again.

"Please repeat after me," he said. "Toward the One."

"Toward the One," Antonio spoke in his sleep.

"The perfection of love, harmony, and beauty."

"The perfection of love, harmony, and beauty."

"The only Being."

"The only Being."

"United with all those illuminated souls . . ."

"United with all those illuminated souls . . ."

"Who form the embodiment of the Teacher . . ."

"Who form the embodiment of the Teacher . . ."

"The Spirit of Guidance."

"The Spirit of Guidance."

"Good, most excellent," the doctor said. "Thank you. Now I am going to take you back in time to a day when you were in the botanical garden and the sun was very bright. It was a day when you were perfectly relaxed and very lazy. The sun was all over your body. You were wrapped in a cocoon of light. You can experience it again, right now. The sun is very relaxing, and all over your body. Your feet are very warm from the sun your legs are very warm you can feel it in your belly and your arms are very warm your chest is very warm . . . very warm and very relaxed . . ."

The doctor went on talking about that sunny day in the garden. He spoke more and more slowly, enunciating each word carefully, coming back to the same phrases over and over, repeating "warm" and "relaxed" many times. Sigismundo almost started to drowse himself, even without the sleep herb Antonio had been given.

"Now," Dr. Orfali said, "please take a deep breath, but very slowly. That's it. Inhale, inhale, inhale . . . keep inhaling. Fill your chest with that warm sunlight. Feel your heart full of golden sunlight. Now open your mouth and let it all out, slowly, as I count from eight to one. Eight . . . seven . . . six. . . five . . . four . . . three . . . two . . . one. *Very* good, *thank you.* Now, if you will look as far as you can see into the distance you will notice a gigantic figure in a red robe. He is the great archangel Rapha-El, who executes the Will of God. Speak his name."

"Rapha-El," Antonio said.

"Good, excellent. You are getting even more relaxed. Now behind you there is another gigantic archangel in a blue robe. His name is Gabri-El, and he communicates the Wisdom of God. Speak his name."

"Gabri-El."

"Good, very good. You are warm and relaxed now, and there is another gigantic archangel in a blue robe. His name is Gabri-El, and he communicates the Wisdom of God. Speak his name."

"Gabri-El."

"Good, very good. You are warm and relaxed now, and there is another archangel at your right, in a robe of glittering gold. His name is Micha-El, and he embodies the Love of God. Speak his name.'

"Micha-El."

"Now you will notice another archangel at your left, in a leafy green robe. His name is Auri-El, and he inhabits all the creations of God. Speak his name."

"Auri-El."

"Now I am going to count from eight to one again, and you will become even more relaxed and go deeper and deeper, because you have nothing to fear here, the angels will always be with you now, and they will make a shield to keep the devil voices out, you will always be protected, and I am starting to count . . ."

There was a great deal more sunlight and relaxation and counting backward and the angels kept returning with more details added at each appearance until even Sigismundo, who hadn't been drugged, was beginning to recognize distinct personalities in each of them, and then Dr. Orfali was counting backward again but at *one*, he asked suddenly, "Who killed your father?"

"I don't know. Four strangers . . ."

"And you will remember it that way from now on," old Abraham said. "You will no longer be mixed up and think you did it yourself. With every breath you take and with every word I utter, the voices of the devils are going further away, and the angels will always protect you. This is true, and you believe me, and you will be much relieved when you wake up, and day by day the voices will go further away, because every time you think they are starting again you will just breathe and count backward from eight to one and the angels will protect you. Now you will rest for a few moments, but it will be like many hours, and when I wake you, you will feel as if you've had a wonderful night's sleep, and you will feel very good all over, better than you've felt in years and years."

Dr. Orfali beckoned Pietro to a corner. Sigismundo, not invited but not warned off, followed them.

"Cases like this," Orfali said softly, "are the hardest of all. Despite what the donkeys and monkeys in the College of Medicine think, it is much easier to get rid of physical symptoms than these mental problems. You had better bring him back once a week, for a while, until I see signs of real transformation. Meanwhile, I can promise you that the improvement will be dramatic enough that his mother will not let the exorcists take their whips to the poor lad."

"I understand," Pietro said. "With physical symptoms you have only to treat one soul. In these cases you have to deal with all three."

Sigismundo decided they must be talking of the three souls described by Aristotle.

"I wish—" Pietro began. But he did not even finish, seeing the look in old Abraham's eyes.

"You know it is forbidden," the old man said.

Sigismundo realized that Pietro wanted to pay and that Abraham could not accept money because of an oath he had taken; and with that, he knew what Abraham was.

"FRC," he blurted out, unable to control himself, realizing that, just once in his life, he had to prove himself shrewder than Uncle Pietro realized.

Two bland faces, revealing no more than a pair of locked doors, looked down at him.

"That was a good guess," Pietro said quietly. "Considering certain *domini-canis*, however, you would do well to never mention that subject again."

Which was tantamount to a confession. Abraham Orfali was a very advanced member of the *Fraternitas Rosae Crucis*—the legendary Rosicrucians—the "Invisible College" that knew all the forbidden arts and sciences but lived in secrecy to avoid trouble with the authorities. Only the highest ranking Freemasons, it was said, could even apply for membership in the FRC.

They returned to Antonio.

"You will wake in a minute or so, feeling better than you have in years," the doctor repeated. "Within twenty-four hours you will decide that you haven't been getting enough exercise lately, and you will take up fencing or some other active sport, because now you have a lot of new energy. You will sleep well at nights, because the angels will always protect you. Your father was killed by four strangers, and you will always remember that correctly after today. Now, when I count to five you will wake up. One . . ."

And when Antonio woke up, he was in fact bright and cheerful again.

When Sigismundo and Uncle Pietro walked home with him, however, he did make a few peculiar remarks. Nothing as eerie as his earlier ramblings, but still somewhat bizarre: "Isn't it strange that people think time flows in only one direction?" he asked once, and later he added, "I know I've been confused, but Jesus *was a woman* when He came to me."

After they left Antonio with Aunt Gina, both looking much improved, Sigismundo said to Uncle Pietro, "I won't ask anything about the FRC," lowering his voice. "But tell me about the three souls. Aristotle doesn't say you can use them to heal diseases."

Pietro turned toward the Orto Botanico, obviously wanting some privacy for this conversation.

"Aristotle didn't know everything," he said quietly. "Actually, there are potentially at least eight souls. We are born with one, but how many we develop is a matter of education and hard work and, to tell you the truth, luck. The three souls Aristotle knew about are just the average at this stage of human development. The FRC," lowering his voice further, "is made up of men with at least four souls."

They entered the botanical garden. "The first soul is vegetative, as Aristotle said. It is the same in you and me and these plants. It feels terror when threatened and happiness when it is fed or nourished, and that is about all it feels and knows. It is quite mechanical. Vico claimed it was the only soul in the most primitive men, the giants."

"I read that," Sigismundo said. "Vico says the Cyclops in the *Odyssey* was one of these giants. He says they survive in the New World and the Indians call them 'Bigfoot.'"

"I haven't been to the Americas," Uncle Pietro said, "so I wouldn't know about that. The point is that this primitive soul—which you can observe easily in newborn infants —cannot speak and communicates in signs. According to FRC teaching," whispering again, "all physical illness, without exception, is the sign language of this vegetative mind. The signs are saying 'I am afraid,' 'I feel helpless,' 'I need Mama,' and so on. The doctors do not know this, so they bleed the victim or cut holes in him, and he gets worse and eventually dies. Dr. Orfali uses certain herbs to put the higher souls to sleep and then speaks to this primitive, infant soul and reassures it. It is said that a Magus must be male and female in one; that means he must become like a mother and speak as a mother to a frightened infant. You heard Abraham speaking that way, if you think about it."

Sigismundo digested this. "Then the animal soul," he said, "is characteristic, not just of beasts, but of the barbaric men, as Vico called them, the men who fight over territory. The Hercules type."

"Exactly. But you must remember that we each contain that barbaric psyche, just as we contain the more primitive vegetative psyche. The human soul, the pure reason, comes in on top of all that and is often overruled by vegetative fears or barbaric angers. In fact, reason very seldom overrules these older parts of the mind: more generally, it perverts itself to find rationalizations to justify them. The vegetative and animal souls are very old and deep, and reason is very new and weak thus far."

"And what happens in the illness of the senses, such as Antonio has?"

"That is a major civil war in the psyche. All three souls are equally confused by shock, and all are in conflict with each other. The cure may take a long time. It is very dangerous to talk of such things. If the Inquisition does not burn you at the stake for such ideas, the College of Medicine will plot your ruin in other ways."

"What about the fourth soul? How many men have developed to that level?"

"Teaching too much too fast makes for confusion," Uncle Pietro said. "Digest what I have already told you. Watch people and see which of the first three souls are acting in them at a given moment. See which souls dominate which people most of the time. Study yourself to see which soul is strongest most of the time. Then you can begin looking around for signs of the fourth soul in some people. But I warn you again: Do not talk about such things in Napoli. The eyes and ears of the Inquisition are everywhere."

But Sigismundo was thinking: No wonder the Inquisitors are often excessive and sometimes completely unfair. They see conspiracies everywhere because, by God, there *are* conspiracies everywhere. In only a few months I have learned of the *Carbonari*, who may or may not be the inner chiefs of Masonry; and the Jacobites, who may or may not be the *Carbonari*; and the Masons themselves, who may be anyone and everyone (including even a Jesuit like Father Ratti); and the *Alumbrados*, who may include the *Rossi* unless it's the other way around and the *Rossi* include the *Alumbrados*; and the MAFIA; and now the FRC. We have more secret societies than a you-know has crabs; more than the Umbertos have florins out at interest; more than my poor head can comprehend.

Uncle Pietro guessed his thoughts. "It is always that way in conquered nations," he said sadly.

▲

There was a piece by Scarlatti, a Sonata in D Major, that was like the human soul trying to free itself from the vegetative and animal souls, and Sigismundo was walking in the market, working on a variation, developing a series of chords that would carry the theme through a circular or "solar" permutation (like some of the old church music) to arrive back where it started in such a way that it would be going forward and backward at the same time. This was very amusing because the mathematics of it was so precise—almost like two Greeks haggling over a contract—and yet the sound would be in the *galant* style, and you'd almost want to dance to it.

And then Sigismundo saw Carlo Maldonado, resplendently

rich in the magnificent brocade of that family, examining silks at a stall. You couldn't miss Carlo. His stockings were the same precise blue as his blouse, his cloak was woven with enough gold thread to make a hoard for a miser, and even in Napoli, where the nobles were not famous for drab or conservative dress, he was as unobtrusive as a unicorn.

Sigismundo's steps faltered. Guilt and remorse gnawed at him as he thought: There's the innocent boy I almost murdered. Because I didn't stop to think. Because I let the animal in me run wild. Because I was the Cyclops, as Vico would say, and not the Odysseus.

But even as he started to turn, Sigismundo suddenly became conscious of many eyes around him. They are not looking at me, he told himself quickly. But still if he turned too suddenly, *somebody* might notice. *Somebody* might say the Malatestas were afraid to show their faces on the streets when they saw the Maldonados coming.

Sigismundo walked forward, not looking at Carlo, walking past him rapidly, staring ahead as if at some goal he must reach in a hurry. And then he collided with a blond man and was catapulted slam-bang, openmouthed as an idiot, right into Carlo's chest.

"Hey," Carlo cried, "watch where you're going—" Then he recognized Sigismundo. "Oh," he said. "A Malatesta. Has the wine finally ruined the brains of your whole family? Can't you even walk straight?"

Sigismundo's hand moved toward his sword hilt, but he stopped it midway. The rational human soul should govern the emotions of the animal soul.

"I am sorry," he said stiffly. "It was an accident."

But the blond man, who was very tall but dark of skin—half Sicilian and half Northerner, probably—was looming above both boys. "'I'm *thorry*,'" he repeated, mimicking Sigismundo. "'It *wath* an *accthident*.' How effeminate the

Malatestas have grown," he added sarcastically, addressing everybody within earshot.

"You stay out of this," Sigismundo said sharply. "It's none of your business." But his ears were reddening; he wasn't sure he did not look like a coward to some of the crowd.

Carlo, only twelve after all, was beginning to see the possibilities of emerging as a real hero and thoroughly humiliating a Malatesta. "*Yeth, thtay* out of *thith*," he lisped, in the same caricature of Sigismundo's tone, making it sound girlish.

Sigismundo considered. "You know," he said to Carlo, "If my dog had a nose like yours, I'd shave his rump and teach him to walk backward."

The crowd was bigger and louder now. "You tell him, Sigismundo," somebody shouted.

Carlo flushed. "The only sheep in Napoli who are still virgins are the ones who can run faster than you," he said.

There was a satisfactory roar of laughter. "You tell him, Carlo," somebody shouted.

"I wonder," Sigismundo said, "does Count Maldonado have any idea who your real father is, or was the list of suspects too long?"

The laughter was louder. Everybody thought this was turning into a great entertainment. Maybe we should add juggling and trapeze and then take up a collection, Sigismundo thought.

Then Carlo bit his thumbnail. The laughter stopped.

Sigismundo sighed. "Don't draw your sword," he said. "You might cut your dork off."

That did it: Carlo had his sword out in a second.

"Take back what you just said about my mother," he demanded, his voice shrill. (He's afraid of me, Sigismundo thought, but he's more afraid of backing down in public. Thus cowardice doth make courage for us all, as Uncle Pietro would say.)

Carlo's sword was pointing nowhere yet, not in the challenge position exactly. "Take it back," he repeated.

"I meant no offense," Sigismundo said stiffly. "It was just banter. I thought we were just teasing each other."

Carlo decided this was weakness.

"Take it back," he repeated, now raising his sword to challenge position.

How do you get free of the damnable books of Romance when everybody else is still living in them?

"Listen," Sigismundo said, "I don't want to hurt you—"

"Two little girls," the blond man said mockingly. "Each one afraid of the other."

Sigismundo's sword was in his hand at once. *Stop and think*, he was telling himself, but the sword was already at challenge.

It was another frieze, just like the horror in San Francesco di Paola on Easter. For it seemed an eternity as he slowly moved his sword to tip Carlo's, making the challenge official. *Moira*: I almost killed him once, through stupidity, and I escaped by luck, and now here I am playing the same scene again. Uncle Pietro is right: he says Destiny is the name we give our bad habits when we realize they cannot be changed.

"The brave fools die first!" said a familiar voice in a tone of withering contempt.

Everyone turned as old Tennone pushed to the center of the crowd.

"What heroic children," Tennone said loudly, "ready to die right now, just over a few stupid words. And what fine citizens we have here, egging these children on, just to see some fresh blood again. What, are you all bored? Has it been a few weeks since the last murder? You, sir," picking a fat fruit merchant out of the crowd, "if you are really in need of excitement, how would you like to exchange a few thrusts with me?"

"Now wait a minute," the merchant said. "You're a professional . . ."

"What?" Tennone cried. "Are you afraid? What kind of Neapolitan are you? Do you lack testicles, my man? Or is there shit in your blood?"

"Stop bullying," the merchant stammered. "Everybody knows you're invulnerable."

"Well, then, who does want a fight?" Tennone demanded. "I'm waiting," he said coldly.

The crowd began to disperse.

"You two simpletons," Tennone said then. Sigismundo and Carlo both blushed. "Go home and tell your mothers you almost gave them a new funeral to celebrate. Go! Or I'll give you both a kick where it won't blind you."

But as Carlo slunk away in one direction and Sigismundo in the other, Sigismundo suddenly realized that the tall blond man had vanished very rapidly as soon as the swords were drawn. He pushed me into Carlo, Sigismundo thought, and he incited us to fight . . .

A *Rosso*? Wheels within wheels, as Drake said.

Sigismundo felt himself in the middle of a world where nothing was ever quite what it seemed, where treachery and conspiracy were as omnipresent as the whine of the professional beggars.

Moira: a knot, a predetermined thing.

▲

And then it was the hottest, most punishing part of summer—the "dog days"—and all of Napoli went quite mad, as usual. The more excitable *signorine* were not content merely to weep loudly at the Teatro San Carlo but often fainted dead away when popular tenors sang the more melancholy *arias*. New miracles were reported every second day, most of them so lunatic that the Church quickly disavowed them. One peasant claimed the Holy Grail descended out of the sky, the Virgin got out of it, and she told him Ferdinand IV would be forced to abdicate but would later be restored to power. The Umbertos, who had come out of God knows where in the South to become one of the richest banking families in Napoli, were suddenly arrested by the Dominicans and held *incommunicado* while rumors went hither and yon about incredible confessions concerning goat worship and infant sacrifice.

Then a gang of drunks went down to the ghetto one night and began burning the Jews' shops. Ferdinand IV sent in the police, and the hooligans were arrested and sentenced to be dragged through town behind mules while being whipped by the public hangman—"giving them air and exercise," that was what it was called in popular speech.

Maria Maldonado came home from the convent school for the summer, even lovelier than ever. Sigismundo suffered every time he saw her, because she was unaware of his existence, and because he could not stop having impure thoughts about her, and because whether this was love or lust did not matter, since it was impossible either way. She was a Maldonado, he was a Malatesta; he had more chance of a happy marriage, a passionate novelistic romance, or even a one-night liaison with that naked stone Venus in Drake's garden.

So it was a great relief when August came and he was able to go with Uncle Pietro on their long-planned trip to Rimini. Between the heat and the you-knows in the market and Maria, Napoli was becoming a continuing invitation to the sins of the flesh.

The ostensible purpose of the journey was to expose Sigismundo to more of the operations of the family wine business. Actually, Pietro was much more concerned with showing the boy the Tempio Malatesta, the incredible architectural grotesque created by their infamous ancestor Sigismundo Pandolfo Malatesta in the 1440s, over three hundred years ago.

Nobody in Italy knew what to make of the Tempio Malatesta, nor of Sigismundo Pandolfo Malatesta himself, but

Pietro never left any doubt that he was damned proud of both of them. He talked of the *tempio* so often, in fact, that most of the Malatestas in Napoli were convinced it was even more glamorous than Saint Peter's in Roma.

Coach travel was new to Sigismundo, and by the time they were halfway through the journey, in Arezzo, he was beginning to think the coach was an instrument of torture invented to persuade wise people to stay home and let the bloody fools do all the traveling. The first day is exciting, he thought—all the new scenery to see; the second day is increasingly boring and uncomfortable; by the third day you begin to suspect that you will never get your body into an uncramped posture again.

When they stopped at Assisi, Pietro insisted on visiting the birthplace and shrine of San Francesco. This slightly surprised Sigismundo, who was growing increasingly doubtful about Uncle Pietro's orthodoxy. Too many trips to England, too many Masonic contacts, too many conversations with Protestants . . . But at the shrine, Pietro began reciting one of San Francesco d'Assisi's poems, and he chanted with such fervor that the boy suddenly thought his enigmatic uncle was as pious as a Dominican, in his own odd way. One line in particular moved him: *"Nel fuoco d'amore mi mise."*

Into the fire of love, Sigismundo thought; it would be wonderful to be that close to God. He never felt that way in church or in any of his efforts at prayer; only music ever raised him to that perspective, where the fire of love was the most important fact about existence. Music, and Maria Maldonado; and what he felt for music was profane, although permissible, while what he felt for Maria was probably sinful lust. If only he could feel that fire for God, he would be a saint like Francesco himself.

He wished he was a saint in love with God instead of an artistic fool in love with the daughter of Count Maldonado.

When they finally arrived in Rimini, it was a shock to see the Adriatic Sea. It was dark as wine—like Homer's *oinopa ponton*—and didn't have the coppery glitter of the Bay of Naples. And the people were strange, too—tall Northerners, many of them blond and red-haired, totally unlike Neapolitans even though they spoke approximately the same language.

If Sigismundo learned anything about the wine business on that trip, it did not stay with him for long. He was overwhelmed by the Tempio Malatesta and the horror that came after it.

Of course, he had known the scandalous legend of the *tempio* for years—who in Italy did not know it? Sigismundo Pandolfo Malatesta was either the greatest man or the greatest monster of the fifteenth century, depending upon whose story you believed. The Church had convicted him of atheism, parricide, incest, adultery, rape, sodomy, perjury, treason, sacrilege, and a few dozen miscellaneous heresies and atrocities. Those were all damned lies, Uncle Pietro said, slander created by Sigismundo Malatesta's enemies.

Actually, incest or no incest, rape or no rape, sodomy or no sodomy, Sigismundo Pandolfo Malatesta, prince of Rimini, was an extremist even by the standards of the uncouth times in which he lived. Almost every prince in Europe had had a war with the Pope by then, but they had always had the decency to claim they had a better Pope of their own; keeping track of all the conflicting Popes and anti-Popes was the hardest part of religious history class for Sigismundo Celine. But Sigismundo Malatesta, his ancestor, boldly told the world that he didn't believe in the Pope, the Church, Jesus, or anything at all, except the atoms of Epicurus, the void in which the atoms are suspended, and his own Will. He did not hide his mistresses either, as other princes did, but flaunted them openly, and year by year their numbers grew to equal any Turk's hareem.

The Tempio Malatesta had been built, in fact, to honor the

last and best loved of Sigismundo's mistresses, Ixotta degli Atti, whom he had finally married. It had not one Christian icon in it, but contained a monument proclaiming *Divae Ixottae sacrum*—sacred to the Divine Ixotta. When Ixotta died, Sigismundo Malatesta entombed her there, under a plaque saying "Ixotta of Rimini, in beauty and virtue the glory of Italy." The rest of the temple was dedicated entirely to the gods of ancient Rome.

If you can imagine a Barbary ape with pepper up his nose, Uncle Pietro said, you can imagine how Pope Pius II, the reigning pontiff, jumped and howled and screamed when he found out about this heathen temple. When it was further reported that Sigismundo Malatesta had once filled the fonts of the Christian churches in Rimini with ink so that he could stand in the streets and laugh at the ink-dabbed foreheads of the faithful as they returned from Mass, His Holiness "had the apoplexy, the falling fits, and blind staggers," as Uncle Pietro robustly expressed it.

The war between Sigismundo Malatesta, prince of Rimini, and Pope Pius II, bishop of Roma, was won by the pope, as everybody knew; and Sigismundo Malatesta did penance afterward by serving five years as commander of the Venetian army and winning several victories against the Turks. "A man must adapt to the facts of power," Uncle Pietro said, "and besides, the Church is our great benefactor in this most enlightened and humane of all nations."

Nonetheless, the Tempio Malatesta remained standing in Rimini, the one indisputably pagan shrine created in Italy since the triumph of Christianity. And Sigismundo Malatesta had imported the body of the philosopher Gemisto Plethon from Constantinople for reentombment in the *tempio*, honored equally with Ixotta degli Atti, the gods of the pagans, and Sigismundo Malatesta himself; for Plethon was the last of the

Gnostics, who taught that the reality of religion was so mysterious that only a minority of illuminated men and women could ever understand it.

Contemporary sources added that Sigismundo Malatesta wrote poetry, studied the Greek and Latin classics, and patronized numerous men of art and science, whose company he preferred to that of his fellow nobles. They also reported that the prince of Rimini thought paganism more beautiful than Christianity but the philosophy of Epicurus more true than either; that he was a Freemason; that he had said many times that the Church went rotten as soon as bishops acquired huge estates and started thinking like landlords; and that he once remarked, in the hearing of men of good repute, although he was admittedly more than a little inebriated at the time, that he almost believed his lips touched God's beatific essence only when he ran them over the body of the divine Ixotta degli Atti and he had never experienced such holy awe when chewing the bread blessed by priests.

Sigismundo Celine was properly horrified, but also somewhat uncomfortably fascinated, by such a sinister ancestor. He was even more fascinated by the *tempio* when he entered the fane and saw the heroic elephants leading inward to the halls of gold and beauty.

"Took years for the Masons to get those elephants right," Uncle Pietro said, but Sigismundo hardly heard him. He was transported right out of his body, as if by a new Scarlatti sonata. He had never seen so much luminous jewelry and so many precious metals before. He had never seen architecture in this promethean, megalomaniac mode before. And he had never seen so many unclothed female bodies before.

The Tempio Malatesta was not dedicated to "the pagan gods" in general, he perceived. It was dedicated to Venus, the ideal female body. Mars was there, and Diana, and Jove, and others, but chiefly it was Venus he saw, and another Venus, and another. All of them golden, glorious, provocatively offering their beauty, as shameless as whores and yet as proud as musicians offering new *sinfonias*. It was to the boy a temple of sensuality and nudity and Satanic pride. Shame did not exist here, modesty was forgotten and almost unimaginable; it was as if the artists had never known sin or had been ordered by the Lord Malatesta to forget everything they ever heard on that subject. There was only flesh and light and joy: golden flesh and clear light and pagan joy.

And then Sigismundo Celine came to Duccio's painting of his monster-ancestor. Sigismundo Pandolfo Malatesta, egotist, anarchist, rebel, was portrayed, unbelievably, kneeling before a statue of San Francesco d'Assisi, his face upturned in rapt adoration. Was this an attempt to dilute the lewd paganism of the *tempio*, a concession to the Church, or did the prince of Rimini have his own heathen, pantheistic reasons for honoring the saint who talked to the birds and wrote hymns to the sun?

How many of the things written against my strange ancestor were true, Sigismundo Celine wondered, and how much was, as Uncle Pietro says, the slander of his enemies?

There was no way to answer that question, ever. Sigismundo Malatesta was lost, back there in the abyss of past time, three centuries ago; the verdict of his enemies got into the surviving chronicles.

But the *tempio* also survived, and in it something of the man remained, something that was not entirely monstrous. This architecture, these paintings and statues were like music: coherent in many dimensions. Sigismundo thought of Pythagoras and the Pythagorean "secret society" in ancient Italy. He remembered the legend that the Masons had secrets, geometrical and mystical teachings preserved since the Pythagoreans, hidden formulas about Cabala and magick. These formulas were in all the great medieval and Renaissance buildings, it was said, but only another Freemason could decipher them.

"Isn't she lovely?" Uncle Pietro said, pausing before a Venus with eyes that seemed alive after three hundred years. "She was our ancestor. The artists were ordered to use Ixotta degli Atti's face on every image of the goddess."

The eyes of Sigismundo Celine's great-great-great-grandmother (or however many greats it took to go back three centuries) spoke to him from the canvas. Duccio had captured the woman's soul in her expression. She was as proud and shameless as her infamous consort.

This whole building, whatever else it was saying, was a love poem in stone. It was announcing to all the world, for all centuries to come, to anybody who wandered in here looking for Renaissance culture, or some insight into the bandit-nobility of the fifteenth century, or just to get out of the sun: *Look, I, Sigismundo Pandolfo Malatesta, spent a fortune to build this, because I loved one woman past all measure, past reason, past limits*. The Inquisitors claimed that Sigismundo Malatesta committed incest with his sister, poisoned his brother, raped a nun once. The temple said: *I loved beauty*.

"He supervised every tiny detail, even writing long letters to the artists when he was away serving as mercenary general to other princes, when he wanted to raise more money to make the *tempio* even more outrageously stupendous," Uncle Pietro said. "All the tracery, you will notice, consists of variations on the intertwining of his initial with hers—*S* and *I*."

Sigismundo loves Ixotta: it resonated from every lovely statue and erotic painting to every soaring arch and illuminated column. Sigismundo Pandolfo Malatesta of Rimini made this monument of excess because he loves Ixotta, and paganism, and the Gnostics. And he doesn't give a flying French coitus for the pope or Christianity. Out of the most Catholic of all countries, in the most Catholic of all centuries, Sigismundo Malatesta had created this symphony in marble and gold to hail his own private gods: against all the laws of probability and history, the first pagan temple in a thousand years.

"And he didn't even believe in God," Sigismundo Celine said, bewildered by this glorification of those powers the Church called lust and pride and sensuality.

"He had his own definition of God," Uncle Pietro said. "To the popes, orthodoxy is God. To San Francesco, love was God. To the Dominicans, killing has become God. To our ancestor, Prince Sigismundo, whom I wished you to be named after, beauty itself was God."

Toward the One, the perfection of love, harmony, and beauty, the only Being . . .

Sigismundo Celine remembered Cousin Antonio raving about Jesus being a woman. In his own way, while trying to get his three souls back together, Antonio had been trying to say what their ancestor had said in this building. It is not just in music, Sigismundo thought, where I first heard it. It can be in a building like this, too. It is inside all of us. It can be the fire of love in which San Francesco had dwelt; perhaps that is why the Lord Malatesta honored him. They were both consumed by the fire of love, in different ways.

And as he stood there, looking at nudity unashamed for the first time in his life, he was being consumed by fire, too.

▲

Sigismundo Celine carried away one further memory from the *tempio*: on the tomb of his ancestor, Sigismundo Malatesta, the family motto

TEMPUS LOQUENDI

TEMPUS TACENDI

"There is a time to talk, and a time to be silent." Uncle Pietro was always guided by that motto, he realized.

On their way back to their inn, Sigismundo wondered about his uncle's connections with Freemasons and Jacobites and Rosicrucians, and about the Freemasonry of their sinister ancestor, Sigismundo Malatesta, and the proportions of music and Masonic buildings, and of the naked goddess who was life and beauty and light in one.

Of course, he thought, my diabolical ancestor was a great sinner, and Uncle Pietro is probably another, and Dr. Abraham Orfali is a Jew beyond doubt, so obviously I am being seduced into heresy and perverted from the true Faith. Obviously. But, then, Father Ratti is probably a Mason, too. Maybe I can learn to be whatever it is these men are and still remain a good Catholic.

Uncle Pietro picked just the right moment to tell me I am named after *that* Sigismundo. That is why he encourages my music. He knows it does not have to come out in architecture each time, but he wants it to come out again. Everything that happens is part of a process of gradual revelation that my genially Machiavellian uncle decided on before I was even born.

He was too excited to resent that.

Toward the One . . . the fire of love . . . Maria naked . . .

He realized he was seeing everything with great clarity, as on Easter Sunday when the atrocity happened. This is a kind of shock, too: time has been stretched out of joint, not by horror this time, but by ecstasy.

It was in that heightened awareness that he realized he and Uncle Pietro were being followed.

He wondered how to steal a peek at the stalker without being obvious.

Meanwhile, he listened, and used more the subtle senses Tennone had hammered into him in fencing class. The follower was remaining about ten yards behind and was large. Large even for a Northerner.

Approaching an inn, they passed a row of shops. Sigismundo quickly said, "Oh, what's that?" and turned as if to look more closely in a window. He saw a row of silks, as gay as a tree full of parrots. But he also caught a glimpse of the stalking man, who was also stopping to look in another window. It was the blond Sicilian who had provoked the quarrel between him and Carlo Maldonado.

"Uncle," Sigismundo said softly.

"I know," Pietro replied quietly. "Keep your voice down. No, no—too expensive," he added loudly.

They walked on.

"That blond man," Uncle Pietro said. "For two days now at least. Don't jump like that. He is just one of di Tanucci's boys."

"The secret police? I do not think so. He is the one who almost got me into a duel with Carlo Maldonado."

"Very well," Pietro said. "He is a *Rosso*. He was one of the four in church last Easter. You didn't notice him then because you were busy wrestling the younger one, with the violet eyes."

Sigismundo took a deep breath. "And why did you try to deceive me this time?"

"So that you wouldn't make a blazing idiot of yourself again."

It is inspiring, the confidence everybody has in me.

"And why do you not denounce him to the police, since you know he is one of the *Rossi*?" Sigismundo asked, still quietly.

"How many chess games have you lost by making the obvious move? If he saw me walking toward a police building, he would vanish like the stars at sunrise. Meanwhile, the other one would still be on our trail."

"The *other* one?"

"Not so loud, damn it." Uncle Pietro took Sigismundo's arm and strolled on very casually. "There are always two on a surveillance team. One is careless, or so it seems: it is easy to spot him. The other is more subtle. All the tricks of mountebanks work the same way. You see something you think you were intended not to see and then, while you are congratulating yourself on your shrewdness, the second trick, the real sting, goes right by you."

"Like the three-card game, where you think the queen turned over accidentally?"

"Precisely. I have been trying to spot the second one for over a day now, and still he eludes me. I almost think they are violating the rules and there *is* only the blond man; but it is not safe to think that way. I keep watching."

But when they were back in their room at the inn, Uncle Pietro said, "I still haven't found the second one. Maybe I am getting old. Anyway, they do not have assassination in mind this time, or they would have made their move by now. They have something else planned, and I hate to think of it. Damn, damn, I am sorry it has to start when you are still so young."

Sigismundo remembered violet eyes looking into his own, in San Francesco di Paola, clearly unwilling to kill him. He had never liked to think about that.

"When are you going to tell me the truth about any of this?" he asked in exasperation.

"These are evil times, and this is a violent part of the world," Uncle Pietro said. "Knowledge, which should be the liberator of mankind, is a terrible burden instead. He who knows too much is in peril. I keep telling myself, 'Wait, wait, when he's a little older . . .'"

"If we are being stalked by assassins," Sigismundo said, "I think a little knowledge might not be as dangerous as total ignorance." But he was also afraid of what he might hear.

Uncle Pietro went to the door and looked into the hall. When he returned, he moved two chairs to the point furthest from either the door or the window. Sigismundo half expected him to complete this performance by looking under the bed.

But, after all, this is the land of the Inquisition, and what was coming was not going to be the kind of thing you would stand up and yell in the marketplace.

"My 'club' is a big one," Pietro whispered. "The FRC. Our work is very dangerous, but it must be done. It is not something you do for glory or for profit. You do it for the reason our ancestor built the *tempio*. Do you understand?"

"You are heretics," Sigismundo said very quietly. I always knew it, he thought. He has given me so many clues that anybody who could count the walls in the room wouldn't miss it.

"*According to one pope long ago*, we are heretics," Pietro said carefully. "One pope is not the whole Church."

"You have Jews among you. Protestants also?"

"Even Mohammedans," Pietro whispered.

"Father Ratti is one of you?"

"Yes."

I knew it. "Does he think he is still a good Catholic, or is he just one of your spies within the church?"

"He is a good and pious Catholic. Abraham Orfali is a good and pious Jew. What we are doing is beyond sect, it is for all mankind."

"That *is* heresy," Sigismundo said gravely. Now I come to the moment of supreme temptation. He was right to keep it from me when I was younger.

"Galileo was a heretic once," Pietro argued. "The Church changes and grows."

"Can I go to confession ever again? If I tell, you will all be arrested. If I do not tell, I will be in mortal sin."

"Many of us go to confession and receive the Sacraments," Pietro said. "It is no sin to work for the enlightenment of mankind. It is no sin to keep quiet about things that will be misunderstood. *Tempus loquendi, tempus tacendi.*"

"That is sophistry," Sigismundo said. "Heresy is sin. To

protect heretics is sin. You can't change that with your merchant's clever word tricks. Papa said once that you could sell sand to the Arabs, but you can't sell me the line that this isn't heresy."

There was a pause. They looked away from each other.

"You will denounce me," Pietro said finally.

This day and this moment will never come again, Sigismundo thought. What I decide now is forever.

"I cannot denounce you," he said. "I think I am a heretic myself and have been for a long time without knowing it."

"When my second daughter was born," Pietro whispered, one outlaw to another, "the midwife warned me. If we had any more children, my pretty Violetta would be in grave danger. I looked, for years, trying to see a sign that my daughters had the power. They didn't. I love them, they are fine girls, but it doesn't always pass directly to one's children. It is part of our oath that we must pass the knowledge on to a child born with the power so it never dies out completely."

"I thought only *strege* had the power?"

"Many have it, in all nations. It is merely the habit of the Dominicans to claim that anyone who shows it publicly *is* a *strega*."

"That is why I do not get along well with boys my age? Not just because I am an artist?"

"Those with the power are always the lonely, at first. Many misuse it, become *strege* or worse. The FRC is to teach how it should be used as God intended it."

"It is also where my music comes from?"

"Of course. You are growing toward the fourth soul."

"Why am I such a fool so often then?"

"It is that way," Pietro said with a grimace. "Our ancestor had the power in very large measure, as you could see in the *tempio*. He squandered his wealth to build that one beautiful edifice. He got into dozens of stupid wars, declared his opinions openly, virtually forced the pope to excommunicate him. He died nearly bankrupt, a considerable feat for a man born so rich. Without guidance, we do not *use* the power, Siggy: it uses and abuses us."

Sigismundo sighed. "And how do Drake and the Jacobites fit into this? If his name really is Drake?"

"Oddly enough, it *is* Drake. Robert Francis Drake. Descended from the famous pirate, he says. As for the Jacobites, they are Freemasons, too, but few of them have reached the rank of the FRC," lowering his voice still further on the initials.

"What is the goal of Masonry?"

"Brotherhood. Peace. To put an end to the damned fool wars that have torn Europe apart."

"And the goal of the FRC?"

"That is harder to describe in ordinary language. It is concerned more with the inner world than the outer."

"And why was Uncle Leonardo killed and why are we under surveillance? There is more than revolution in this, right?"

"The *Alumbrados* have their own ideas about the power and who should use it and how it should be used. Your Uncle Leonardo was one of us, the FRC. Like the Inquisitors, the *Alumbrados* wish us abolished, exterminated. If possible, they would like even the record of our existence expunged, so that none would know of the power but themselves."

Sigismundo remembered Father Ratti talking of mind control, strange drugs, powers that were not flesh and blood. He involuntarily made the sign of the cross.

"Yes," Pietro said. "You have heard enough for now. Some things will have to wait until you are older."

Sigismundo did not protest. He had a deep, crawly sensation that there were some secrets he did not want to confront yet.

▲

In Arezzo, on the way home, Sigismundo saw the blond Sicilian again. Just once; but he suddenly realized that every face on every street is as incomprehensible a mystery as the dogma of the Holy Trinity. You have no idea what any of them are really thinking or planning. You are alone, completely alone, and always vulnerable.

This quiet man who does not even seem to notice you might be an assassin who has been waiting for you to pass this way. More strange and terrible: you don't even know what the harmless ones are thinking. This unfriendly, irritable woman may be mourning a dead child; this cheerful man may have been maddened by the French pox and think he is Cato the Elder.

Suddenly the whole street was foreground and he, Sigismundo, was just background—no, he was hardly there at all. An overwhelming sense of the reality and fragility of the world descended upon him: it was huge, it was full of people, all of them were different, and all were important to themselves; millions came, millions passed, millions died, and Sigismundo Celine was not the center of all Creation by any means. I am lost in the mass and vertigo of everything that is not me, he thought; I am, somehow, outside this world looking in, and it is all glass, and spinning rapidly, and it shatters easily.

He felt the Horror coming closer, and knew he would find part of the secrets Uncle Pietro had not told him, very soon and very unpleasantly.

▲

The torrid "dog days" were over when they returned; Napoli was enjoying its usual balmy climate again.

"Come walk in the garden," Father Ratti said one day.

Sigismundo accompanied the Jesuit to the Sacred Heart garden, wondering what was coming now.

"Ever since you asked me about the Jacobites," Father Ratti said, "I have been remembering a song about the battle of Culloden Moor. I thought you might find it interesting, since it is in the kind of English that the Scots speak. It is not at all like ordinary English." His face was as bland as that of a three-card-monte artist.

Ratti opened a book of English verse and read "Lament for Culloden." It was a dramatic monologue about the sufferings of the Scots at the hands of the English army. Sigismundo was especially moved by the last stanza:

> Now wae to thee, thou cruel lord,
> A bluidy man I trow thou be;
> And monie a heart thou hast made sair
> That ne'er did wrang to thine or thee.

"It is indeed unlike ordinary English," Sigismundo said awkwardly, waiting for the trap to be sprung. Then he blurted: "It is most stark and tragic. I hate the world for being that way."

"All decent men hate it," Father Ratti said. "The question is: How do we change it?"

Life is one test after another, Sigismundo thought. "Who is the man denounced in the closing lines, the cruel lord?" he asked, stalling for time. Ratti is one of them—a Jesuit but a heretic, too.

"William, duke of Cumberland," the priest replied, and in the guise of further historical background to the song returned to his real theme: "He was indeed a 'bluidy man.' After the victory, he pursued the clans who had supported Bonnie Prince Charlie back to their hills and homesteads. *All* members of these clans were killed, even those who had not joined the rebellion. Several clans were exterminated, down to the last man, woman, and child. Infants were not spared. William's troops were given free reign to burn every barn, every house, every granary they passed. Thousands of women were raped. Children were bayoneted to death. We have no word for this, my child: it was the murder of a whole culture, a people, a way of life. Do you understand?"

"It is sickening," Sigismundo said bitterly.

"And it was not madness or blind fury," the Jesuit went on, his mouth as tight as that of a Dominican discussing Voltaire. "The English crown had decided to teach a lesson in reality to the Scots, as the Roman senate decided to teach a lesson to the slaves after the Spartacus uprising by crucifying fifty thousand men along the Via Appia. This is the truth of history, my child. This is what government is all about; this is what power means."

"I hate it," Sigismundo repeated. "I thought such monstrosities happened only in primitive ages."

"The crown was most pleased with William of Cumberland," the Jesuit went on. "They actually named a flower after him—isn't that touching? It is called Sweet William. The Scots have never accepted the name. They call it Stinking Billy."

So now I know what the Jacobites are, Sigismundo thought. They are the survivors of a holocaust.

"Such things are more common than you realize, Sigismundo," Ratti said. "History texts are not chosen by disinterested scholars seeking only the truth. They are chosen by government censors. I know of no subject more likely to destroy one's faith in the moral order of the universe than the true record of what princes and prime ministers have done."

Sigismundo was now sure he knew where all this was leading.

"Suppose there was one group concerned only with truth and justice," he said abruptly. "They would be abused and denounced by the fanatics of all parties, is that not so?"

"Undoubtedly," the Jesuit said carefully.

"Such a group would have to include men of all nations," Sigismundo went on. "There would be both Catholics and Protestants among them, and even Jews and Moslems."

"It could be."

"That would make them heretics," Sigismundo said bluntly. Let us have it out in the light of day, he thought.

"If they were condemned by an ecclesiastical court and if they then remained obdurate," the Jesuit said precisely, "they would certainly be heretics. Since that has not happened to the, ah, hypothetical group we are imagining, it is for each man to search his conscience in the matter and decide if it is heresy or not. When I say 'search the conscience,' I mean nothing casual, I hope you realize. One must be totally sure of one's sincerity and of the rightness of one's course. One must not act out of vanity or childish romanticism, do you understand?"

"Thank you, Father," Sigismundo said. "I always find your talks on religious knowledge most helpful."

He was thinking: Are the Jesuits a stalking horse for the Jacobites, or are the Jacobites a tool of the Jesuits? Or does the FRC run both of them?

And: No wonder the Jesuits have been expelled from so many nations. Nobody knows what they are really plotting; they are as enigmatic as a cat's eyes.

▲

The horror came quite unexpectedly, one day as he was returning from school, just after the beginning of the autumn term.

He had found a short cut lately, an alley between two *palazzi* that saved nearly five minutes of circular uphill huffing and puffing.

That day, a Thursday it was, he saw the blond man again, in the alley ahead of him.

And so there was the exquisite pleasure of stalking the stalker, spying on the spy: through one alley after another, across this *palazzo* and that garden after that garden and another *palazzo*, proud of his skill and stealth, never thinking of who might be stalking *him*, more skillfully, more stealthily.

The blond man finally entered a seedy, run-down inn with

peeling paint and dirty windows—the kind of place patronized only by the poor.

Sigismundo lounged in a doorway and watched. Others entered the inn, and they had the look of *Rossi* about them: peasants, yes, but peasants without humility, with rage and violence in their faces. They were the kind of men who would sell you their daughters for two lire, slit a throat for five lire, dump the archbishop in the bay, well weighted down, for a florin. The sane, sensible thing to do at this point, he realized, would be to remember the name of this place (Osteria Dante) and report it at once to Drake in the palace. That was obvious. So naturally he found a way to enter the garden from the other side and climb the wall of the adjoining coffee house. From the roof he quickly made the jump to the roof of the inn.

He had entered enemy territory unobserved.

Now he might really have something to tell Drake, if he saw them before they put their hoods on.

There were a thousand and one potted plants, as on any roof in Napoli. He found his way among them to the staircase.

He inhaled, held the breath to the count of four, exhaled to the count of eight. He was empty and emotionless.

He stepped onto the staircase, then paused. The only sounds were from the tavern.

YOUNG MUSICIAN EXPOSES REVOLUTIONAR-IES: It would be in the journals all over Italy.

He descended slowly. As he expected, the second-floor landing led to a hall that passed him to a balcony above the tavern.

He crept forward to the balcony.

There were thirteen men in the tavern—the same number as comprises a witch's coven—and the street door was bolted. They were hooded already. Their solid black again reminded him of a caricature of a religious order.

Black candles were being lit on the walls.

The tallest man—the blond *Siciliano*, Sigismundo guessed —raised a dagger to the north, east, south, west.

"Tana, who is our green mother," he intoned solemnly. "Orpheus, who is our golden comforter. Aradia, who is our blue skies. Lucifer, who is our red rage."

Uncle Pietro and his friends did not know the whole invocation or would not say it even to frighten me, Sigismundo thought.

"Tana, Orpheus, Aradia, Lucifer," all chorused.

"What is the first duty of a Master Mason?"

My God, he thought, they actually do think they are the real Freemasons.

"To see that the *baraka* is secure."

From then on it followed the formula Pietro's friends had used to hoax him. Until suddenly a statue was unveiled and all cried, "*Magna Mater, Magna Mater, Magna Mater.*"

It was a naked goddess, but not beautiful at all, not like the ones in the Tempio Malatesta. She had no face—no eyes, no nose—and was grotesquely fat, with huge breasts. Somehow, looking at her, Sigismundo knew she was incredibly old, older even than Sicily.

"Mother Tana, who is the woods and the wind and the silvery stars," the tall man chanted.

"Mother Tana, who is the woods and the wind and the silvery stars," all chorused.

"Mother Tana, who wishes all of her children to be free and equal."

"Mother Tana, who wishes all of her children to be free and equal."

"Mother Tana, who gives birth in blood, whose sacrament is blood, whose regeneration is blood."

"Mother Tana, who gives birth in blood, whose sacrament is blood, whose regeneration is blood."

They do have a demented Gothic poetry about them, Sigismundo thought.

"*Konx om pax*," intoned the leader. "This session of the Temple of the East is now open."

"What is the first order of business, El Eswad?" asked a voice.

"We must bring down our uninvited guest on the balcony," El Eswad said.

Sigismundo leaped to his feet immediately, but four men had quietly come onto the balcony behind him, and he was seized before he could draw his sword.

"Heroism is the admirable quality we attribute to damned fools who have survived their follies," he remembered Uncle Pietro saying. And: When you think you see what the magician does not intend you to see . . .

Rough hands dragged him rapidly down the stairs, banging his head brutally against the wall every time he struggled to break free. He was dizzy and his scalp was bleeding when he arrived in the center of the circle.

This was no joke this time. If they all enjoyed a good hearty laugh afterward, it would be while they cleaned up the bloodstains.

They released him after taking his sword. He was surrounded, and every hand held a dagger. His heart was pounding wildly again. Maybe I'll get used to it, he thought. If I get out of this alive, by divine intervention maybe, and keep on getting into messes, I might eventually notice only the times when my heart isn't banging like a bass drum at the opera.

He looked about him. The eyes behind the hoods were cold and black and about as jovial as a pit of cobras. The black candles created an ideal atmosphere for human sacrifice, and they would probably chant more heathen invocations while they sliced him up. He looked again at Mother Tana. She was indeed unbelievably old and had been carved with primitive tools many aeons ago. She might date back to the time Dr. Vico wrote of, when men were mute giants and lived in caves.

A hero would leap to the table like greased lightning, bound quickly up to the chandelier, swing across to the window, and crash out into the street. Somehow, Sigismundo thought, I don't think I'm quite that good yet.

"Greetings, brave little musician," El Eswad said with a mockery of aristocratic speech.

"Greetings, great big brave rebels who slash and stab when there are four of you against one unarmed man," Sigismundo replied. Uncle Pietro and his friends prepared me for this scene, he thought. I will not pee in my pants. I will die like a man, no matter how my heart pounds.

"Note those r's," El Eswad said, with mock geniality. "Only a true aristocrat can roll them like that. They practice all day, except when they are busy foreclosing mortgages. A son any man would be proud of."

"*You are going to spare me again,*" Sigismundo blurted. He didn't know why he said it or how he knew it.

There was a murmur of astonishment among the hooded figures.

"It is as I proclaimed," El Eswad announced pontifically. "He has the *baraka*, do you see? He is one of us."

"I have the power sometimes," Sigismundo said. "But I will never be one of you. You filthy butchers."

"You will learn," El Eswad said. And then he removed his hood, reminding Sigismundo of the time this scene was only a joke. The head that emerged was the blond man's, as Sigismundo expected. None of the others repeated the same indiscretion, which meant they were indeed going to spare Sigismundo; that was why he would not see their faces.

"Look at me, boy," El Eswad said. "You will join us someday, and you will do it of your own free will, because you will come to understand our divine work in this world."

"Never," Sigismundo said. "I hate you and your murders."
El Eswad quoted:

> "'We have the Mason Word and second sight:
> "'Things yet to come we can see aright.'

"I see you wearing my hood someday," El Eswad pronounced, with absolute certitude. "You will travel to many countries and cross the ocean. You will flee your true nature in every way. But eventually you will come to us."

A hooded figure spoke, in a youngish voice. "Brother, it is true. You are one of us. You were born under stars that made you one of us." He was the one with violet eyes.

They really believe it, Sigismundo thought. That is why they spared me in the church on Easter. I am in the hands of fanatics who kill one man by the conjunctions of two planets and spare another by the trines of two others.

"You murdered my uncle. I would sooner join the foul Mohammedans."

"As for that," El Eswad said. "You have already joined the 'foul Mohammedans.' Where do you think the real control of the FRC comes from?"

The younger voice spoke again, those violet eyes staring passionately at Sigismundo through the slits in the hood. "It is not murder to fight for what was stolen from you by violence. Killing and more killing is what history is made of. What is the story of your glorious Catholic church but butchery and more butchery, against the pagans first, then against the Jews, then the Mohammedans, then the Protestants? What is the history of Napoli and Sicily but butchery? How did our gracious majesty, Ferdinand IV, come to rule us, except that his French and Spanish ancestors butchered *our* ancestors? So it has been and so it will be, until all priests and governors are killed and we are all free brothers together."

"Every national border in Europe," El Eswad added ironically, "marks the place where two gangs of bandits got too exhausted to kill each other anymore and signed a treaty. Patriotism is the delusion that one of these gangs of bandits is better than all the others."

"And you will change all that through more butchery?" Sigismundo exclaimed. "You are destroyed by the French pox; it has gone to your brains."

"Listen," violet eyes said, "your wonderful uncle we killed —he was a heartless usurer."

"There are a hundred beggars who were once farmers before they got into debt to your lovely uncle," El Eswad said. "There are two hundred whores who would be leading virtuous lives as farm girls now if the farms had not been foreclosed by your noble uncle."

"I will explain," Sigismundo said reasonably. "You are uneducated men. My uncle was most generous, most kindly. But when a man lends money and the money is not returned, he must collect the warranty. Otherwise he will be the beggar and his daughters will be the whores. It is the science of economics. It is in books."

"It is the science of murder and banditry," El Eswad said. "Enough of this chatter. Nobody is convinced by mere words. You will come to us eventually; it is written in the heavens. You will learn that we are the wave of the future."

"Never," Sigismundo repeated hotly. "I will piss in the milk of your mothers first. I will fuck your eyes. I will damn you to the stinking bottom cesspool of hell."

El Eswad merely turned and said, "Bring the cup. The ritual begins."

Sigismundo was forced into a chair, and a cup was brought. Oh, Mother of God, no, he thought. They wouldn't kill him—the power was real and he trusted it—but there were some things worse than death. They knew how to put him to sleep as Dr. Orfali did and work on his mind. Oh, bleeding Jesus, no, he prayed. Let them kill my body and leave my soul alone. Dear Jesus, don't let them poison my very being with drugs and black magick. Please Jesus. Please.

It took eight of them, but finally his jaws were pried open. He went on struggling, he spat out as much of it as he could, he prayed to Saint Jude (patron of hopeless cases), and none of it helped in the slightest. They got a large portion of the drug down his throat.

In a few seconds his heart was pounding so fast he thought he might die of it. He was trembling all over, and then he began to have violent spasms, like a man with the falling sickness: it was as if he was freezing and being boiled in oil at once.

That is the primitive vegetative soul, he told himself. Dr. Orfali uses a drug that pacifies that soul, but they are using one that throws it into emergency. My body feels fear and impending death, but my mind, my human soul, knows better. It is only a drug agitating the vegetative part of the psyche. I can detach myself from it by remembering it is only a drug. I can. I can. I *think* I can.

Then they released him, and El Eswad said, "Now the magick begins to work in you. Now the old gods return," and then Sigismundo noticed that King Ferdinand had been hiding in a corner all along and His Majesty raised his royal purple scepter and chanted like a priest at High Mass, "To Buggeranthos let this charge be given, and let them bugger all things under heaven," and the black candles suddenly became yellow and soon there were fireworks and flying cockroaches, pinwheels, and rockets, a vertigo of rainbows, and they were soaring through the air, Sigismundo and El Eswad and Uncle Pietro and Don Quixote, some of them already turning into birds, and he realized he almost knew the worst secret, the one they had been hiding from him since his birth.

And the gorilla with testicles for eyes and a rotten leper's nose said, "The clash of our cries for peace. Or say that stone is the speech. Do not murmur. Nor know. For the lions."

And then he saw his hands getting older and older, bent and splotched and wrinkled, old man's hands, and he thought, They are moving me ahead in time. I am locked in this home for the mindless forever.

But no, he told himself, this is hallucination. It was a long time ago that somebody gave me a drug, and I am still hallucinating.

And they pricked Sigismundo's finger, using his blood as the ink. It didn't seem to matter, out here among the dead planets with the vegetable people, and then he threw the pen across the room, refusing to sign.

"Now repeat after me," El Eswad said. "'Unto Lucifer I pledge my soul, for this lifetime and all future lifetimes.' Repeat."

But the further down they went, the more of the horned dog-faced things Sigismundo noticed. The ceilings were getting lower; eventually they were crawling on all fours. The horrible smell, Sigismundo decided, was bat shit; he was crawling in the filthy stuff.

"I don't understand," Reverend Verey said. "A chicken in the Vatican?"

Looking at it rationally, Sigismundo decided that it was a good idea to get rid of his clothes and put on these animal skins. No sense getting bat shit all over your best silks, he told himself. Still, he didn't exactly remember putting on the bearskin he was wearing.

"'Unto Lucifer I pledge my soul,'" El Eswad repeated.

Sigismundo had the pen again, wet with his own blood.

"Just sign here," El Eswad said gently.

Sigismundo signed the parchment. Bells tolled solemnly; a million damned souls screamed in horror; giant spiders rushed about devouring citizens on the streets. I don't have to believe any of this, Sigismundo told himself. I didn't sign; this is hallucination.

The reptile men groveled in worship to the Faceless Goddess and the wheels interlocked and he was on collision course—religious fanatics raving about earthquakes, last product of moon ash and blood septums. "When we came out of the mud like crippled monkeys—strictly from insect—"

And Sigismundo noticed that the cave walls were decorated with paintings, mostly showing men in bearskins (like himself) shooting arrows at bisons, and then he saw a painting of a man sleeping with an erect penis, and after that they got to the bottom, gorillas and bishops fighting in the dung. The man with goat horns was waiting for them, and the statue of Mother Tana had fresh blood on it from a goat lying with its throat cut, and the voices said, "They'll all go mad in that house. They'll all go mad in that house. They'll all go mad in that house."

Sigismundo realized he had been in this room for many years, his whole sense of time had been warped, he only imagined he was still in the cave with the mute giants, they had destroyed his mind, and he was in this home for the feeble-minded for decades and decades, his hands wrinkled and corpselike, growing older, and he had to stop hallucinating so the doctors would release him and let him go home.

"Step on the crucifix now," El Eswad said.

"Noses and noses!" Sigismundo screamed. (I mean *no*, why can't I say *no*?)

They lifted his foot and placed it down hard on the crucifix. Jesus, tiny as he was, screamed in pain, and blood spurted up Sigismundo's boot.

And then another demon was sodomizing him. He remembered in shame and horror that he had been raped many times already. That was another hallucination, he told himself. I must believe it is a hallucination; but the demon had leathery wings and scaly skin and his foul breath was hot on Sigismundo's neck.

But the tree-people were mocking him, repeating over and over, "Your mother is a whore, your mother is a whore, your mother is a whore," and he knew that was the secret, but it couldn't be, and he was with Miskasquamish at the golden springs of the *wakan*, because the creatures of this *bolgia* lacked eyes and Dante was being eaten alive by them, but that could happen to any artist: do not call up any that you cannot put down.

"Of course," Sigismundo said to the Devil reasonably, "I am no longer a human being. That is the secret, right? I am glad I signed that contract with you, sir, and I am sure my immortal soul is in good hands now. Antonio and I are the same person but not the same apostle."

El Eswad was still chanting, "Tana before you, Orpheus behind you, Aradia at your right side, Lucifer at your left side." Then he came very close and looked right into Sigismundo's eyes again. "You see our four gods," he said, "but now look within and find the creator of all gods."

Sigismundo turned to fire and light.

He understood suddenly that the *Rossi* were his friends after all. Everybody was his friend. It was worth all the terror of transition to arrive at this ecstasy. The whole world adored him. He became the whole world: God and Goddess, male and female, human and animal, life and death.

They had made him emperor of the universe.

The walls were pornographic. Winged penises flew through the gardens, and young ladies chased them. Some had captured a few and were raptly sucking on them, eyes closed in bliss like nuns at prayer.

Sigismundo looked around groggily. He was back in his own clothes again, but the bearskin was thrown in a corner.

The adjoining wall was an orgy: permutations and combinations like mathematics. How could they do all that with only twelve bodies?

All is permissible, he thought. I am the emperor of the universe. I will run up the hill and fuck Maria at once.

Then, with a snap, things came into focus again.

He realized that he was in Pompeii.

A woman in one of the murals began to move, inviting him to join the orgy.

Sigismundo stared at her, willing the hallucinations to go away. She stopped moving.

The first real shock came when he started to stagger toward the door. There was graffiti on the walls—part of the evil glamour of Pompeii, ancient obscenities—but he could not read the letters.

He tried again and again. It was all a blur.

Part of his mind had been destroyed by what the *Rossi* had done to him. He had lost the human soul. He was as illiterate as a newborn or an animal.

He lurched into the street, fighting against despair. The Orsini family had a child with a huge head, deformed. He was sixteen or seventeen now but still a baby. He could not read or feed himself and spoke only in terrible, pitifully slurred grunts. Sigismundo wondered if the devil drug had done that to him, if he would be like that for the rest of his life, chained in a room and hallucinating, watching his hands turn old and wrinkled.

"All of Gaul is divided into three parts," he said aloud, in Latin, testing himself. His speech was normal. "And then set sail upon the wine-dark sea," he tried in Greek.

The human soul was not destroyed; it was just that his eyes were out of focus.

He saw an ancient street sign: VIA GRACCHI.

He could read large letters. It was only the small ones that were blurred.

Belladonna. The Greek drug. His pupils were dilated,

obviously; he had not lost his literacy. When women put belladonna in their eyes to look beautiful at the opera, they could not see small things either.

He found the sun and started the trek westward and downward, back to Napoli.

His memory of last night was full of holes; that, too, was the effect of the belladonna. He would never remember all of it. He could remember only going down into a very deep cave and seeing Carlo Maldonado point a pistol at him.

His right index finger was sore. He looked at it and saw many prick marks. He almost remembered how that happened, but then the memory disappeared into chaos and confusion.

Gradually his eyesight returned to normal. He kept checking his palms, and eventually he could see every line clearly.

Every ten minutes or so he had to stop, because the world would spin and he couldn't walk straight for a while.

A peasant from Ottacelli, driving an ox cart, gave him a ride part of the way. He kept looking at Sigismundo dubiously. *Maybe he can see that I am not in all respects rational right now,* Sigismundo thought.

Sigismundo did not go directly home. He went to Uncle Pietro's house on Via Capodimonte.

"Where have you been?" Pietro demanded at once. "The whole family—"

"Never mind that," Sigismundo said. "I just spent a hilarious evening with the *Rossi.* I know the secret. *Who is my father?*"

Uncle Pietro sat down wearily. "I knew this day would come," he said.

"I knew, too," Sigismundo said. "The reason I was always closer to you . . . Papa is strained with me. I am not his child, am I?"

"Listen," Pietro said. "You must not be too harsh on your mother. That beast forced her."

"Never mind that either. *Who is my father*?"

"The blond man, the assassin from the church. His name is Peppino Balsamo."

"And you kept it from me for my own good, of course. So: I am Sigismundo Balsamo, not Sigismundo Celine. 'The common people are lazy and ignorant,'" he quoted himself bitterly. "And I am one of them. Sweet Christ, I am a bleeding *Siciliano* even. I am a Sicilian's bastard, my mother has been enwhored, my father murdered my uncle, and everybody I know is involved in one conspiracy or another. We are living in *The Lives of the Caesars*."

"Stop it. Get a grip on yourself."

"There is a chicken in the Vatican."

"What?"

"You wouldn't understand," Sigismundo said. "There are tunnels, vast systems of tunnels underneath Europe, and things haven't changed at all. After Culloden they murdered the infants; Moloch rules still. Antonio was right about time. But who was the other—the one with the violet eyes who would not kill me in church?"

"He is Balsamo's son also. By another woman, in Sicily. Your half brother."

(Yes, he called me brother. I thought it was revolutionary rhetoric.)

"Splendid," Sigismundo said. "Most marvelous and lovely entirely. I have been born in the middle of a grand opera but we bleed real blood. Do you wish to hear the latest, the cream of the jest? The tunnels go down, under the earth, but also backward, into earlier ages. But no, that is not it. What you should know is that they want to recruit me. Isn't that hilarious? Peppino Balsamo—I mean, my father, the one who arranges murders when he isn't plotting revolutions—you know, the real one, not the one who married my mother, not that weak sister who lets strange birds foul his nest—"

"Stop it."

"No," Sigismundo said. "You must hear it. My real father, the devil worshiper, says the stars have picked me to succeed him. And I will agree of my own free will, he says. And to tell you the truth, Uncle, I am not at all sure I have any free will left after last night. I don't know what they did to my head. But my mother *is* a whore, and Jesus *is* a naked woman, and I see huge chickens driving the popes out of the Vatican. I tell you my three souls are all sick, and I know in the future that I will be the worst of all monsters."

▲

PART TWO

THE EMPRESS

Cruelty has a Human Heart,
And Jealousy a Human Face,
Terror, the Human Form Divine,
and Secrecy, the Human Dress.

William Blake, "A Divine Image"

Liliana Celine thought she was lying when she told Guido that Peppino Balsamo had raped her.

Because it was not rape, at least as she understood rape, even though it was not seduction either—there was no romance, no passion. But Guido could never understand what actually happened, since Liliana had no words to explain it at the time. Nobody, she thought often as the years passed and Sigismundo grew, *nobody* anywhere in God's world could understand it. There was no reason in it anywhere; it was simply the kind of deviltry that, inexplicably, happened whenever a thing like Peppino was loosed in the world. It took half her adult life before she understood that she had not lied to Guido, that it really was rape: rape of the mind.

She had loathed Peppino from the beginning. He was insolent, and cruel to the animals, and he obviously hated her and Guido for being rich; but that was only part of it. Basically, it was her intuition of what Peppino was and what he could do, what he might do, that made her wary of him. Guido had hired

Peppino to do some carpentry; he was very good with his hands, all kinds of repair work. Guido kept him on for several weeks, having many small jobs done, because he was so quick and clever at such things.

Liliana wanted to discharge him from the first day, because of his arrogance and the bad way he treated the animals. And his insolence. He thought he could have any woman he wanted; his eyes showed it when he looked at her, and he made coarse jokes, implying that he had seduced even noblewomen. His confidence, his conceit, was unbearable. So Liliana kept asking Guido to discharge the man, and Guido didn't understand. Men never understood such things—not normal men anyway. Only monsters like Peppino Balsamo understood. Guido thought she disliked the tall blond Sicilian with the sulky good looks because he did not have the humility of the average peasant. That was the irony of it: Guido assumed, until it was too late, that she was just being a snob—an eighteen-year-old girl, married only two years, accustomed to being protected from the world by her brothers, the mighty Malatestas, who were almost as rich as the Maldonados. He thought she was vain and silly to be so upset that a peasant who was smarter than average was also a bit uppity. "The bright ones are always troublesome," Guido told her.

But at last, thank the saints, Peppino left. There was no more repair work to be done, and Guido finally realized how much Liliana feared the man, even though he still did not know why. Not then. Because you can look at the sky sometimes and know a storm is coming, far away; or you can look at a dog and know it is vicious. That really was what Guido could not comprehend. Liliana had looked at Peppino, that first hour, when he was fixing the broken leg of the kitchen table, and had known he had it in him to leave a town where he had been wronged, or imagined himself wronged, and he would leave very quietly with nothing said, and he would stay away many years, until everybody forgot him—forgot his name, forgot his face, forgot that Peppino Balsamo had ever been there—and then he would come back, once only, at night and kill a small child of the man he thought had wronged him, and vanish again, nobody but himself to understand the motive of the atrocity. It would be like a stroke of lightning, and only he would know he was lightning. If they made him a general, she knew, he would tell his troops, "Kill them all. The children, too. Destroy the village down to the last pig, the last stray dog; leave no brick standing on a brick." Without compunction.

It was absurd, too, that he had a name like Peppino. But it was clever for a demon to pass himself off in the world as just another Peppino, your standard average peasant; there must be as many Peppinos in Napoli, she thought, as there are stars in the sky or fleas in a stable. Peppino this and Peppino that, everywhere, hundreds of thousands of them, not just in Napoli but all over Italy. And among them, one alone, this demon with enough hatred to fill the hundreds of thousands. In Spain, she thought, it is Pablo, in England it is Bill or Will, in France it is Pierre, here it is Peppino. Maybe that is why he became a monster, so he would not get lost among all those Peppinos, all those servile peasant faces. And so, when he left, Liliana thanked God and the Holy Virgin and San Gennaro that the outrage would happen somewhere else.

But then next summer, when Guido was in Spain on business, Peppino returned. He came to the back door, of course, and took off his hat; even he could pretend to courtesy when it was in his interest. Liliana told him there was no work.

He smiled at her; it was more like a shark showing its teeth. He said it was obvious that her husband was away and she was afraid of him because she thought all peasants were brutes. She tried to be brave. She told him there were five servants in the house and that if he made another insolent remark she would have him horsewhipped.

But she was still only eighteen and too well-bred to know how a clever liar can get around you.

Peppino stood there in the garden and apologized, most abjectly. It almost seemed as if he might weep. He said that he had had no work in a long time and that he had a family to support. He told her that she had humiliated him, because there are always a few odd jobs for a man with his mechanical and manual talents. He said that when he realized she was afraid of him, he was pained and lost his head, and that a fine rich lady like her could not imagine how hard life was for a poor man with a wife and three children. He apologized over and over, and then he asked Liliana if she knew of any neighbors who might have odd jobs they needed done.

She didn't believe him, not really. But he made her doubt herself. She wondered if she *was* just a silly snob and perhaps had wronged this hulking giant who now seemed so desperate for honest work. Maybe, she thought, she was afraid of him only because a peasant who can read and write (she had learned that about him last winter) is something strange, like a dog walking on its hind legs. With two male servants in the house and three maids to scream for help, Peppino would not *do anything*, certainly, and her fears were childish. And she thought of his wife and family. She was uncertain, and that made her vulnerable.

She decided to give him a few small jobs and some coins and be rid of him.

So she let him in. And then it began in earnest, the struggle for power in her own household: she, the noble lady with all the weight of tradition and the police to help her if she called for help; he, the homeless and propertyless man with (seemingly) no power but his brute strength, which he dared not use (of course). And yet she was the one who was on the defensive, always.

Everything she did or said was taken as an insult. He was not angry again, and he did not complain openly; but he let her know. She was rich, and he was poor, and she was afraid of him because she was a silly girl who didn't trust peasants. Somehow, she had to prove—not to Peppino, but to herself, or to God maybe—that she wasn't the cruel, prejudiced, cowardly girl-woman he had made her seem.

Later, she finally understood. Everybody knows about the tyranny of the powerful, but there is something worse, and Peppino knew how to use it. It is worse because you cannot understand it, you feel too guilty to fight it, and you cannot even define it until it has taken what it wants from you. It is the tyranny of the suffering.

Peppino suffered. And suffered. And suffered some more. And every chance he got, Liliana heard more about his children, his great love for them, the hardships of his life, the life of a peasant too independent to work somebody else's farm, too proud to join the professional beggars on the streets, a man forced to live by his wits for the crumbs of life. More and more it became a trial in which she had to prove that she was not personally responsible for his suffering or for the suffering of all the poor people in the world—she didn't know which offense was worse, or more her fault; but he had those two injustices firmly identified in his mind, and then in hers.

Liliana never did really pity him; still, she distrusted him. But she was unsure and felt increasingly guilty about distrusting him. She found she could not bring herself to tell him that all the work was done. That would be another sign of her cruelty, the cruelty of her class, not just to Peppino Balsamo, but to all the Peppinos everywhere.

So she kept finding new work for him, afraid of the accusation that would be in his eyes when she told him to go.

And she kept hoping Guido would come home from Spain. And every week Peppino told her that he sent his wages to his wife and children and that they were all praying for her because she was such a kind and charitable woman. Somehow, he made it sound as if kindness and charity were two more insults, two more abuses she was heaping on him.

Somehow it became a question of how close he could get to her, how close she would allow him to be without showing her anxiety. She feared him still, but he had made her ashamed of her fear. Because there is an area around the body that is like a second skin: when you let somebody inside that space, you are intimate with them. We let only our family get that close, normally. And yet, she could not keep Peppino out of the space—not without thinking she was a fool and a snob and personally, uniquely responsible for every hungry child in Napoli, for every injustice committed since the followers of Spartacus had been crucified.

Then he persuaded her that the chimney in the bedroom fireplace needed repairing. And after that he made her know that if she avoided the bedroom while he was in there hacking and plastering, it would be another prejudiced condemnation of an honest, hard-working man; and so they came to the moment, staring at each other, an inexplicable flicker of fear in even his eyes for one brief second; and then it happened.

In a courtroom, she knew, she could not honestly say that he forced her. But it was not voluntary, either: it was the storm she had sensed when she first saw him. His rage and his lust and his need to seize the world and be its master—that was all part of it. And her fear and her guilt and, most of all, her attempts to convince herself that she was not merely acting from fear and guilt. It was not lovemaking, just as it was not (legally speaking) rape. It was an explosion, as if all the poor people in the world brought their suffering and resentment into that bed and she had to give them all she could give to make them leave, to take

that suffering somewhere else. Somehow, she was proving to
him that she did not think of peasants as animals; somehow,
letting him use her as a receptacle was the only proof she had
left. Perhaps she was trying to bribe him, the way one tries to
bribe one's conscience at times. He had become conscience
and rage and judge and executioner all in one.

Guido would never understand; neither would her clever
brother, Pietro, who understood so much. No normal man
would understand. Only other women might know—other
women and those who prey upon them, the true spawn of hell
like Peppino. Because she could have cried out for help—five
servants in the house, after all—and that would be the logical,
practical question any man would ask: Why didn't you scream?
And how could she answer logic when there was no logic in
Peppino's crazy, hate-filled world? She was ashamed: that was
part of the answer. And because Peppino was so fast and so
brutal, she had thought, *Well, in a few minutes it will be over*.
Knowing that if she did call out for help, it would never be
over. Peppino would stand trial and be hanged, but half the
town would think she had led him on. They would say (men
always say), "It wouldn't have happened if she had not really
wanted it." As if anyone would want to look the Devil in the
face, with all the servility and hypocrisy removed, with eyes that
showed only hatred and rage and contempt for life.

But she could never explain any of that to Guido; it was
easier to call it rape in the ordinary sense. Because the act itself,
despite what the priests say, is no big thing to a married
woman. Sometimes, with Guido, it could be tender and quite
wonderful; and sometimes it was just what a woman must do,
to keep her man happy, and she did not resent that. Guido did
many things to keep her happy. But it is not like opera; it is no
cataclysm. With a demon like Peppino, all you can think is:
Don't make a fuss. Let it be over quickly. Because if she
screamed or resisted, he might really lose his head, and he was

capable of any atrocity (she was sure of her intuition now). Get it over with and *try try try* to forget it: that is what she thought with such a huge creature as Peppino pinning her beneath him.

How could she tell Guido, how could she go into court and tell the judges, "There were no stars spinning in the skies, no glory and magic, such as foolish men write in novels about adultery? It was not even painful, as I am told real rape is; it was merely foul and hideous, like having your face pushed into something nasty on the street." The terror, the degradation was all in the intangible—the opening of her body to a man she did not love but hated, and the fear, the sickening fear that he would go wild completely and kill her afterward, so that she could not denounce him and have him arrested.

But Peppino Balsamo did not kill her or even threaten her. He was sure she would not tell anyone; he who was such a clever liar was even more superlative at deceiving himself. He was convinced that she had capitulated because she could not control her passion for him. The pig.

He stood there, afterward, buttoning up, and bragged about his power over women and told her what a silly person she was. He said that she had believed every brazen lie he ever spoke. His wife and three children were a myth, he said, laughing in her face. He spent his money on weapons, to make a revolution, to kill all the rich. He did have children, he said—many of them, probably, all over Italy—but he did not know the names of most of them, nor care. He had never been married.

He said she had wronged *him*, last year, by acting surprised when she found out he could read. He said peasants had brains as good as anyone's and all could read given a chance; it was a lie of the rich that peasants were too ignorant to learn. For that lie and that insult he had decided to punish her. The punishment, he said, was to show her her own weakness and to prove he could give her greater pleasure than her fancy rich husband. He was sure of it. He stood there, after it was over, and it had taken only a few minutes, and he bragged about how he had taught her real passion. He said that the rich were all effeminate and that only a peasant who worked hard all day had the vigor to please a woman truly. He believed it, the colossal deceiver and self-deceiver that he was.

He would not see that she had no feelings but loathing and humiliation. Because she had cried out once in terror and because her body had shaken with his crudity and violence, he believed she had been in spasms of pleasure. He made quite a long speech about it; he liked making speeches. He said all women were whores, and many things like that, and he named all the other rich women in Napoli he had conquered by one dirty trick or another. It was strange, but as he talked about women, this libertine, he sounded very much like the Dominicans.

And then he was gone. Peppino Balsamo: Joe Everybody. Just another face in the crowd. Anybody's serf, on any *latifondi* in Italy.

Or a Demon from Hell.

She was never sure which was the true way to think of such a being.

And Guido did not for a moment consider putting her aside. He *wept*—not that he was humiliated, but that she had been used brutally. And when the boy, Sigismundo, was born, Guido tried, he honestly tried, to be as good a father to him as to his own children.

But as the years passed, as Sigismundo grew, Liliana had her own private hell, knowing the storm would come back yet again, in a new form. When Sigismundo's temper flared and he stormed about the house like a wild animal, she told herself: All boys do that sometimes. It is not Demon blood, I must not think that way; he is usually a good child. But in his music she heard more and more of Peppino: the same force, the same uncompromising passion to go beyond all limits, to surpass human boundaries. It is art, she told herself: it is the same force, but it is turned toward creativity this time, not toward destruction. He is only trying to go beyond melody, not beyond morals and pity and all reason. He is not trying to impose his Will upon the whole world, just upon the structure of music.

I must not be afraid of my own son.

▲

PART THREE

THE MAGICIAN

Therefore, as logical metaphysics teaches
that man contains all things by understanding them (*Homo Intelligendo Fit
Omnia*), this poetic metaphysics reveals
that man contains all things by not understanding them (*Homo Non Intelligendo Fit Omnia*).

Giambattista Vico, *Scienza Nuova*

For Sigismundo, it was back down the hill, round and round the curving roads, past one mule after another—for the first time, he wondered if there were more mules or fools in Napoli, but in either case he was a prime candidate for king of either species—and then into the ghetto again.

Some of the shops had not been repaired yet, after the looting in August, but Sigismundo saw a group of people working to refurbish the walls of several buildings.

The drunks who came down here and burned and looted and beat up old men thought they had a good reason to hate the Jews, he reflected. My perfect devil of a father thinks he has most excellent reasons to hate the nobles. The Dominicans have intricate and theologically orthodox reasons to hate anybody who reads the wrong books. The Jacobites hate the king of England, and he hates them back. Everybody has somebody to hate: it just proves that God's Creation is above all perfectly balanced and orderly.

My father is a cuckold, he thought, wonderful comic figure

in every farce. No, I mean the man who pretends to be my father is a cuckold. My father isn't my father. My real father is some kind of archfiend and thinks I'm a likely apprentice demon. As Antonio said, we have been sentenced to hell because Napol isn't yet quite bad enough for us.

Perhaps, all things considered, I *am* a demoniac. That would explain why I thought I sensed God in my ancestor's heathen, un-Christian temple and why I now have the delusion that the holy Dominican fathers are mad dogs who have turned the Pope into a giant purple rooster. And that my mother is a whore.

Uncle Pietro told me once that hysteria is a chaotic and irrational emotional state caused by seeing how the world really operates.

But now they were in Dr. Orfali's shop and the old Jew was whispering with Pietro. Talking about me, Sigismundo thought.

"Now you will work on my head," he said ironically. "Everybody takes turns working on my head. There are liars in this town, sir, do you know that? They tell me my father is the Devil and wishes me to succeed him as emperor of hell, that is to say, of this world."

"I will not work on your head," Dr. Orfali said gently. "That is not necessary. You have the power. You can work on your own head. You are one of us."

"That is what they all say," Sigismundo remarked cynically. "The devils say I am one of them. Is this some standard line all you magicians use?"

Old Abraham smiled. "You are one of those with the power," he corrected himself. "Which side you join is your own free choice. Now, just as an experiment, can you repeat one sentence? Try it: *Atoh Malkuth, ve-Geburah, ve-Gedullah, le-olahm.*"

"No," Sigismundo said. "Tell me what it means first."

"You see?" Abraham said to Pietro. "He is actually quite

rational. Even prudent. Very well," he said to Sigismundo. "It means, 'For Thine is the kingdom, the power, and the glory, forever.' I say it before each healing, because it is not I, Abraham Orfali, who heals people; it is God working through me. Now you are to become a healer, starting on yourself. So ask God to work through you. Say *Atoh Malkuth, ve-Geburah, ve-Gedullah, le-olahm.*"

"There is a huge purple cock in the Vatican," Sigismundo said. There was a dog-faced Thing in the corner, but each time he stared hard at it, it went away.

"No," Abraham cried, suddenly much taller. "Stop that in the name of the angel Emmanuel, whose name means the presence of God is with us. In the name of Emmanuel, who appeared beside Shadrach, Mishac, and Abednego in the furnace of ineffable fire and was their protector. In the name of Emmanuel, who is here and everywhere, who is yesterday, today, and the brother of tomorrow."

Sigismundo gulped, staring at the old man who spoke suddenly like thunder itself.

"I know all about chickens in the Vatican and demonic dogs and little green men with egg in their beard," Abraham said bitterly. "They do not belong in this space but in another, crazy space. In the name of Emmanuel, I summon your spirit, Sigismundo Celine, back to this space. Be perfectly aware and impartial, right where you are sitting now."

Sigismundo came back into Euclidean space, back into the small rear room of Dr. Orfali's shop.

"Now repeat the invocation," Abraham said. "*Atoh Malkuth, ve-Geburah, ve-Gedullah, le-olahm.*"

Sigismundo repeated the invocation.

"Good. Excellent. *Thank you*," the doctor said. "Now just visualize the four archangels. Do you remember their names?"

"Rapha-El, Gabri-El, Micha-El, Auri-El," Sigismundo said, immediately seeing them quite vividly.

"Now, with no drugs and nobody 'working on your head,'

all by yourself, pull the angels into you. Bring them in, from the four compass points, to the very center of your forehead."

Sigismundo tried. After all, he thought, I am doing it myself. He is not forcing my mind like those demoniacs last night.

The angels coalesced in the center of his head. There was a tingling and a sense of light. Quite suddenly, there was no amorphous figures lurking in the corner of his vision, and, for the first time since the drug had been forced on him, he was not dizzy or light-headed at all.

"Now, listen," Abraham said, sitting down himself and talking in his ordinary voice. "Why do you suppose they gave you that belladonna last night? If they want you to be their next leader, they should not be trying to drive you out of your mind."

"I don't understand that," Sigismundo admitted.

"That drug, pernicious as it is, will *not* drive you out of your mind," Abraham said. "At least, not with one dose. You are in no sense suffering the same civil war inside that your poor cousin suffered last year. What the *Rossi* have done is to push you to the edge of an abyss-"

"Yes," Sigismundo said. "It is like standing on a cliff and also as if I could see to infinity. But in between are these crazy places."

"They have opened you to the fourth soul," Abraham said. "In a brutal and sudden way. This is most dangerous. We in the FRC," lowering his voice, "believe it must be done most gradually and carefully. *They* are not so scrupulous. They believe that if you cannot bear the shock, you do not deserve to be one of them. Now tell me about the things you have been seeing since the drug was administered."

Sigismundo frowned. "They keep slipping away," he said. "My memory doesn't seem to work properly yet."

"That is typical of belladonna," Abraham said. "Tell me what you do remember."

Sigismundo recalled Carlo Maldonado pointing a pistol at him. Then suddenly that faded, and he had a rush of images of dog-faced Things, green dancing tree-men, winged lions, black men in turbans, a veiled goddess on a golden throne.

"Typical of *Yesod*," Abraham said thoughtfully.

"What does that mean?"

"They are old acquaintances," Abraham said whimsically. "They are hallucinations only if you cannot control them. If a man can summon them at will and master them, they are keys to the deep levels of the psyche. But do not attempt that at your age. You want to be rid of them. Only when you are much older should you consider trafficking with them as we in the FRC sometimes have to do.

"You will find," Abraham went on, "that they will fade away over about two weeks' time. When they are annoying, summon the angels to banish them. Keep a diary every day, and write down every odd new idea that comes to your head. We will go over that diary together, every few days, and I will help you through this period. The *Rossi* will not have you, I assure you. They do not understand the power, really; they are like drunken men playing with weapons, and eventually they will blow their own heads off."

"They said it was destined that I come to them," Sigismundo replied uneasily. "But they also said I would do it of my own free will."

"Very well," the doctor said. "I now tell you that it is divinely ordained that you will join us in the rose cross order. There appear to be two rival prophecies at this time. Who will decide which prophecy will come true?"

"I will," Sigismundo said hesitantly.

"You *what*?"

"I *will*."

"You see?" Abraham said. "Nobody has to work on your head. You understand the basics already. Now, I'm sure a lad of your curiosity has heard something of the goals of our order. What are they reputed to be?"

"The medicine of metals, which changes all substances at the pleasure of the magician. And the stone of the wise, which some say is a code name for the Holy Grail. And the elixir of life, which gives longevity. And true wisdom and perfect happiness."

"Now, suppose I tell you that all those are just different metaphors and symbols for the same thing?" Abraham smiled. "I wager you will be able to tell me at once what that thing is."

"The fourth soul," Sigismundo said, quite certain.

"And another name for it?"

"My will," Sigismundo said.

"No," Abraham said. "The fourth soul is your will united with the will of God."

▲

That was the real beginning, not the end of anything. Sigismundo returned to Dr. Orfali's shop many times; they discussed many things.

Abraham talked of *Yesod*, which is a level of consciousness existing in all men but usually operating without the awareness of the ego: all the supernatural figures Sigismundo had seen since being given the belladonna were denizens of *Yesod*. "They are part of you, not outside at all, but they are not your creation since they are part of all men and women," Abraham said. "Notice how many coincidences are connected with their appearances. That will show you that they are a link between all individual minds." Sigismundo did not understand that at all, but he did begin noticing coincidences.

They spoke of the Next Step, which is the goal of the FRC, the information of the fourth soul in all humans, whereby humanity will be completely transformed "as in a refiner's fire, the scriptures say."

Often, they talked of Peppino Balsamo.

"I hate him," Sigismundo said bitterly.

Abraham waited and waited. "Now tell me the truth," he said finally.

"He is my father. I wish I didn't have to hate him."

"You are wishing you could love him."

"Yes. I wish he was not what he is."

"It is natural. All boys want to love and admire their fathers. Between father and son, even hate is just frustrated love."

"Then he will have me, eventually. He is a murderer and a devil worshiper and God knows what else, but there is a destiny in it. Every day, now, I remember: I am not really of the nobility. I am a half-Sicilian half-peasant. What evil joke is it that I wear silks and eat what I want, while my brothers and sisters and cousins on the farms are in rags and starving? He has put a spell on me. This red revolution, cruel as it is, will lure me in the end."

Abraham was silent again, waiting. "Now say the rest of it," he prompted.

"I hate the violence," Sigismundo cried. "I think the *Rossi* are madmen. Certainly there is injustice in the world, but it will never be changed by lunatics like them. If I knew where they are, I would turn them in to the Inquisition to be burned like the garbage they are. I would *like* to see them burn—all of them, including my father."

"So, who is the real Sigismundo speaking?" Abraham asked. "The one who will join the *Rossi* or the one will turn them in to the Inquisition?"

Riposte. Parry. All life is fencing, Sigismundo thought.

"I wish I knew," he said wearily.

"You will know, when the time comes."

But that night Sigismundo dreamed that dog-faced *Rossi* were in his room. He knew it was a dream, and he forced himself to wake—but they were still there. Battling terror, he reasoned: I did not wake, I just dreamed that I wakened. With another effort, he struggled toward consciousness again.

They were still there.

Yesod: the other world, between nightmare and reality, the crazy space.

He prayed: Toward the One, the perfection of love, harmony, and beauty . . .

The images of nightmare faded. Sigismundo was fully awake now. It was only the drug, he told himself. They cannot linger after the dream ends, except for that cursed drug, and each week there is less of the drug left in my bloodstream. This is most educational if I do not let it scare the living Jesus out of me: I can see a part of my mind that most people never see.

Then another dark figure moved suddenly between him and the window.

When you keep trying to wake and the nightmare still goes on: that is the true horror.

"Sigismundo?" It was Mama's voice. She moved closer, and he could recognize her face even in the dark. "Were you having a bad dream? I thought I heard you cry out."

He had been brave when the *Rossi* surrounded him with drawn daggers, and he had defied them; he had been brave for over a month since then, whenever the dog-faced or faceless Things appeared, staring at them and willing them to go away. He was suddenly, in the middle of the night and in the dark, too tired to be brave anymore.

"Mama," he said. "I'm frightened."

She came and held him, and he thought: What Peppino did to her was worse than what he did to me.

As if she guessed his thoughts, Mama said, "*He* will not last much longer"—she would not speak Peppino's name. "Pietro is spending all kinds of money, through every contact he has. *He* will be caught, and punished."

And then, Sigismundo thought grimly, the others will be ready to receive me as his successor.

▲

The next week Frankenstein came to Napoli.

The rumor ran through town like Mercury himself: the most famous alchemist in all Europe was in the marketplace. He had set up a tent and was performing miracles that astounded all witnesses. Of course, if you wanted to see him, the rumors added, you'd better hurry: as soon as the Dominicans get wind of this, he is sure to be arrested.

Sigismundo could not resist a show as promising as this. After all, everybody in Europe knew about Johann Dippel von Frankenstein, who had allegedly performed more wonders than all the sorcerers in Bavaria combined. Many had actually seen him turn lead into gold (or thought they saw that, as Uncle Pietro would say). He was widely believed to be between 90 and 120 years old, although he always looked young, and he once had a spot of bother with the Inquisition in Tuscany when he told a crowd that, like Elijah, he would never die.

Most marvelous and incredible of all was the legend that Dippel von Frankenstein had once achieved the greatest of all alchemical feasts: he had built a *homunculus*, an imitation human being, perfect in every detail, except (of course) it didn't have a soul. So many in Bavaria had allegedly seen this machine, or this creature, or whatever it was, that the authorities were moved to condemn von Frankenstein for black magick. He couldn't go back to Bavaria, it was said, and he didn't dare show the Thing (whatever it was) anywhere else; but many claimed he still had it hidden somewhere, and it was getting bigger and stronger all the time.

Of course, Sigismundo had seen some of the clever automatons that other mountebanks exhibited in the market from time to time: figurines that would dance to music or come out of their tiny houses and bow to the audience and sing, or heads

that would move their eyes and answer questions. But whatever
the mechanical technique of each such wonder, they all looked
like painted creations of plaster and metal. Frankenstein's
imitation man, the legends said, looked and acted like a real
man; he even smoked a pipe. There were more sinister tales,
too, saying that It, the Thing, whatever it was, had a foul
temper and you wouldn't want to meet It on a dark street.

At twilight, the tent was opened for business. Dippel von
Frankenstein was a tall man, not blond like most Bavarians, but
dark, with a great hawkish nose like Julius Caesar and crafty,
calculating eyes. He did not look a day older than thirty, despite
the fact that he was known to have been born in 1673.

Frankenstein removed his hat and bowed, waving the hat in
a wide arch. Abruptly he drew the hat back and held it before
his chest. With his left hand, he produced a live rabbit out of it.

A few small children cheered. Most of the adults muttered;
they had seen that trick a thousand times.

Frankenstein held the rabbit above his head and suddenly
slapped his palms together. The rabbit was gone.

"Things come out of the void for no reason," Frankenstein
intoned in a rich, solemn voice, "and they return to the void
for no reason."

Sigismundo sat up, curious. Mountebanks were apt to say all
sorts of vaguely mystical-sounding things, but was this not
daringly like the Epicurean heresy?

Frankenstein leaned forward, almost kneeling, and clapped
his hands again. The rabbit was suddenly hopping about in
front of him on the floor.

"And things can be made to come back out of the void,"
Frankenstein said hermetically, "by those who know the secrets
of the will."

Of course, Sigismundo thought, it is probably not a rabbit at
all. Something that folds up and expands again, made of paper
with springs inside perhaps . . .

Frankenstein raised the rabbit (or whatever it was) by the ears and carried it back to a table full of strange apparatus. He held it aloft and suddenly produced a razor to slit its throat. There was a gasp, and the blood gushed into a basin.

Orange dye inside the mechanism, Sigismundo guessed.

"We are not subject to the angels or to death entirely, save by failure of the Will," Frankenstein intoned.

He threw the dead rabbit into a bin and poured the blood, if it was blood, into a large, clear glass beaker. Then he stepped back and produced a pistol. He fired at the beaker. Amid shattered glass and red blood (or dye) the rabbit leaped out and hopped across the stage.

There were several more tricks of that sort, and even the adults were excited by now; each trick had a new twist that they hadn't seen before. Sigismundo noticed that the patter kept returning monotonously to the themes of the void and the Will.

"I have a message for P.," Frankenstein said suddenly. "Is there a P. here?"

It would be a real miracle, Sigismundo thought, if there were no Paolo or Pietro in a crowd this size.

"Is it for me?" a shopkeeper asked. "I'm Paolo Marconani."

"Somebody has been stealing from you," Frankenstein said solemnly.

"Yes, yes," Marconani said. "And I think I know who the fatherless one is."

He suspects his clerk, Sigismundo guessed; what clerk doesn't feel underpaid and "borrow" a little now and then?

"He is a man you have trusted, a man you have done great kindness for," Frankenstein said. The clerk would see it somewhat differently, Sigismundo reflected.

"You will do the right thing," Frankenstein said ambiguously. "You will think it over tonight and you will know the proper course."

The clerk will find a new job in Roma, Sigismundo thought.

"S.B.," Frankenstein said suddenly. "I am getting the letters S.B."

Nobody responded.

"Wait," Frankenstein said. "I see more clearly. You do not use that name. You would rather forget it."

Sigismundo Balsamo. Oh, no; it's just a coincidence, a lucky guess. Don't get suckered in like that shopkeeper.

"You are right to resist your father," Frankenstein said. "He is an evil man. But your future is not with the white-haired old man who calls up angels either."

Sigismundo controlled his face. I will not give him any clues. I will not be played for a fool again.

"You must find your own path," Frankenstein said. "But you cannot abandon the power. Not ever. If you ever try, it will almost kill you."

He was looking directly at Sigismundo. But then his glance moved on (To protect me? Or is every imaginative adolescent getting a few seconds of that meaningful gaze?).

"You will hear from me again," Frankenstein said. "I will help you find the true path."

Holy Mother of God, Sigismundo thought, *he's* trying to recruit me too. Everybody wants me to learn their secret handgrips and join their very own special conspiracy.

"Remember this prophecy," Frankenstein said in his organ-solemn tones, again addressing the whole audience. "The son of the hawk shall appear in the East. He shall be marked with the sign of the Beast. His mother a whore, his father a thief. The earth will shake in a violence and grief. These words are a riddle, their meaning unclear. Understand only: Ye have nothing to fear."

▲

"When was Frankenstein born?" Sigismundo asked Father Ratti the next day.

"In 1673," the priest said calmly.

That was what Sigismundo had always heard; but the man he had seen simply did not look to be 92 years old.

"And he died in 1734," Ratti added. "At the age of 61."

"I don't understand."

"I have seen two Frankensteins in my time," Father Ratti said. "And often it seems that he is performing miracles in two different cities at the same time. That is even more remarkable than climbing out of his grave and going on tour, is it not?"

"Oh," Sigismundo said. "You mean any traveling mountebank can call himself Frankenstein."

"Exactly. I even saw Faustus once, in a fair at Hamburg, and he died in 1580. Or at least his friends took the liberty of burying him then."

Sigismundo returned to the market that night to see what further mystifications the alleged "Frankenstein" would offer.

But the tent was gone. The mountebank had left as abruptly as he had come.

▲

"We are most fortunate," Father Ratti said one Monday. "The good Dominicans—the ornament and glory of Mother Church and the model toward which all other, and hence lesser, orders can only aspire—will be holding a retreat for all the boys in the local colleges. The retreat will begin on Wednesday afternoon. Friday afternoon confessions will be heard for all those who have found blemish in themselves.

"I can only pray," Ratti added without a smile, "that this solemn occasion will bring us all closer to that holy sanctity and Christ-like spirit that the Dominicans exemplify."

On Wednesday afternoon, Sigismundo and the rest of his class and dozens of boys from other colleges in Napoli filed into the Dominican chapel.

The Dominican preacher was a monk with a shaved head and eyes that had not liked anything they had looked on in this world. Sigismundo wondered if this man worked in the interrogation branch of the Inquisition when not holding retreats for young boys. He looked like he'd know how to apply the thumbscrew, counting five beads on his rosary for five turns of the screw and praising God all the while.

"I'm sure this is not the first retreat you boys have attended," the Dominican said, "and, if God protects you and you remain good Catholics, it will not be the last. Some of you may even regard it as a rather boring ordeal you are forced to undergo once a year. It would be more fun to be playing ball in the park or going to fencing class, I'm sure. I can understand that; I was a boy myself once."

And he probably pulled the wings off flies, Sigismundo thought.

"Still," the Dominican said, "Holy Mother Church has a reason for demanding periodic retreats. The world is a vile place these days; it is full of sin and temptations to sin. It is also full of worry and anxiety and problems of all sorts. Living in this world is not conducive to contemplation of God, and it is almost impossible to achieve union with the Will of God while we are in the world. That is why some orders are cloistered and do not come out into the world ever, for all their lives. And that is why retreats from the world, like this one, are necessary. We must depart from this wicked and fallen world occasionally if we are to see through its evils and delusions and come closer to the Light that is God, the Light that was in the beginning, is now, and ever shall be.

"To retreat from the world, we must begin by considering the final things, the things that the world ignores in its bustle for money and pleasure and success. You all know the final things: they have been mentioned many times in Religious Knowledge class. Every one of you can name them: death, judgment, Hell, and Heaven. But the purpose of a retreat is not merely to name them, my dear children. The purpose of a retreat is to think deeply about them. To come to know them. So that when we return to the world, we shall not be deceived by the world. So that we will know that the proud man is proud only for a while, the lust-filled fornicating man is groveling in his swinish pleasures only for a while, the rich man is rich only for a while. At the end, they all must face—you and I must face—the last things. Death. Judgment. Hell. And Heaven.

"Death, you all know, may come at any time. The typhus might come back to Napoli. A flowerpot could fall off a roof and crush your skull. And, after death, each of us—man, woman, and child—must face the judgment. And after the judgment, it is either Heaven or Hell, forever. That is the purpose of a retreat. To face this fact of existence. To stop for a while avoiding it and to look at it honestly. We must die. We must be judged. And then, dear boys, will it be Hell or Heaven?

"Satan is subtle and tireless and has many traps. And this is especially true for those of you who are almost becoming adults. It is easy to lead you to the ways of impurity, to sinful thoughts and carnal desires, even before you are aware that you are allowing the Devil to enter you. There are many artists who claim to be good Christians, and yet their paintings seem calculated only to arouse lustful and impure thoughts. Do you turn your eyes away from such paintings quickly, or do you allow Satan to enter you for a few minutes—do you allow sinful fantasies to form? Have you allowed lewd companions, with jokes and sophistries, to convince you that such things are not really serious?

"Oh, my little brothers in Christ, the Word of God assures us that such sins *are* serious. And they quickly lead to worse sins. I tremble to think of it, but many boys are led from these impure paintings to acts of self-pollution, to the mortal sin of Onan, to the destruction of the seed that was given us only to populate the earth.

"Sin always enters the soul with a lie, a perversion of reason, a plausible deception. It is said that Lucifer's sin was pride, but in a sense all sins are sins of pride. In every case, we set our fallible, personal judgment against the revealed Word of God.

The greatest poet the world has ever known, the great Dante, said it: The path to Hell is easy. We enter without admitting to ourselves that we have chosen that path—like Paolo and Francesca, the very first sinners we meet in Dante's Hell. They read a book they should not have read. What harm is this, they probably thought: the Church is too strict; we can read and judge for ourselves. And so they went their way to eternal damnation.

"Oh, my little children, it is a hard thing for mortal man to understand eternal damnation. At your age, you probably do not think further ahead than the next holiday. The farmer plans for the harvest, the man of business may plan for five or ten years ahead, but nobody can plan for eternity. It is too large for our small minds.

"This is only one day in all the history of the world. And yet this day has been full already. You can remember waking, and washing, and eating breakfast, and walking to this chapel. You may remember those you spoke to before coming in. Every hour is full of incidents and events. And yet eternity is not made of a thousand hours, nor a million, nor a million million. It contains an infinite number of hours, an infinite number of days, an infinite number of years. This is impossible for mortal man to understand, but we can form some image of it.

"Imaging waking, not in your bed at home, but on a bed of coals. Imagine that the fire burns forever but consumes not. You have all been burned at some time, I'm sure; but that is only natural fire. The pain of Hell is the pain of supernatural fire; it is infinite pain, endless torment. It burns forever, but it never consumes the victim; it is supernaturally renewed, so thatthe pain never ends.

"And I suppose some of you remember being afraid of the dark when you were smaller. Even adults sometimes do not like to go into dark and strange places alone. And yet Hell is always dark. The supernatural fires burn forever, but just as they never devour the victim totally, they never shed even a glimmer of light. It is a place of inky darkness, inhabited only by fellow sinners and by fearsome demons who afflict the sinners with torture and mockery. Monstrous demons who cannot be seen but whose leathery wings and scaly skin and buzzing speech are loathesome and whose only ambition is to torment the sinners forever. This is the punishment for those who depart from God's law, Lutherans and other heretics and fornicators and those who think impure paintings and lewd books are 'no serious matter.'

"Many of you go to Jesuit colleges. It is an admirable thing about the Society of Jesus, that they build so many colleges and staff them with so many scholars of great erudition, even if their theology is not always perfectly accurate. They are fine scientists, the Jesuits. Their mathematicians are among the best in Europe. Those of you who have studied with them know what infinity means. You know that if you write 1, and then 10, and then 100, and then 1,000, and keep on writing like that for the rest of your life, no matter how many zeroes you add, you will still be no closer to infinity. And this is the final agony of Hell: the knowledge, sure and certain and unchanging, that every pain, every terror, every hour of agony will be repeated, and repeated, and repeated, forever and ever and ever, without end. That is eternity."

There was a muffled sob. Sigismundo looked around covertly. The sob came from a child who looked about eleven. He's fair ready to urinate needles, Sigismundo thought.

"Some ask how a just God can inflict such tortures on His creatures," the Dominican went on. "But it is precisely because God *is* just that Hell is necessary. God is infinitely good, as you all know, because if He were not infinitely good, then by definition He would not be God. Therefore any departure from God's laws—the laws of infinite goodness —must be infinitely evil. And an infinite evil demands in logic, in justice, an infinite punishment.

"San Tomasso d'Aquino, the greatest of the teachers of the Dominican order, was so wise that some have named him 'the angelic doctor.' Even though he wasn't a high-toned Jesuit. Um. And San Tomasso wrote that for Hell to be infinite, it must be metaphysical. That is, the pains I have described are only the lesser of its evils. The supreme evil, the final horror of Hell, is a metaphysical pain, the *poena damni*, the pain of damnation. Let me explain that.

"God is with us every minute, every second. We do not feel His presence, usually, because we are too concerned with our own little minds. Yet He is always there. When you laugh. He laughs with you and through you. When you play, He plays among you. When you look at the starry skies and feel awe and wonderment, He is within you and within the stars themselves. All things that are are reflections of the Divine Light of Godhood. We are never deprived of that Light.

"*Except* in sin. In lustful thoughts, in impure jokes, in foul sensuality, in the company of whores, in unnatural vices, in lies and heresies and other offenses, we separate ourselves from God. The Light goes out of our lives. Things become problems, worries, anxieties. That is the beginning of the absence of God; that is the state of mortal sin. Hell, you see, is *the total absence of God*. The darkness there is both physical and metaphysical. There is no light there, because there is no mind that reflects God, no mind that reflects anything but its own vices, no mind not perverted by hatred and guilt and self-pity. There is no hope, because eternity never ends. There is simply despair. Forever! Forever and forever and forever! Eternal darkness and eternal despair: that is Hell.

"We will think more deeply on these things tomorrow. In the name of the Father and of the Son and of the Holy Spirit. Amen."

That night Sigismundo dreamed that he was being initiated into the *Rossi* by his blond murderous father, Peppino Balsamo. Everybody was wearing crocodile masks instead of hoods, and when they invoked their four fallen angels, all four appeared quite solidly. Orpheus said that Sigismundo was his to claim, because those who love music more than God are sons of Orpheus; but Aradia claimed him also, because he wanted to see Maria Maldonado naked and put his dirty thing inside her; and Lucifer said Sigismundo was *his* son, because no man ever lived with such diabolic pride. But Mother Tana took him as her own because he was secretly her ally and the ally of her children who were poor and angry and knew the sacrament of the dagger.

Was the dream sent by God, to warn him of his dangerous tendencies? For that matter, was the retreat especially for him, because he was so far gone in heresy?

When Sigismundo entered the chapel Thursday morning, he did not feel at all superior to the boy who had let out that involuntary sob the day before. I will be defecating purple boulders before this is over, he thought.

"Today," the Dominican said, "we are going to consider the sins that are most hateful to God and most likely to entice boys your age. I refer to the sins of impurity.

"What is impurity? It is a blemish, as when we say the color is not pure in a piece of cloth, because a stain has gotten into the dye. It is a poison, as when we say the water is not pure, meaning that it will kill you to drink it. It is a discord, as when we say the music is not pure, because perhaps the violin has hit a wrong note.

"Stain, poison, discord: these, then, are the synonyms for

impurity. In each case, there is an ugliness, a foulness, a danger. We wince at impure music, we reject an impure color, we fear impure food.

"God in His mercy has made the sins of the flesh equally foul, so that we will instinctively avoid them.

"Ah, but Satan is always busy, busy, *busy*, always plotting, always fertile in new tricks and deceptions. He knows well how to offer us that perversion of reason, that plausible lie, that will lure us to our damnation. He knows how to disguise the foulness of womankind so that even the holiest, the most pious, the best among us, can at times be drawn toward the cesspool of vice, seeing it in delusion as the fountain of blessedness."

Sigismundo was sweating profusely. The air in the chapel was dead; all the doors were closed. This is what it means to be stifled, he thought.

The priest went on, but Sigismundo tried to think of music so he would not grow faint and disgrace himself. The words still hammered at him; neither Vivaldi nor Telemann could drown them out. "Satan has invented *paints* and *rouges* for women, the better to lure us. But what do they lure us to? You have all seen the copulations of dogs, of donkeys, of pigs. Is that not an ugly and grotesque sight? Yet Satan would put a myth over our eyes and lead us to believe our fornications are not equally bestial and obscene.

"Why did God make woman inferior to man? He wishes us to avoid these 'occasions of sin,' as the great San Tomasso called them, these 'sacks of dung,' in Origen's words . . ." I will not faint, Sigismundo thought, even if the air is unbreathable. I will hold my dignity. "Do you know what the French pox does? The boils, the pains in urination . . ." I haven't done it, I've only thought about it . . . "Some go blind and must beg on the streets, in eternal darkness, living in the black pit of Hell in this world even before being condemned to it after the judgment. And there is no cure for this hideous disease . . ." It went on, and on, and on.

"And remember, I implore you, the last things. Death. The judgment. Heaven. And Hell. Remember the black and bottomless pit where no sane voice is ever heard, where the flame burns and scalds and torments but consumes not.

"*Hell is forever.* That is what we must think upon in this retreat from the world. Hell is forever. May we avoid it, I pray. May we find our way to God and to the peace that passeth understanding. May we beware of the painted woman who is all perfume on the outside and a foul, rotten, stinking cauldron of blood and urine and pox within.

"In the name of the Father and of the Son and of the Holy Spirit. Amen."

At a signal, the boys all knelt to examine their consciences. The Dominican, sweating like a runaway horse, left the podium.

The boys were alone with their thoughts. Another monk, in the back, watched them so that they would remain kneeling and contemplating their sins for the required amount of time. After forty-five minutes, the boys were allowed to leave the chapel and file into the dining hall, where bread and water were served to remind them that they were here to leave the world and its superficial pleasures behind and contemplate the eternal things: death, judgment, Heaven, and Hell.

That afternoon the Dominican spoke of heresy.

"All Europe is an armed camp," he said. "We live in a permanent state of war and preparations for war. This terrible condition is no accident: it is the way Satan wishes it to be; it is the proof of his success in misleading and deceiving men.

"There is no heresy that is not boldly proclaimed among the so-called intellectual classes in Protestant countries such as England. Even in France, the Inquisition is hamstrung by meddlesome aristocrats, and the most vile, satirical books are freely published. And yes, even here in Italy—less in Napoli than in the North, of course—many books circulate that our ancestors, in their wisdom, would have thrown into the public bonfire at once. And even here in Napoli the heresy of liberalism has, at times, appeared. Most of you are not old enough to remember Don Carlos, the uncle of King Ferdinand. You all know that Carlos built that wonderful opera house, the largest and most beautiful in the world. But Carlos also did a terrible thing. Misled by French fads, he passed an edict of toleration for the Jews. He gave them permission to practice their religion here in Napoli! A religion without Christ in the center of Catholicism! Heresy, you see, had reached even into the court at that time.

"Your fathers will tell you what happened. God turned his face away from Don Carlos. That unfortunate king waited year after year, but his queen produced no male heir to the throne. Finally, beginning to listen to the wise words of the Grand Inquisitor at last, King Carlos withdrew that absurd, that blasphemous edict of toleration. The Jews may live among us, he said, but they may not practice their black and blasphemous religion, which denies Christ.

"How has Satan accomplished so much in only a few centuries, so that even a king in this most Catholic part of Italy would fall into such error? How has the Prince of Darkness led men into the 'war of all against all' that is modern Europe? It has been done through *conspiracies* and *secret societies*.

"That is why the Inquisition can never rest. A little spark may ignite a thousand acres, as any farmer will tell you. I remind you again that Satan is always busy, busy, busy! I am sure many of you have heard tales of the old *Carbonari*, who would appear out of nowhere, in the night, like the Three Wise Men who come at Christmas. A poor family would hear a knock at the door. They would open, and the *Carbonari*, with lampblack on their faces, would hand them food and clothing and money. And then they would disappear again, saying only, 'We do it for the widow's son.'

" 'What harm is that?' you might ask. Many have asked and have seen no harm in it. Some men of business, they thought, who like to dress up in strange costumes and do charitable works anonymously. *That was what it was meant to look like*. But it was actually the work of Satan.

"In this way, men's minds were influenced to think that secret societies might be benevolent. They forgot that every group that acts clandestinely might be a portal to the powers of the darkness and Old Night. And then, behind the scenes, the real male-factors would pull the strings: the *illuminated ones* of Spain, who are actually Mohammedans pretending to be Christians. Now, all over Europe there are these groups, usually calling themselves Freemasons, doing these charitable works 'for the widow's son,' as they say. And the foolish ask, 'What harm is that?' And more and more each year are lured into Masonry and its allies and affiliates. 'What harm is that?' Oh, dear little brothers in Christ, these Masonic lodges are the chief sources of the heresy of toleration. It makes no difference, they say, if a man is a Catholic or a Protestant; he can still be a Mason. It makes no difference if he is a Jew or a Moslem; he can be a Mason. It makes no difference if his loyalty is to an Italian prince, a Swiss parliament, or a caliph in Baghdad; he can still be a Mason. And so, with the perversion of reason, with the plausible lie of toleration, this secret society grows and grows, and the Unity of the Faith is corroded. If there is no one true religion, if all religions are equally true, then why bother with the sacraments? Why bother with confession and repentance? Why burn books with improper language or doctrinal error in them, since no man can be sure of the truth? And so it goes, until the Church will be destroyed utterly, and Christ's message will be lost, and each man will be his own Pope and Christ and Bible, and there will be Satan's kingdom on earth: universal anarchy.

"If you know of a boy who collects books with improper language, not suitable for young adults, you must report this. It is your duty. Such books are poison. It is the same with books of moral and doctrinal heresy and subtle satire on God-given institutions. They must not be allowed to corrupt innocent souls; they must not lead others into eternal damnation and the fire that burns forever and is not quenched.

"But what about a mother, a father, a beloved relative? It makes no difference. *I come to set brother against brother*, our Lord said. And: *I come not to bring peace but a sword*. It must needs be so. The Church Militant on earth *is* our family, our true father and mother. The sheep who obey and are docile must be separated from the egotistic and self-willed goats who rebel against all authority. Satan's work must be stamped out. Remember the last things: death, judgment, Heaven, and Hell. Will you go with the gentle sheep, directed by those wiser than themselves? Or will you join the goats who say, *I know better than anyone* and plunge, like Satan, the father of pride, to doom and perdition?

"Let me add this: in the thirty-eight years that I have served the holy office, I have sat on tribunals that judged over nine hundred heretics. That includes mass trials of whole families and whole lodges of secret societies, of course. And do you know how many of those accused were actually turned over to the civil authorities for public execution? Only fifteen. Only fifteen were so stubborn and obdurate in their pride as to be considered beyond redemption. All the others—all—made submission and confessed their errors. And they were given very minor punishments. Some were sent to prison for life. Some, especially repentant, were allowed to enter monasteries or, in the case of women, nunneries, to spend the rest of their lives in prayer and mortification. And a great many were merely assigned a simple penance, such as making pilgrimage to a holy shrine and there doing public mortification for a period of weeks or months.

"So: if you know of secret societies or passwords, or of heretical books or pamphlets, it is your duty to tell your confessor tomorrow. Think upon these things. Search your consciences. Pray all night long, I beg you. In the morning, confessions will be heard.

"In the name of the Father and of the Son and of the Holy Spirit. Amen."

▲

Sigismundo searched his conscience all day and much of the night. The next day, as time for Confession approached, he was still in turmoil: dog-faced Things were beginning to appear again near the edge of his vision.

He knew the Dominican's final argument had been true: there were very few burnings these days in Napoli. Most heretics just lost their property and went to prison. Huge mass burnings occurred only in Spain, and not so often there anymore either.

He thought of Uncle Pietro in prison, Father Ratti sent off to a monastery to do perpetual penance. And Giancarlo Tennone was in the "club," too: what would happen to old man Tennone? In his fearless and taurine way, he would tell the Inquisitors to go intercourse themselves if they asked him to name names. Sigismundo also thought of Abraham Orfali. An old Jew who practices magick and has no property worth confiscating—that *could* turn into a burning offense.

The reason there were so few burnings these days, really, was that opponents of the Inquisition were gaining in power: the erudite Jesuits, the noble families who had had relatives

condemned in the past, the merchants who resented the
constant snooping that accompanied all Inquisitorial activities.
But you could not depend on such trends continuing: politics
was full of surprises. If the Dominicans were in favor with the
Vatican again, if they wanted a demonstration of their continued power, everybody might burn. Uncle Pietro, Dr. Orfali,
Tennone, Father Ratti—all.

And the whole Church, not just the Dominicans, taught
that to make an unworthy Confession, to conceal sins, was
itself a mortal sin.

I have gone far, far into heresy, into the *selva oscura*, the
mental spaghetti, Sigismundo thought, but have I gone far
enough to doubt the whole Church? Can I deliberately make a
mockery of the Sacrament of Confession? Especially when that
Thing that has been following me around since yesterday, the
one with the lion's face and bat's wings, might actually be a
Demon?

("They are old acquaintances. They are hallucinations only
if you cannot control them.")

What was Pascal's Wager? Sigismundo reconstructed the
famous argument of the great mathematician. The value of a
wager is equal to the value of the *possible gain* multiplied by
the *probability* of achieving that gain. If you obey the Church,
like the gentle sheep, the *possible gain* is infinite bliss in
Heaven. Say the *probability* of this is very low, as low as any
French skeptic claims. Say 0.00000000001 percent. Still, the
value of the wager is infinity times this probability, and infinity
times anything, however small, is still infinity. And on the other
side, if you join the proud and rebellious goats, the same
mathematics yields the same result. The possible loss is infinite, so even if the probability of Hell is as low as
0.0000000000000000001 percent, the total value emerges as
infinity again: infinite pain, in this case. The probabilities

simply disappear, as insignificant, when the gain is infinite bliss and the loss is infinite torment.

That was Pascal's mathematics, and you couldn't refute it.

The retreat of the past three days had made infinite pain a very real concept to Sigismundo. Could he risk that, setting his adolescent judgment against the wise teachers of the whole Church? He who was so often a fool? If he confessed fully and honestly, as the Sacrament demanded in order to be valid, the people arrested would only suffer finite pain, during interrogation. Even if they were burned, which was not really likely these days, that would still be finite pain. And besides, he thought, I won't feel it. (That was a vile, selfish thought.) But: If I do not confess fully, I will face infinite pain. There is just no scale that can measure the finite against the infinite. (And besides I will not feel their pain.)

Sigismundo suddenly felt an enormous revulsion, not against himself alone for having these thoughts, but against the Church for forcing him to make such choices.

Infinity doesn't change it, he thought angrily. It's my pain versus the pain of those I love, those who have trusted me. That and that alone is what they are forcing me to decide.

Pascal's Wager might be mathematically sound, but did not Pascal himself say that "the heart has its reasons that the reason knows not"? I cannot betray my friends, and that is all there is to it. To hell with mathematics, to hell with probability, to hell with logic, to hell with theology, to hell with all the philosophical spaghetti. I do not turn on my friends because I am afraid. I am not a donkey to be led by the carrot of salvation and the stick of damnation without thinking of where they are driving me and what they are making me do.

So: I shall now enter into mortal sin knowingly: and that is the definition of mortal sin, that you do it knowingly. And then, if the Church is right, the Devil will have my soul. My father will win in the end. As Dante said, the path to Hell is easy. First a lie in Confession and then downward, downward, downward to every abomination, whores and books with coarse language and the *Rosso* madness.

I am not meant to be a saint, he thought. I have too many passions, too much pride and fury and rebellion in me. And I am not an ordinary boy: I have the power sometimes. Perhaps I am destined to be the greatest of sinners, the king of the diabolists.

It was his turn to enter the confessional.

Sigismundo knelt, seeing the priest's shadow through the screen.

"Forgive me, Father, for I have sinned."

"What do you have to confess, my son?"

"Impure thoughts, frequently. I do not always resist them . . ."

And so on, and so on. He had been through it once a month for eight years, since his first Holy Communion at six. Always the same sins—"anger," "pride," "bad language twice"—but never before this tension of the One Great Sin held back, not confessed.

"Anything else?" the priest said finally.

Tempus loquendi, tempus tacendi.

"No," Sigismundo said. "That is all, Father."

"You are experiencing the normal temptations of your age," the priest said kindly. "You must pray, and I will pray for you."

And then it was over. Sigismundo was outside the confessional, kneeling in prayer at the altar rail. His prayers were jumbled, his mind wandered; he was swinging wildly between anxiety and resignation. It is done. I am cut off from the Church, whatever Uncle Pietro and Father Ratti say. Seventeen hundred years of theology pronounces that I have damned myself. Jesuitical equivocations cannot change that.

But then if working for peace and brotherhood, even if by

means of Masonry, is not a sin, there was no need to confess it. The Dominican lied, and I am not damned.

I have no certitude left about anything.

Sigismundo remembered the day he heard the Frenchman mock the miracle of San Gennaro's blood. He had thought that day that some things were sure: flaming rocks do not fall out of the sky, priests do not lie (but either Ratti or the Dominican *had* lied), and Mama had never been unfaithful to Papa.

Is there anything I am still sure of? Oh, yes, he thought wryly, the last item on that list: I am Sigismundo Celine of Napoli, not the man in the moon. Well, I am Sigismundo Balsamo of Napoli, not the man in the moon.

▲

The crisp but sun-bright season of winter in Napoli was now upon them. Life goes on, Sigismundo thought, even for us Damned Ones. It is as I felt it that day in Arezzo: millions come, millions pass, millions die. The fabric is always changing but always the same. Life goes on.

Then they heard that a *Rosso* had been burned in Palermo. He died cursing, the reports said: he called up 777 demons, even as the flames engulfed him, and implored them to fall upon the Pope, the king, the cardinals, the landlords, and especially the oral-copulating secret police, inflicting all with blindness, pox, and idiocy.

Whomever this demoniac was, he was not one of the four who had killed Uncle Leonardo. Uncle Pietro had obtained a full description; this man had never been in Napoli at all. Nobody recognized him.

Finally, as Advent began and everybody was preparing for Christmas and the visit of the Three Wise Men, the Dominicans announced that they were finally bringing the Umbertos to trial—the banker's family who had been arrested for witchcraft on July 23.

"Very speedy work for the Inquisition," Uncle Pietro

commented, in a low voice, to Sigismundo. "Usually, they hold people two or three years before having all the confessions they want."

Since school was out for the holidays, Pietro suggested that Sigismundo come with him and observe a day of the Umberto trial.

"I am sure it will be full of fun and rollicking good humor," Sigismundo said grimly. "Like the mating rituals of spiders."

Uncle Pietro did not smile. "It will show you a face of the Catholic faith that Father Ratti does not present to you," he said. "He, in fact, would like to see it abolished. I think you should come. Education consists of knowing what the world is really like."

The day they attended was the highlight of the show for everybody. Signor Umberto was making his confession.

"Why did you join the *strege*?" the Grand Inquisitor was asking as they entered. He was a kindly looking old man with a sorrowful face. He really believes in what he is doing, Sigismundo thought, and regrets that inflicting pain is part of it. Some of the *domini-canis* were just thugs in theological uniform, but this man had the self-lacerating sincerity of Saint Kevin, who had let his sweetheart die outside the monastery gate because he had sworn never to look upon a woman again.

Old Umberto, on the other hand, looked exactly like the end result of that kind of sincerity. He was a hideous caricature of the proud rich man he had been only half a year ago. His face, his hands, even his legs were monstrously swollen; his eyes might have been looking into the deepest mine shaft in Finland, seeing nothing but darkness and endless abyss.

"It was my aunt," Umberto said. "She taught me."

"She was a *strega*?"

"Yes. She said it had been in the family since the Roman Empire."

"How old were you when your aunt led you into the paths of Satan?"

"Fourteen."

Sigismundo remembered Abraham saying he should keep a record of coincidences.

"Why did she wish you to join in her evil works?"

"She said that it must always be passed on to a child, so that it never dies out." Sigismundo jumped at the words. But the quality of Umberto's voice was beginning to register on him: it was an actor's voice, but not very professional. The confession had been rehearsed many times, but the banker still did not speak with total conviction.

"Did she take you to a sabbat?"

"Yes. In Eboli, before we moved north. There were thirteen at the sabbat."

"Was there a leader?"

"She was the priestess herself. The male leader, her consort, was called only the Black Man."

Il Negro, Umberto had said in ordinary Italian; *El Eswad*, the *Rossi* said in Arabic. But the meaning was the same.

"Was the Devil worshiped?"

"Yes. They called him Lucifer."

"Were other devils invoked?"

"Yes. A she-devil named Aradia. And a Greek musical devil named Orpheus. And the devil's mother, Dana. She was the devil to invoke for success in hunting."

The connection leaped into Sigismundo's mind: Diana . . . Dana . . . Tana. The *strege* and *Rossi* both had kept parts of a tradition that went back to the most ancient moon goddess of Southern Italy. Was it possible that the fat and faceless Tana was the oldest form of the idea, going back to Vico's age of cave dwellers?

"What did you do at the sabbat?" the Inquisitor asked.

"We danced and sang."

"And then?"

"One of the women was possessed by Dana. She answered questions."

"What sort of questions?"

"Where lost objects were, who would get married soon. She always answered in poetry."

"How long did this demonic possession continue?"

"All night. She answered many questions. Sometimes she made jokes."

"Blasphemous jokes?"

"No, just jokes about people in the circle."

There was a long pause. The Inquisitors conferred in low voices.

"Let the prisoner be taken out," the Grand Inquisitor said sadly, with real pain in his voice. "Show him the instruments again."

"No," Umberto said hurriedly. "I didn't remember. Please, your honors. It is clear to me again."

"Were there blasphemous jokes?"

"Yes. She ridiculed Jesus and the Blessed Virgin."

"Were there further blasphemies?"

Umberto looked around vaguely, like a man who was not sure what city he was in or how he had gotten there.

"We blasphemed the holy sacraments of the Church," he said, almost mumbling. "We said the Lord's Prayer backward. We urinated on a Host."

"And then?" the Inquisitor prompted.

Umberto looked at the floor, "We murdered an infant and ate its flesh."

There was an outburst in the audience, and soldiers had to be called to restore order.

"Well?" Uncle Pietro asked, when the holy office recessed

for the afternoon *siesta*. He and Sigismundo were walking in the Palazzo Reale, which was mostly deserted at that hour.

"I don't know what to think," Sigismundo said. "His swollen hands—that was the thumbscrew?"

"Of course."

"Then the other swellings . . ."

"Similar instruments."

Sigismundo moved closer to the center of the empty *palazzo*, further from all neighboring houses.

"Are there real *strege*?" he asked.

"How can you doubt it when so many infallible Popes have declared—"

"No more irony. Please. Just tell me."

"I think there are *strege*," Uncle Pietro whispered. "There are many with the power, in every country. Village healers, people with second sight, old women who know herbal remedies and then learn other secrets because, well, people always tend to form 'clubs.' There are as many occult 'clubs' probably as there are styles of painting or forms of music. There is a legend that once there was only one 'club' and all those with the fourth soul were members. But then came the Inquisition and the burnings. The 'club' was destroyed. Maybe it happened that way. Or maybe whenever two or three people with the power get together, they start inventing a 'club' to organize what they are doing."

"Do the *strege* really eat babies, or do the Dominicans just make them say these things, with the thumbscrew and other instruments?"

"What do you think?"

"I told you. I don't know what to think."

"Well, neither do I," Uncle Pietro said. "Some 'clubs' are very nasty indeed, as you have reason to know. The Dominicans also have inflamed imaginations and tools that would make the Pope himself confess that he is the pigeon who made Mary heavy with Christ." Pietro sighed. "That is what is devilish about the *domini-canis*," he said. "One never knows what to believe about a confession obtained with their methods. Let us stroll down to the Osteria Pompeii and have some *scampi*. I'm famished."

That afternoon old man Umberto confessed to increasingly bizarre deeds—sodomy and incest and cursing people's cows so that they could not give milk and flying through the air to a giant sabbat in Bavaria where witches from all over Europe meet on May Eve.

The Dominicans expected to hear all that from a *strega*, Sigismundo reflected. As long as Umberto denied such things, he was by definition "obdurate in his heresy" and the torture would continue. The *strege* might be as innocent as a country dancing society, or they might be as vicious as the *Rossi*. It was impossible to judge from outside. But it was not impossible to judge the Inquisitors themselves. The Grand Inquisitor might be very sad and very sincere, but he presided over an academy of torture.

Sigismundo remembered Father Ratti explaining the Spiritual Exercises of San Ignatius Loyola. These exercises used the imagination to train the will; the technique was to make an imagined scene so real that the mind reacted as if it *were* real. For instance, every Jesuit had to go through the Crucifixion of Christ in his training: Father Ratti himself had done it. The candidate had to imagine each detail vividly and more vividly, until it was as if he had been put to sleep by Dr. Orfali and lived it. He had to imagine and live the pain of being whipped, and the agony of the crown of thorns, and the cruel nails being driven through his palms, and the wrenching of every muscle when the cross was lifted, and hanging there in the hot sun all afternoon. To be a Jesuit, you had to feel all that, and feel the blood run out of your side as you were pierced by the centurion's sword, and you had to die willingly for all humanity, as He did; and as you died in this vivid fantasy, you had to sincerely forgive those who crucified you, as He did. In that way, in that heightened imagination, you became one with Christ. That was what it meant to be a Jesuit.

The Dominicans, Sigismundo thought, have their own spiritual exercise, without realizing what they are doing. By contemplating Satan and Hell so vividly in their imaginations, over and over and over again, they have gradually become one with Satan and Hell. That is what it means to be an Inquisitor.

Umberto was being asked to name the Black Man who led the coven of witches in Napoli.

"He was merely *Il Negro*," the old banker said. "Names were not exchanged."

"Describe him then," the Grand Inquisitor said.

"He was young, very young. A *Siciliano*, I am sure, very dark. A thin face. About as tall as I am. And he had a touch of violet in his eyes, as if there were some blue-eyed Normans among his ancestors."

Sigismundo started. He knew that *Siciliano* face with violet-flecked eyes. It had spared him once in San Francesco di Paola. "Brother," it had said, another time, "you were born to be one of us."

So: There was a connection between the witches and the *Rossi*. And, as usual in this peninsula of tangled plots and endless conspiracies, this kingdom of philosophical spaghetti, the inevitable question was: who is using whom? Are the witches infiltrating the *Rossi*, or vice versa?

He suddenly wondered if the pseudo-Frankenstein, whomever or whatever he was, had just happened to come to Napoli *by accident*. And did he have words of ambiguous advice for "S.B." just by picking two initials out of the air? And what experiments by the real Frankenstein had led to all those terrible legends in Bavaria?

Sigismundo was beginning to see connections, links, patterns everywhere. *And I am trapped in the center of the web* he thought. *Even the stars have conspired to put me there according to the Rossi. What did I ever do to the stars that they should have such malignant intentions toward me?*

And why did Uncle Pietro want me to hear this?

▲

Federico Umberto was burned on San Stefano's day, right after Christmas.

Sigismundo did not attend the *auto-da-fé.* He had never seen a public burning and had no desire to add such a spectacle to his education. He was revolted enough by the celebrations that broke out in every neighborhood in Napoli.

It began at nine in the morning, when Umberto was being torched. All the churches in Napoli started tolling their bells at once, to thank God for this deliverance from evil. Then people spontaneously came out of their houses and started bonfires. Soon wine bottles were being opened and street dances were beginning. At noon the cannons were fired for the first time, and thereafter, every hour until midnight, there was another blast. It seemed to get louder as the day wore on—somebody had found some extra cannons, Sigismundo supposed. All the dogs in the city were hiding under beds and howling in protest; a sane man, Sigismundo thought, might consider the propriety of joining them.

In the afternoon, the crowds prevailed on the priests at San Domenico Maggiore and the Madonna was brought out, in Her robes of woven gold, and paraded through the streets for the rest of the day. By then, musicians with horns and drums and trumpets and fiddles were going from one neighborhood to another; it was turning into a classic Neapolitan holiday. *All we need,* Sigismundo thought, *is the indispensable drunk to fall through a stained-glass window in one of the churches.* Half the population was falling-down drunk by sunset; another half was in the churches singing the litanies.

As twilight came on, the cannons were joined by fireworks

of every description. The sky was soon as brilliantly chaotic as Sigismundo's hallucinations on belladonna—at times you couldn't tell the moon and stars from the other lights. And the cannons seemed to fire continuously now, and the church bells seemed never to stop clanging either. The dances grew wilder and more licentious; the Dominicans would not like this part of it. ("There will be a hundred brand new ex-virgins tomorrow," Uncle Pietro said. "And a hundred sudden marriages next month.")

By now it was as if Mardi Gras had come early, as if the wine had been spiked with strange drugs. People began shooting pistols and muskets into the air to add to the booming of the cannons and the banging of the fireworks: as if all the pent-up passions from the time of Adam himself were running amok in a delirium of celebration that seemed always on the razor's edge of madness. There was no street not alight with torches, not resounding to trumpets and hunting horns and shrill, demented-sounding violins. If the fourth soul is innate in all things as Abraham says, Sigismundo thought, this must be what Nature feels like in the spring when she begins to sprout forth new buds and bushes and trees of all sorts; but why does it take a man's death to unleash this energy? Are we still Dionysians, only pretending to be Christians? He remembered from the Bible:

> But who may abide the day of His coming?
> And who shall stand when He appeareth?

Does that really refer to the Messiah, he wondered, or to the dark side of the fourth soul that the Rossi wish to unleash? Are the Dominicans serving the same demonic force without even knowing it?

Finally, a group of drunks went down to the ghetto and began burning and looting at random. The police were called, and then, the frenzy having risen higher, the battle spread backward from the ghetto to the main parts of Napoli. People who had been singing and beating drums and dancing now decided to express their opinion of Bourbon rule by hiding on roofs and hurling bricks and rocks at the police. Some even emptied their chamber pots, which was called giving the cops a "Sicilian Bouquet," although Uncle Pietro said people in the North called it "Neapolitan confetti."

By dawn a semblance of order had returned; but then the most disgraceful details became public knowledge. Two policemen had been killed, their skulls cracked by flying bricks. One drunk had blinded himself by igniting a Roman candle the wrong way round, and another (as Sigismundo had expected) actually did fall through a stained-glass window—at the Cathedral, no less. The woven gold robe of the Holy Virgin was stolen by miscreants during the riot. And a little 11-year-old girl had been brutally gang-raped and beaten by hooligans from God-knows-where.

"Most edifying," Uncle Pietro said. "How holy we have all become, now that the witch is burned and evil driven out of our city."

But Sigismundo suddenly realized that behind his uncle's habitual irony there was, always, a terrible sadness and weariness.

▲

On January 17 the notorious Casanova arrived for a secret meeting with the Malatesta family. The formidable rascal had come by night and very secretly, it appeared. He was at Uncle Pietro's, and something of importance was afoot.

Papa Guido had a strange look in his eyes when he told Sigismundo that all the men of the family were meeting Casanova up there on Capodimonte. At least Sigismundo was now regarded as one of the men, perhaps because he had passed his fifteenth birthday, perhaps because they had all grown tired of trying to exclude him from the men's business.

There were many legends about Giovanni Jacopo Casanova

de Seingalt; most incredible of all was that even cynics agreed that more than half of the legends were true. This was the man who had been imprisoned for sorcery in Venice and had escaped so marvelously that some insisted he must have walked through the walls. Others, however, said that Casanova was a ringleader in the international Masonic conspiracy and his brother Freemasons had gotten him out by outrageously huge bribes at all levels, from the duke and the bishop down to the common jailers and the hangman's assistant's cousins.

Some said that he was not Casanova de Seingalt at all, but just plain Casanova—the child of a common actor—and that he had invented a noble title for himself to gain entry to high places. That he had served as a spy for more than one prince was established beyond doubt; how many state secrets he knew—and how many he had sold to the highest bidder—was a subject of endless speculation. Yet despite this uncouth background—spying was bad enough, but to have an actor for a father was positively sordid—Casanova de Seingalt, or plain Casanova, whichever he was, had become rich and mighty in France, selling alchemical secrets to the nobles. He had chemicals that doctors did not know about, it was said, and could show you Heaven while you were still alive; he could also heal wounds of all sorts. In fact, he had once shot a nobleman in a duel, healed him with one of these elixirs, became his friend, and—exploiting that connection for all it was worth—obtained a royal charter to run the state lottery.

It was also known that Casanova had a diploma in law and had performed as a violinist in leading opera houses, and it was furthermore alleged that he was a notorious cardsharp who had made his original fortune cheating at casinos. And there was the legend, too, that when Casanova was in town, wise men locked their wives in the attics, hid their daughters in the cellars, and hired guards for their elderly aunts.

When Papa Guido and Sigismundo arrived at Uncle

Pietro's house, Casanova was in the middle of a long story. Naturally, he was the hero of the anecdote, which involved an argument with Voltaire. To hear Casanova tell it, he had made a ring-tailed monkey of the French philosopher.

I'm sure Voltaire tells the story otherwise, Sigismundo thought, looking over the man who had such an astonishing reputation as magician, spy, musician, seducer, alchemist, novelist, cardsharp, and master of conspiracies. Casanova was about forty but quite athletic-looking still. (He'd better be, Sigismundo thought, with his unsavory reputation trailing behind him like hired mutes moaning behind a hearse.) He had an actor's handsomeness, or perhaps it was an actor's skill at comporting himself to show his best features. And nobody in the world was dressed in such gaudy and stupendous attire: in all Napoli the only object more astonishing was the Teatro San Carlo itself. It must take a day and a half to get him dressed, Sigismundo thought. But that is how he inspires confidence, of course. Princes look a bit drab next to him.

"So I said to him," Casanova was finishing his story, " 'Pigs will become sculptors and horses will paint murals before man truly becomes a rational animal.' "

He teaches lessons to philosophers, Sigismundo thought, when he isn't walking through prison walls, performing alchemical miracles, or contending for the International Bastardy Award.

By now most of the Malatesta and Celine men were in the room: Uncle Carlo, Uncle Francesco, Cousins Antonio and Paolo, Uncle Benito, Uncle Alfredo, Uncle Eduardo, Papa Guido, and Sigismundo himself. And Aunt Gina was present, too; the only woman there. Sigismundo began to realize what was coming. Mama had spoken of the money Uncle Pietro had distributed to his "contacts"; Casanova had even more "contacts." Networks of conspiracy crisscrossed Napoli, the Papal States, Genoa, Tuscany, and France. Anything was possible with enough money, enough time. Justice, as Pietro said once, is so high and holy a thing that it belongs exclusively to those wise enough and rich enough to know where to buy it.

"Where is the swine?" Aunt Gina asked suddenly.

Sigismundo looked at her. She was not as haggard as in the first months after the murder; she was almost pretty again, if somewhat older-looking than her real age. She would be pretty, he thought, if it wasn't for that look in her eyes, that look that reminded him of gargoyles on old cathedrals.

Casanova dragged a large box in from the back hall. A box big enough to hold a man, Sigismundo thought.

"There is, ah, the balance of my fee," Casanova said.

Without a word, Uncle Pietro handed him a bag. Sigismundo was startled by the size of it; even if it was only full of lire, it would be a great deal of money.

Pietro accompanied Casanova to the door, where they shook hands with the grip that Sigismundo now recognized as Masonic.

"We met *on the square*," Pietro said.

"And we part *on the level*," Casanova replied.

"Ride like the wind," Pietro said. "We just had a burning last month. The Dominicans are gaining power again."

When Casanova left, Aunt Gina asked impatiently, "The leader?"

"I wouldn't pay so much for anyone else," Pietro said.

Something happened in the room; nobody made a sound, but everything changed. It was like the hour when the air becomes stifling before the thunder crashes, Sigismundo thought.

The leader. My father.

Pietro and Papa Guido and Uncle Carlo took the box apart with hammers and chisels. Peppino Balsamo, bound and gagged, sat amid the splinters, looking at all of them.

Sigismundo could not bear to meet those eyes for the first

moment. Then he nerved himself and glanced at his natural father, the man who had raped his mother and murdered his uncle: the Archfiend, the Demon, the Satanist. Peppino was, even trussed up, a tall and handsome man, and he looked no more nervous than a barrel of wine.

Oh my God, Sigismundo thought, life *is* a grand opera to this one. He will die formidable to the end. He will not even beg for mercy.

"It is your decision," Uncle Pietro said to Gina.

"No," Gina said with that look on her face, the look that made Sigismundo want to turn his eyes anywhere else, even at Peppino. "Let Antonio speak. He suffered the most."

Everybody glanced at Antonio, who had been normal for months. Now he had the same look as his mother.

"A short death is not enough," Antonio said. "We must exercise our ingenuity. It is now about midnight. The pig should not be dead until dawn."

"Wait a minute," Papa Guido said unexpectedly. "We are men, damn it. Certainly, this filth must die. The world is not worth living in while such creatures breathe and walk. But torture is vile. Must we go so far?"

"It is Antonio's right to decide," Aunt Gina said bitterly.

"Yes, Antonio must decide: that is the code," Papa said. "But cannot we discuss it first? I say death, yes, absolutely; but not torture. In the name of Jesus and our hope of salvation."

Sigismundo looked again, very quickly, at his real father, to see how Peppino was reacting to this discussion. He looked at the wrong moment, because Peppino was looking right at him then, and there was demonic glee as well as contempt in his expression.

"Do it," Peppino said. "Torture your own father. Then your soul will truly belong to the Devil forever."

No, Sigismundo thought; he is gagged, he did not speak. My imagination is running away with me. I must not think that he spoke directly to the mind, that the power in him is transferring itself to me, that he is literally a Demon.

Dear God, you don't make it easy on us down here.

"I will never speak to any of you again," Aunt Gina was shouting, "if you refuse this. My door will be locked and bolted. I will have no relatives, do you hear? I will regard you, not as men of my blood, but strangers. Worse: I will consider you *poodles*, not men at all. Little toy French poodles that have been gelded. Christ Jesus, are there no testicles in the Malatestas anymore?"

Do it, Peppino's voice said in Sigismundo's head. Then you will all belong to the Devil. This is my sacrament, the Devil's Mass, the sacrifice of blood, the ritual of hate, and I am a willing victim, so that hate will increase in the world, so that Lucifer will own more of mankind's essence.

"Let me stab him once, where it will not kill him," Papa said. "Then I am part of it. I have obeyed the code. But then I will leave. Such abominations as you have in mind are not fit for the eye of God to look upon."

Everybody nodded, one at a time, like automatons at a carnival. Papa had been defeated, so they would be kind to him now. We have ethics of a sort, Sigismundo thought wildly, just as we have human souls—of a sort.

Papa grimly took one of the daggers from the wall and walked over to Peppino Balsamo. "You deserve to die," Papa said, his voice suddenly shrill. "And you, *you*, you excrement, maybe you deserve all the rest that is going to happen to you." Papa's lips were white.

"Wait," Uncle Pietro said. "I agree that Tony decides the punishment. But we are men, as Guido says, and this creature is still a man. Let us give him a chance to pray and repent."

Jesus no, Sigismundo thought. He did not want to hear what Peppino would say when the gag was removed.

But it was like the church again: time moving slower as if

Zeno's Paradox were true and the arrow could never leave the bow. Nobody said anything; agreement was reached again with slow nods. And in that frieze, Pietro moved very slowly forward and very slowly removed the gag, like a man moving underwater. Like the figure in a nightmare that comes closer and closer in slower and slower motions. Like the man the Dominican preacher spoke of, writing 1 and then 10 and then 100 and then 1,000 and then 10,000 and then 100,000 . . .

"Make your peace with God," Pietro said, almost gently.

"Whose God? Your rich people's God?" Peppino was not even bitter; he seemed to speak with a contempt that had lasted so long it was almost weary. "I have a better God, a God who never says, *submit, submit, submit*, a God who is the bravest and boldest within mankind. A God who says, *resist, resist, resist*."

"You will be dead soon," Pietro said gently. "Give up these fantasies. Die with peace."

"I shit on peace as long as there are some of you rich and all the rest of us poor. I shit on your God and your mealy-mouthed Jesus and on all of you while I am bound and helpless." Peppino was actually grinning in defiance. "You think Leonardo Malatesta was a big deal in my life? I have arranged thousands of assassinations, you fools, *thousands*. And I have not one regret."

"Stop him," Aunt Gina screamed.

"You'd better stop me," Peppino cried. "My God is real, not a myth like yours. He gives me the power. I know all about your sins, you hypocrites. Shall I tell you about the girl you hired in Spain, Signor Celine, and what you made her do?" Papa blanched. "And this noble, long-suffering widow," Peppino leered, "do you want to know what she does to console herself on some lonely nights when she can't sleep without it?"

"Stop him," Gina screamed again. "Stop him!"

Papa Guido slashed Peppino across the face, making a thin red line of blood.

"Huh!" Peppino grunted, but Sigismundo could not tell if it was a cry of pain or of perverse triumph. Blood was running down Peppino's chin onto his shirt, but he went on: "I have fucked every rich woman I ever met, some with one trick, some with another. And the children. Let me tell you. I do not like sodomy much, but teaching it to a little rich boy, knowing he might get to like it and then land in the hands of the Inquisition later—"

Antonio leaped forward, panting in rage, and brutally jabbed his dagger into Peppino's right eye. Not deep enough to reach the brain, Sigismundo noticed; Tony still wanted to be sure this would last until morning. Blood was now all over Peppino's shirt and trousers.

"You cannot make me scream or cry out," Peppino panted. "My God gives me powers you do not understand." But then he grimaced involuntarily. Thank God, Sigismundo thought, he bleeds, he does feel pain, he is not really a Demon.

"You are all so noble, so gentle, so fine," Peppino was going on, "not like us brutal peasants . . . Your wife asked for more," he said to Papa suddenly. "We went at it for hours, like hogs in heat. She couldn't get enough."

He lies, Sigismundo thought. He lies. He lies. I know he lies.

Antonio screamed—no words, just animal rage—and sliced at Peppino's left ear.

"I shit on your God," Peppino repeated, beginning at last to look a bit dazed. "I shit on the Virgin Mary," he added, blood splattering all over him. He is running down, Sigismundo thought; he will faint from pain soon.

But Aunt Gina hurled herself forward. "Yes, yes," she screamed. "Die with blasphemies. Die damning yourself to an even deeper pit of Hell. Go down lower than Judas, pig. Go to the bottom. Curse God some more, please. Make your

damnation absolute." She was kneeling, and for a moment
Sigismundo could not understand, would not allow himself to
understand, what she was doing. Antonio was right, he
thought: we are in Hell all the time: Napoli is just a delusion, a
false front. When we see through to the true essence of things
there is nothing but hatred and pain and eternal darkness and
demons howling curses at each other. "Curse God some
more," Gina repeated, still hacking at Peppino's crotch. Her
hands were bloody as she threw the testicles to the floor.
"Curse God," she screamed again, hacking at Peppino's penis.
Blood was running down both his legs, making a crimson pool
on the floor.

We will get a page in the history books, Sigismundo thought,
right after Caligula and the Borgias. I think I am dizzy again
and not in full possession of my reason.

But, certainly, now the worst was over. Even Peppino could
not shout more blasphemies with so much blood spurting from
so many wounds.

"I fuck your God up the arse," Peppino roared. "I fuck the
Virgin Mary! And the Pope!"

It will go on forever, Sigismundo thought; we will go on
stabbing him, and he will not die or even faint, because his
God *is* stronger: all history proves it. He will just shout more
blasphemies until we are exhausted and have to sleep; and then
when we wake and start again, he will start again too. This is
Hell: infinite hatred, eternal fire. We will grow old and gray
stabbing him, and we will be filthy with blood, and finally we
will all die of old age. And he will sit there, trussed up in ropes
and physically helpless, still defying us.

"I bugger San Gennaro," Peppino continued ranting, but all
Sigismundo could think of was that this man's blood was in
him: demon blood.

"I let Him possess me," Peppino shouted. "When there was

no Peppino anymore, when there was just Lucifer, then I became invulnerable and free. Free of your laws, your morals, your tyrant God. I am He and He is me, you fools, don't you see? I will live forever because only in Him is freedom from limits."

Papa Guido staggered toward the door. "No more," he said. "No more. No more." He stumbled out into the garden.

Aunt Gina had blood all over her dress now and was still slashing at Peppino, but in her fury she was stabbing at random now all over his body. Uncle Pietro seized her and dragged her back.

"Enough," he said. "You will lose your reason if you continue like that."

Sigismundo lurched forward. My turn. Let me strike one blow and get out of here, like Papa.

Peppino looked at him with his one remaining eye, bloody and inexorable. He could still speak. "My son," he said. "You will finish my work. It is in the stars."

"No," Sigismundo screamed. But he faltered.

"Yes," Peppino said. "Tana before you, Aradia at your left side, Lucifer at your right side—"

Sigismundo raised the dagger furiously.

"—Orpheus behind you," Peppino concluded. He smiled, as bloody and hideous as the saddest Christ in the most terrible Byzantine Crucifixion ever painted, smiled and then even laughed one more time, a laugh like the howl of a hyena, savage and primordial and undefeated: the willing martyr to hatred and rage, the Satanic messiah. Pure grand opera to the end.

The fireworks started again, and Sigismundo went into the crazy space.

"In the name of Emmanuel," Abraham chanted, *"I summon your spirit, Sigismundo Celine, back to this space. In the*

*name of Emmanuel, who is yesterday, today, and the brother of
tomorrow."*

Sigismundo was signing the parchment with his own blood.
"Now you are mine forever," Peppino said. "Your name is in
the book of the Devil. You will never rest, no, not for a
moment, while there is a single aristocrat alive anywhere in
Europe."

*"In the name of Emmanuel whose name means The
Presence of God is with us, I summon you, Sigismundo
Celine."*

Uncle Pietro was splashing water on Sigismundo, bucket
after bucket. I am being baptized again, Sigismundo thought.
They were in the garden by the well. Pietro was tireless,
hauling up one bucket after another to dump them on
Sigismundo's head.

"Libertà!" Peppino's voice shouted from the house.

"What happened?" Sigismundo asked. He felt like the
bottom of the junk box in the cellar after the dog had puppies
in it.

"You went into a trance," Pietro said, studying him carefully. "Do you know where you are?"

"I am in your garden," Sigismundo said. "And I remember
everything, the whole lovely Neapolitan evening. Except—"

"Libertà!" came the shout.

"Except what?" Pietro demanded.

"I was about to stab him, and he said something, an
invocation, and then . . ."

"Then you went into the trance," Pietro said.

"Libertà!" screamed the voice of Peppino Balsamo.

"Jesus," Sigismundo said. "Is he yelling that each time they
stab him now?"

"Are you really normal again?" Pietro demanded.

"Almost. I went back in time—"

"No, you didn't. He keyed you with that invocation and you started hallucinating again."

"Uncle, you do not know everything. I went back in time. I was in the cave again, under Pompeii, where the *Rossi* have their sabbats. Abraham helped me escape. And I remembered."

"What did you remember?"

"He made me sign the book. In my own blood. I pledged my soul to the Devil."

"Listen to me," Pietro said. "He gave you a drug that night, belladonna. And he keyed you to remember your hallucinations when he repeated the right words. It's an old trick, drugs and key words. It can make you believe anything if you do not understand that it is only a trick. You do not belong to the Devil. You belong to yourself. You have free will."

"*Libertà!*"

"Christ, Christ, Christ," Sigismundo cried. "Can't they put him out of his misery? Are we as bad as he is?"

"I know," Pietro said. "Do you think I am proud of any of this? But it must be this way. In this kingdom, one does not talk to the government about such matters; one handles them personally. It is not the best way, but it is our way, and it is necessary. We were conquered long before the Bourbons, even before the Normans. We may be the most frequently conquered people in the world."

"I know all that," Sigismundo interrupted. "But—"

"But it is terrible, what is happening in my living room," Pietro said sadly. "I *know*, I tell you. We are simply a people who have never had a government that was not our enemy. Our code grew up because we had to be our own police and judges and executioners. Because the government was never anything but a gang of foreign *banditti* living on us and exploiting us."

"Yes, yes," Sigismundo said. "But Uncle, torture, castration —Jesus—"

"I hate it," Pietro said fiercely. "But *it must be*, I tell you. I would rather just give him a drink of poison and be done with it. But when a people makes their own laws and acts as their own enforcers, the only way it works is if the injured party decides on the punishment, and if the injured party is half-crazy with grief and rage . . . well, these atrocities happen."

"*Libertà, libertà, libertà!*" came the howl. Peppino was still not dead.

"He makes it sound like another of his obscenities," Sigismundo said.

"And he is your father," Pietro said with sophoclean pity. "This night will curse us all. At least I can tell you one thing that makes it less abominable. These brothers of mine are amateurs, compared to the Dominicans. Peppino will be finished soon, because they have already lost their heads. It will not last until dawn as Antonio wishes."

"*Libertà!*" came the shriek, as if Peppino wanted to assure Sigismundo that Pietro was wrong and he would last for a long time yet.

"My God," Sigismundo said. "What is he?"

"He is a man. Like you and me."

"No."

"Yes. A man full of hatred, one more product of the terrible history of this tragic kingdom, but still a man."

"No. He was born a man, but he made himself something else. As old Abraham Orfali is something else, in the opposite direction."

"Listen to me carefully," Pietro said solemnly. "Abraham was much like Peppino once. So was I."

"No."

"Yes. To be alone with God, to be naked in the infinity of existence, is how you become like Abraham. There are many traps and pitfalls on that path, and Peppino fell into one of them. He has to be killed, like a mad dog, but from the bottom of my heart, I pity him."

"No."

"Listen. There is a path, as you suspect, to the beyond-mankind, but it is a path of darkness before it becomes a path of light. The alchemists call it *negrito*, the witches symbolize it by the Black Man in their rituals, Saint John of the Cross called it the Dark Night of the Soul. It is the Chapel Perilous of the Grail legend, to which only the perfect fool can be admitted. Do you understand? You have to lose *everything*, and everything includes what you think you know about God. You may decide there is no God, or that God is the spirit of destruction Peppino worships. It is very lonely and very frightening. I speak from experience, not theory. The only difference between Peppino and Abraham is that Peppino never came out the other side. Why do you think he put you in that trance?"

"To keep control over me," Sigismundo said bitterly. "To make one last effort to get me for the Satanists."

"Maybe. And maybe more. You didn't stab him."

"*Libertà!*" Peppino screamed. "*I will return as millions!*"

Sigismundo shook his head. "You mean he wanted to spare me?"

"It is possible," Pietro said. "He may not repent, in any Christian sense. He may blaspheme the Christian God with his last breath. But perhaps he is human enough to want to save you from that unspeakable crime: patricide. My God, this night has been Hell enough for all of us without adding that to the horrors."

"I don't believe it," Sigismundo said. "Not him. He wants us all to become what he is."

"In every human soul," Pietro said, "something of God remains. Even if the man deny it and try with his last moment of consciousness to escape it, it is there. Maybe that is why he used that spell to stop you."

"So Satan serves God without knowing it?" Sigismundo asked. "That is a Gnostic heresy, Father Ratti says. At least Peppino has stopped screaming about liberty. You must have been right about the family. They lost their heads and finished him."

But I will never be finished with him, he thought. I will always hear that voice, my true father's voice, telling me to kill every aristocrat in Europe.

▲

Sigismundo did not sleep the rest of that night. He prayed, or tried to pray.

Toward the One, the perfection of love, harmony, and beauty, the only Being.

Dear God, I can recognize You at times. Mostly in music. Occasionally in other arts. It comes in brief flashes, but I can see You then as the perfection of love, harmony, and beauty. The trouble is, God, most of the places I see You are tinged with heresy, they tell me. When I try to find You in the Church, I get lost in the theological spaghetti. Listen: I am only fifteen years old. I know that one cannot bargain and haggle with God as with a merchant in the marketplace. I know that is forbidden. Our duty is to accept Your mysterious workings and keep our faith, no matter what.

But I need to bargain and haggle with You. I am terribly confused. Let me tell You, it is not at all easy to find love and harmony and beauty in most of this world. I don't mean to be sarcastic, God, but sometimes it looks as if You're keeping all the love, harmony, and beauty to Yourself. What we have in abundance is hate and discord and horror. I almost killed my father tonight, and all that stopped me was a Satanic invocation. Please forgive me, God, but I can't help asking: Where are You when we need You?

I want to tell You, I act like a fool often, and I try to achieve humility and always fail, but God, You don't make it easy on us. I mean, liquifying the blood of San Gennaro is all very well and good, but it just isn't enough anymore. It is too easy to think the priests might be faking it, as that Frenchman said. It would be nice if You would be a little less ambiguous some of the time. I am not asking much. I know I can't demand anything of You: that would be worse than my other heresies. But I would like to ask, most respectfully, that You help us a little. Aunt Gina had a way with color and fabric that was like a great painter's ability, and tonight I saw her doing abominable things. Now, really, God, she wouldn't have acted that way if You hadn't made the kind of world where women are driven crazy with grief.

Please understand me. It has been explained to me many times that these things are not Your fault. It is the fault of mankind. But I saw a man mutilated and tortured tonight, and he deserved it if anyone ever did, even if he was my father, but damn it damn it *damn* it, God, I tell You that scene was not the perfection of love, harmony, and beauty. Not at all. I assure You on my word of honor as a Christian, it was most unlovely, inharmonious, and unbeautiful. What I don't understand is why You spend so much time torturing Your enemies in Hell. That's what they tell me: You spend infinities of centuries at infinities of varieties of pain. I can't believe it anymore. It makes You sound crazier than Peppino himself or my poor grief-stricken family when they finally got their hands on him.

You know what I think, God? I don't believe they lost their heads at all. They were deceiving themselves. They killed him fairly soon, after all, because the mutilations were making them sick. They wanted to be more monstrous than the monster

Balsamo, but they didn't have the hearts for it. So it was all over in less than an hour, I think, although I lost track of time for a while because I was a little crazy again.

But You see my problem: If I don't believe in Hell, and I don't believe in the Inquisition, and I don't believe all heretics are evil people, then I am really lost in that *selva oscura* of Dante. I don't know what to believe anymore. For all I know, You aren't even there and I'm just talking to myself. The Epicureans may be right: there's nothing out there but atoms and the void. And things come out of the void for no reason and go back into the void for no reason, and we invented You because we were lonely.

This is terrible, I know. I am really insulting You now. This is not a prayer at all but a diatribe. I am ashamed. Honestly, God. But this is still really a prayer, because I do need You. If You aren't there, what happened tonight had no more moral significance than a pride of lions devouring a zebra. If You aren't there, we might as well eat Peppino, instead of letting the meat go to waste.

If You aren't there, what the hell is my music all about?

So: Give me just one sign, God. Nothing big, nothing dramatic. I keep telling You, I know we aren't supposed to demand such things. But I need a sign, or I don't know what will become of me. And if You can take the time in Your busy schedule to liquify the blood of San Gennaro two or three times a year, You can slip in one minor revelation for me. Please.

And one more thing, God. I'm sorry if some of this sounds bitter or ironic. I'm under a lot of strain right now. It's not every boy who gets to see his father castrated and murdered, You know.

▲

Toward dawn, he finally dozed a while. And woke up,

gagging, with a half dream still possessing him: blood on his hands, blood on his nightshirt, on the bed sheets, on everything. A rising ocean of blood.

There was no time to bolt down the stairs to the jakes. He hauled out the chamber pot and vomited, again and again and again, visions of blood circling around and around in his head.

Negrito, he remembered. The alchemists called it the Blackening of the First Matter.

PART FOUR

THE PRIESTESS

For Mercy has a human heart,
Pity a human face,
And Love, the human form divine,
And Peace, the human dress.

William Blake, "The Divine Image"

At first Maria Maldonado was aware of Sigismundo Celine only in the vague, half-annoyed way you become conscious of a bug crawling on your neck.

It had begun when she was thirteen. Napoli was, of course, full of faces of people who were not close friends of the noble Maldonados—faces that she could associate somewhat confidently with family names ("He looks like an Orsini," "Isn't she one of the Portinaris?"—that sort of thing). But there was one face that she began to notice more than the others in the amorphous cloud of the half identified. This one special, *annoyingly* special face was constantly appearing at the periphery of her vision; she would catch it staring at her in the most intense manner possible (as a knight might stare at the Grail, she thought), but then it would look away, furtively and guiltily, when their eyes almost met.

It was the face of a good-enough-looking boy, about her own age probably, short and stocky like most Neapolitans, with a ridiculous little beard he no doubt considered debonair. He must be an extraordinarily stupid boy—maybe feebleminded —because he was always tripping over things or banging his head on the signs outside stores. Only gradually did she realize that he was not exactly a half-wit, but, strangely, that there was something about herself that made him abnormally nervous. That was why, when she caught him staring at her in that peculiarly obsessive way, his mouth was often open: it wasn't that he was short of brains (like the poor Orsini boy with the huge head, who could not speak and lounged about with his mouth open); this Celine nitwit could not breathe properly when she looked at him simply because he was acutely, painfully shy.

It was a long time before she realized that this clumsy and clownish youth was in love with her.

She began to understand that when she started reading novels. Of course, the nuns at Saint Theophobia Convent School in Roma were hell on novels; you could catch *the very devil* if they found you with one. Still, all the other girls read them, and Maria found some of them quite exciting actually, even if the ardent characters in them, allegedly adult, reminded her more of her younger brothers and sisters than of any adults she had met in the real world. But there was no doubt about it: men in novels, when they were in love, acted exactly like that absurd boy who kept trailing her around Napoli every summer when she was home on holiday.

Unfortunately, the novels did not tell you what you should do when you were not yourself madly in love with the male who was suffering these melodramatic symptoms. It was more than a nuisance by then; it was a continuous irritation, like her brother Carlo and his incessant target practice—*bang, bang, bang,* guns firing all summer long, enough to drive you to distraction.

Mother Ursula, the abbess, had a class on Saturdays for especially promising girls; Maria was a member. The girls were encouraged to ask questions concerning just about anything, and Mother Ursula would tell them how to find the answers for themselves, usually, or, when the subject was not very *nice* and a bit embarrassing, she would answer in full, and in a way that got rid of the embarrassment. Generally, she sent the girls on a search for their own answers because, as she often said, "I am here to set your brains in motion. It profits nobody if I just keep pouring my words into your ears until they start overflowing out of your mouths without any real mental activity on your part."

One day—it was a Sunday, after Mass, in the garden —Maria mustered up the courage to ask Mother Ursula about Sigismundo Celine.

"And how do you feel about him?" Mother Ursula asked.

"I think he's terrible," Maria said bluntly.

"Of course," Mother Ursula said, "but that is because he makes you feel terrible. His obsession is annoying because you are intelligent enough to know that it is more or less accidental: if it wasn't you, he would have some other girl to be obsessed with. That is the way it is with boys his age."

Maria nodded, a bit unsurely. "He makes me realize what other men probably think when they look at . . . my body . . ."

"Yes," Mother Ursula said. "Now listen closely, my child. A few girls in this college may decide to give themselves to Christ, as I have, but most of you will eventually be married off to men of the correct social rank. You will be expected to have children. That means that you will have sexual union with your husband, often. Don't fidget like that! This is a sacrament, ordained by God to perpetuate humanity. I am going to be even more blunt. In the early years of marriage this will probably occur many times a week. Five times, seven times, maybe more. Later, when the children start arriving, there will be more distractions, more responsibilities, and this will happen less often. But you will still have it, after marriage, for the rest of your life. How does that make you feel?"

"I'm frightened," Maria said. Even Mother Ursula seldom spoke this frankly.

"Of course you are," Mother Ursula said. "But look into yourself honestly, and be honest with me: Haven't you on occasion had somewhat romantic feelings about certain men? Be honest," Mother Ursula repeated.

Maria felt herself blushing. "I thought," she said awkwardly, "sometimes . . . it would be nice to have Giancarlo Tennone fall in love with me. I have thought of him . . . kissing me. And, and, *and*, well, saying he couldn't live without me."

"You have been reading novels," Mother Ursula said, smiling. "All the girls here read novels. I read novels, too," she said secretively. "The other nuns would be horrified if they knew. Every age has some new art form that is supposed to be a threat to morals and civil order; in our time, it happens to be novels. The human race has survived all such innovations. However, I will now tell you five things about this Signor Tennone, whom I have never met. He is at least fifty. He is the best in his trade, whatever trade that is. He has a wife and several children. He is a man of honor and will not be unfaithful to his wife. He is brave and also kindly. Am I wrong in any respect?"

Maria felt as if Mother Ursula might be a *strega* in disguise. "How do you do it?" she asked nervously.

"It is easy," Mother Ursula said, smiling again. "That is a rough description of the man I was in love with at your age. It is the kind of man nice girls always have fantasies about. Do you know why? Because he is safe. You know it is all fantasy. If you started having such thoughts about a boy your own age, you would frighten yourself. Do you understand?"

Maria nodded. She was too petrified to speak.

"Sin is a terrible thing," Mother Ursula said gravely. "But

God is very wise and very forgiving. Wiser and more forgiving than most people here in Roma or back in Napoli. The sin that you are afraid of—so afraid that you are even embarrassed to think of it—is more hated by men than by God. Do you know why? Because essentially marriage is a property transaction. The buyer wants undamaged goods. It is all male prejudice. That is why this silly, insignificant kind of sin is regarded as more terrible than murder, which is the kind of sin God really hates."

Mother Ursula took Maria's hand. "I was married once," she said. "I gave myself to Christ only after my husband was killed in an accident at sea. Let me tell you something about *sexual intercourse*." (This time she was absolutely not going to let Maria avoid the idea by veiling it in euphemisms.) "That can be the most beautiful part of marriage. Usually, it is not: it is the chief source of resentments, angers, and even violence. This is because both men and women are ignorant. You will be married in a few years, Maria. Come to me often with all your questions and anxieties on this subject. There is no reason why you should enter adulthood in fear and ignorance, just because the Church happens to be run by males who are full of fear and ignorance."

Maria had never heard anything like that before, and she realized Mother Ursula was taking a certain risk in talking so bluntly. Of course, Mother Ursula was not quite like any other nun. For one thing, she had long engaged in correspondence with Maria Gaetana Agnesi, who lectured at the University of Milano on such topics as conic sections and analytical geometry and was something of an expert on hydraulic systems —subjects in which women were not supposed to be competent. And Mother Ursula had also corresponded with Signora Mazzolini, who taught *anatomy* (and actually handled male bodies!) at the University of Bologna, and with the incredible Laura Bassi, of the same university, who taught Natural

Philosophy and how to use a telescope and was accused of the heresies of Galileo and Newton. Mother Ursula said that women could do anything men could do, and someday they might even be *priests* or *bishops*, although she did not say the last part in public. The Dominicans would be sure to swoop down on the convent like weasels on a chicken yard if that opinion were ever broadcast publicly, Maria knew.

So that if Maria learned a great deal about marriage and reproduction from Mother Ursula—and even learned to use the ghastly word *"penis"* without blushing, in their private discussions—she also learned many other things, beyond the musical skills and embroidery that were considered proper for girls. She learned that women had once *owned property* (in Sparta and Egypt, for instance); and that geometry was not impossible at all, but actually quite interesting and showed you how to think accurately; and that there had been women *judges* in Babylon; and that the further north you went, the more people despised the Inquisition and wished it abolished; and that you could analyze music mathematically, as Pythagoras had discovered, thereby showing that even something as mysterious as beauty had a rational foundation.

The most amazing thing about Mother Ursula, however, was revealed to Maria only when Hercules took ill. Hercules was one of the mules the school owned, to pull the carts for their trips into the hills to study botany.

The local horse doctor was called, and he examined Hercules carefully, then gave the beast a purgative. "It is something he ate," he said. "Whether he will live or die, I cannot say; it depends on how much of the toxin is in his blood already."

Maria was very fond of Hercules because he was the most intelligent mule she had ever known and had very sad, weary, contemplative eyes, as if he had figured out long ago that being a mule was mostly hard work and offered little reward. She went out to the stable a few hours after the horse doctor left, hoping that Hercules would be recovering as a result of the purgative.

Mother Ursula was in the stable before her and was kneeling, as if in prayer, but her hands were not clasped; she was holding them over Hercules's body, about six inches from each side of his head. Maria hesitated in the doorway, not sure of what she was seeing; and just then Mother Ursula said, half aloud and half to herself, "It is finished. *Heal!*"

Maria jumped back, almost terrified, as Hercules lumbered to his feet. She couldn't have been more surprised if the sad-eyed beast had followed that feat by singing the *Oratorio* for Easter. "That's right," Mother Ursula was saying, tickling the mule's ears and patting his head, "you *deserve* to live. You are God's child, too."

And Hercules was frisking and playing as if he had never been ill at all.

Then Mother Ursula became aware of Maria in the doorway.

"My prayer was answered," she said simply.

"You did it," Maria blurted. "You are a saint, aren't you?"

"Nonsense," Mother Ursula said sharply. "God did it. Don't talk heresy, child."

Maria rushed forward and grasped the abbess's hands; as she expected, they were warm and tingling. "God did it," she repeated, "of course. But you were God's vehicle. I can feel the power in your hands."

"I wasn't even here," Mother Ursula said. "If I had been here, it couldn't have happened. All praise should go to God."

Maria did not perfectly understand that, but she did know that Papa sometimes talked about an uncle (long dead now) who could do healings of that sort. "You could feel the power in his hands," Papa said; that was why Maria had grasped the abbess's hands, to check that. Every village had a healer with that talent, to judge by stories the other girls told; such healers had to be very careful, and very discreet, to avoid troubles with the Dominicans' committee to theologically investigate claims of the unusual, who usually decided it was witchcraft.

"How do you do it?" Maria asked, enthralled.

"I don't do it," Mother Ursula said. "I just go away and God does it. And never again accuse me of being a saint. That could lead me to the very serious sin of vanity, and if it were repeated, it might even lead some of the other nuns to the sin of envy. That is why Our Lord says, 'Let not thy right hand know what thy left hand doeth.'"

And that was that: Mother Ursula absolutely refused to allow the subject to be mentioned again. Maria did not guess even then why Mother Ursula gave her such special attention.

But Hercules was perfectly well from that day onward and never had a relapse; and every time Maria looked at the baffled, intelligent eyes of the animal, she thought of that strange kind of healing. She had to agree, of course, that God did it—that was theologically correct—but God didn't do it for just anyone. He didn't do it for the horse doctor, for instance. You had to be a special person, with the capacity to be *not-there*, as Mother Ursula called it, so God could work through you.

Maria remembered two times she herself had been *not-there*. Once, at home, in the garden, she was looking at a very special kind of butterfly—she didn't know its name because it was a species she had never seen before. Just then Carlo fired a gun at the other end of the estate, shooting at targets, as usual. Suddenly there was only the butterfly—there was no Maria looking at it. It was a wonderful experience, but she was always afraid to talk about it to anyone, because she had her first period that evening and she always thought it was some kind of strain that had unhinged her mind for a minute. That was when she was twelve and didn't know Mother Ursula yet.

The second time had occurred when she was fifteen. Papa had taken the whole family to the Teatro San Carlo to hear an *oratorio* by a German named Handel, called the *Messiah*. Near the end there was a chorus made up of the one word *hallelujah* repeated over and over and over in counterpoint, and suddenly Maria was *not-there* again: there were just the voices and the joy and (it seemed) God Himself singing in each of the voices. And no Maria. It was as if space had been abolished and time stretched out to infinity.

And, sure enough, she had her period that night too; and still she did not understand.

And then a few months after her talk with Mother Ursula about that repulsive Celine boy and a week or so after the healing of Hercules came the incident of the peasant's cart. Classes were finished for the day, and Maria was in her room studying for the test in Religious Knowledge. She was reviewing some Bible texts and came to Matthew, chapter 10, verse 7:

> And when he had called unto him his twelve disciples, he gave them the power against unclean spirits, to cast them out, and to heal all manner of sickness and all manner of disease.

Maria idly wondered: If all twelve had the power, and they passed it on to so many others (the early history of the Church was full of stories of miracle healings), why had it become so atrophied in later centuries? Why did only a few have it now, such as Mother Ursula and the (usually ignorant) healers among the peasants? But then the next verse struck her:

> And he said: as ye go, preach; the kingdom of heaven is at hand. Heal the sick, cleanse the lepers, raise the dead, cast out devils. Freely ye have received: freely give.

"The kingdom of heaven is at hand": That was what Jesus, the Son of God, had said. And yet seventeen hundred and sixty-six years had passed, and the kingdom had not manifested. It was heresy to think that Jesus had lied or even that He had made a mistake. Was it possible that the kingdom of heaven *was* at hand, all the time, and we had only to open ourselves to receive it? The way Mother Ursula opened herself to let God heal Hercules through her?

"Freely ye have received": But suppose you did not know what you had received? That would explain why the kingdom was not manifest to us. Were we like an ignorant man who has a million florins buried in his cellar and doesn't know about it?

That was when she heard the crash and the scream.

When she raced downstairs all the girls were rushing out the gate toward the road. The nuns, who had been praying in the chapel at the other end of the college, were far behind the crowd.

As Maria came through the gate, the Portinari girl from Firenze came back from the road, white-faced, and turned to vomit in a corner, behind the rose bushes. Puke and red roses, Maria thought: it was like the design of an artist gone demoniac. But then she braced herself. Somebody had been hurt, and the mature thing to do was to try to help, not to stagger off and get sick like a child. She stepped into the road.

A peasant was lying in a pool of blood. (Roses and gore: the crimson of beauty and the crimson of agony. Stop thinking like that!) There was a wheel off his cart; obviously the wheel had come loose and he had been thrown sideways, banging his head badly on the cobblestones. Maria felt tears rushing to her eyes, but then instead of weeping she just *opened* again, as she had during the "Hallelujah Chorus."

Freely ye have received; freely give.

She rushed forward and knelt by the fallen man, tearing her petticoat to make a bandage for the wound. But she was also thinking: *Heal. Heal. If I go away God can do it. Let me go away, Let God come in. His wife and children need him; it is a hard life for peasants. Heal. Heal. Let Your mercy flow through me.*

Mother Ursula was suddenly standing beside her.

"Beatrice," she said to one of the girls, "run as fast as you can to Via Dante and get the doctor." Then she knelt beside Maria, looking at the man's face.

"His breath is coming back," she said. "Somebody dip some rags in the well and bring them here."

Maria put both hands over the bandage, as if straightening it. She could feel the tingling power in her fingers. She looked nervously at Mother Ursula.

"You are doing fine," Mother Ursula said. Then, for the others, she added, "It was very cool and intelligent to make a bandage so quickly."

"*Jesus,*" the peasant said vaguely.

"Hush," Mother Ursula told him. "You will be all right. Just rest and don't try to get up."

"I have to go to market," he said.

"No, you don't," Mother Ursula said calmly. "That will be attended to eventually. You just have to rest now."

"Who did it?" he asked. "What fatherless one hit me?"

"Rest," Mother Ursula repeated.

The peasant closed his eyes again. He was breathing normally, like a man going to sleep at night.

And when Dr. Mazzini arrived, he was astonished. "With a wound like that," he said, looking extremely perplexed, "he should have bled to death, even with your makeshift bandage. Very strange. Well, God's mercies are mysterious. Isn't that what you would say, Mother Abbess?"

The peasant survived; and a few weeks later, he came to the gate of the school and insisted on donating a big barrel of fresh tomatoes and peppers.

And Maria finally understood that she had the power too.

So it was no surprise when Mother Ursula invited her to take a walk in the garden again.

"There are many superstitions in the world," Mother Ursula said.

Maria had known it would begin like that.

"If people see certain things," the abbess went on, "they are very quick to jump to conclusions. Some, especially the young and innocent, may say that the person who does these things is a saint." (Maria blushed.) "That is always wrong. Nobody is a saint until the Church infallibly says so, and that can happen only long after the person's death, and there must be extensive investigation, as you know. So it does no good to talk of such things, and it leads to vanity. On the other hand, there are more dangerous superstitions. Anybody can be accused of being a *strega*, you know—even the daughter of the great Count Maldonado."

Maria nodded.

"We must be merciful," Mother Ursula said softly. "If we can help others, it is our duty to do so. But in this wicked world we must also be, as Our Lord said, 'gentle as doves and subtle as serpents.' Like the fabulous Rosicrucians—who probably do not exist at all outside of legend—we must figuratively 'wear the garb of the country and adopt its customs.' We should not stand out at all. Ostentatious display of the power is not only vanity but folly. Do you understand? It can be extremely dangerous."

Maria turned and confronted the abbess directly. "You don't think the Inquisitors are very bright, do you?" she asked bluntly. "You are saying that even harmless people can be condemned by them."

Mother Ursula smiled tiredly. "Read the life of Joan of Arc," she said. "Then tell me if you think Joan was really a witch, as the Inquisitors claimed."

And Maria knew that, whomever Papa married her off to, whatever else happened in her life, her days would not be those of an ordinary Neapolitan *contessa*.

PART FIVE

THE WORLD

The great and direct end of government is liberty. Secure our liberties and privileges, and the end of government is answered. If this be not effectively done, government is an evil.

Patrick Henry, speech against the U.S. Constitution, June 25, 1788

All at once I felt myself dazzled by a thousand sparkling lights . . . [I realized] that man is by nature good, and that only our institutions have made him bad.

Jean Jacques Rousseau, letter to Malsherbes, January 12, 1762

All of Napoli awoke one morning to learn that a horribly mutilated corpse, of a tall blond man, was hanging from a tree in the Piazza Medaglia d'Oro. On its chest was a scroll saying

SO PERISH ALL THE ROSSI

The police pronounced themselves mystified by the atrocity; Sigismundo assumed that Uncle Pietro and his friend Drake had pulled the right strings and greased the right palms, to guarantee that the police would officially remain mystified forever.

And so, he told himself, the worst was over. Other *Rossi* were still out there, somewhere, plotting and scheming (his half brother among them), but things would never be as they were when Peppino Balsamo was alive. Whatever malice they possessed, however violent their aims, the other *Rossi* were only human beings and did not have cloven hooves. There could not be another one like Peppino.

And maybe, Sigismundo thought, God will not be insulted by my frantic prayer last night. Maybe He will send me a sign that He really is there and that I wasn't just talking to the atoms and the void.

So when he was returning from classes that afternoon and took his short cut through the alley off of Piazza Bellini, he was not so much frightened as outraged, almost furious, at what he saw. This is my answer, he thought; this is the Sign. God wants me to know He doesn't give a hoot in Hell about any of us down here.

Because a figure had stepped out of a doorway ahead of him; it had drawn a dagger; it was waiting. (That is precisely the final horror, he thought: that there *is* no final horror, that it goes on, and on, and on . . .) For there was no mistaking that face, those dark Sicilian eyes with a touch of violet in them.

Sigismundo quite forgot his nausea at the memories of last night's butchery, his vomiting into the jordan until he could vomit no more. Right now he wanted more blood; he had been pushed to his limit. He had his sword, he had his training, and at this moment he had a good share of his father's fury. I will slice the bastard to a million pieces, he thought, and feed his nose to my dog when I get home.

But then—by the sheer power of Tennone's training, automatically—he looked behind him, almost unconscious that he was checking the path of retreat, if retreat were necessary. "Plan for everything," Tennone said, "and count on nothing."

Two men had stepped out of another doorway behind him. Like his half brother in front, they were not hooded, but their clothes were solid black. They wanted him to make the connection and identify them as *Rossi*. And, of course, their daggers were already drawn.

Sigismundo unsheathed his sword, unable to feel even a twinge of fear because he was overwhelmed by blind fury—at God, at the order of nature, at whatever it was that kept doing these things to him. Three against one, it was, and two of them *behind* him; it didn't matter. He would almost certainly die; it didn't matter. He was going to hack and slash and chop as long as he had even one arm left to wield the sword—not against these three alone, but against It, God, the order of nature, whatever tormented him continually from behind the scenes, against the stars themselves if they were the forces that had elected him to this damnable destiny.

Sigismundo's brother approached. He was smiling. I will kill him at least, Sigismundo thought; I am good enough for that, even with two at my back.

Young Balsamo charged.

Sigismundo lunged with his sword, a perfect thrust, Tennone would be proud of him, and—he could not believe it—he missed entirely. And, spinning around, trying to understand, he saw that his brother had run past him, not at him, and that the other two were running also: three black figures looking almost like crows as they vanished around a corner.

Sigismundo, panting, incredulous, looked about. There were no policemen on the horizon. There was nobody outside any of the houses at all. If anything moved, it was as unobtrusive as a pickpocket's fingers.

The *Rossi* had not been frightened off. They had not planned to harm him at all.

He wanted to scream in rage. He wanted to run his sword through the first cat that moved on the street. He wanted to dash into the nearest church and denounce God from the altar. So he merely resheathed his sword, breathed the relaxing breath Abraham had taught him, and—when that did not work immediately—turned and kicked a rock.

This was what he had feared in San Francesco di Paola last Easter, when his life had been spared the first time. The oldest, most vicious Sicilian trick of all. *We could have killed you, but we didn't.* Now it was just a matter of waiting. They might be back tomorrow or next week, or they might wait a year. They might even box him in again and let him go again. Cat and mouse.

Sometimes, if this technique were sufficiently prolonged, some men actually went looking for *them*, to beg for mercy or to offer a deal, any deal they wanted. "Take my daughter," some had said, after a few of these visitations. Or, "Take 50 percent of my business." Or, "Whose throat do you want me to slit?"

And, of course (everybody knew it), sometimes when you got that point and went to them to beg and plead, it turned out that they didn't want anything except to kill you. They simply liked you to know you were a coward and a fool, going to them almost on your knees, while they waited like spiders to devour you.

I wish they had attacked, he thought. Even though I was outnumbered. But if I could fight and (miraculously) win, or even if I could fight and die, at least it would be over. But now it will go on as long as they desire. And it makes no difference if the Inquisition or the secret police somehow catch this group. A Sicilian vendetta never ends. If they all hang in the public square or burn at the stake, the men who will replace them are already picked. My name is on their list.

There was the story everybody had heard about the landlord who was particularly cruel, monstrous even for Sicily. And the M.A.F.I.A. got him one day, four of them, and carried him to a cliff. They held his legs and dangled him over the abyss. It was said that they held him that way, upside down like the Hanged Man in the Tarot, and never spoke a word, never answered his pleas and his screams. It went on for ten minutes—which must have seemed like an hour to the landlord, waiting to die—and then they abruptly hauled him up again and set him on the ground, alive.

At last one of the M.A.F.I.A. men spoke, one sentence

only; and then they all vanished. The landlord could not stand up straight and walk home for nearly two hours, it was said.

The M.A.F.I.A. man had said, "Next time we let go."

The landlord killed himself a month later, went out to his barn and took a gun and put it in his mouth and blew the back of his head off. He could not stand one more day of waiting for "next time."

Sigismundo breathed the relaxing breath again and invoked the four archangels. There are people like Abraham, he reminded himself. The world does not consist entirely of monsters battling monsters.

When he got home, he went at once to his room. Playing the *clavicembalo*—any tune would do right now—would certainly help calm him.

And then, as if he had found a five-legged horse, he saw *it*. Beautiful, he thought. I must admire the artistic restraint of this. So nicely inconspicuous and understated, but still as hard to ignore as a cobra in the bed sheets.

It was only a book; but it was very old, and it was not one of his books. Somehow he knew it was not a gift from a friend, that he should be afraid of it.

Sigismundo walked over to the table and picked it up, wondering if it might explode like a bomb. They are doing a nice job, he thought, in making me see threats everywhere.

The Key of Solomon, it said. And close up he saw that it was even older than he had thought from across the room. I wonder if they informed the Inquisition, he thought. The Dominicans might be at the front door right now, to investigate a report that I own a copy of the most infamous Black Magick *grimoire* in Europe.

He took the book between two fingers and carried it out onto the veranda. There was a potted palm balanced on bricks so the excess moisture could run out the bottom after it was watered. Not the cleverest hiding place in the world, but it would have to do for a while. He inserted the book between the bricks, under the pot.

He sat down on the swing chair and thought. It did not fly in the window, he told himself. I may be the most perfect approximation of pure idiocy since Quixote, but I am not simple enough to believe that. Somebody put it there. They did not just walk into the house and put it in my room and walk out again, all without being seen. They are human and palpable.

He went looking for the upstairs maid, Carlotta, and found her dusting in Papa's study.

"Carlotta, did somebody deliver a package for me?"

"Yes, master." She looked frightened.

I must control my face. Don't scare the wits out of the servants. Breathe slowly.

"Did you take it?"

"Yes, master."

The true peasant. She would never say more than was directly asked.

"It was a book?"

"Yes, master."

Thank God she can't read. She has no idea she was handling something people have been burned for owning.

"The man who delivered it," Sigismundo said easily. "Was he a *Siciliano*?"

"No, master."

"What did he look like then?"

"A tall man. Very dark hair. A great hawk nose."

Frankenstein. No, I mean the man who pretends to be Frankenstein. He isn't really Frankenstein. Just as my father isn't really my father, and the *Carbonari* are not necessarily the real *Carbonari*, and the miracles of San Gennaro may be a fake, and nothing is for sure or certain anywhere.

Sigismundo returned to his room and then to the veranda.

Mama was trimming flowers in the garden, singing softly to herself. Nobody else was outside. He looked over both shoulders anyway. One can't be too careful these days. He slipped the book out of the bricks, inside his cloak. Like a thief in my own house, he thought.

He breathed again, counting backward. It was a beautiful Neapolitan day. The sun was low on the horizon, and the bay was turning green as fast as a peasant girl's wedding ring. The plants in the garden were lush and fat, like bishops or any other creatures that get fed without having to hunt or work.

Uncle Pietro, for all his cynicism about local mores, agreed there was no city in Europe more beautiful than Napoli. There may be no city in the world with as many splendid views, Sigismundo thought. I wonder if I should hire a food taster.

He slipped back into his room and began exploring *The Key of Solomon*. Many geometrical figures, a scattering of Hebrew words, the basic text in Latin. Then he noticed the bookplate in the front:

EX LIBRIS
JOHANN DIPPEL VON FRANKENSTEIN
SCHLOSS FRANKENSTEIN
FRANKENSTEIN-AM-RHEIN

The real Frankenstein, he reminded himself, had died in 1734. This was all an elaborate hoax. Of course. He did get out of his grave and come to Napoli to haunt me because of something the stars say. Besides, astrology is a heresy. Like the Doctrine of Toleration or the idea that flaming rocks fall out of the sky.

No: even alchemists do not climb out of their graves.

Unless there had been a "gypsy switch" like in the three-card monte game and they had buried the wrong man.

Next I will be looking under the bed for crocodiles.

Sigismundo rummaged about in the closet and found an old shirt. He used it to wrap the book, making a bundle that showed no square edges.

He quickly went down the outside stairs to the garden.

"Lovely day," Mama said.

"Yes, God be praised," he answered.

He threw the bundle into the incinerator. Lorenzo, the gardener-handyman, would burn it that night.

No Dominicans came to the house that evening. So, Sigismundo thought, having me arrested by the Inquisition is not the game the *Rossi* intend.

The next morning he woke with the sun in his face and larks singing in the garden.

He felt his chin. The beard was becoming more luxuriant every day. I am becoming a man, he thought. I have the brains and the balls to deal with whatever is coming at me. I am almost sixteen. I haven't hallucinated in months—except when they were torturing Peppino.

Then he looked at his writing table.

The Key of Solomon was back.

And for some reason he remembered his crazy father's dying words:

Libertà! I will return as millions!

▲

Sigismundo thought of Schloss Frankenstein. Castle Frankenstein. It got that name because *stein* means "mountain" as well as "rock" in German, and the Franks held that mountain as a fortress in the ninth century. about the same time we Malatestas were made governors of the western Empire by Charlemagne. Always build your castle on a high mountain: that was the first rule of survival in those days.

And a hundred years ago, almost yesterday in that perspective, Dippel von Frankenstein had lived in that castle, conducting forbidden experiments. And he is still walking around, or somebody is going to a great deal of trouble to make me think he is still walking around.

Sigismundo looked at the book of magick that had apparently come back out of the void. If Epicurus was right, the book was made out of atoms. When the book burned, the atoms weren't destroyed, merely reconstructed. Sigismundo tried to imagine an act of Will that would cause the atoms to return to their original structure and form the book again. It was a weird thought, like that macabre passage in Shakespeare about the atoms of a king being eaten by a worm that was eaten by a fish that was eaten by a peasant, thereby proving a king can pass through the intestines of a serf. And a book could come back out of the void and Antonio and I did travel backward in time and a dead man came to the door yesterday and the Pope does have feathers.

If you didn't believe in Hell or the Inquisition, you were not really a Catholic anymore. Faith was shattered, and you had to figure out the universe one piece at a time.

Maybe one man's Will had caused a book to re-form itself out of the void after being reduced to ashes.

Or maybe *they* simply had two copies of the book.

He laughed out loud. The essence of the human soul, above the animal and vegetable, was reason. The square and the level and all the other symbols of Uncle Pietro's "club" were implements of the rational mind.

Sigismundo dressed rapidly, rushed through his washing, and went to the garden. He found Lorenzo collecting manure from the hut where they kept the family mule.

"Good morning, Lorenzo."

"Good morning, master." Lorenzo removed his hat and smiled, then looked at the ground.

"Did you find a book in the garbage last night?"

"Oh, yes, master." Lorenzo smiled more broadly. "I knew it must be a mistake, so I returned it to your room."

A victory for the square and the level. The universe was rational after all.

"That was very observant of you, Lorenzo," Sigismundo said. "A thousand thanks."

"You are welcome, master."

Sigismundo returned to his room, wondering why that "master" business was beginning to get on his nerves. All his life the servants had called him "master." It was always "*Si, signor*" or "*No, signor*" or "*Grazie, signor*." It was something that had always been part of his world, like Vesuvius smoldering up there like a wounded dragon that might belch fire again anytime. But now it was all different: what would Lorenzo think, what would any of the servants think, if they knew he was half-peasant himself, and half-Sicilian on top of it? Would they say "*signor*" in exactly the same tone then? And even if they did, what would they say to each other, behind his back?

Alone in his bedroom, Sigismundo succumbed to temptation. He opened *The Key of Solomon* and began browsing.

The geometric diagrams he had noticed last evening concerned magickal circles. First you were supposed to draw a circle on the floor, then put one of these diagrams (pentagon or octagon or whatever) inside it, then use the proper incenses or perfumes, then recite a formula, and then an angel or a demon would appear.

Sigismundo read an invocation to summon Set and Beelzebub and seventy-five lesser demons, to unleash them upon an enemy. I do not believe in Hell anymore, he reminded himself. I wonder, though, if I am so far gone in skepticism that I would dare to try this, confident that it is all nonsense and seventy-seven demons would *not* appear. The answer was clear: he was still enough of a Catholic not to want to experiment upon summoning devils. Besides, he thought, who knows what's in those incenses and perfumes? You can certainly summon demons with belladonna—demons real enough to haunt you for weeks or months afterward.

He remembered Abraham saying, during one of their

conversations, "Magick is just the art of changing the focus of consciousness at will." With drugs and repetitious chants, Antonio and Sigismundo had both experienced such shifts in focus. It could even be done by ritual alone; a cripple had walked out of the Cathedral, healed, only a few months ago, after a Solemn High Mass.

Dr. Vico said every country was a group of people living in a common myth. Uncle Pietro said every "club" had its own myth. If every myth is a metaphor, as Vico also claimed, then the *Key* was just a system to experiment with alternative metaphors . . . Sigismundo stopped himself at that thought. I will end up committing worse heresies than the *Alumbrados* if I am not careful, he thought.

Turning the pages at random, he found detailed instructions on how to create a *homunculus*. This passage was heavily underlined, and Sigismundo visualized Dippel von Franken-stein, ninety-some years ago, reading it with great excitement. (But that was not the man who came to the door yesterday. It couldn't be.)

First you must procure warm horse manure, the *Key* said, and place it in a hermetically sealed jar. At the full moon, add to it your own sperm. (This is the Sin of Onan, Sigismundo thought. Black Magick indeed.) Every seven days, for seven times seven days, add more fresh sperm. On the fiftieth day, at dawn, a transparent wraith will appear above the jar. Feed this with fresh blood every day for twenty-one more days. It will then become solid and grow into a man.

Sigismundo slammed the book shut. Enough. Now I know how Frankenstein created that Creature they still tell mon-strous tales about in Bavaria. It is not well to know such things. This book definitely comes from one of the more unsavory "clubs."

And somebody (not Frankenstein himself; that was impossi-ble) wanted him to have this kind of knowledge.

Because of the bloody stars and their damnable messages about him.

Sigismundo was very observant on his way to college that day.

He saw no *Rossi*.

And coming home in the afternoon, it was the same. But of course he had known that the second visitation would be very nicely calculated to come when he least expected it. He had thought that they would assume he would expect a long delay before the second visit, so he had guessed they would come again very soon, to shock him; but they had guessed that he would think that way, and hence they were waiting. It was a game of torture with all the exquisite subtleties of chess strategy.

That Dominican at the retreat was right about one thing, Sigismundo thought. This world is a monstrous place, and the only way to catch even a glimpse of God is to withdraw from it entirely, as the cloistered orders do. But that would not work for me. I would be in my cell one day, meditating and trying to find union with the Divine, and a knife would come through the window and whizz past my throat to plunk into a wall. To remind me: They never forget. A Sicilian vendetta never ends.

They have their own mad sense of balance, he thought. I am being tortured in a more refined way than Peppino was tortured; it has its own delicacy, this Sicilian revenge.

Measure for measure, in their account book.

▲

But that evening, something else was afoot in the Celine household. Mama was busy in the kitchen, supervising the cook, which meant that this was going to be a special dinner. And Papa had a look that Sigismundo read easily: there was a surprise in store for somebody.

Then Uncle Pietro and Aunt Violetta arrived. At a glance, Sigismundo knew they were in on the secret.

When the servants brought in the antipasto, Sigismundo

knew this was a very special occasion: diced octopus and *prosciutto* and black Greek olives along with the usual peppers and cheeses.

Aunt Violetta, typically, dominated the conversation, and therefore they all talked almost entirely about *novels*. Either Aunt Violetta had never heard the Malatesta motto about a time to talk and a time to be silent, or she simply didn't believe it. She had always declared that there was nothing wrong with novels, no matter what the Dominicans said, and she read even more of them than Mama did. She read them in English and French as well as Italian and refused to believe they were inferior to the classics. She often said that some of the novels would be classics themselves someday, which (to most educated people) was like saying a monkey might be a man someday.

Tonight, Violetta was especially keen on something called *The Castle of Otranto* by some Englishman named Walpole.

"It positively scared the blue *hell* out of me," she said, "but all the time I was enjoying it. I kept asking myself why I enjoyed being frightened. I decided it was because I knew, really, that it wasn't real."

"Aristotle had a different theory about why we enjoy being frightened," Uncle Pietro offered.

"You mean that catharsis idea?" Aunt Violetta asked. "Well, that's true enough, but only when we know it isn't real, as I was just saying. Nobody enjoys a real catharsis."

I'm not enjoying mine, Sigismundo thought.

Aunt Violetta had ordered *The Castle of Otranto* from London. "God only knows when there will be an Italian translation," she said. "Probably in a hundred years. If all the Dominicans go away."

"Be *careful*," Papa said.

"They don't care what women say," Aunt Violetta replied. "They don't even know we exist, most of the time."

It was after antipasto and pasta and salad, during the meat course (beef in the French style), that Papa made his announcement.

"We have decided," he announced, "that this year I will go to London and Paris to sell our wines, not Pietro. And you, Sigismundo, will accompany me."

"But"—Sigismundo objected. This was too good to be true. Escape from Napoli, from *Rossi* and witches and conspiracies and black magick and the maybe-dead maybe-Frankenstein character . . .

"I know," Papa said genially. "The college. We have discussed this already with the Rector. He agrees: such a trip will be more educational than keeping you in school at this point. You are ridiculously far ahead of your classmates in most subjects."

Sigismundo felt his ears reddening. "Thank you, Papa," he said awkwardly. I will reread every play of Shakespeare's, he was thinking; my English will be perfect when we get off the boat.

After dinner, Sigismundo asked if Uncle Pietro would come to his room to look at something he had written about the theory of harmony. Everybody accepted that at face value; if Pietro suspected more, his face did not show it.

When they were alone in Sigismundo's room, Pietro revealed at once what his face had not confessed. "Is it only harmony," he asked, "or something not so aesthetic?"

Sigismundo hauled *The Key of Solomon* out from under the potted palm on the veranda. He told the whole story of the last two days, in a whisper, of course.

"Well," Pietro said, "I congratulate you on several points. Especially, I congratulate you on deducing how the book got back and checking your reasoning against the evidence by going and asking Lorenzo."

"Do you think the *Rossi* will kill me?"

"No," Pietro said at once. "They may frighten you in a thousand cruel ways, come up with more bluffs than a million card players, but they will never really harm you. At least, not kill you. They really believe you were born to lead them. Never, never, never forget that. The terror cannot destroy you if you remember that these men are limited by their belief in that astrological nonsense."

Sigismundo had been pacing. He stopped by the *clavicembalo* and strummed a few bars by Telemann, thinking. "I wonder if the astrology is still binding on them," he said, "now that we have killed . . . Peppino."

"I have studied astrology," Pietro said, "and so have Dr. Orfali and many in our 'club.' There is something in it beyond all the humbug, and we keep hoping we will someday rediscover it. Meanwhile, we have cast many horoscopes to collect data. I assure you, I have never been so astonished as when I cast yours. It is unique." Pietro looked at Sigismundo somberly. "The *Rossi* read your horoscope the way Peppino made them read it, because he always imposed his will, wherever he went. What is significant is that if one believes in such things at all, you will have an extraordinary life. You will travel to many countries and influence millions not yet born. You appear to be virtually invulnerable until your destiny is achieved.

"It is," Pietro continued, "as if no force on earth can stop you. I have seen only three horoscopes that compare in any way with yours, and since it is very dangerous to say even as much as I have said already, I am afraid to tell you which three men had those particular horoscopes. I will say only that everybody alive has been influenced by them."

"Uncle," Sigismundo said. "Please."

"I know it is a burden to be told this," Pietro said. "For years I have hidden things from you, so you could have a normal life for a while at least. Even now I dare not tell you all."

Sigismundo played some Vivaldi to calm himself. Can I imagine, he thought, that people might not just say Scarlatti and Vivaldi and Celine some day, but Jesus and Mohammed and Celine or Euclid and Newton and Celine? How am I to avoid vanity if the stars themselves set such traps for me?

If this is the Sign I prayed for, God has a very bizarre sense of humor.

"But this astrology is all nonsense," he said finally.

"Of course. At least, it's mostly nonsense. The point is that the *Rossi* want you alive, as their leader, and that is your shield against the hideous games they play. They are trying to bend your mind and your will, but they will not kill your body."

"What do I do about that accursed book?" Sigismundo asked, finishing off Vivaldi with a bit of his own that seemed to fit. "Take it out and burn it myself this time?"

"Put it in the bottom of your trunk," Uncle Pietro said. "Take it to England with you. Read it there, with no fear of Inquisitors looking over your shoulder."

Sigismundo stared at his uncle: no, it was not a joke. "You mean it," he said.

"Nothing in a book can harm you," Pietro said. "Your fear can destroy you utterly if you do not destroy it first. I have read sixteen books that claimed to be *The Key of Solomon*."

Sigismundo digested this. "And they didn't harm you," he said, drawing the lesson.

"There were some real principles of healing in some of them, but they were mostly drivel."

"Then why should I waste my time on this book?"

"To see that what I say is true. If you don't read it, you will always fear it."

Sigismundo thought about that. "Tell me," he asked then, "the formula for making a *homunculus* . . ." He reddened again. "You know, mixing manure with your . . . seed . . ."

Uncle Pietro laughed out loud that time. "There," he said. "That is why you should read the book and see what nonsense it is."

"Frankenstein did not create his . . . Creature that way?"

"No. For reproduction a woman is absolutely necessary. There is something in the womb—like an egg, the natural philosophers believe—that is just as important as the seed. God would not go to all the trouble of making two sexes if only one was needed."

"Thank you," Sigismundo said. "The Church makes so much embarrassment about . . . these matters."

Pietro laughed again. "That formula for a *homunculus* is in many *grimoires*," he said. "Since the invention of the printing press three hundred years ago, it must have been read by thousands, hundreds of thousands. Imagine how many of them stood in their alchemical laboratories, pulling themselves off into manure and waiting for a miracle. Whoever first put that formula into a book had a most heavenly sense of humor and a very accurate opinion of the intelligence of most students of magick."

▲

Guido Celine and Sigismundo left Napoli on a coldly sun-bright March day with the sea calm and the sky hopeful, aboard a two-rigged sailing ship called the *San Francesco*.

The first few hours, Sigismundo would not leave the deck and go to their cabin. He knew that Greece was in the other direction and Africa too far south to be visible, but still he felt midway between the European present and the almost-mythical age of the classics. Scholars forever argued about where Odysseus had sailed or whether Odysseus had ever existed, but Sigismundo could not take such nitpickers seriously at a time like this. He was on the sea Homer had known; tomorrow they would lay over in Spain, and some scholars claimed that Odysseus had met the Cyclops there. It was not a windmill in that case, but a real giant—even Dr. Vico said so.

Sigismundo started repeating to himself, *"Polyphloisbois thalassas"*—"The loud-roaring sea"—and, by God, Father Ratti was right: it did sound exactly like the noise of the waves against the prow.

"Polyphloisbois thalassas," Sigismundo chanted.

Polyphloisbois thalassas, the waves answered.

He should really be practicing his English, not reviewing his Greek; but this was Homer's sea, damn it, and he was excited by it. He was sailing over three thousand years of poetry.

He wondered if he could think of any words in English that were as purely onomatopoeic as *thalassas*. He thought of *crash*, which did sound like something crashing. And *wolf*, which was the noise of barking: *Wolf! Wolf!* According to Vico, these minor miracles of language proved that all our ancestors were poets once; and out of poetry and poetic myth came the laws that shaped a society, which was why one nation could never fully understand another. All peoples are living in different myths.

So, standing at the rail and quoting Homer himself, the father of Greek culture, he was literally in transition between Neapolitan mythology and English mythology. Maybe he needed the Greek myth as a bridge from one world to another.

▲

At sea
March 31

Dear Uncle Pietro,

The philosophers are right: Travel expands the mind. I spent one day in Spain, and already Napoli seems different to me! I wonder what England will do to my mind when we get there next week.

As soon as we docked in Málaga two days ago, I set off, as you can imagine, to find some students of my own age, since with such a group I could ask anything and everything that curiosity suggested. To make a long story short, I found a group of boys from the local Jesuit college, and to my astonishment they were so bigoted and superstitious that already Napoli seems to me like a place of flaming liberalism.

The students are angry at Don Carlos because he has banned bullfighting. However, they are all quite sure that he will be made to see the light and the ban will be lifted, because (they say) Spain without the Sunday afternoon bullfight is unthinkable.

You know that I am not an experienced traveler. I made a mistake. I told them honestly what I thought of baiting and tormenting an animal for sport. At first they were more amused than shocked, and they set about enlightening me about the virtues of the *corrida*. I made another mistake. I argued with them. You can guess what happened. I hope that at least my nose will be healed by the time we dock in London City. In any case, there are only a few places that still hurt.

The number of beggars I saw astonishes me. I already begin to understand your ideas about free thought and free markets. By comparison with the general condition of Spain, our own Napoli seems rich beyond measure; what I thought was the abyss of abject poverty at home is the norm in Spain. And, correspondingly, the Inquisition is stronger and intolerance more entrenched. Just recently (I was told) they tried to burn a Jesuit for a book he had written, and they were very indignant when Don Carlos intervened. He allowed them to burn the book but not the author. The students say this shows Don Carlos is corrupted by French Bourbon ideas from that side of his family.

Students!! In a Jesuit college!!! and they not only do not know anything, they do not even suspect anything. If I told them the Pope urinates pure holy water, they would believe it and buy two vials.

I will have this posted to you when we arrive at London City next week.

Your loving nephew,
Sigismundo Celine

▲

One week later that letter was posted to Napoli, and Guido and Sigismundo were sitting in the Turk's Head Tavern on Gerrard Street in London City. Sigismundo had insisted on coming there because Uncle Pietro said it was where the intelligentsia gathered.

They had mugs of ale before them. Sigismundo was sipping slowly and cautiously; the drink tasted so foul to him that he was convinced it must be many times more intoxicating than any wine in Italy.

The English were all absurdly tall. Maybe that's how they got their empire, Sigismundo thought; perhaps it comes from looking down when you talk to other races and nations. They were not all blond, however—it had only seemed that way to his Neapolitan eyes when Papa and he first got off the boat—but they were so light of skin that it almost appeared they were made up to play ghosts in the theater.

The two men at the next table were discussing something called the Stamp Act. Parliament had just passed this act, whatever it was, and both men viewed the event as a kind of criminal lunacy. The taller man—tall even for an Englisher, and red of hair—was particularly vehement on the subject.

"The fools will not allow themselves to perceive what they are doing," he said bitterly. "They somehow persuade themselves to forget that the colonists are British, too, and can read Coke and Blackstone as well as we can."

"It is more asinine than that," his companion, a darker man, said. "I was talking to Burke the other day, and he told me there are more copies of Blackstone in the colonies than there are in all England. *Everybody* studies the law there, Burke said; it is their singular passion. God's hooks, they farm all the bleeding summer and read law all the bleeding winter. The most litigious people on earth."

"You were talking to Burke?" the redhead asked. "I was

passing the time with him just last night—at Dr. Johnson's
—and he was addressing the same subject. He came out with
one of those marvelous phrases of his. Said the colonists were
the resultant of the Protestantism of the Protestants and
dissidence of dissent. God's blood, I could tell Dr. Johnson
wished he had said that first."

"That *is* rich," the darker man said. "Too good for a drawing
room. I am quite sure a man like Edmund Burke will find a
way to slip it into one of his speeches eventually."

"If our beloved monarch and his lackeys do not find some
excuse to expel him from parliament," the redhead said drily.
"The Wilkes case is a good precedent, you know. Anybody can
be hurled into the outer darkness now, if he becomes too much
of a thorn in George's side."

"Shite and onions!" the other cried. "That is a tender
subject with me, sir. Hell and damnation, if the king's coterie
can remove Wilkes from parliament on mere personal spite, we
might as well invite the Stuarts back to rule us; the revolution
has come to naught. Christ's nightshirt, you should hear Burke
animadvert on the subject."

"I can imagine," the redhead said. "Edmund Burke's
eloquence is never more sublime than when he is absolutely
furious."

"Jesus and Mary Christ, sir," the other burst out, "do you
know how the bleeding Tories are trying to discredit Burke?
They are spreading some cant that he is a Jacobite, by
God."

"Anything can happen now," the redhead said glumly.
"God alone knows what the colonists will do, and Wilkes
might return to parliament to dissolve it, like Cromwell." He
drank some more ale and sighed deeply. "Have you heard of
Mr. Patrick Henry?" he asked mournfully.

"No. Who is he, in the name of God?"

"In the colonies. The Virginia House of Burgesses. He almost went over the line in discussing this damned Stamp Act. My American cousin, John Drake, who lives in Philadelphia City, sent me a news story about it. This Mr. Henry, who must be a more enthusiastic demagogue than Wilkes himself, actually said—this will loosen your bowels, sir—he actually said, 'Caesar had his Brutus, Charles the First had his Cromwell, and George the Third—!' " He paused ominously.

"Hellfire and damnation, sir, did he—?"

"He was interrupted, as you might expect, by shouts of 'Treason.' He waited until they had died down and then finished, as demure as a whore at a coronation, '—and George the Third should learn from their experience. If this be treason, make the most of it.' How does that taste going down your gullet?"

"*Ora pro nobis*," the darker man said. "Lord-fuck-a-duck, I need more ale."

Sigismundo could contain himself no longer. He had been listening in fascination, and the mention of the name Drake emboldened him.

"Pardon me," he asked excitedly, "but is your name Drake?"

Both Englishmen stared at him.

"Excuse my son," Guido said hurriedly. "He is sometimes impetuous."

"I am Charles Putney Drake," the redhead said simply. "And who, in the name of the Lord Harry, are you two gentlemen?"

"I am Guido Celine, a wine merchant, of Napoli," Papa said.

"I am Sigismundo, his son, a musician," Sigismundo added quickly. Papa kicked him under the table, but he went on. "Please do not consider me eccentric. It was prophesied once that I would go to Philadelphia City, and at the time I did not even know where that was." Papa kicked him again, harder.

Sigismundo realized that these men might not understand Abraham's ideas about coincidences, but it seemed too late to stop now. "And there is something stranger. I think perhaps I know another cousin of yours."

Charles Putney Drake suddenly looked like a man who had just discovered a turd in the punchbowl. "In Naples—that is, in Napoli?" he asked cautiously.

"Yes," Sigismundo said. I have really put my hoof in my mouth, he thought.

"That would be Cousin Bob," the redhead said. "I assume you do not know much about our politics. It is not advantageous to be related to Cousin Bob; in fact, at times it has proved a decided annoyance."

"We mean no trouble," Guido said hurriedly.

"I understand that Robert Francis Drake—Cousin Bob —cannot come back to this country," Sigismundo said. "But the coincidence—as if our meeting were predestined . . ." He felt himself running out of words.

Charles Putney Drake grinned finally. "Damn their eyes," he said bluntly. "They would accuse me of being a Jacobite even if there were no Cousin Bob. They accuse everybody they don't like of being a Jacobite."

"They will accuse me of being a Jacobite next," the darker man said. He held out his hand to Papa. "Sir Edward Babcock," he said. "It is a pleasure to meet you, Signor Celine."

Sigismundo thought he saw a slight exploratory movement of Babcock's fingers. Papa seemed to notice it, too, because he stared curiously for a second. Then Babcock extended his hand to Sigismundo. There was no strange movement of the fingers this time. But that means nothing, Sigismundo thought; I am too young to be a Freemason, so he wouldn't bother testing the grip.

Things thawed out considerably, although Papa continued to cast warning glances at Sigismundo, who could not resist

questioning the Englishmen at length about the political issues
they had been discussing.

Papa still acts as if we are in Napoli, he thought.

John Wilkes, he learned, was a former member of parliament, now declared an outlaw and living in France. He was a
Whig, like Drake and Babcock, but they did not entirely
admire him: he was a "demagogue," one who appealed chiefly
to the "mobile party," or "mob," for short—the propertyless.
Nonetheless, Wilkes's removal from parliament had violated
the Bill of Rights, and Babcock and Drake could not tolerate
any such "experiments upon our liberties," as they said.
Sigismundo asked what the Bill of Rights was. It turned out to
be a document George III's grandfather, William of Orange,
had signed as a condition of parliament accepting him as their
new king when they passed over James II, the Catholic
Scotsman whose grandson the Jacobites were still supporting.

Sigismundo again felt that the more he learned the less he
understood. If the Jacobites were behind Masonry, these men
were on the opposite side—but their ideas sounded very
similar to those of Uncle Pietro and his "club." And he *did*
think he had seen the grip tested when Babcock shook hands
with Papa . . .

▲

From Sigismundo Celine's journal:

> I am starting this journal, and will write a little essay every day,
> because I wish to retain a record of this strange and wonderful
> Nation, and there are some things I dare not put into a letter to
> Napoli, even using Uncle Pietro's code.
>
> Due to Mr. Drake and Sir Edward Babcock, I have met a most
> singular Irishman named Edmund Burke, who talks (all the
> time!) in classic metaphors, the way the great Shakespeare wrote.
> I am told this is because he was born in Dublin, where eloquence
> is studied as passionately as music is in Napoli. Mr. Burke says
> things like, "Oh, let us not plumb the ultimate metaphysical

meaning of property or law; that is the great Serbonian bog where armies whole have sunk," and has a strange Dublin accent called a "brogue."

Mr. Burke was raised by the Quakers, a most eccentric sect unlike any group I have ever heard of or read about; they might almost be called nonviolent *Rossi* if that were not oxymoronic. They will not take off their hats for the king. They wish to abolish the slave trade. They are peculiar in dozens of ways, and, in fact, they were once persecuted. But in this remarkable Nation, all eccentrics become acceptable eventually.

In Napoli, a man like Mr. Burke would be leading a secret society; here he is part of the government itself. He and the other Whigs are forever obstructing the king: they tell him *what he may do* and *what he may not do*. Of course, the king does not like this at all, but when the Whigs have enough votes in parliament, the king himself may not disobey them. This is because of the Bill of Rights they made his grandfather sign.

I try to imagine our Ferdinand IV being made to sign and obey such a document. It is easier to imagine a cow giving birth to two monkeys and an ostrich; it is easier to imagine Sigismundo Malatesta's naked goddess replacing the Holy Virgin in Notre Dame de Paris.

*   *   *

The ale is not so strong as I thought at first; it only tastes strong. Last night I drank six full glasses of it at the Turk's Head Tavern and felt only a little bit light-headed for it. Mr. Drake, who was also there and kindly invited me to his table, drank nearly three times as much and did not seem any the worse, although he did begin speaking loudly and in a silly fashion after a while. He made several remarks about the king's German ancestors that were quite amusing, although very indiscreet; and I doubt that it is biologically possible for such unnatural unions to bear progeny. Then he began discussing local buildings—he is an architect—and ended by proposing a second London fire on the grounds that nothing built in the last century is worthy of being passed on to posterity. He was most droll especially about Sir Christopher Wren, who he said should have worked for a Baker designing Wedding Cakes, but then he lost his balance and fell out of his chair backward. It made a most terrible Crash; but I do not think he was really drunk, because he kept his good humor and spoke most wittily about the mishap, comparing himself to a Mr. Humphrey Dumpty (of whom I have never heard) and imploring all the king's horses and all the king's men to come to his aid.

* * *

I was too hasty in forming my opinions of the English ale. Last night I drank twenty or more glasses of it with Sir Edward Babcock, whom I met at the Turk's Head. All was going most pleasantly when all of a sudden the tavern began to spin around and around and around like a child's top. I tried to explain that I was not entirely well, but Sir Edward was weeping most piteously about a tombstone in Dublin and the lacerations of Christ (I think), and then he fell out of his chair sideways with a Thunderous Awful Thump. I don't remember what happened after that.

Papa says I must promise not to drink so much ale when I go out alone again, or he will forbid me to go out alone at all, since this city is full of "other temptations worse than ale," he says.

It seems I was brought home in a wheelbarrow.

* * *

Papa took me to see a factory today. The owner was a noble lord who had ordered much wine, and Papa asked if we could see the clever machines for which the English are so famous.

The factory was outside London City in a place called Westminister, and at first glance it reminded me of one of the lower *bolge* in Dante's *Inferno*. And yet when the Machines were shown to me and their Workings explained, I understood at once why Uncle Pietro believes that where thought is free, almost anything is possible. Every machine, and every part of each machine, was the concrete expression of some man's intelligence; it demonstrated that one part of the universe had been understood correctly. This is what natural philosophy can accomplish (the English call it "science"), and it is aweinspiring. It is indeed because natural philosophy is hounded by the Inquisition that Napoli is poor compared to England and why Spain, where the Inquisition is stronger, is poorer still.

Every machine is a thought that produces wealth, as Uncle Pietro wished me to understand.

And yet the factory was also depressing. The people who work there are all of them—men, women, and children—almost as famished looking as our most backward peasants. When I attempted to question one of them, he removed his hat and looked at the floor, just like a peasant, and, like a peasant, he answered everything briefly, and I had the impression he was saying what he thought I would want to hear.

Of course, all these "workers" (as they are called) are former peasants.

He called me "sir" at the end of each sentence, just as our servants call me *signor*. I wonder how many thousands of years of atrocities were required before one part of humanity was trained to look down and say "master" when they spoke to the other part of humanity.

This ex-peasant was named Joyce, and he was Irish. Our host told me later to believe nothing he said because the Irish are all liars, scoundrels, ignorant, and superstitious. It sounded just like what everybody in Napoli says about Sicilians.

* * *

I keep thinking about that man named Joyce, and I feel there is a specter haunting Europe: but I do not know its name.

* * *

I suddenly find myself wondering why Sir Edward Babcock has been so kind to me, considering that I am only a boy. Could he be a sodomite and plotting my seduction? I do not think so; it is probably only that he misses his own son, who is always traveling on the Continent, he says.

* * *

Sir Edward is indeed a most unusual man. When I was enthusing to him about the freedom of this country (where there is no Inquisition), he said, ironically, "We have our own tyrants, called Good Taste and Common Sense. No book yet says all the writer knows and means. The Inquisition is the same, even if it changes its name." The Whigs, I think, are all like that: dreaming of a total liberty that is forever impossible in this fallen world.

Yet when I read Mr. Gibbon's *Decline and Fall*, I could see that Sir Edward was not completely wrong. It is obvious that Mr. Gibbon dares not say what he really means, in many passages, and can only hint and make inscrutable jokes, to force the reader to guess what was omitted because of the restrictions on freedom that exist even here. Will there ever be an age when a writer is free to say all he knows?

Another example of how Sir Edward's idealism is entangled with his cynicism: I told him a syllogism I had constructed after seeing the wonderful factory in Westminster, to wit:

S: A machine is a concrete thought.

M: When our thoughts are perfectly accurate, our machines will be perfectly efficient.

P: When our machines are perfect, our wealth will be infinite.

Sir Edward replied at once, "Yes, but who will own that wealth? The most bold and predatory, I daresay."

* * *

Papa is taking me tonight to hear a performance by the English Bach. That is, Johann Christian Bach, not his famous brother, Carl Philipp Emanuel Bach, the German Bach. Everybody says the German Bach is the better of the two, but I heard J. C. Bach when he was in Napoli four years ago, and I think everybody is wrong as usual. J. C. Bach is as startling and brisk as Scarlatti.

There will be three other performers: a man named Leopold Mozart, who is said to be good, and his fourteen-year-old daughter, Nannerl, who will probably be bearable (most girls can play competently by that age), and then there is the alleged *wunderkind*, Wolfgang Mozart, age nine, who can play anything, according to legend. This must be a hoax: no nine-year-old can be worth hearing.

J. C. Bach will make the evening memorable, I'm sure.

* * *

I heard it, but I still don't believe it.

* * *

The Monster is being investigated by the Royal Scientific Society (which was founded by the Jacobites but somehow still survives). I almost wish they will find some evidence that he is fake. Maybe some adult hides offstage and does the playing for him?

This must be the sin of Envy. Maybe that is what growing up is—learning that you are capable of every vice you despise.

* * *

I saw Nannerl Mozart again today. The Monster was crowing about his success with the Royal Scientific Society. They have decided he is not a fake.

In one test, it seems, they employed Bach, who is as puzzled by the Monster as anyone. Bach began a very complex fugue and then stopped suddenly; the Monster was asked to proceed. He did so immediately, without missing a beat, and finished it appropriately.

I must admit that the Monster is likable in certain ways and that my envy of him is most malign and unfair. But, my God, he does with such ease things I cannot accomplish after years of frantic effort!

And he is a foul-mouthed little brat.

* * *

Swearing, blasphemy, and profane language are as common among the aristocracy here as among the sailors on the *San Francesco*. I keep expecting Inquisitors to leap out from behind a curtain and arrest everybody; and yet I must admit such earthy language had its own comic poetry to it. As an admirer of the methods of natural philosophy, I decided to keep a record of what I heard in a single evening at the Turk's Head Tavern. My tally sheet shows 137 abuses of the name of God, 231 abuses of Jesus, 333 scatological references to the Virgin Mother, and 358 indelicate references to saints or Old Testament figures. Unfortunately, this record is not complete, since—despite my promise to Papa—I again took a bit more ale than was good for me.

Sir Edward Babcock drank much more than I and again complained bitterly about his son, who is always gadding about the Continent and seldom home. Then he started weeping about Tombstones and Lacerations again, and the next thing I knew I was being conveyed home in a wheelbarrow again.

This is a nation of drunkards. I will learn to be more prudent.

* * *

I have read most of David Hume's book on "the human understanding." I was especially curious because the Dominicans always denounce him as the most dangerous heretic of our age.

My head is spinning.

Hume has pulled the carpet of certitude from beneath the feet of all previous philosophers and landed us upon our backsides. All that we know, he proves in dozens of ways, are our own impressions; everything else that we think we know is only deduction and may be extremely probable but never certain.

The universe of San Tomasso d'Aquino, with man at the bottom and various hierarchies of angels culminating in the Holy Trinity at the top, is a deduction; so is the universe of the French atheists, with Epicurus's hypothetical atoms floating in his conjectural void. All San Tomasso or Epicurus ever *knew* were their own sensations; all I *know* are *my* sensations. Mr. Hume demonstrates that every philosopher who reasoned from these sensations to some general principle committed an error early on, by which he wishfully confused himself and promoted an inference into a certitude.

My head is still whirling. We are all walled cities shouting at each other over the armaments of our preconceptions.

* * *

Nannerl and the Monster and I went to the Royal Zoo today. I must admit it is very difficult to hate him in person; he is so full of fun and jokes (just as his music is), and even his self-importance is comical rather than obnoxious, considering how small he is. When he plays the *clavicembalo*, his tiny legs stick out straight in front of him, and he looks like some clever Toy that a king might own.

We heard some of the city peasant children (who are called

"cockneys") doing a kind of routine that is probably amusing to them only because it offends passing adults. The recital goes like this: "'Oo shit on the stairs?" one of them asks. "Bert shit," another answers. "Bullshit," Bert objects. "'Oo shit?" "Frank shit." And so on, and on, and on, until they get bored (which can take quite a long piece of time indeed) or until some passing adult attacks them with a cane and disperses them.

The Monster thought this was hilarious and kept repeating it endlessly. I was quite mortified that his sister had to hear such language; but Nannerl was not disturbed. She is accustomed to his infatuation with scatology.

He seems to be two Shakespeare characters in one: the noble prince and the foul-mouthed clown.

It later occurred to me that this crude form of childish humor has the same structure as a fugue. Is that why it amused the Monster? That is such a bizarre thought that I reflected further and decided it is also similar to Mr. Hume's analysis of consciousness (which runs around in circles when it tries to find itself). I must think more about that; it is provocative.

* * *

Harpsichord. That is the one English word I keep forgetting. It is not a *clavicembalo* in this country: it is a harpsichord. Harpsichord, harpsichord, harpsichord.

* * *

The Monster tells me he is writing a symphony. Not a *sinfonia* merely, but a full-fledged modern French-style symphony, in four movements with all the harmonic developments and counterpoint and everything.

The worst part is that he can do it. He has already written eight of them. The little Monster.

* * *

I have found out why it is that I virtually never see a beggar in London City.

In my ignorance, I had imagined that this was because there were so many jobs in the factories that nobody needed to beg; but that is only part of the story. Begging is a crime here, and anybody caught at it is whipped by the sheriff's men and taken

to the highway, with a warning that he will be hanged if he
returns.

Mr. Drake explained this to me, and when I asked him what
becomes of these persons, he said that some do eventually find
work in factories, some starve, and some become "highwaymen"
or "cut-purses" who live by stealing. There are even gangs, he
told me, who are called "Mohawks," after a tribe of Red Indians.
These are ruffians who roam London at night, not merely
stealing, but slashing their victims across the faces with knives
they carry for that purpose. These Mohawks seem to hate the
rich as much as our *Rossi* do.

Every country is different, but injustice and vengeance are the
same everywhere.

*   *   *

It all happened so fast I didn't even have time to think.

I was walking in Grosvenor Park with Nannerl and Wolfie. (I
can't call him the Monster anymore.) We were crossing a path,
and Wolfie was reciting another piece of scatological lore he had
picked up from the cockneys. Nannerl, as usual, was being
aloofly indifferent to his obsession with such language.

Suddenly, I heard a great clattering and clashing about and a
woman screaming. I looked back, and there was a runaway
carriage—the horses had been frightened by something and were
galloping as if the Devil himself were at their heels. The
coachman was doing everything he could to stop them or at least
slow them down, but the animals were mad with fear. My blood
went cold when I saw they were headed straight for Wolfie.

I threw myself in their path and gave Wolfie a shove that sent
him spinning yards out of harm's way. The horses barely missed
me by a finger. In fact, I suspect that they did not entirely miss
me, since my left side is sore. Perhaps I was too excited to feel the
pain at the time.

I leaped at once to Wolfie, to reassure him and calm him.
Damn, but he threw his arms around me and started weeping.
(Well, what did I expect? He is only nine years old.) I found
myself holding him, muttering reassurances, as if he were my
own son. I felt like an adult for the first time in my life! And, for
the first time, I saw him as a little boy—a boy who happened to

have more musical genius than a hundred adult performers, but still a child; and, at the moment, a terribly frightened child.

I was abruptly sickened and ashamed about all my bad feelings toward him. Nannerl was kissing both of us and calling me a hero, and all I could think of was that I had actually hated him just because he had more talent than me. It is easier to see a beetle's hind leg at twenty paces than to see your own vices.

The worst part of it is that, shamed as I am, the envy is still there. I keep thinking that when histories of music are written they will mention that the great Wolfgang Amadeo Mozart was once saved from runaway horses by "Sigismundo Celine of Napoli, who wrote a few minor works for harpsichord himself." No; that is not the way of history. They will say he was saved "by an unknown Italian merchant or, as some claim, a Polish count."

* * *

Today I finally had an audience with the great J. C. Bach. It was even worse than I expected.

I played my latest sonata and he was most polite about it, but I could tell he was *only* polite. Somehow, I nerved myself to offer a second sonata, terrified that he would make some excuse to get rid of me. He graciously said he would be happy to hear more of my work. I then played the most complex and experimental sonata I have ever attempted, a piece I am very unsure of; but I was determined to get something out of him besides mere politeness.

When I was finished, I hardly dared to look at him.

"Amazing," he said, most warmly and sincerely.

I turned, and he was studying me with the expression Cristoforo Colombo might have had if he had sailed to the edge of the world and actually fallen off. "What *were* you trying to do?" he asked simply.

I tried to answer; but nobody has ever been able to explain music, not even to another musician. I quoted Telemann on harmony and then got increasingly obscure and recondite—I might have been a Jesuit explaining transubstantiation—and worrying that I sounded like the most pretentious young ass in Europe.

"I thought so," he said mildly. It develops then that he

understood me perfectly: Telemann was his godfather and an old friend. But then he asked if I had ever heard anything by his father, Johann Sebastian Bach. I was astonished and felt like an ignoramus. I admitted that I knew only some of his own works and a few by his brother, C.P.E. Bach.

"Don't be embarrassed," he said. "Few people outside Saxony have ever heard of my father. His work was too special for most audiences. The odd thing is that you sound as if you are trying to imitate him, even though you have never heard any of his works."

The upshot of it is that I have the name of a publisher in Saxony, from whom I can order some of the works of Johann Sebastian Bach; but meanwhile, that afternoon, J. C. Bach played several of his father's works for me. I was especially thrilled by one called "Jesu, Joy of Man's Desiring," although a long piece called "The Goldberg Variations" is closer to what I am trying to do.

Johann Sebastian Bach died in 1750. I am like a man who with great effort and struggle has succeeded in devising a crude printing press, fifteen years after Gutenberg.

* * *

Last night I dreamed of the *Rossi* again. They all had knives to my throat, but they were not threatening me; it was a ritual, part of an initiation.

When I woke, I realized that I had been keeping them out of my mind by deliberate effort. It is easy to drench myself in the sights and sounds and exciting people of London City; but back in Napoli, and Sicily, and God knows how many other parts of Italy, these maniacs wait, confident that when the stars are in the right conjunctions, I will accept my destiny and become their new *capo*.

I decided to invoke the four guardian angels to calm myself and get back to sleep. But then I started thinking of David Hume again. It was most amazing, but Hume would say the angels were constructs of my mind—just like a French atheist. But Hume would add that the table, the chairs, and the bed were also constructs of my mind; and my mind itself, insofar as I can know it, is a construct trying to construct itself. In a world of mental constructs, the angels are no more arbitrary than any other image the mind projects. Strange that Hume didn't see that implication; or did he? Is he trying to undermine the atheists as well as the theologians and leave us in a vacuum?

When I joined Papa for breakfast the next morning, I knew at once that something was wrong.

"What is it?" I asked, thinking of a million possible horrors.

"Have some tea," Papa said; he has acquired the English notion that this drink is as soothing as an opiate.

"It's a letter from Pietro," he told me. "Your Aunt Gina is dead." Then all the details came out in a rush: it was the disease of the heart. She had chest pains, and when the doctor came it was already too late.

The only reason Papa was not weeping outright was because he was surrounded by Englishmen in the dining room. An Italian weeping would just confirm their idea that we are all emotionally unstable.

"It was the *Rossi*," I said finally.

"No," Papa said. "The doctor was sure. It was the heart."

He didn't understand me, and I was too stricken to explain. The torture of Peppino had not accomplished what she had hoped: it had not ended the grief. To say that her heart was broken is not a metaphor. It goes on and on—hatred and death and still more hatred and death.

What will this do to poor Tony? Now he has lost both parents in a year.

*   *   *

I had a strange experience crossing the English Channel. It was not seasickness—after all, I sailed much further on the trip from Napoli to London City—but something unholy and eerie. Perhaps the death of Aunt Gina was preying on my mind. The waves suddenly looked colder than the Atlantic, and I kept obsessively thinking that I was going to be cast overboard by some freak accident. No matter how I tried to banish it, the image kept coming back to my mind: cold waves and myself drowning in them. And all the time I was remembering lines from the *Odyssey* in Greek, about the rage of Poseidon, as if the sea was a living god and wanted to devour me.

When I sat in a deck chair and did the relaxing breath, I suddenly remembered my baptism; but that turned into a fantasy, too. The priest did not just dab my forehead; he poured on more and more water, more and more . . . like Uncle Pietro that night in the garden.

I was very glad to set foot on dry land again.

* * *

I have been in Paris one week and haven't written down a single observation in this journal, because I have fallen into sin. Yes, I visited one of the *maisons* that the nobility patronize. The girl I picked was from Algiers and was named Fatima. She was most talented and, in the full meaning of the word, *formidable*. The most remarkable thing about the experience is that it did not feel like sin at all; it was very much like writing a sonata. I know this is more terrible than any of my other heresies, but I could not find anything "coarse" or "animalistic" about our play—it seemed not only artistic but spiritual. I even understood, briefly, why the ancients allegedly worshiped the generative organs. Is it possible I will end up becoming a pagan like my infamous ancestor, the prince of Rimini?

* * *

Anxiety has been gnawing at me ever since that night of pagan sensuality. I don't really trust the Church anymore; but the French pox is not one of their myths; people really do contract it in such *maisons*. The humiliating truth is that I went to Notre Dame today, prayed to the Virgin for protection, and then saw a doctor.

He assures me that I don't have it, thank God. He also said, with some asperity, that it should be called the Italian pox, not the French pox; he claims our navigators introduced it to Europe. I didn't argue that, since I don't know the facts. I just thanked him, paid him, and returned to Notre Dame to pray again. I am still a Catholic when I am frightened enough.

* * *

Nobody can understand the state of this nation today; in a hundred years not even the French themselves will believe it.

The Inquisition is powerful; this is a Catholic country. Books are burned, men are placed on trial for heresy, some are even condemned—just as in Napoli. At the same time, here in Paris, the most radical ideas circulate freely. The aristocracy has decided that it proves their enlightenment to defy the church and encourage heretics of all sorts. Our *Rossi* would hardly be noticed here; they would almost be quaint.

There is a man named Rousseau who is all the rage. He denies Original Sin and claims all men are born good. (Obviously, he has never visited Napoli or Sicily.) He is in exile—the Inquisition has that much force—but his ideas are discussed everywhere. If there is no Original Sin, people say everywhere, then there is no limit to human perfectibility. I wish I could believe that; it sounds like "the kingdom of Heaven is at hand."

Then there is a man named Meslier who is dead and buried but still raising Hell; like Copernicus, he was sly enough to wait until he was on his deathbed before authorizing publication of his ideas. His book is suppressed, but every dandy and every lady with a *salon* has read it; it cheerfully urges murdering all the kings in Europe (!) and then electing a parliament of fathers over fifty years old, on the grounds that such men would have a sense of responsibility.

Another philosopher named Morelly agrees with Rousseau in rejecting Original Sin, but he also rejects private property. He wants everybody to own everything. This will be accomplished, he says, by taking children from their parents and educating them in state schools, where all tendencies to individuality will be scientifically suppressed. No Leonardos, no Michelangelos, no Scarlattis, no Newtons—just a herd of contented cows! It sets my teeth on edge. As Uncle Pietro says, a hundred men can invent paper Utopias for every one who can manage a chicken farm successfully.

Morelly is fond of a slogan that, I think, will have great appeal to all poor people as soon as they learn to read: *"Chacun selon ses facultés, a chacun selon ses besoins."* Roughly, "From each according to his abilities, to each according to his needs." Christ, that is enough verbal gunpowder to blow Europe sky-high.

No wonder Mr. Burke regards this country with dread. They are so in love with Reason that they have completely lost contact with common sense.

*   *   *

Their music isn't as good as ours either.

*   *   *

Tomorrow we take the coach southward, back toward Napoli. Thank God, Papa dislikes these long coach trips as much as I do, so he has booked us onto one that changes horses frequently without overnight stops. We will make good time that way and not be bored stiff with endless bouncing and jouncing around for days and days.

There is one long stop when we get near the border: a little town called Abbeville. I hope it will be peaceful and restful there.

▲

July 1 dawned bright and sunny in the little town of Abbeville. Larks were whistling and chirping above the square, making endless circles in the sky. There was scarcely a cloud to be seen.

But already an ugly animal was moving through the tiny, curving little streets. The animal had many parts, and each part was a man or a woman; some had been awake even before dawn, coming from farms far off. They were silent—there was no joking and hardly any conversation—and as they all converged on the square and became the one big animal, Sigismundo, leaning out the inn window in his nightshirt, knew at once that this was no saint's day or any local carnival. "Papa," he said, "come see."

Guido Celine, also in his nightshirt, stumbled wearily to the window and looked. The animal was getting bigger and uglier every minute. "*Jesus*," Guido said.

"What do you think it is?" Sigismundo asked.

"I don't know," Papa said, "but I wish to all the saints that our coach was leaving right now." The coach was not due to leave until about noon, so that the passengers could sleep late.

Looking into the distance, Sigismundo could see the foothills of the Alps. This surely is a beautiful place to live, he thought; I wonder why that mob has such an ugly mood about it.

"Wash quickly," Papa said, "and get into your clothes. I think it would be a good idea to take a walk, far away from the town square."

Sigismundo was already moving to obey. He remembered the festivities after old Umberto was burned; a mob of moralists gets excited by violence, and after a while, anything can happen. He and Papa could be set upon and beaten—or worse—just because they were not locals.

One lovely lark, separated from the flock, sailed past the window, gliding easily and slowly. Far off, a rooster crowed.

That is a fact I will remember, Sigismundo thought: when something God-awful is happening, most of nature doesn't even notice; it just goes about its own business.

But when he and Papa were dressed and descended to the ground floor of the inn, they found that the angry animal was now even bigger. People were jammed together like fish in a net right up to the door of the inn. Opening the door to step outside, he and Papa would be engulfed in the press of bodies.

"Well," Papa said simply. "It is, after all, none of our affair. We will have breakfast."

They found their way to the dining room and discovered the other passenger from the coach, a fat Bavarian named Hans Zoesser, who was already eating.

"Sit down," Zoesser said cordially. "It is not very—ah —hospitable outside."

They took a seat with the blond Bavarian, who, they had learned on the coach, was a lawyer.

"What is happening?" Guido asked cautiously.

"An *auto-da-fé*," Zoesser said cooly. "The southern French still have these nostalgic medieval rituals occasionally." He broke off a piece of *croissant* and chewed it. "The guest of honor," he added, munching, "is a young nobleman named La Barre."

"They are going to burn him?" Guido asked, barely concealing his revulsion.

"God in heaven, no," Zoesser said, still munching. "They are too civilized for that in France these days. They are merely going to chop his head off. Much more humane, *hein*?"

"What did this La Barre do?" Guido asked.

"A terrible, terrible thing," Zoesser said, scraping some egg off his plate. "It takes a great deal to bring the death penalty down on a nobleman, you know. If it were one of the ordinary peccadilloes of the rich—if he had been sodomizing peasant children for support, say, or poisoning his wife—he would probably have gotten off with a sentence of exile. He is a *chevalier*, and you know what that means." It meant he was related, however distantly, to the royal family, Sigismundo knew. "No, this was a *serious* offense," Zoesser said. "No family connections could help in a case like this."

"Well, for God's sake, what was it?" Guido asked, growing impatient with the lawyer's irony.

Zoesser munched some more *croissant* and washed it down with that devilish new drink the French were so fond of, coffee. "The Chevalier Jean François Lefebre de La Barre," he said with a poker face, "was found to have a book by Voltaire in his house."

Sigismundo could scarcely believe it. But the lawyer, despite his penchant for florid sarcasm, was obviously not joking about the facts. His face was sober and had the expression of a doctor who has decided this case is hopeless and he had better forget it and move on to the next one.

Sigismundo lost all caution. "But that is absurd," he exclaimed. "In Paris, everybody regards Voltaire as old-fashioned and reads books much more radical than his."

Zoesser nodded. "But that is Paris. This is the country. The Church does not have so many rich and powerful enemies here. These are pure, simple, uncorrupted workers of the soil. 'Noble Savages,' Rousseau would say. And so, in their simple, pure, uncorrupted savagery, they are eager to see this man's head cut off, because their priests say he is evil. Faith may not have the power to remove mountains, as we are told, but it certainly can remove common sense and common decency."

The innkeeper arrived. He looked as if he hadn't changed his shirt since the days of Louis XIV, and had an expression that might make a cattle stampede swerve in the other direction. He set down *croissants* and eggs for Guido and Sigismundo and trudged off sullenly, obviously not liking what he had heard of Zoesser's remarks. He suspects us of secular humanism, Sigismundo thought.

"Somebody informed on this La Barre," Papa said thoughtfully. "Even the Dominicans wouldn't just crash in on a chevalier and start ransacking his library without some provocation."

"You haven't heard of the terrorists?" Zoesser asked. Sigismundo and Guido at once thought of the *Rossi*, but Zoesser went on: "There is a group—or a lone lunatic; nobody knows—going about doing, well, perfectly obscene things to churches. After all," and at this point even Zoesser lowered his voice, "the Church owns almost all the land. If you walk north, east, south, or west from here, for weeks on end you will never see anything gaudy but a cathedral and nobody fat but a priest. If there is going to be resentment, the Church is going to be the target."

"La Barre is suspected of being the vandal who attacked the churches?" Guido asked.

"From what I've heard," Zoesser said, "dozens of suspects were arrested. La Barre finally got elected because of the book by Voltaire in his house."

"My God," Guido said. "Even in Napoli—" He checked himself.

"Yes," Zoesser said, "This *is* extreme, even for the holy office. And I sit here and stuff myself with pastry and make bad jokes because, gentlemen, there is not a damned thing strangers like us can do about it. Do you want to go out and lecture on the laws of evidence to that mob?"

Sigismundo pushed aside his eggs. He took a sip of coffee, unable to digest anything solid.

"What were those . . . desecrations . . . that La Barre is being blamed for?"

"You don't want to hear it at breakfast," Zoesser said.

"I can't eat anyway," Sigismundo said.

"I'm not hungry either," Papa added.

"You'll be sorry later," Zoesser said. "We have a long ride ahead today. You must learn to grown a certain amount of callus around your feelings."

Just then, the tumult finally came: the young chevalier was being led through the mob by the jailer. Separate voices began to reach the dining room, more shrill than the surrounding roar:

"*Pig!*"

"*Atheist scoundrel!*"

"*Filthy dog!*"

Gradually, the roar and the shrieking subsided into a tense silence. The executioner was making his preparations.

"What *did* the vandal do to the churches?" Sigismundo asked, trying to keep conversation going, to avoid listening for the sound of the ax.

"Well, since you're not eating anyway," Zoesser said, "he—or they, since it might have been a group—threw human excrement all over the crucifix and the altar."

"Mother of God," Guido said hollowly.

"You might say that both religious and antireligious feelings are running high in this country these days," Zoesser said, sipping coffee with a hand that shook slightly.

Suddenly the inn door opened; a Dominican stood there. "Everybody out," he said in a tone that precluded argument.

Papa Guido argued anyway. "We arc just passing through," he said. "This isn't our country . . ."

The innkeeper glared at all three of them.

"This is a *public execution*," said the Dominican, a jowly but muscular man with the eyes that most of them had, eyes that suspected literally everybody of virtually everything. "Its purpose is to demonstrate justice. It is to be seen by all, as a lesson to all. Are you atheists? Shall I call the bailiff?"

"We're coming," Zoesser said smoothly. "We were just finishing breakfast, Your Reverence."

As they arose, Papa Guido whispered, "You don't have to look. Keep your eyes on something neutral in the distance."

The Chevalier Jean François Lefebre de La Barre was a young dandy of about twenty-five, Sigismundo guessed, and looked surprisingly robust in view of the fact that he must have been held in a dungeon for many months between the arrest and the execution. He was dressed in a penitent's robes, as prescribed for heretics, but looked as if he were still in his best brocade. It is the disdainful way he stands, Sigismundo thought; he is still a *chevalier*, and they are trained for war. Only in rare periods of peace do they live into middle age. He has been preparing for death all his life, in a sense.

A Dominican on the execution platform finished a prayer. The jailer whispered something to La Barre. The *chevalier* knelt obediently, without any last words, without any visible emotion, and coolly placed his head in the cavity of the executioner's block. He is making his speech through his behavior, Sigismundo thought; he is showing them how a brave man dies.

"Look away," Papa repeated urgently.

But Sigismundo could not avert his gaze. I wouldn't look when they burned Umberto, he thought, but this time I will not be a coward. This is *my* possible future being enacted up there: I am a heretic myself. I must look Death straight in the eye and know the true face of the Church that may kill me someday.

The executioner raised his ax. The whole crowd seemed to hold its breath.

The scatological Cockney refrain ran through Sigismundo's head: Who shit in the church? La Barre shit. Bullshit. Who shit?

The ax descended. The head fell into the basket, and an unbelievable geyser of blood sprayed out of the neck, ten times worse than Uncle Leonardo's wounds in the church, a fountain, almost a flood. We will be drowned in it, Sigismundo thought, almost starting to vomit, clenching his teeth, holding it down, misquoting Shakespeare to himself: Who would have thought the young man had so much blood in him?

He clenched his teeth again and did not vomit. The crowd was cheering wildly, and all the church bells began to chime. *Kill, kill, kill, and kill,* they seemed to say to Sigismundo; *I am the God of the Iron Rod and this is my Will: kill, kill, kill, and kill.*

This is my future, Sigismundo thought. No, my possible future. I will be too smart for them. I will go back to England. I will never set foot in a Catholic country again. I think I am going to vomit after all. You can't blame it all on the Dominicans. Our whole religion is a blend of the sublime and the bestial. Like our politics. Lord, I mustn't get hysterical and start thinking about chickens in the Vatican again.

But then the executioner, following tradition, held the head aloft for all to see, and Sigismundo almost felt he was full of

belladonna again, because the *chevalier*'s eyes were still conscious and full of pain. Of course, he had heard about that: life
remains in the brain for a few moments, and the eyes show
awareness. But if the mouth opens and he talks, I will finally go
mad.

I didn't know it was going to be this bad, the eyes of La
Barre seemed to say.

But then the eyes ceased to focus, and death was complete.
Glittering diamonds stared out of a dead face.

La Barre had been brave and true, Sigismundo thought, but
it didn't really make any difference. His death was as ugly as the
death of a coward. It was foul, foul, foul; and the mob rejoiced.
Sigismundo was suddenly aware that in the effort to avoid
vomiting, he had clenched his teeth until his jaw hurt.

Nobody noticed as Papa quietly edged Sigismundo back into
the inn. Herr Zoesser followed unobtrusively.

"Wine," the Bavarian cried as soon as they were seated.

The innkeeper set the bottle on their table. "That is how we
treat monsters here," he said grimly, as if all foreigners were
probably monsters, too.

Sigismundo and Guido drank along with the lawyer.

"To the Holy Roman Catholic and Apostolic Church,"
Zoesser said. "The civilizer of Europe." He raised his glass in a
toast.

Lutherans have done terrible things, too, Sigismundo reminded himself. They once forced children to watch as their
mothers were burned for witchcraft. It is not one church or one
sect: it is anybody anywhere who becomes fanatic.

"Jesus," Papa said softly. "I'll never forget this day."

I don't hate the whole Church, Sigismundo was telling
himself, I don't, I don't, *don't*. It's only the Inquisition. I must
not become a fanatic myself.

But it was not true: At that moment, if he could have
destroyed the Church with one blow—demolishing every

building, every altar, every nave and ciborium—he knew he would strike that blow.

▲

His first week home, it seemed as if Napoli had changed completely.

That was an illusion, of course; it was he, Sigismundo, who had changed. But everything that people did and said was no longer natural and taken for granted; it was distinctly, peculiarly Neapolitan.

He had always thought tourists were rather rude; they seemed to stare in the most impolite manner as they scuttled about Napoli. Now he understood them. They were staring because half or more of what they saw was alien and incomprehensible, as half or more of what he had seen in Spain, England, and France was shocking to him at first sight. It was as Vico said: People made up a world by talking to each other, and then they lived in the world they had talked into existence.

When Sigismundo met Antonio again, he was startled and distressed. Tony was waxy pale again and had that strange smell.

"Have you been to see Dr. Orfali lately?" Sigismundo asked, knowing Tony's illness had come back because of his mother's death.

"That sodomite?" Tony asked angrily. "We shouldn't associate with sodomites. They want to seduce all of us."

Sigismundo tried to be reasonable. "Dr. Orfali is not a sodomite," he said. "You are letting your imagination run away with you."

"I can *recognize* sodomites, no matter how they try to hide," Tony said, calm and certain. "They caused the fall of the Roman Empire. They are everywhere, and they are always plotting."

There was a great deal more of that, and gradually the horrible truth came home to Sigismundo. The last time, he thought, Tony knew he was ill and wanted to be cured. This time he does not even suspect that he is ill.

Sigismundo went straight to Malatesta and Celine Wine Exports and found Uncle Pietro.

"Tony is ill again," he said.

"I know, I know," Uncle Pietro said wearily.

"He won't go to Dr. Orfali."

"He doesn't want to go," Pietro said. "I've been dragging him there once a week anyway. But it is much harder this time. He is full of hostility."

"He suspects Dr. Orfali of being a sodomite."

"It is worse than that," Uncle Pietro said gravely. "He suspects everybody of being a sodomite. He has an infallible method, he says, of detecting sodomy, no matter how well it is hidden."

Sigismundo sighed. "What can be done?"

"I don't know," Uncle Pietro said. "There is nobody in Napoli who understands these things as well as Abraham. And even if I found such a person, Tony would just decide that person was a sodomite, too. So I take him to Abraham and Abraham tries to help him, but this is a different illness."

"Yes," Sigismundo said. "This one, in some sense, he enjoys."

Pietro shook his head. "He doesn't really enjoy it," he said. "It is just preferable to the other choices he can imagine at this point. After all, it is not as frightening as hearing demon voices and not being able to concentrate on anything but noses. It makes him feel important, too. He thinks eventually all fairminded people will agree he is right and join him in a crusade to drive all the sodomites out of Napoli. Don't, for Jesus' sake, *argue* with him; he will go on for hours, producing evidence to support his delusion."

"It is what the French call an *idée fixe*?"

"It is an *idée fixe* to an exponential power. I have seen it a few times before. I once knew a man who was a brilliant natural philosopher, and then he began seeing Masonic symbols on the moon. The more other astronomers tried to reason with him, the more he became convinced they were all part of a conspiracy. That is the way it happens with this illness. The sufferer seems to enjoy it, as you thought, because he is continually involved in exciting quarrels and continually hoping he will be proved right. Actually, his anger is growing all the time, until it blinds him, and he is getting lonelier and lonelier. We can only hope and do our best. Sometimes there is remission."

And so the matter rested, for a while.

Sigismundo met Antonio on the street one day and received a venomous glance.

He has proved I am a sodomite, Sigismundo thought. His infallible method has detected it in my walk, or my music, or something.

▲

The sun had set. The bay waters were the glittering purple of good Burgundy, and Sigismundo was working on a new sonata he called "The Two Nations." He hadn't seen any *Rossi* since his return, dead men had not come to the door with black magick *grimoires*, and he was thoroughly absorbed in the music.

He had been working lately on a new exercise Abraham had given him: to look, each day, for ten beautiful things in Napoli he had never noticed before. "It reminds you that the things you worry about do not comprise all of existence," Abraham said.

Sigismundo heard the raised voices in the living room before he realized what they were saying.

"In the bay—"

"—ten minutes ago—"

"Divers are still jumping—"

He was irritated at being interrupted in a beautiful

semifugue structure; and then, of course, he was immediately ashamed of that selfish attitude. He raced downstairs.

Papa was already on his way out the door. Sigismundo caught up with him at the street gate.

"Is it Antonio?" he asked; but he knew.

"Yes, God help him."

"I can run faster, which part of the bay?"

"Down by the Piazza Reale—"

Sigismundo was already racing downhill.

Down, down, down, he thought, like the day I was going to kill little Carlo; and I thought of the *bolgia* of the suicides that day. Dante has them turned into trees . . .

He could see the Teatro San Carlo. The best thing Don Carlos ever did for Napoli, and now he's trying to abolish bullfights in Spain . . . Everything is connected . . .

He was panting, but the bay was closer.

I know why Tony did it, he thought. He had finally proved that everybody in Napoli was a sodomite. He was all alone then, surrounded by perverts who lusted for him. That's the way this illness works. You lock yourself in a cage of suspicion and then grow the more terrified because you are now alone. Because he couldn't accept the deaths of his father and mother and needed an explanation for what was wrong with the world. Because the only explanation that made sense to him, in that state, was one that allowed him to hate everybody.

As soon as Sigismundo crossed the Piazza Reale, he knew where Antonio had jumped. There was a crowd gathered by the pier on Via Ammiragliato.

Sigismundo stopped to catch his breath. I never even liked him, he thought, but that does not matter. He is a Malatesta; I have my duty.

There were several boys and young men in their undergarments, dripping. They had been diving for several minutes.

With a shock, Sigismundo saw Carlo Maldonado come to

the surface and breathe deeply. Then, in thirty seconds, Carlo dived again. The boy I almost killed, trying to save my crazy cousin.

Sigismundo tore off his boots and outer clothing. It's probably pointless now, he thought, but I've got to try. Suicide is the worst sin, the sin against the Holy Spirit. That is why even strangers are diving.

Several people looked at him evasively, out of the corners of their eyes; they knew it was probably too late. Christ, he thought, the Church won't even let us bury him in sanctified ground. Not when half the city knows he jumped.

Sigismundo dived.

The water was colder than he expected, almost frigid. It's after sunset now, he told himself; it always gets colder when the sun goes down. But he was thinking of his nightmare vision of drowning in icy water, while crossing the English Channel.

I won't drown. I'm a good swimmer.

Carlo Maldonado was swimming near him. Then, his eyes adjusting to the darkness, he saw a fish of a species he had never encountered before. God knows what's down at the bottom of the bay that I've never seen, he thought.

Sigismundo came back to the surface and breathed. He realized that he was much further out than he had thought; the tide was ebbing, the current was outward, Antonio could be a long way gone by now.

Another head came to the surface, further out still. It was getting darker, but Sigismundo thought he recognized one of the Portinari boys. Sigismundo swam north and west for a while: that was the direction of the current, which would be carrying Tony.

He dived again and almost collided with an octopus. A tentacle touched him, but then it moved away rapidly in a purple spray.

Sigismundo swam back from the inky excretion.

Fish, fish, fish; no human bodies anywhere, not even other divers.

When he came to the surface again, he could hardly see the pier. It was getting darker rapidly, and there was less visibility below the water also.

"What can I do?" he asked out loud, almost hoping God would answer.

Keep diving. Don't give up. He may be alive.

Sigismundo swam further north. He noticed that his teeth were beginning to chatter. Peppino was more than human because he would not admit limits. What I must do is be like that: do not admit any limits. Anywhere.

He dived again.

He was lost in inky blackness, and for a moment he thought he had collided with another octopus. No, it was just the absence of the sun.

He came up.

"What can I do?" he asked again.

Then he saw the torches coming, golden flames in the twilight. Some of the fishermen had put out in their boats to assist the divers.

He dived again.

Inky blackness, but his eyes were getting accustomed to it. Down, down, down, and nothing but fish.

He came up. "Over here," he shouted, and before the fishermen arrived, he dived again.

Down, down, down, and no sign of Tony.

A boat arrived as he came up again. Friendly, anxious faces.

Sigismundo clutched the side of the boat, panting, listening to his teeth chatter.

"You'd better come out," the pilot said. "You're turning blue."

Sigismundo shook his head, too exhausted to reply.

"It's the boy's cousin," somebody said.

"Well, take some of this," the pilot said, holding a bottle to Sigismundo's lips. Sigismundo drank briefly: too much would not help at all. It tasted like Malatesta and Celine muscatel.

If only his teeth would stop chattering.

You've wrestled with a professional assassin. You've been drugged and terrorized by Satanists. There's a gang of maniacs out there, determined to coerce or cajole you into becoming their leader. You saw your father tortured to death. Your uncle murdered. Your aunt dead of grief. Now it's time to show some real courage. Dive down into that ice-cold water again.

He dived.

He could make out more in the reflected light of the torches, but all he saw were fish and more fish. The divers were far apart now, trying to cover the whole bay.

Later, he never knew how many times he had dived, how many times the boat had found him again, how many times the pilot had begged him to stop. He remembered plunging again and again into the inky caverns with only the torches shedding faint visibility. He remembered clinging, time after time, to the side of the boat, panting, teeth chattering, his body shaking with spasms of cold and exhaustion. He remembered diving again and again. As if the sea was a living, devouring god . . .

He was driven now by fury, by outrage at the sheer unmitigated stupidity and cruelty of Antonio's act. I don't care how crazy he was, he thought bitterly, he had no right to do this to the family. We've been through enough and more than enough. He was freezing, he was (possibly) drowning, he was lost in cold and in pain. His fury drove him on. Do not admit limits. I will find the bastard and tell him to his face, "You had no *right* to do this."

Down and down and down . . .

"This night will curse us all," Uncle Pietro had said.

He was clinging to the side of the boat again. It wasn't the same boat. He was completely lost now.

"Come out, you're purple, you'll catch pneumonia . . ."

He dived again. I'll find him, I'll bring him home, we can at least have a funeral.

Down, down, down into the freezing inky blackness. Gold flames making strange patches of illumination. A dolphin went by suddenly—big as any crocodile—and Sigismundo was glad dolphins are not hostile to man.

Back to the surface, hanging over the rail of a boat.

Hands were pulling him up. A blanket was thrown around him.

"No," he said. "I must go back down."

"Shut up. Drink this." Wine was poured into his lips. A cheap Chianti this time.

He became aware that his whole body was jerking with spasms. Cold and exhaustion; but it was like the belladonna, the same internal explosion of the vegetative system.

"I have failed again," he said, teeth chattering.

"I stopped diving a half hour ago," said a voice.

Sigismundo looked across the narrow boat. Even in the dark, he recognized Carlo Maldonado.

"Everybody stopped a half hour ago," Carlo said. "I don't know what kept you going."

Fury, Sigismundo thought. When you have nothing else left, that will keep you going. It comes from my father's side of the family, with a little madness thrown in.

"Drink some more of this," a fisherman said, passing the Chianti again. "Do not feel ashamed. You lasted longer than the professional divers."

"He was my cousin," Sigismundo said numbly.

"*Che mala fortuna*," the fisherman said sympathetically.

He should go to England, Sigismundo thought bitterly; he has a talent for understatement.

They rowed in silence for a while, and Sigismundo stared morosely at the lights of Napoli coming closer.

"Carlo," he said finally.

"Yes?"

"This feud between our families . . . my Uncle Pietro says it is a great folly."

"My father says the same."

"You were very brave today. I will see that my whole family hears about what you did."

"I had to do it," Carlo said. "I felt so sorry for him. He looked so sad when he jumped."

They didn't say anymore. They were both numb with exhaustion. The lights of the city came closer.

▲

PART SIX

THE HANGED MAN

I will not cease from Mental Fight,
Nor shall the Sword sleep in my hand:
Till we have built Jerusalem,
In England's green & pleasant Land.

William Blake, "Milton"

John Babcock was born in 1745 in Dublin, Ireland, where his father, Sir Edward Babcock, was serving as a judge; but the ancestral home of the Babcocks was in Lousewartshire, and the family returned there by the time the boy was six years old.

"I shall never go back to Ireland again—not for the king, not for my country, not even for God," Father often said. He had found in seven years that not one Irishman existed who did not loathe the English (*Sassanach*, they called them, which was Gaelic for "Saxons"). Father, though a Whig, began to advocate Irish independence, not on humanitarian grounds, such as were urged by other Whigs, but simply on the grounds that the English would never be able to govern that country. Even Cromwell, who had acted like Attila the Hun when he invaded Ireland, had not destroyed the Irish rebellious spirit. The Irish had just become more fanatic and more secretive. Even the battle of Boyne River, which crushed the Jacobites in Ireland, did not crush Irish intransigence. They just became even more fanatical and founded more secret societies. Or so Father said.

The boy did not remember much about the Dublin years. He knew, the way small children know such things, that Father and Mother both feared and respected the Irish but that the fear was stronger than the respect. He was never left alone, not for a minute, since some of the Irish were capable of atrocities against English children. In later years, he remembered the beautiful leafy acres of Phoenix Park, the looming hulk of the Hill of Howth (where the castle door was always open at dinner time, because of some inscrutable Irish superstition), and the dark-hued river Anna Liffey sparkling and dancing as she came pouring down from the green hills; and he remembered that it was not safe to go "beyond the pale"—beyond the small area surrounding English Protestant Dublin, the area controlled by English troops. Beyond the pale—out there in the wild lands—were only Catholics and Jacobites and the monstrous White Boys, who rode by night in white hoods and were capable of any cruelty against the English.

And he remembered the Field of Clontarf, where Father had taken him, in the interest of history, to see the spot where the aged Irish king, Brian Boru, had defeated the Vikings on April 23, 1014. Little Johnny thought it was an odd coincidence—April 23 was Shakespeare's birthday—so he never forgot that date.

But most of all he remembered one grave Father had taken him to, the grave of a man Father said was the greatest writer of the century.

"It would be a great waste if you grew up in Dublin and never saw this," Father said; and John was properly impressed. Father was quite gray already, at forty, and wore his beard full and long: John often imagined that God looked a great deal like Father and had the same strict standards of honor.

The gravestone was in Saint Patrick's Cathedral, which was Anglican and not a den of Papist idolatry at all. "Let's see how your Latin is progressing," Father said. "Can you translate it?"

And little Johnny (he was five at the time) translated, a bit haltingly, " 'He has, er, gone um where lacer—uh, he has gone where fierce indignation can no longer lacerate his heart.' Yes, I have it. 'He has gone where fierce indignation can no longer lacerate his heart. Go, traveler. Imitate him if you can. He served liberty. Jonathan Swift, 1667–1745.' " He died the year I was born, he thought.

"Damn fine epigraph," Father said. "Hope they can say as much about me when my time comes."

"What did Mr. Swift do?" Johnny asked timidly.

"He raised merry hell," Father said. "He was dean of the cathedral here, by profession, but by avocation he was the greatest enemy of tyranny and humbug the world has ever produced. Young lawyer named Burke comes here regularly and stares at that tombstone. I'll wager a lot of others come here, too, as I do on bad days. Remember this, Johnny lad. Try to live so that words like that might be appropriate to your stone at the end of your days."

"But what did Mr. Swift *do*?" Johnny repeated. "Was he in parliament?"

"He was more dangerous than any politician," Father said. "He wrote books. A book can be the most deadly weapon in the world, if it can get past the censors. He was so clever that nobody realized how subversive his books were until they were in circulation a long time." Father smiled. "Some people still complain about his crude words and coarse language, as they do about Shakespeare; but he got his message across. He served intellectual liberty, you see, not just political liberty."

Johnny knew what *liberty* meant. It was what Father and all the Whigs lived for, adored, worshiped. "He served liberty": any Whig would want that on his tombstone. But he did not understand those words about the lacerated heart, not at the age of five.

Father's real hero, though, was Lord Edward Coke, who had also served in Ireland, although a long time ago. In fact, Lord Coke had not so much *served* there as he had been *exiled* there. Edward Coke had been lord chief justice under James I and had tried to make James understand that there were some things even a king could not do, because the Constitution forbade them. But nobody could tell James I what he could not do, not even the lord chief justice. James sent Coke off to serve in a minor bureaucratic post in Ireland. And the result of that, Father said, was that James I did whatever he pleased and raised his son, Charles I, to be equally pigheaded; and the result of that was Cromwell and revolution and Charles I having his head chopped off. That was exactly what could be expected, Father implied, for any royal family not intelligent enough to listen to a man like Coke.

And, of course—Johnny learned by the time he was at Eton—Lord Coke had triumphed in the long run. The Stuarts were not kings at all anymore (although a handful of wild Irishmen and crazy Scots, the Jacobites, wanted to bring them back), but Lord Coke was studied in every college of law in Great Britain, and you had to read some parts of his work even in an ordinary public school.

It was after Father met Mr. John Wilkes, the demagogue, that John, by then in his teens, began to hear about those passages in Coke that said parliament, just like the king, could not do anything it pleased but must obey the constitution. And about Thomas Reid, the Scotsman, who argued that "the pursuit of happiness" was the only rational goal of man and the only justification for government. But Reid and Wilkes and even Lord Coke were all, somehow, implicit in that early experience of that one ineluctable Dublin tombstone that was to remain forever, as Father had intended, the goad and goal of John's sense of conscience:

HE HAS GONE WHERE FIERCE INDIGNATION
CAN NO LONGER LACERATE HIS HEART

GO, TRAVELER: IMITATE HIM IF YOU CAN
HE SERVED LIBERTY

Something else that had an equally powerful impact on John's mind occurred when he was at Eton. The master of the geometry class was a man named Robert Estlin Drake, a tall blond man who had a habit of using geometry as a launching pad for excursions into logic and philosophy generally; he delighted in presenting the class with paradoxes for which there was no known solution. John learned all about Achilles and the tortoise in that class, and the arrow in flight that never moved, and even about Bishop Berkeley's proof that nothing existed until it was perceived.

Then one day Drake discussed Plato's idea that we would not be able to conceive of equality if there were not another world in which perfect equality did exist. This must be true, the argument ran, because we cannot deduce equality from this world, where only approximations of it exist.

One student, a boy named Geoffrey Wildeblood, decided Plato was right. The other world, where equality exists, he said, must be the mind of Bishop Berkeley's God.

"Ah," Drake said delighted. "I have actually prodded one of you to read the good bishop. But think of the implications, Wildeblood Major. Perfect justice must also exist in that ideal realm, as Plato also pointed out. And perfect knowledge. And perfect music. Does that not all follow, Wildeblood Major?"

"Yes, sir!" Wildeblood said boldly.

"Nobody has ever seen a perfect chicken coop," Drake said and paused. "Every chicken coop in England, or on the Continent, or far off in Asia, is just an approximation of perfection. Therefore, in that perfect realm of Plato's, or in the mind of God, there must be a perfect chicken coop toward which we can only approximate. And it would include perfect hens, perfect roosters, perfect eggs, and *perfect chicken shit*. Is that not a remarkable thought?"

The class was in an uproar. Drake pounded his cane on the desk to restore silence.

"Babcock Major," he said. "You look uncommonly perplexed. Do you think my example of the chicken coop has reduced Plato to absurdity?"

John rose, as was required. "No, sir!" he answered sharply. "I think there is something wrong with our logic, sir! We invent better machines all the time, sir. I think someday we will invent a better logic and all these paradoxes will be solved, sir!"

Drake nodded thoughtfully. "I had forgotten that your father is a judge, Babcock Major. That is the most interesting answer I have ever heard to that problem. If you ever succeed in inventing such an improved logic, pray make haste to inform me of it at your earliest convenience."

Somehow, this led to a new nickname being appended to John; throughout Eton, not just in his own class, he became "Better Logic Babcock." Worse: he was continually being asked if he had found the precise second, t, when A turned into not-A. Various wits inquired of him if he had found a new geometry yet or if he was currently working on the foundations of a new number series.

All these matters of ontological analysis became quite concrete and urgent when John happened to think of them while receiving a caning from an apoplectic master named Murdstone—a nasty old twit with all the warmth and sentiment of a female praying mantis. Murdstone was always eager to find an excuse to cane a boy. John, of course, accepted caning as he accepted the moon and stars; it was part of the way things were. But this time, suddenly, John thought of the tombstone in Dublin declaring a love of liberty so fierce that it lacerated the heart; he abruptly suspected that his original rage at being caned might have been justified and that learning to tolerate it merely showed that he was afraid to question some things that really deserved to be looked at skeptically. If Lord Coke could, at least posthumously, convince the kings of England that their powers were limited, could not somebody, someday, tell the masters of Eton that their power over the students was also limited?

It was only a thought. John knew full well what would happen if he seized the cane and tried to fight back against Murdstone.

Then something even more dramatic occurred.

John fell in love.

The boy was the other heretic in geometry class, Geoffrey Wildeblood, who believed there was a perfect chicken coop in the mind of God.

▲

One day in 1760 all the boys at Eton were excused from their classes and taken to the chapel. The masters were very grim, and everybody knew that somebody was going to catch blue hell.

The chaplain, Father Fenwick, had once been a Papist —everybody knew it—but he had been a good Anglican for more than twenty years now, and all the old rumors about his involvement with Jacobite plots were discredited. He was around fifty and was considered a good sort by the boys—your cheerful, kindly clergyman, not your stuffy, stiff-necked variety. But today he looked like thunder and lightning when he stood up in the pulpit.

Some of the boys have been stealing wine from the sacristy again, John thought.

"I must speak today about a terrible, terrible subject," Father Fenwick said, in a tone that suggested that at least grave robbery and black magick were involved, if not ax murder. "I would to God that I did not have to let words of such vile matters pass my lips, but it is necessary to speak out at this time.

"There are many kinds of sin, but some are so loathsome that even to name them is revolting to people of sensibility. There is one sin in particular that is known to appear often in schools such as this, where many boys are living together in close proximity for long periods of time. I speak of the abomination that is both against nature and against Scripture. You all know the story of Sodom and Gomorrah . . ."

Oh, Jesus, John thought. They *know*. Perhaps I will shoot myself with a pistol as soon as I get out of here.

Father Fenwick talked at length about the sin of sodomy. He said that God had destroyed the whole city of Sodom with fire and brimstone because this sin was so hateful to Him. He said that this vice was so vile that gentlemen never even talk about it, although they may make jokes about other sins of the flesh. He said that the authorities at Eton did not want to believe, at first, that a nest of monsters was among them, but there were so many rumors that an investigation had been made. He said that eighteen practitioners of this hideous vice were now known.

My God, John thought, who are the other sixteen?

Father Fenwick said that if the culprits came to him and confessed, they could receive absolution; but they must swear to God to forsake their unspeakable vice, or the absolution would be a deception of God and magnify their guilts. And we will all be watched, John thought, from that day forward; we will be policed as if we lived in the lands of the Inquisition. He was wondering if some of this cant might not be a huge bluff. Suppose his name were not on their list? Then by confessing he would just be sticking his neck in the noose for no reason at all. But if his name *were* on their list and he didn't come forth—

"Those of the eighteen who do not come to me to confess in privacy," Father Fenwick said, "will be regarded as obdurate in their vice. The school will have no choice. Such boys will be expelled, and their parents will be informed of the reason for their removal."

Suppose Geoffrey doesn't confess, John thought; then, if I confess, I must name him—they will insist on that—and he will be sent home in disgrace.

But: Suppose I do not confess, and Geoffrey does. Then I will be the one sent home in disgrace.

Father Fenwick talked on and on and on. John realized that this had all been rehearsed, plotted out like a Neapolitan conspiracy. The talk would go on, and on, convoluted and repetitious and rambling as an old man's yarns, and the monotony would raise the apprehensions of the guilty. None of the boys would be let out of the chapel until the emotional effect was exactly as planned.

They have done this before, he thought. Maybe they do it every six years, or every ten years; they may have made a science out of it.

He was beginning to analyze the situation. Probably, he thought, they will have some way to keep us apart so that we cannot talk. If two of us promise not to betray each other, the whole system fails. It depends on each of us thinking that he cannot be sure the other will not inform first.

He dared not look around, to try to catch Geoffrey's eye. *They* were probably watching like hawks, to see which boys were looking at which other boys.

Father Fenwick went on talking about the dreadful effects of the vice. He spoke of emasculation, feeblemindedness, insanity, and incurable diseases. He said that practitioners seldom survived into adulthood unless the sin was relinquished. "Their hands tremble," he said gravely. "Their eyesight begins to fade. They cannot concentrate on their studies . . ."

How much can I trust Geoffrey? He said he loved me, but . . .

Suddenly, the talk was coming to an end.

262 ROBERT ANTON WILSON

"I will now go to the rectory," Father Fenwick said. "You will be let out of chapel, one by one, in intervals of five minutes. You will each come to the rectory, and either you will tell me that you have nothing to confess, or else you will make your confession, and we will pray together that God will forgive you and give you the strength to resist this bestial vice in the future."

The priest left the pulpit.

"Ainsley Minor," shouted Mr. Murdstone.

Bleeding Christ, John thought, they are doing it in alphabetical order, of course. I will go very soon; and Geoffrey Wildeblood will have a long, long wait, wondering if I peached on him or not.

It seemed an eternity before Murdstone called "Babcock Major."

John crossed the quad very aware that the chestnut trees were blooming beautifully, very aware that the sky was the same shade of blue as Geoffrey's eyes ("eyes that go all the way back to heaven," Dubliners say), very aware that he was about to make the most difficult decision of his young life.

It doesn't matter, he thought in an instant of total despair, whether I confess at once. He will see it in my eyes. And he will keep me there, hounding me, until I do confess.

He opened the door to the rectory.

Father Fenwick was seated at his desk. He looked up blandly. "Yes, Babcock Major?"

"I have nothing to confess, sir."

Pause. A long, searching look from dark eyes.

"Are you sure, Babcock Major?"

"Yes, sir!" You old swine.

Another pause. Let me sweat a minute.

"You may go, Babcock Major."

"Thank you, sir."

John crossed the quad again, heading back to his room. I never knew I could lie to an adult and get away with it, he thought. And: I was able to do it because I remembered the caning and realized what *they* are.

This is not just a school, he thought. This is an institution for the production of automatons. It is run by automatons who were produced by other automatons, long ago, and now they have forgotten what it is to be human and are engaged in turning us into automatons in turn.

He remembered the story that had been in the London newspapers a few months ago. It had been written in very veiled language, but everybody knew what it meant, and many of the older boys made jokes about it. A brothel had been uncovered that specialized in caning men. Of course, he thought: some of the automatons get to like being caned. And some of them get to like doing the caning, and they come here and become masters or headmasters. And when the gears turn a certain way, a boy gets caned, and nobody dares to question whether it is fair or not, because we are all becoming automatons here and automatons do not ask questions. They move as the gears move them.

He was back in his room, alone. Henson Minor and Montgomery Minor, who shared the room, would not be back for a while, since the Inquisition was proceeding alphabetically.

No, they were not exactly automatons, but they did not know what they were doing. They take down a boy's britches. They stare at his buttocks. They cane him until the buttocks bleed. And they believe this is virtue, because it is done in a school, and it becomes vice only if it is done in a place with a red lantern over the door.

How long would it be before he learned if Geoffrey had confessed?

John tried to distract himself. He opened a book by his

favorite writer, the man whose tombstone spoke of fierce indignation. He found himself reading over and over, with no amusement at all:

> Last week I saw a woman flayed, and you will hardly believe how much it altered her person for the worse. Yesterday I ordered the carcass of a beau to be stripped in my presence, when we were all amazed to see so many unsuspected faults under one suit of clothes. Then I laid open his brain, his heart, and his spleen; but I plainly perceived, at every operation, that the further we proceeded, we found the defects increase upon us in number and bulk; from all which, I justly formed this conclusion to myself: that whatever philosopher or projector can find out an art to sodder and patch up the flaws and imperfections of nature, will deserve much better of mankind, and teach us a more useful science, than that so much in present esteem, of widening and exposing them (like him who held anatomy to be the ultimate end of physic). And he, whose fortunes and dispositions have placed him in a convenient station to enjoy the fruits of this noble art; he that can with Epicurus content his ideas with the films and images of things; such a man truly wise, creams off nature, leaving the sour and dregs for philosophy and reason to lap up. This is the sublime and refined point of felicity, called, the possession of being well deceived; the serene peaceful state of being a fool among knaves.

John had enjoyed that passage before, but now the irony seemed tinged with something more than a little sinister. This was as comic as the murder of Christ; it was the joke of a man who jokes because the only alternative is to scream down the house.

Lord, how many hours will this go on?

"I saw a woman flayed": yes, and you could still see that, anytime you cared to go to Newgate Hill. One could be quite sure it would alter her person for the worse; and it would alter all the other persons on Newgate Hill for the worse, although they might not realize it. You could see a boy caned any day, at Eton, and caning was not really very different from flaying.

Henson returned finally; and, a little later, Montgomery. They both put on great airs of amusement and cynicism; but John was wondering if either of them had been guilty, unbeknown to him; and he knew they were wondering the same about him—and maybe about each other.

Mystery and suspicion will hang over this class for years, he realized.

Finally, it was time for dinner. No word had come for John to come to the headmaster's office; Geoffrey had not confessed. John felt a faint guilt for doubting Geoffrey at all.

Mr. Murdstone made a brief speech when all the boys were in the dining hall. He said that thirty confessions had been obtained—not the eighteen they expected, John noted. Murdstone added that one boy had run away somewhere but would probably soon be found. Then he told them all, in solemn tones, that no further discussion of this matter would be allowed, inside the school or out, and warned them all that the school itself would be disgraced if any breath of this scandal ever went beyond the walls.

Father Fenwick then made another speech. He said that all thirty culprits were truly repentant and that nobody should attempt to learn their identities. "That must remain a matter between the boys themselves and Our Father in Heaven," he said.

And everybody will know in a week, John thought. Or at least everybody will pretend to know.

Then he noticed that Geoffrey was not in the dining hall. Geoffrey was the boy who had run away.

Jesus, Jesus, he thought. Just when I thought it was over. The worst is yet to come.

He never remembered what was served for dinner that

night. Somewhere, out there in the darkness, Geoffrey was wandering, frightened. Where could he go? Not home, certainly. Was he fantasizing about running away with gypsies, becoming a cabin boy on a ship to America, or was he just in a blue funk and walking on and on like a horse with the blind staggers? God help him, John thought, if he falls into the hands of the highwaymen.

Probably the sheriff's men would pick Geoffrey up tomorrow. With that starched collar, they would know at once he was from Eton and would bring him back here. And then, terrified, weak after the night's ordeal, Geoffrey would confess everything.

Expulsion.

John tried to imagine the look in Father's eyes when he returned home, a convicted sodomite.

That was legally a hanging offense, but John had never heard of anybody actually being hanged for it. Probably you were just sent off to America or to the Continent. Still, according to the books, they could hang you if they wanted to.

Geoffrey was probably thinking about that, out there in the dark. Geoffrey knew all about sodomy and its implications: he said he had always known he was that way, as far back as he could remember. John was not sure about himself; he often had fantasies about girls. If girls had been available—well, then, he might be in another kind of trouble. But that was pointless now. Whatever calamity was going to befall him, it was because he had loved Geoffrey, not a girl.

It was not only sinful but *dangerous* with a girl, because she might get pregnant. It was unnatural with a boy, because he *wouldn't* get pregnant. That seemed to leave the sheep; but no, that was *abominable*. There was your own right hand, but that led to blindness. I think they are lying to us about some of that, John thought.

Damn it, where was Geoffrey, and what was happening to him out there in the dark?

At eight in the evening, the news arrived at West Hall where John lodged.

Geoffrey Wildeblood had been found in a pond, dead. "We must in charity assume that he fell in by accident," said Mr. Drake, who had brought the story. "The poor lad will then be given a Christian burial. For the sake of his grieved parents, let none of you breathe a word to the contrary. Remember, I pray you, that all we know for certain is that the poor lad drowned; all else is inference. Spreading unfavorable inference is the sin of scandal condemned in Holy Writ."

John realized that he felt nothing.

Maybe I am just numb with shock, he thought.

Or maybe I am one of those monsters without normal human feelings.

John pictured Geoffrey floating in the pond, and nausea swept over him; he thought for a minute that he would lose his dinner. But that was horror, not true grief. What has happened to me? he wondered. Has part of me died today, along with Geoffrey?

All those starched Eton collars, he thought, and nobody knows what goes on in the heads above them. Future prime ministers and future leading figures of all sorts. All learning to hide emotion and become English gentlemen. Thirty confessed; Geoffrey and I did not confess; and the others? God alone could answer.

He was awake long after the candles were extinguished, still not feeling anything. Perhaps grief is this way, he thought; it takes a few days before you feel it. *"Then I laid open his brain, his heart, and his spleen; but I plainly perceived, at every operation, that the further we proceeded, we found the defects increase upon us in number and bulk . . ."*

Geoffrey was too sensitive, basically. He could not stand the normal teasing and the cruel wit of the boys at Eton; he was easily hurt and depressed. Geoffrey killed himself because they put him in a trap and he broke under the strain.

Everything that appears imperfect here on earth has a perfect model in the mind of God; Geoffrey really had believed that. Then there is a perfect Eton in the mind of God, John thought. The system works perfectly there. Everybody confesses; nobody lies; nobody jumps in the pond. And they all graduate and turn into perfect English gentlemen. And the best of them, the cream of the cream, the pluperfect of the perfect, arrive eventually in a perfect House of Lords and snore perfectly while perfect bills are perfectly debated.

And the hangmen are all perfect there; when they flay a whore, they use perfect whips.

I know why Geoffrey killed himself, John thought. He would not betray me, but he could not walk into the rectory and lie to Father Fenwick. He might have walked toward the rectory door many times, but each time he would walk away, walk around the quad again, probably stopping to look at the old whipping block from the 14th century. (Do they keep that there to show how far we have progressed since then, or to warn us of what they are capable of doing if rebellion ever appears?) He would walk back and forth, trying to get his courage up. But he could not look at the priest and lie.

So he threw himself in the pond and died.

Around dawn, John thought: I will never see him again. That is what death means. Shakespeare put it in five words: never, never, never, never, never.

No part of him that I haven't kissed; no part of me that he hasn't kissed. And I will never never never never never see him again.

John began to feel something, finally. Not grief; his mind

still held that at bay. He felt a fierce indignation that lacerated his heart.

It will be a lonely life, he thought, living a lie. But that is the condition of survival in this place at this time. And I will throw the lie in their teeth eventually.

Someday. Somehow.

▲

PART SEVEN

THE DEVIL

But there is one dangerous element [in Freemasonry] and that is the element I have copied from them . . .

Adolf Hitler, quoted in Hermann Rauschning, *Hitler Speaks*

At eighteen, Sigismundo Celine was attending the University of Napoli, where the great Tomasso d'Aquino had once taught.

Sigismundo was majoring in mathematics, not music, because he had decided nobody in Napoli could teach him anything about the kind of music he wanted to write. Someday, in a few years, he would go to Hamburg and study with those who had been pupils of Telemann; in the meanwhile, he was still composing experimental sonatas.

He had almost finished one symphony in the French style but had thrown it out as hopeless.

Mathematics more and more obsessed him: the relation between music and mathematics seemed to him the most exciting and most mysterious of all areas of knowledge. Ever since he had understood those wonderful English machines as concretized thoughts, he had wanted to learn more and more and more about the kind of coherence that appears only in equations. That kind of knowledge could yield machines that would endlessly magnify human wealth; he believed it also brought humanity closer to the real structure of the universe, the way God thinks.

And one day after his eighteenth birthday, Sigismundo had gone to Uncle Pietro and said, "I think I am old enough now to join your 'club.'"

"I must ask you three times," Pietro said somberly. "Are you sure you are ready to commit yourself?"

"Yes," Sigismundo said fervently.

"Think, now, as I ask again. Are you truly sure?"

"Yes."

"Think again, and don't answer so fast. Are you sure you are ready to commit yourself?"

Sigismundo thought: The *Rossi* will never stop dogging me. This means that the Inquisitors will dog me also, someday. "Yes," he said flatly. "I am absolutely sure."

"Very well," Pietro said. "We are, as you have guessed, the Ancient and Accepted Order of Freemasons, also known as the Order of the Oriental Temple. We were driven underground in 1307, when the Inquisitors stumbled upon some of our secrets, which they could not understand. We have changed our name many times—and even now we have a different title in Arabic countries than we have in Europe. There are many others who claim to be Templars and Masons who are not of us. They are mere pretenders and charlatans. We alone possess the original unbroken tradition of the inner Light, preserved since the days of Solomon. Do you believe that?"

"No," Sigismundo said promptly. "Every 'club' claims to be the original and genuine. I believe you and your friends are the most rational people around here, but that's all I believe, so far."

"Very good," Pietro chuckled. "Sometimes I believe we are

the original—on Sundays, Tuesdays, and Thursdays. The other four days I am not so sure who invented our club or when. It doesn't matter. Speculative Masonry, in our form, seems to me the best hope for improving the lot of humanity in a world full of fanatics."

"When can I be initiated?" Sigismundo demanded.

"In a few days. I must call a meeting of the lodge. Meanwhile, there is a piece of paper I must give you, with questions. You must think about them every minute. Even give up music and neglect your university studies for these days. Think about *nothing* but these questions."

Pietro went to his bookshelves and rummaged about. "Here it is," he said.

Sigismundo looked at the parchment.

Who was Adam the son of?

Morte de Cristo, he thought, that's as bad as the old one about where did Cain get his wife? He looked at the rest of the questions:

Does God have an opposite?
How many sons of God are there?
Are the sons of God also gods?
Are any sons of God less than others?
What is the goal of prophets and teachers?
How many minds are there?
What is a human being?
Is mankind finished or in process?
How much can we and should we attempt?
What is the purpose of life and consciousness?
What is the next step?

Sigismundo grinned. "Thanks a lot," he said. "If the belladonna didn't drive me crazy, these riddles certainly will."

He spent most of that day rereading Genesis many times. Adam, of course, did not have a father. The first question was either pointless or very sneaky.

He tried pondering the next question: "Does God have an opposite?" The obvious answer was "Yes, the Devil." Was he supposed to deny this? That wouldn't be too hard, since he already doubted Hell. But if there was no Devil, how account for evil? That was a subtle trap; you might end up attributing evil to God.

And then the third question: "How many sons of God are there?" There was only one, the Perfect Man, Jesus—any other answer was heresy. And yet Abraham, who was a Jew, could not accept Jesus as the only son of God in orthodox Catholic fashion, and Abraham was a Freemason. So there was some other, clearly heretical answer.

He remembered Peppino's words, "As for the 'foul Moham-medans,' you have joined them already."

Was he supposed to think that Mohammed was also a son of God? And maybe there were others . . . The Chinese had their own prophet, Confucius. The Hindus had many prophets and seers. Was the Masonic heresy that all these men were equally the sons of God? Did they hope to unite mankind with that relativistic idea? If so, and if that doctrine ever leaked out, the Masons would be condemned by the Church at once.

Sigismundo skipped down the page to

What is the purpose of life and consciousness?

That was a rare beauty, that one.

Let me try it from the other end, he decided. I am about to become a Freemason. If I know what that means, I will know how to approach these questions.

Free: free to do what? He thought of the free market and the abolition of tariffs; of freedom of thought and the end of the Inquisition; of freedom from every form of tyranny. He liked the sound of all that, but it didn't tell him who Adam was the son of.

Mason: builder. A free mason was a free builder. Not just in the literal sense, obviously. The man with the steam engine in Scotland, Watt, was a free *mason* in the sense that he had built something new, out of the freedom of his own mind, not being told what he must and must not think.

Wealth increases where ideas are free, Uncle Pietro always said.

I am free when I write a sonata, Sigismundo thought, but music is not wealth. Or is it? Publishers pay to print our melodies, people buy the scores to learn to play them, other people pay to go the opera house and listen. By God, music is a kind of wealth. Even poetry is wealth: how many innkeepers in Stratford are making money every year because tourists go to see the place Shakespeare is buried?

Any product of the mind is wealth if people want it. To set the mind free, totally free, everywhere, in everybody, would increase wealth just as rapidly as Uncle Pietro claimed. All kinds of wealth; dozens of kinds that we can't even imagine yet.

How many sons of God are there?

Sigismundo could not sit still. Despite Pietro's instructions, he went to the *clavicembalo* and began improvising. He had too much energy; he could not think about these questions anymore. He began trying variations on "The Goldberg Variations" of J.S. Bach. He constructed new counterpoints, he returned to the original, he went back to variations again, then back to Bach. This J.S. Bach had indeed written the music Sigismundo longed for, the music of the human mind, above animal emotion, the music of the clear light. And yet it was music that delighted the animal soul, too, and reached down to the vegetative levels, too, because it included all three souls. More: It was groping toward the fourth soul.

He played on and on, adding more and more, making permutations on Bach's permutations. This was music for the *clavicembalo* only; to imagine it adapted for a string quartet, say, or even a trio of any kind, was to imagine a different beauty, not this special stark clear lucid unique loveliness. Old Bach, father of J. C. and C. P. E., must have been in ecstasy when he wrote this; he was seeing more of the naked essence of being than anybody but the greatest mathematicians.

Sigismundo was suddenly drained. He could play no more; he was exhausted.

Who was Adam the son of?

Sigismundo came out of his body again, as often happened with the best music. But this time was different: he was not outside the world itself, as in his previous ecstasies, not at all, he was emphatically still in this room. He seemed to be somewhere near the ceiling. He was looking down at himself, seated at the *clavicembalo*.

This is most amusing, he thought. I look like eleven dozen other Neapolitan youths: the same curly black hair, the same dark Mediterranean skin, the same Mephisto beard and mustache. I am stocky, but not fat. God, I look tired.

Am I really out of my body, or am I so excited that I am imagining things?

What is the purpose of life and consciousness?

He was back in his body and his chest hurt. He thought, in alarm, That's what killed Aunt Gina, the swelling of the heart.

The light was still with him. Everything in the room was shining, brilliant, incandescent. His eyes watered, not from emotion, but from something else. It is like looking into the sun, he thought. But I can't look away from it, the way you look away from the sun. This light is everywhere.

And the light was everywhere for the next three hours. He tried to escape it by taking a walk, but it was the same in the streets. The whole world had changed, as if the sun had become a thousand times brighter. The burning coal symbol of the *Carbonari*, he thought: this is what it means. His eyes were watering continually, but at least the pain in his chest was going away. He was happier than he had ever been. If the *Rossi* jumped out of a door—finally—and stabbed him, he would die with a smile.

By dinner time he was mostly back to normal, but his appetite was immense. Mama made a joke that he would get fat. Nobody seemed to notice that he was in a distinctly odd frame of mind.

Very provocative questions, he thought when he returned to his room.

Who was Adam the son of?
How many minds are there?

He didn't go out of his body again; he just became increasingly abstracted. The intensity of colors faded away; the world faded away. He might have been working on a mathematical problem.

After dark, when everybody else was asleep, he was sitting on the veranda, staring at the stars but hardly seeing them.

There might be minds out there asking the same questions, more or less.

That was why the Church had burned Giordano Bruno at the stake, in Roma in 1600: for saying there were other minds out there—minds like ours, and minds nothing like ours at all; minds of all sorts. Infinite minds. Bruno said the universe did not have a beginning or an end and that human beings were a very small part of it. If Bruno was right, there were minds everywhere in space. And the microscope had already shown there was a city, a whole kingdom, in any drop of water.

How many minds are there?
How many sons of God are there?

Sigismundo went to sleep in the swing chair, looking at the red glare of Sirius in the south and wondering if he was traveling to that star or only dreaming about it.

▲

From Maria Maldonado's journal:

Mother Ursula told me that anyone could learn to interpret dreams, just as Joseph did in the Bible. She says the whole art is in three steps: first, one must learn to remember one's dreams; second, by meditating on them, one can eventually understand them; and third, with this knowledge mastered, one can begin to interpret the dreams of others.

To remember one's dreams, Mother Ursula says, it is necessary to keep foolscap by one's bed and write down all that one remembers of the night's dreams the very first thing on awakening. She says that if one does this every day, one remembers more every day.

1, February 2: Last night, I dreamed that a snake got into the convent garden. Papa killed it.

* * *

5, March 3: The images of the Egyptian gods Isis and Osiris. Somebody talking about ghosts. I think: I must get out of this place before it is too late.

* * *

8, March 23: A boy has fallen into a well or pond. He is drowning. I want to save him, but then I realize this is very far away and I can't reach him in time. He has a starched white collar, and I am terrified to see him sinking. My brother Carlo dives in to try to save him.

* * *

17, March 31: Mother Ursula gives me a book. It is called *How to Find a Lost Cat*. Somehow I know that this book is very important. I open it, and the first chapter is called "North Gods Versus South Gods." Papa comes in and is most angry. He says girls should not read such books.

* * *

23, April 23: I am being condemned by the Inquisition for hoarding darts. I become terribly angry and indiscreet. I tell the judges that they have made themselves stupid by refusing to collect their own darts. I suddenly realize that what I am saying does not make sense.

* * *

56, May 7: Very strange. I dreamed of ants infesting my room. When I woke, there was a cloud formation over the sun, making a splotched pattern on the floor, just like the pattern made by the ants in my dream.

* * *

93, June 6: Papa is very worried. He tells me that there are no more snakes in any of the Italian states. I try to tell him that we do not need snakes and some of them are venomous anyway. He says that I do not understand. "It is the snakes that bring prosperity," he says.

I realize that this man is not Papa at all, but some sinister Black Magician who is impersonating Papa. I try to leave the room, but the door is locked. Suddenly, he grapples with me, attempting to tear my clothes off.

Somehow, I am outside in the garden. But the evil magician is pursuing me, so I try to find my way to the street. There is a black woman who offers to help me. She says her name is Fatima. We go to a place where a huge black dog keeps guard. The dog sits with tremendous dignity, and I have a feeling that he is not a dog at all but some pagan god in the form of a dog.

Fatima tells me, "You need never fear us. We are your Dark Companions." I realize that she is secretly in league with the evil magician.

Of course, it gets easier to read the meanings, just as Mother Ursula said. This dream means that Father wants to get me married off soon.

▲

Sigismundo Celine's initiation as a Speculative Freemason occurred on the night of July 23, 1768.

He had been puzzling over Uncle Pietro's questions for five

days and had gone through stages of ecstasy, irritation, bore-
dom, increased sensitivity, and sudden flashes of anger at the
whole mystifying business. If the Masons had something
important to teach, he thought in these moments of rebellion,
why not just teach it and be done? But he knew the answer.
From music, he had already discovered that some things simply
cannot be taught; they can only be learned.

On the evening of July 23, Sigismundo was in the living
room of Giancarlo Tennone, his fencing teacher, with Uncle
Pietro.

"The lodge meets in the garden," Uncle Pietro explained.
"You can probably guess why."

Sigismundo understood: Tennone's house had the traditional Mediterranean architecture, with four wings, each wing
being the side of a square. The garden formed the middle and
was therefore the furthest spot from any streets or neighboring
houses. It was the place most invulnerable to spies, especially if
each wing of the house had a lookout stationed to ensure that
no stranger approached uninvited.

Tennone stepped into the room from the garden. He was
wearing a lamb-skin apron with five Hebrew letters on it. Even
though Sigismundo's knowledge of the language was scant, he
could read that word. The letters were *yod he shin vau he*,
יהשוה —Yeshuah, or, in Greek, Jesus. Without the *shin*, it
was *yod he vau he*, JHVH or Jehovah. The *shin*, which
looked like a flame, ש , represented the descent of the Holy
Spirit of Jehovah into the flesh in the form of the man,
Jesus.

"Prepare the candidate," Tennone said in a tone that
conveyed no admission that he had known Sigismundo for
seven years.

Tennone quickly stepped back into the garden and closed
the door behind him.

"By now," Uncle Pietro said, "the questions I gave you have

turned into monstrous problems. I will now give you the answers. Read them quickly, because you will be summoned to the garden in only a few minutes." He went to Tennone's bookcase and removed the Holy Bible. With a solemn glance, he gave it to Sigismundo, who noticed at once that it had a parchment sticking out of it.

"Read the parchment and consult the Bible," Pietro said. "I will leave now. You will be called shortly."

He immediately exited into the garden, leaving Sigismundo wondering if the parchment might say, "This is the final joke. Beware the damnable books of philosophy along with those of Romance."

Sigismundo removed the parchment. It began:

Who was Adam the son of?
See Luke 3:38.
Does God have an opposite?
See Exodus 3:14 and Ephesians 4:4–6.

And so on. Oh, damn and blast, Sigismundo thought. Why didn't they just write in the texts, instead of forcing me to look each one up for myself? But the answer was clear. Hunting for each text under a time limit would increase his sense of urgency.

He turned to the first question and its answer. Luke would be near the back of the Bible, of course. He quickly found chapter 3, verse 38:

Which was the son of Enos, which was the son of Seth, which was the son of Adam, which was the son of God.

Sigismundo couldn't believe his eyes; he felt like Galileo seeing the blasphemous, unbelievable, non-Aristotelian spots on the sun. He scanned rapidly back through several verses. This was the genealogy of Jesus (whose name was on

Tennone's apron . . .). It began at verse 23, saying Jesus was
the son of Joseph and Joseph was the son of Heli which was the
son of Matthat and so on, David and Solomon and all, until
Enos, "which was the son of Seth, which was the son of Adam,
which was the son of God," in verse 38, from which he had
started.

But Adam was "the son of God" only metaphorically,
wasn't he? (But Vico said all thought was metaphor.) The text
did not seem to be speaking poetically; it repeated "which was
the son of" in what seemed to be a very literal sense each time
until it reached that astonishing conclusion. It seemed to be
saying that Adam was the son of God as literally as Joseph was
the son of Heli.

The Masons were indeed leading him into most extreme
heresies. The idea that Mohammed was literally the son of
God, and so was Confucius, and so were many others, could
easily follow once you accepted that Jesus was not the only
one, that Adam had been another.

Sigismundo quickly turned to the next question.

Does God have an opposite?
See Exodus 3:14 and Ephesians 4:4–6.

He turned the pages rapidly. Exodus 3:14 said:

> And God said unto Moses, I AM THAT I AM: and he said,
> Thus shalt thou say unto the children of Israel: I AM hath sent
> me unto you.

And Ephesians 4:4–16 was even more startling:

> There is one body, and one spirit, even as ye are called in
> one hope of your calling: one Lord, one faith, one baptism, one
> God and Father of all, who is above all, and through all, and in
> you all.

Sigismundo thought of God as I AM, as one body and one spirit, in all. Even in Peppino? Even in Caligula? This was pantheism, another doctrine for which Bruno had been condemned. Were the Masons secret followers of Bruno?

He rushed on to the next question.

How many sons of God are there?
See Romans 8:14–17.

Here we come to the heart of the heresy, he thought. But he looked up the text:

> For as many as are led by the Spirit of God, they are the sons of God; For ye have not received the spirit of bondage again to fear; but ye have received the Spirit of adoption, whereby we cry, Abba, Father. The Spirit beareth witness with our spirit, that we are the children of God: and if children, then heirs; heirs of God, and joint-heirs with Christ; if so be that we suffer with him, that we may also be glorified.

Everybody was a child of God—not just Adam and Jesus—and the Bible said so. Sigismundo had never heard that in Religious Knowledge class. He went on to the next question.

Are the sons of God also gods?
See John 10:34.

Sigismundo turned pages impatiently.

Jesus answered them, Is it not written in your law, I said, Ye are gods?

There it was in black and white.

Are any sons of God less than others?
See Colossians 3:4.

When Christ, who is our life, shall appear then shall ye appear with him in glory.

In other words, Sigismundo thought, when you can *see* Christ you *are* Christ. When your will becomes one with the Will of God, as Abraham said.

What is the goal of prophets and teachers?
See Ephesians 4:11–13.

And he gave some apostles, and some prophets, and some evangelists, and some pastors and teachers; For the perfecting of the saints, for the work of the ministry, for the edifying of the body of Christ: Till we all come in the unity of the faith, and of the knowledge of the Son of God, unto a perfect man, unto the measure of the stature of the fullness of Christ.

We are to be raised to *perfection*, Sigismundo thought. Just as the French atheists say. But here the Bible is saying it, too. He rushed on, turning pages rapidly.

How many minds are there?

He had thought: billions and billions, all over space. What he read did not contradict that, but gave a new perspective on it:

See Deuteronomy 4:39 and Exodus 3:14.

Know therefore this day, and consider it in thine heart, that the Lord he is God in heaven above and upon the earth beneath: there is none else.
And God said unto Moses: I AM THAT I AM . . .
Sigismundo rushed on.

What is a human being?
See Genesis 1:26.

And God said, Let us make man in our image, after our likeness.

Is mankind finished or in process?
See 1 John 3:2.

Beloved, now are we the sons of God, and it doth not appear what we shall be: but we know that when he shall appear, we shall be like him, for we shall see him as he is.

How much can we and should we attempt?
See John 14:12.

Verily, verily, I say unto you, He that believeth in me, the works that I do he shall do also; and greater works than these shall he do.

But that was the heresy of the *Alumbrados*: the doctrine that we could all perform the miracles of Christ if we were illuminated.

What is the purpose of life and consciousness?
See 2 Corinthians 9:8 and Luke 12:32.

And God is able to make all grace abound toward you; that ye, having always all sufficiency in all things, may abound to every good work.

Fear not, little flock; for it is your father's good pleasure to give you the kingdom.

And the last question, finally:

What is the next step?
See Romans 8:19.

This will be the knockout blow, Sigismundo thought, turning pages. The text leaped out at him:

> For the earnest expectation of the creature awaiteth the manifestation of the sons of God.

"*Pssst!*" Uncle Pietro whispered. "Come out now."

Beautifully timed, Sigismundo thought. They were watching to see when I finished.

He walked toward the garden with his mind in a whirl of confusion and excitement. They have me, he thought, in a state where any shock will be like great music or that moment of first walking into the Tempio Malatesta.

The whole garden had been transformed. A huge tent had been set up in the middle of it, there was a silver altar with a Bible in the east, the well in the west had been painted gold, and everybody was wearing those lamb-skin aprons and had blue garters on their thighs.

Abraham Orfali, in the Arabic robe, stood before the tent.

"Fellow soldiers," he said, "assist me. What is the first duty of a Master Mason?"

"To guard the camp," said Uncle Pietro, now also in Arabic garb. ("You have already joined the 'foul Mohammedans,'" Peppino had warned.)

"Let the camp be guarded," said old Abraham. Two strange men, in Arabic clothing, left the garden.

"Most Mysterious Master," Uncle Pietro said, "the camp is guarded."

"What is the second duty of a Master Mason?" Abraham demanded.

"To see that all present are true brothers," Uncle Pietro replied.

Sigismundo by now recognized Tennone in the gloom, and Father Ratti, and Robert Francis Drake with his blond hair, and (life is full of surprises) Count Maldonado. Others were merchants he had noticed at one time or another around town. A few were strangers.

"Are all true brothers?" Uncle Pietro demanded.

All raised their arms to make an L in the air, then moved them into a V, then crossed them in an X.

LVX: light, Sigismundo thought.

"How many officers has the camp?" Abraham asked.

"Three visible," Uncle Pietro replied.

"And eight invisible," Tennone stated.

Sigismundo felt a shiver. They're really giving me the full treatment, he thought: eight invisible?

"Who have you here?" old Abraham asked.

"The son of a widow lady, who has been drawn to our oasis and received the hospitality of our camp," Uncle Pietro said. "He is a seeker for the Grail."

"Halt!" Abraham cried. "Do you understand," he asked Sigismundo coldly, "that by entering our camp you have incurred the penalty of death?"

Sigismundo stared, unable to answer. The first time was a joke, he thought; the second time was a Horror; this time may make the second time look like another joke by comparison. They are magicians, like the *Rossi*; they also want to use me.

"Say yes," Uncle Pietro whispered.

"Yes," Sigismundo said, unconvinced.

Tennone, Count Maldonado, and Father Ratti suddenly surrounded Sigismundo and put daggers to his throat. He again recalled his experience with the *Rossi*.

"Do you consider the honor of enrolling yourself among us as a full compensation for this doom?" Abraham asked.

"Yes," Sigismundo said, bewildered.

The daggers were withdrawn. Sigismundo was led around the garden by Uncle Pietro. At each of the four corners —where the guardian angels would stand if Abraham were doing a healing; where the four demons would be if this were a *Rosso* ritual—a man in a lamb-skin apron stopped them. In a hostile tone, he demanded to know who Sigismundo was. "The son of a poor widow lady," Pietro answered each time.

This is Chapel Perilous, Sigismundo thought. I am in the role of Parsifal, the poor widow's son—but then the castration of Peppino would be the wound of Klingsor, and that wasn't part of a ritual. What did Abraham tell me about coincidences being part of the Path?

Sigismundo was returned to Abraham.

"In all cases of difficulty and danger, in whom do you put your trust?" Abraham demanded.

"In God," Sigismundo replied.

"Take him out," Abraham cried, with a great show of anger. "He is not one of us!"

Sigismundo was led back into the living room by Uncle Pietro, who did not appear at all friendly.

"A Freemason does not know more than one mind," Pietro explained impatiently. "You spoke as one still blinded by false dualism. You will never get out of Chapel Perilous or find the Grail that way. Go back in and give the right answer this time. You will not be given a second chance."

Sigismundo and Pietro returned to the garden. The whole ceremony started again from the beginning. "Fellow soldiers, assist me . . . Let the camp be guarded . . . Three visible and eight invisible . . . the son of a poor widow lady . . ."

"In cases of difficulty and danger, in whom do you put your trust?" Abraham demanded a second time.

There is one body, and one spirit . . .

"In my self," Sigismundo said.

"I am glad that your faith is so well founded," Abraham said.

'But I am bound to explain to you that it would have been better if you had never approached us. For this night you must surely die, and what will rise will not be you. Will you still persevere?"

"Yes."

"Repeat after me," Abraham said somberly. "I, Sigismundo Celine, a fool and a sinner . . ."

"I, Sigismundo Celine, a fool and a sinner . . ."

". . . in the presence of the powers of birth, visible and invisible . . ."

The oath went on and on. It seemed to contain many repetitions. Sigismundo began to fear that Dr. Orfali was putting him to sleep . . .

When the oath was finally finished, somebody in the garden began beating a drum softly. Another began playing the flute. Sigismundo recognized the tune as Scottish; then he recognized "The Boy Who Was Born to Be King,"—a lament for Bonnie Prince Charlie—or for every man who did not know how to use his powers?

Sigismundo was again taken on a tour of the north, east, south, and west. This was called "travels with the moon." At each quarter a man in a lamb-skin apron emblazoned JESUS said one sentence to him in turn:

"Learn to Know."

"Learn to Will."

"Learn to Dare."

"Learn to Keep Silence."

He was back at the tent, facing old Abraham, who now looked darker and more Arabic than ever. This whole ritual is doing something to my mind, he admitted to himself.

"Most Mysterious Master," Uncle Pietro said. "The candidate has fulfilled the travels with the moon."

"Prepare him for the ordeal of fire," Abraham said in a most sinister tone.

Sigismundo was suddenly seized and blindfolded. He was dragged around the garden again, but not in a regular path over the four quarters; this time he was deliberately being disoriented. Oh, Christ, he thought, the ordeal by fire. He hated that kind of pain, and it reminded him of the Dominican howling about eternal fire. How much would he be burned, and how severe was the ordeal in general?

Suddenly, he was loose; nobody was holding him. He had no idea where in the garden he was. Blindfolded and waiting in suspense, he did the relaxing breath, vowing to be brave. All was silent. The drum and flute had stopped. Nobody spoke.

The seconds passed like giant turtles lugubriously trekking across the sands toward the water.

"And the earth was without form and void," Abraham's voice said suddenly.

Sigismundo, in total blindness and anxiety, waited.

Nothing happened.

Nobody spoke.

Get it over with, he thought. Burn me and complete it; don't keep me sweating like this.

Several rocks hit him at once. They were thrown from nearby, with careful aim—he was not seriously hurt—but the slight pain of each rock, and the shock of the unexpected, made him jump and yell: an inarticulate shout, like a baby at birth, he thought.

Hands grabbed him, and he was lifted.

Oh, Jesus, Jesus, he thought.

He was dropped.

The whole world had ceased to make sense: he was falling further than seemed possible. CHAPEL PERILOUS: PRICE OF ADMISSION, YOUR MIND. He had been waiting for fire but instead was hit by rocks and now he was flying (it seemed) through space. Fire . . . earth (the rocks) . . . air . . .

Then he hit the water.

"*Mama mia*," he cried involuntarily, angry and frightened. This was becoming as much good clean fun as a public hanging.

He had landed on his knees and banged his head. He stood up carefully, still blindfolded, up to his belly in cold water. I am in the well, he reasoned. That is why they hold the ritual in the garden: so they can throw the poor fish in the well when he's waiting to get burned. *Fire and water are the same*, the alchemists said. It was one of their riddles; only another alchemist could understand. I am being put through a dramatization of that riddle, he told himself. After *negrito*, the Dark Night, comes the union of opposites . . .

"And God said: Let there be Light! And there was Light!" Abraham chanted ecstatically above him.

Sigismundo was in a different space again. He was far above the city looking down at Vesuvius and the bay. He was plunging toward the sun; then he *was* the sun—there was nothing at all but limitless light. He was an old man, going blind but still writing music—that was in Leipzig; but then he was coming up out of the water into Napoli again crying, emerging from his mother; then he was back in the camp again, but the old man was not Abraham Orfali, but Saladin; all this had happened long ago, during the Third Crusade; he was wearing the white tunic with the red cross on it that was the insignia of the Oriental Templars. Then he was in Philadelphia City, and a tall, redheaded man who spoke a peculiar English with a drawl in it was arguing that "unalienable rights" was more correct than "inalienable rights." Sigismundo could not keep track of all the new things that were happening. He would still fight a duel with Carlo Maldonado. He had crossed a desert. He was a woman giving birth. He was captain of a strange yellow ship that traveled *under* the water. He could step in and out of space and time whenever he wished.

Maybe I've gone as crazy as Antonio, he thought.

He was blindfolded at the bottom of a well, and these people he trusted were definitely doing things to his mind that he did not understand. Maybe they were all *Rossi*, too—in a conspiracy within a conspiracy. Maybe everybody had lied to him all his life. Maybe he was being possessed by demons. Maybe this was the fulfillment of Peppino's prophecy that he would join the *Rossi* of his own free will. Maybe he had never been released by the *Rossi* but was still in their cave, hallucinating. Maybe the last four years were all hallucination.

Then he was being raised out of the well by several hands. He almost seemed to be floating.

"And on the third day," Abraham intoned in the darkness, "he rose again."

Sigismundo, wet and dripping, was set on his feet.

"See the face of the eternal God," Uncle Pietro whispered.

The blindfold was whipped off. Sigismundo was staring at a young man's face that stared back at him with a look of total astonishment: the perfect fool who understood nothing. Then the eyes (his eyes) became less astonished and laughed, as he realized they were holding a mirror in front of his face.

He looked about, not sure if he were in eighteenth-century Napoli or eleventh-century Jerusalem.

"Were you afraid?" the old man—Abraham or Saladin, whoever—was asking him.

"Yes."

"That is the first lesson of wisdom," Abraham said, still looking like Saladin in his Arabic robe. "Always remember this, I implore you: All men are savage beasts and will kill each other promiscuously if the goal of True Brotherhood is not attained."

Sigismundo was led back into the living room. Tennone, without speaking, gave him a pure white robe. Sigismundo got out of his wet clothes, thinking he had been Osiris as well as Parsifal and Jesus in this ritual, wondering how his mind had created that pure blinding white light, thoroughly shaken in body and spirit. When he had donned his robe of white, Tennone led him back to the garden. They approached the tent.

"The Lord Saladin will now address you," Uncle Pietro said.

Abraham came forward and put a hand on Sigismundo's shoulder, looking deeply into his eyes.

"During this initiation, which is only a first initiation," he said, "you have been exposed to many terrors and discomforts. You were alone. You were completely helpless to defend yourself if we had been inclined to malice or evil. Remember this every day of your life, I pray you. Hold it in your heart whenever you encounter any human being in nakedness, rags, poverty, danger, illness. For the widow's son, whose death you have partially relived, whose rebirth you have partially understood, remember when you were alone and frightened and helpless. Give freely, as we give freely to you. You are now a True Brother and a Free Man. You will become more, more than you can imagine. Now, whence comes all light?"

"From the sun," Sigismundo ventured.

"What is the center around which all planets revolve?"

"The sun."

"You speak with understanding," Abraham said. "But such understanding comes only from reason and imagination. To the unaided eye, the earth seems to be the center. Men learned the truth only slowly, and some who understood the truth before others were ready for it were killed or persecuted. Know, Dare, Will, and Keep Silence. Think about that many days.

"I must tell you that you have not found the center of your self yet. You have, if you were lucky, seen a few rays of the light this evening. The truth of the mind is no more visible to ordinary sense than the truth of astronomy. The self that you know is like the earth: it only seems to be the center. The Inner Light, which you may have seen somewhat in this ceremony, is the true center, as the sun is the true center in astronomy. To find the inner sun or fourth soul or Holy Grail is the aim of Speculative Masonry. Beyond that, there are further secrets of power, which you may some day attain if you persevere and reach the inner order of the Sanctuary of the Gnosis, FRC.

"Look at these tools," Abraham said abruptly, producing a compass and a triangle from his robes. "By using these instruments, we have already learned many secrets of the universe. By using them properly, you may learn some of the secrets of the inner universe. Take them, keep them, contemplate them.

"Now kneel," Abraham said. "You have been Raised and now you must be Accepted."

Sigismundo knelt.

"Take him out," Abraham screamed. "He is not ready to be one of us!"

Uncle Pietro led Sigismundo back to the living room again.

"You don't kneel," Pietro said impatiently. "You answer, 'A Freemason kneels to no man.' Damn it, I thought you were ready to understand."

The humiliation was deliberate, to ensure that Sigismundo would remember. He understood that, but he was still mortified.

They returned to the garden.

"Now kneel," Abraham said.

"A Freemason kneels to no man," Sigismundo recited.

Abraham took his hand and arranged their fingers into the grip, thumb-nails interlocking.

"This is the sign of True Brotherhood," he said, staring into Sigismundo's eyes passionately. "You are now an accepted Mason."

Sigismundo was led around the garden again, sharing the grip with everybody.

"It is in my heart to tell you the legend of that grip,"

Abraham said. "I do not assert that this legend is true, but that it has long been believed by the wisest of our order. All men who have joined hands that way, it is said, are true brothers, for if one man anywhere in the chain deals unfairly or treacherously with any other man anywhere in the chain, then all the men in the chain will surely die that day. I say not that this legend is true, but ponder it. If this trust be broken, we are not Free Men and True Brothers but mere beasts again only."

Abraham stepped back.

"This session of the Temple of the East is now closed," Uncle Pietro shouted.

Somebody pounded on the stones three times, then five times, then three times.

Everybody began informally filing into the living room.

"Now we have a meal," Uncle Pietro said, unbending and becoming himself again.

A banquet table had been set. There was a white tablecloth with a gold trim; the wall behind it bore a white tapestry with a gold design of an eye in a triangle. Abraham took the head of the table.

"Why is it necessary to eat?" he asked, ritualistically.

"To replenish our bodies," Tennone said.

"To what end?"

"To carry on the Great Work," Tennone replied.

There was no more ritual after that. Malatesta and Celine muscatel was served with an antipasto of cheeses and cold meats and peppers.

As soon as Sigismundo got home, he carefully found the family Bible in the hall and took it to his room. He checked every reference the Masons had given him; they were all there. The Masons had not printed up a special edition with their own heresies inserted. The Bible was simply a book he had never understood before.

He took out the compass and triangle and looked at them.

Dimly, all the pieces began to fit together, and he understood part of what it means to be a Freemason.

▲

From Sir John Babcock's journal:

Back in Paris again and still terribly depressed about Father' death.

Thank God that I could be with him at his last moments Strange how his final words haunt me: "The same bleeding nonsense all over again." I can't imagine what he meant, but a the time I had a most eerie feeling, as if the reincarnation idea were true after all and Father was looking straight at his next life It would be like him to decide it was "the same bleeding nonsense."

He knew. I know he knew. When he asked where Peter Hammersmith and I had been after Heidelberg and I said, "The Greek Isles," he nodded and looked at me most peculiarly. Yet before God, I believe there was no contempt in that expression; it was just curiosity, wonderment. I think he suspected for years. A man who travels as much as I do and never marries eventually arouses that suspicion in those who know the ways of the world.

When I remember my anxieties nine years ago, at Eton, I am almost amused. Now, I know the rules: I know exactly what will happen if I am ever discovered. Certain doors to certain positions of power will close forever; certain men will never invite me to their homes again. But that will be all. Our class does have a sense of union, and the lower orders are not allowed to hear about such things when one of us is involved.

Still, now that I am Sir John Babcock, every door is open—if I evade discovery, and that is not difficult if one is careful.

(Sir John Babcock: every time I sign a cheque or a letter I feel guilty. It is as if I were responsible for Father's death. I wish I could drop the damned "Sir" entirely, but, of course, that would be too much of an eccentricity for the career I have in mind—if I ever recover from this depression.)

I will go to the Maison Noir tonight; they are said to have

several new boys fresh from the country. That will cheer me up, even if I still hear that dying voice saying, "The same bleeding nonsense all over again."

It is not just my Platonic proclivities. All men face this abyss once a year or more. Loneliness is the tax we pay to nature for being conscious enough to know our own mortality.

▲

From Sigismundo Celine's journal:

One year ago, in 1768, shortly after I became an accepted Mason, there were massive arrests of *Rossi* in Roma, and then, a few months later, in Napoli and Palermo. I heard some true tales of horror about how these fanatics reacted to Inquisitorial interrogation: one actually bit his tongue in two when he was on the point of confessing. Other tales were even worse. Over six hundred men were executed or sent to the galleys when it was all over; I dared to hope that the power of the *Rossi* was broken.

I should have known better: there was no violet-eyed Balsamo among those arrested.

Then, a few months ago, in the spring, a rich lady in Turin was robbed of jewels worth half a million florins at least. Somehow, the notorious *Verità*—a publication that comes out of Parma once a month and is always in danger of being suppressed—got the inside details of the story. It seems that the thief did not break into the house but was invited in. He was, in fact, the lady's lover. He had spent six days with her, while her husband was away on business, and then snatched the jewels one night while she was sleeping.

The power is with me more often these days: I had an immediate premonition when I read that.

Sure enough, today the Napoli police posted pictures of the suspect (there are probably similar drawings hanging on walls all over Italy), and even though it is a pen-and-ink sketch and the violet eyes look black, there is no mistaking that face. I remember those eyes peering at me through a black hood when he said, "Brother, you were born under stars that make you one of us."

I suspect that he will go to France, where the best "fences" are. Even if he realizes only a quarter of a million florins on the jewels, he will be rich enough to pass himself off as a count, if that be his pleasure.

Whatever he does, I have a conviction that we will meet again

He resembles our father more than I do; he has learned from the *strege* as well as the *Rossi*. He will be formidable.

I have learned a great deal from old Abraham and from the "club." I will be formidable, too.

I damned well better be.

▲

When Maria Maldonado returned to Napoli in the summer of 1769, she found that an Englishman named Sir John Babcock was staying as a guest of her father's. It had something to do with business, she was told—Babcock was a cousin of the Greystokes, who were almost as important in England as the Maldonados were in Southern Italy.

She very quickly surmised that more than commerce was afoot.

Maria, at eighteen and a half, realized that most girls her age had been married off already. Papa had delayed so long, she knew, only because he approved of the kind of education she was receiving from Mother Ursula. Papa had said once that a stupid wife was the worst misfortune that could befall a man and that a society that expected women to be ignorant was not in all respects rational itself.

So Sir John Babcock was the first candidate being presented to her. There was no great pressure, and nothing overt was said—Papa was not that old-fashioned—but she understood: if Sir John were to be rejected clearly by her, another candidate would be around very soon. Her time had come.

Sir John seemed to be about twenty-five or so, maybe a bit younger than that, and was quite handsome in an English way, once you got used to the fact that his skin always seemed pale and wan. But the English were all like that, and, besides, Sir

John had black hair and dark eyes, so he didn't seem as extremely pallid as all those blond Englishmen she had seen around Capodimonte. He was tall by Italian standards—almost five feet nine inches—and he spoke Italian perfectly.

The courtship began in the ritual form. Everybody left the living room one evening, almost on cue—except Aunt Bianca. Sir John and Maria were "alone," more or less—as much "alone" as was considered decent.

Sir John did not fidget or look uncomfortable, thank the Lord. He asked what she had studied in school.

Maria described the curriculum Mother Ursula had devised for her girls.

Sir John was impressed. "Conic sections," he repeated. "A most progressive woman, this abbess of yours."

Maria asked about his studies.

"I've been at Oxford and Heidelberg," he said casually. "And wandered here and there, studying a bit of this and a bit of that. Political history mostly."

"Political history?" Maria asked. Then she said boldly, "I always find that depressing."

Sir John looked at her with interest. "It *is* depressing on the surface," he said. "But if you looked deeper, you might actually find it inspirational. It is not just wars and treacheries and great atrocities, you know. It is also the story of mankind's collective search for justice. A blind search, full of frustrations and tragedies, but a search that always starts over again after every seeming defeat."

Maria, having been bold for a girl, decided to be bolder. If Sir John could not stand an intelligent woman, so much the worse for him. "That search may never come to an end, within history," she said. "We may have to look outside history for true inspiration."

"Outside history?" Sir John asked. "Do you mean outside time?"

"Perhaps. Outside the world of ordinary experience certainly."

Aunt Bianca frowned. This was no way to attract a man.

Sir John, for all his seeming self-assurance, seemed to think the frown was directed at him. He looked about vaguely, and his glance lighted upon the *clavicembalo*.

"Do you play?" he asked politely.

"A bit," Maria answered. This was more ritual; any educated girl was expected to play a musical instrument.

"I would be most delighted," Sir John said, "if you could, ah, favor me with a sample of your art."

Maria moved to the instrument and seated herself, erect, not slouching, just as she had been taught. "I hope you will like this," she said, continuing the ritual by lowering her eyes modestly.

She played Vivaldi's "Winter Winds" theme from *The Four Seasons*.

Sir John leaned forward, listening intently.

"My word," he said when she finished. "That was exceptionally well played. My compliments, Signorina Maldonado. Do you think that music came from beyond history and ordinary perception, perchance?"

"Yes," Maria said. "Where else?"

"And yet it was manifested within history and ordinary perception," Sir John said with a chess player's smile. "Cannot other things from higher realms also be manifested here, then? Even in politics?"

"*Touché*," Maria laughed.

He talked a while, then, describing how Napoli seemed to him—a place of extraordinary beauty, full of noise and bustle and excitement, but always a little bit mysterious and incomprehensible. "England would seem like that to you, of course," he concluded. "If you ever came there, that is."

The first hint.

Aunt Bianca coughed.

"Would you be so good as to show me about the garden?" Sir John asked.

"I would be delighted," Maria replied.

They walked among the flowers, beneath a full moon, with Aunt Bianca exactly ten steps behind, so she could watch but they could pretend (or hope) that she did not also hear.

"What music do you like best?" Sir John asked.

"The German *wunderkind*. Wolfgang Amadeo Mozart."

"Ah," Sir John said. "My own favorite. He has changed his middle name to Amadeus lately, for some reason I fail to comprehend. I had thought the fad of Latinizing one's name went out two centuries ago. But isn't it incredible what he has written? He is only fourteen."

"I am only eighteen, sir."

"Oh, ah, yes, I didn't mean—"

Maria laughed. "I was teasing."

Sir John smiled. "You are doing very well," he said softly. "I appreciate that this whole situation is a bit awkward for you. Your father has told me you have never been courted before."

Ah, he admitted he was courting.

"You are doing well yourself," Maria said.

"Listen," Sir John said. "Suppose we both jump dear old Aunt Bianca and stuff her in the potting shed or some such convenient place. Then we could be alone and decide what we really think of each other."

"Most marvelous," Maria said. "Then my reputation would be ruined in the morning, and you would have to marry me, or else one of my brothers would have the melancholy duty of shooting you dead. Carlo is the best pistol shot in Napoli, I must warn you."

"Splendid," Sir John said. "It sounds like a most adventurous opportunity. It would be exciting to wake in the morning knowing that I must choose between death and marriage."

"Are all Englishmen as mad as you?"

"Only a few. But it is the national tradition to be at least eccentric. My father was a most righteous and dignified personage, a judge in fact, yet he was seldom sober after twilight."

They walked in silence for a few moments.

"Seriously," Sir John said, "if it is agreeable to you, *signorina*, I would enjoy seeing a great deal more of you, and if you can bear my presence for a few weeks, we can then discuss how much more of me you could find likable and the obvious purpose of my attendance upon you."

"Yes," Maria said. "I would enjoy walking and talking with you on other occasions."

Aunt Bianca coughed again. Maria and Sir John had had as much "private" conversation as was considered proper at that stage.

When Maria returned to her room, she was both excited and bewildered. She had observed men looking at her lustfully at times; she knew that she would marry eventually; there was the constant annoyance of the demented Celine fellow, staring at her like a saint seeing a vision of the Virgin; but all of that was suddenly much more real than before.

She knew that the idea of being in love was exciting—the novels all said it was better than finding gold, better than flying to the stars like an angel—but it was not just novelistic romance that was making her feel this way. It was that special pleasure, the most secret of all pleasure, the pleasure that was so strictly forbidden and could get you into all sorts of trouble before you were married and was then, all at once, no longer forbidden the *very moment* you were married. Some of the girls at the convent school had experimented with that pleasure, upon themselves or upon one another, but Maria had been afraid to attempt such experiments because of the power in her hands, the power to heal. She was worried that any sin could do something terrible to the power, turn it in a dark direction, send her hurtling toward the abyss of witchcraft. After all, there were only two types of people who had that power: the saints and the *strege*. You could easily cross the line, become a saint or a *strega*, without even realizing you had gained or lost your soul itself.

And yet, although the thought was sinful, she could not stop thinking what it would be like to be married to Sir John and to have sexual intercourse with him. It was like a forest fire, she knew, and not just in novels. People in real life did all kinds of wild, crazy, even violent things once they had been initiated into that secret ecstasy. Some rich men had so many mistresses —despite the Church's prohibitions—that it was obvious they lived chiefly for sexual pleasure; it was to them what God was to the saints. And there were even women, and not a few women either, who committed adultery, who had lovers because they had grown bored with their husbands or had never liked their husbands in the first place. Sometimes a whole town would know about such affairs before the husband himself learned. Sometimes murder would result; and then, if the wife's family was the richer of the two, the husband would be hanged, or if the husband's family was richer, the judges would decide that the evidence was inconclusive, and they would set him free. There were always a few known murderers like that in Napoli and in other cities. Sometimes, such a man would die mysteriously, and there would be rumors of the wife's family having taken revenge with unknown and undetectable poisons such as the Borgias had supposedly used.

There was nothing else in the world—except money—that caused so many violent passions. That was why the Church said it was "an occasion of sin" to even think about it.

And yet when you were married, it was not a sin anymore.

What would sexual intercourse be like with an Englishman? With Sir John specifically?

Everybody said Italians made the best lovers; but nobody anywhere, in history or in legend, had ever said they made the best husbands.

If she married Sir John, if that seemed like the wise choice she would always be faithful to him. That was virtue, and besides Maria detested sneaking and lying. But it would be strange to have grown up in Italy and never to have sexual intercourse with anyone but an Englishman.

One thing was certain: Sir John was not an ordinary man. When he spoke of justice as something that kept trying to manifest itself within history, he was speaking of his deepest beliefs; you could tell that from his tone. The heroes of novels always had high ideals like that. And they were sensitive and a bit secretive about some guilty secret hidden in their past; but the guilt was not really something *terrible*, and the heroines always loved them in spite of it.

Maria wondered if Sir John had some guilty secret. A man who spoke so passionately of justice had probably experienced injustice. Well, anyway, she decided, he's not as absurd as that clownish Celine fellow.

But when Maria finally went to sleep that night, she had a dream in which a man was having sexual intercourse with her, and it didn't hurt at all, even though it was the first time, he was very delicate, and it was quite lovely, almost like the nuns singing "Ave Maria" at Mass; and then she saw that the man was that horrible Sigismundo Celine, and she woke up, knowing that it was more than a dream, that it had happened to her in her sleep.

▲

Two nights later, Papa took Maria and Sir John to the Teatro San Carlo, to hear a new performance "by our most controversial local musician," as he said. Maria did not want to go to a performance by that mad Celine, *ick*!, but she could not think of any excuse to get out of it. One couldn't tell one's father about something as silly as the yearning stare with which

Celine haunted her days, or something as intimate as the fact that Celine had now invaded her nights and *intercoursed* her in her sleep.

Sir John was most curious when Count Maldonado told him about the mixed reception Celine's music had received thus far. Frankly, Sir John was all for innovation and eccentricity in art. Most of it was trash, of course, but it was a challenge to the audience, because great works always seemed intentionally irritating at first, before people got accustomed to them.

The concert began conservatively enough. Sigismundo Celine, who looked as if he might still be a year or so shy of twenty, played pieces by Vivaldi, Scarlatti, and somebody named J. S. Bach. He played well, except for a tendency toward overemphasis, as if he was forcing more emotion than was appropriate to the music. At the intermission, nobody was either greatly disturbed or greatly impressed; the main question discussed was whether this J. S. Bach was a brother or a cousin of the famous J. C. and C. P. E. Bach.

When the audience returned, Sigismundo announced a new composition by himself, which he called Sonata 23, "Fire and Water."

As Sigismundo began, nobody in the theater had any doubt that the opening bars were the fire theme. Sir John recognized that the structure, a permutation of triplets, seemed to be going forward and backward at the same time; then he realized that there were actually two structures involved, that the "fire" was itself a conflict of inner tensions, as if a man might feel himself drawn to the divine and the diabolical with equal force in both directions, so that in the music, as in such a man, combustion was a symptom of explosion, of some inner fission or earthquake of the soul. This was hardly music; it was Job's complaint. Judging from a few murmurs elsewhere in the audience, some people thought it was not beyond music but *beneath* music, some species of barbarism or deliberate insult.

But the second movement, arriving so abruptly that the laws of harmonic development seemed to have been stupidly or brutally violated, was a series of *arpeggii* so tranquil, so humorous, so limpid that it was not just an answer in the traditional argument structure of the sonata, but a leap to another level of discourse: this watery progression did not deny the fire, but merely reflected it; and—Sir John thought, absorbed—it reflected like light itself, like one of the incandescent thrones of Dante's *Paradiso*. Then, somehow, Celine had found his way from this celestial or "brilliant" opening to something that was suspiciously like Neapolitan *bel canto* —which seemed, Sir John realized, as if it might be one of the two-in-one fire themes permuted in conscious self-mockery. But the resolution, the last part of the second movement, was a structure of both fire and water, passionate *staccati* and languid *legati*, as if Celine were trying to leap beyond the limits of both music and logic, affirming and bitterly grieving at once.

Somebody laughed rudely, and a voice said, "He's willfully being annoying."

"Ranting and raving," another voice said.

Sir John, however, was remembering his first initiation, at the Scotch Rite Temple in London. *"Fire and water are one"*: this composition was not merely a joke at the expense of musical decorum but a very private in-joke for fellow Masons. It was like writing a book that only one reader in a thousand could understand.

The third movement did not combine fire and water—that possible denouement having arrived unexpectedly as the climax of the second movement—but consisted of variations on water, repeating all the watery themes in new ways that seemed extraordinary. There were gasps of delight in several parts of the audience—this movement at least was winning over many—but then Sir John noticed that each variation was progressively a little more pathetic than the last, until a

definitely dirgelike quality had come into a theme that had
seemed at first as wild as a *tarantella*. The water was becoming
a watery grave; the mood plunged down, down, further down,
to melancholy and doom. (Sir John thought of poor Geoffrey,
years ago at Eton, but he also recognized several parodies of
death *arie* from popular operas in there.) But then, by some
miracle of logic turned on its head, the most melancholy bar of
this pathetic theme repeated itself and then repeated again with
only a slight variation, and then it was back again with a
(seemingly) equally slight variation, except that now it was part
of the fire theme that had been hidden in the water theme all
along—a masterpiece of disguise, Sir John thought. This was
very humorous music indeed, ridiculing itself every step of the
way, and yet it also sadly confessed all the emotions it parodied.
And now, as the melancholy death by water and ecstatically
bizarre death by fire joined in the climax that was both
necessary and absurdly unexpected, they became united in a
triumphant and definitely drunken-sounding caper off into
various traditional forms of resolution until (logically but
incredibly) arriving at the opening theme played once and
hanging there: a conclusion that was not recognized as such by
most of the audience for nearly ten seconds before the wild
applause, and the angry boos, began.

Sigismundo Celine bowed, somewhat sardonically. He is
determined, Sir John thought, to accept the boos as well as the
applause, as homages to his originality. Or else he has steeled
himself to such a reception and is putting on a damned good
mask of indifference.

Sigismundo returned to the harpsichord.

"Now," he announced, "to finish the evening, I will play
something less conservative." (Cheeky bastard, Sir John
thought.) "This is my Sonata 56, which I call also 'The Two
Nations.'"

Such clashing and crashing about had never been heard

before in the Teatro San Carlo and would not be heard again
for fifty years. "He thinks the *clavicembalo* is a percussion
instrument," somebody muttered angrily near Sir John.

But out of this cacophony a theme surprisingly emerged: it
had been implicit all along, hidden among the howling
discords. It was a waltz theme, suitable for a state ball in any
palace in Europe; Sir John could almost see exquisitely gowned
ladies and periwigged gentlemen dancing to this sensuous
legato. Then the roaring and clashing began to return: it was
like a mob of peasants storming the palace. No; as Sir John
listened, it seemed more like goblins and clowns. The waltz
struggled onward, seeking to reassert itself, but each sensual
galant upsurge led, by perverse artistry, back into one of the
weird, angry sounds of the invasion. It was no longer quite
clear to Sir John whether the invaders were revolutionaries, as
he had imagined at first, or mischievous wood sprites, as it later
seemed, or some barbaric tribe from the outskirts of civiliza-
tion, reanimated Vikings gone berserk.

The structure of this musical conflict, Sir John realized, was
densely packed: it made each minute seem longer and larger
than a more orthodox structure would. A feeling of giganticism
began to emerge, a sense of cyclopean or titanic figures, not
threatening the waltzers, but merely towering above them,
indifferent, moving on some mission of their own that mortals
could not understand. But the waltz itself was being magnified
in the course of this musical "argument": the waltzers were not
merely people, they themselves were growing to the stature of
gods. Was it mere repetition—a redundance that a more
polished, or more traditional, composer would have avoided as
clumsy—or was it some subtle variation that the ordinary ear
could not catch? Somehow, by whatever means, Celine was
turning the innocent dance theme into a force stronger than
the threatening invasion theme.

And out of this a sunny Neapolitan song gradually revealed itself: it was, in fact, the invasion theme with the bombast and heroism removed. Celine was revealing that all that had been heard was a set of variations implicit in the real theme, and it was a theme that all ears could recognize as normal and quite lovely. Except that now, with these inner tensions having been explored, this ordinary Neapolitan melody sounded like an evasion or an apology. The conclusion was not a concession to contemporary taste but a mocking joke at the expense of such taste. It ended with trills so lovely that only those who had listened very closely could realize they were hearing melodic satire.

The applause this time was louder and more passionate; so were the boos and catcalls.

Sigismundo bowed again, with great dignity, and left the stage with a haughty and arrogant stride, as if he had not heard the boos. The effect was slightly spoiled when his eye caught Maria in the Maldonado box and he fell over his feet, landing on his backside.

Returning home, Count Maldonado discreetly acquired a companion—an old man named Pietro Malatesta, uncle of the Celine fellow—and the two of them dropped back several paces. Maria and Sir John were being allowed their second interlude of (comparative) privacy.

"I think this evening was most provocative," Sir John ventured. "When he grows a bit and loses the desire to be merely astonishing, this Celine will have quite a future, I would say."

"He will be another Casanova, I think," Maria said, with an emotion Sir John did not understand at first. "With such a character, he will abandon music eventually to become a mere adventurer."

"I hope not," Sir John said thoughtfully. "I found it all more entertaining than annoying, myself. As if he had taken us into his workshop and shown the struggle out of which the music emerged. Most extraordinary."

"He is an obsessed fellow," Maria said angrily. "He once almost killed my brother Carlo in a silly quarrel. There is more *fire* than *water* in him."

"Well, as for that," Sir John said, "I wouldn't know. I am commenting only on his music."

"He is a madcap, a harlequin."

"Perhaps," Sir John said, "he should come to England. Nobody would notice him there, since we are all mad, as you have noticed."

Maria smiled finally. "You are droll."

"And you do not really dislike this Celine," Sir John said calmly. "I think you are attracted to him and do not know why. That is what makes you angry."

"Do not talk like that in Napoli," Maria whispered urgently. "People will think you are a witch."

"Ah," he said. "You are beginning to worry about my welfare. That is a promising sign."

But later Maria realized that she had not denied what he said about her attraction to that obsessed Celine. And she knew that in some sense he was almost correct: she still remembered the dream, which was more than a dream, in which Celine had taken her psychological, if not her physical, virginity.

▲

That week there was a meeting, at Giancarlo Tennone's villa, of the Order of the Oriental Temple, Free and Accepted Masons. Present as an honored guest was Sir John Babcock, a member of the Scotch Rite Freemasons in England.

Sir John, having decided that the "Fire and Water" sonata was a Masonic initiation set to music, was not surprised to see Sigismundo Celine among the Neapolitan Freemasons. He

vas a bit startled, however, by the inadvertent hostility in
Sigismundo's glance, which was not quite successfully hidden
by a pretense of cordiality. Of course, Sir John thought, he has
seen me with Maria and is jealous; he must have courted her
unsuccessfully once, or tried to.

After the usual preliminaries, everybody adjourned to
Tennone's dining room for antipasto and abundant wine.

Pietro Malatesta began by discussing the reforms of the
Empress Catherine in Russia.

"Everybody says she is a whore," the other Englishman
present, Robert Francis Drake, commented.

"People always spread such scandal about a strong-minded
woman," Pietro said. "The fact is that Russia has had religious
freedom for almost three years now. I very much fear that we
can no longer consider Russia the most backward nation on
earth. Would anybody care to guess which *is* the most
backward?"

An elderly priest, who was named Ratti, if Sir John had
caught that correctly, spoke up. "I know where you are leading
us, Brother Pietro. Another expedition to Roma to argue for
relaxation of the Inquisition, no?"

"Not at all," Pietro Malatesta said. "We have tried that often
enough. I think it is time that we become braver. I suggest an
expedition to the Holy Father to argue for total abolition of the
Inquisition."

"Excellent," Giancarlo Tennone said. "And next let us
build a ladder to the moon and teach our donkeys to fly."

"It has already happened in Tuscany and Parma," Pietro
said stubbornly. "It is possible."

"Tuscany and Parma are not Napoli," Father Ratti said. "I
am willing to join in this effort, because only by such repeated
attempts will we achieve our goals, but I am not optimistic.
Right now, as you must know, our new Pope, Clement XIV, is
being beseiged by cardinals who wish to *strengthen* the

Inquisition. They also want to abolish the Jesuits," he added darkly.

"I say," Sir John interjected, "why is there so much prejudice against the Society of Jesus in Catholic countries lately?"

"There has been aroused a suspicion," Father Ratti said briefly, "that many of us are Freemasons. Perish the thought."

"You see, Brother John," Pietro Malatesta commented, "in Parma, they not only abolished the Inquisition but also expelled the Jesuits. That may sound paradoxical, but it is simply rising anticlericalism in the North. The duke of Parma does not like either Dominican conservatives or Jesuit liberals. He wants priests out of politics completely."

"In this climate of conflict," Sigismundo Celine said, "the new Pope may move in any direction. I say Uncle Pietro is right. We have nothing to lose by petitioning for abolition of the Inquisition."

The matter was put to a vote. It was decided that Father Ratti, Count Maldonado, and five others would go to Roma to speak to the Pope personally.

The next issue was raised by Giancarlo Tennone. It had been a long time since anybody had seen the *Carbonari*, he said; perhaps worry about the Inquisition had made us all too cautious.

"You are, as always, subtle as a rhinoceros," Robert Francis Drake said. "Who is it this time?"

Tennone told of a fisherman recently lost at sea. "His wife, she does the best she can, but there are many children . . ."

Pietro Malatesta took a coin bag from his cloak and emptied half of it on the table. In a few minutes, everybody had followed suit, and a stack of lire was being passed to Tennone.

"I haven't been out in blackface for a long time," he said. "It will be fun."

"For the widow's son," Count Maldonado said solemnly.

"For the widow's son," all chorused.

Sigismundo blushed, thinking of his wrong guess (during his first initiation) that the widow's son was Parsifal. Now that he knew the answer it seemed that he should have guessed long ago; it was in the Bible after all.

Robert Francis Drake then took the floor. There were always wild rumors about the Masons, he said, and it must be so—"as long as we must act in secrecy, as long as Europe is an armed madhouse." Nonetheless, one rumor was more and more prevalent, because there was occasional truth in it. "In some places," he said, "sodomites have formed Masonic lodges as a cover for their, um, er, real purpose in getting together, and when such things are discovered, all Masonry receives the same brand."

"What are you proposing?" Father Ratti asked.

"'Grand Inspector General' is virtually an honorary title these days," Drake said. "I think it should be more than honorary. We should uncover such lodges, before the outer world does, and expel them to avoid the scandal that ensues if they are uncovered by others."

"That sounds like a good idea on the surface," Pietro Malatesta said, "but I do not like the implications. We are an odd bunch of birds, if you ask me, to propose in one breath that the Church end its Inquisition and then, in the next breath, to start an inquisition of our own."

Old Abraham Orfali spoke up. "Spies we do not need. Better we have a hundred sodomites than one spy."

"Exactly," Sir John Babcock said. "Sodomy is a dreadful and revolting vice, but when men are asked to inform on each other, malice comes to the surface, false charges are made, and we end up with our own inquisition, as Brother Pietro said."

"Well," Tennone said, "I think we have exhausted the

subject of sodomy for a while. Anybody want to pursue it further? I thought not. Brother Babcock, as an honored visitor what can you tell this lodge about the working of the Craft in your own country?"

Sir John said, "I believe some of you know of John Wilkes?"

"He was in Napoli a while back," Pietro Malatesta said. "A great wit and raconteur and a brother in the Craft. Some of our brothers, however, do not understand the full ramifications of his case, so you had better explain."

"John Wilkes," Babcock said, "has been expelled from parliament three times now—"

"He had been expelled only twice when I was in England," Sigismundo Celine said.

"He was declared an outlaw after the second expulsion," Babcock explained. "This year, he finally returned and risked imprisonment. The king's party was quick to oblige him, and he is still in gaol tonight. Meanwhile, the voters have elected him to parliament again—even while he sits in prison—and parliament has expelled him again."

"What are the issues involved?" Tennone asked.

"The original issue was freedom of the press," Babcock said. "Wilkes was expelled the first time for publishing a criticism of the king that was deemed libelous by a judge of the king's party. But after the expulsion, the issue became the right of the voters to be represented by the man they chose. Seventeen counties have petitioned the king to let Wilkes sit in parliament, where the voters want him. The king turns a deaf ear. We of the Craft have formed an organization, the Society of Supporters of the Bill of Rights. Our original intent was merely to agitate for the legal return of Wilkes to parliament, but once we started our ball rolling we found many allies from odd quarters. The Society of Supporters has become more radical than we planned. It has demanded that the whole parliament be dissolved, as not representing the people, and a new parliament be elected to replace it. It has also demanded universal adult suffrage."

"You mean," Count Maldonado asked, "that every adult could vote? Even the peasants?"

"Exactly. *Everybody*—well, except the women. That will probably be the next demand. We are moving rapidly toward a new age."

"The world is on fire," Sigismundo Celine said quietly.

▲

A similar meeting was held later that week in Bordeaux, France, but the ideas of those present were somewhat different from those of the Neapolitan lodge.

Louis Philippe, duke of Chartres, representing the Social Contract Lodge, was officially in charge, as the highest ranking Freemason present. Philippe, who was the richest man in France, would have dominated the meeting even without his 32° initiation: as the leading supporter of liberal causes among the nobles, he had already won the admiration of the nation. His well-publicized charities had also endeared him to millions. Only a few suspected that behind all his deeds he had one goal in mind: to become King Philippe, benevolent despot—after the present king had been good enough to die a natural death, and a few others in succession were removed.

As duke of Chartres, Philippe was next in line to become duke of Orléans; with proper management, he could move from there to king in a few steps. If all went according to plan . . .

The men in the room understood and supported this goal. Only one of them, thus far, had considered the possibility of accelerating the process by persuading King Louis XV to die sooner than nature intended.

"The overt atheism in the Paris lodges has to stop," Philippe was arguing. "It may guarantee that every new member is a liberal, I'll grant you, but at what cost, gentlemen! We drive away thousands of possible recruits every day with that policy."

"I quite agree," said Count Casanova, who was the only man at the meeting dressed more expensively than Philippe. "No man can understand the world or understand how power is actually grasped and used until he has mastered the principles of Machiavelli and Hobbes. Everything is ultimately settled by strength and stealth. But it is stupidity *in extremis* to proclaim such views openly. Such ideas are only for those whose intelligence has qualified them for the higher degrees in the Craft."

"Exactly," said the guest from Bavaria, a fat lawyer named Hans Zoesser. "Admit everyone who wants to be a Mason. Challenge their false ideas and superstitions gradually, as they proceed from grade to grade."

"We are all of one mind about that," said Count Cagliostro. "The question is: What do we do about it? I hardly imagine we can persuade the fanatics in Paris to come around to our way of thinking."

Philippe was ready for that challenge. His answer seemed so brilliant to him, in fact, that he had quite forgotten it had been suggested to him earlier that day during a long talk with Cagliostro. Philippe had even forgotten how drowsy he had become during one part of that talk.

"This is what we should do," Philippe said. "We must form a completely new order, a bigger one than has ever existed before. It should be the best-financed Masonic order in the world, and I will undertake to finance its rapid growth personally. I think it would be wise if I were also its grand master, since my close family tie to the king will be advantageous in lending prestige and preventing suspicions of subversion."

"That is an excellent idea," Cagliostro said smoothly. "You

are indeed far-thinking. When this new order becomes large enough, everybody will regard it as the only Masonic group that is really important."

"What about the *Illuminati* in Avignon?" asked Casanova. "Are they really *Alumbrados*?"

"No, they were founded by an alchemist named Pernety," Philippe said. "I have had several meetings with them. They will pose no problems. Their heads are all lost in a maze of Cabala and Rosicrucianism and other mystic hogwash. Very much like the Italian Masons, I might say. If our new order has the proper mystical trappings on the surface, they will accept us, as long as we keep the secrets of the higher degrees from reaching their ears."

"I have been an alchemist myself," Casanova said quietly. "The mysteries of that art, I assure you, are not incompatible with our own goals."

"Of course," Cagliostro said softly. "*Et ego in Arcadia*, eh?"

He and Casanova exchanged cryptic looks.

"Sometimes I don't know what you two are talking about," Philippe complained.

"*Sometimes*?" Zoesser protested. "I *never* understand them. I know only that they have the same motives as the rest of us: the destruction of the Inquisition and the Popes."

"And a better king for France," Cagliostro added blandly.

Casanova observed Philippe's smug smile. How easily that man swallows flattery, he thought, and how skillfully Cagliostro feeds it to him. Snug and cozy as two jackals at dinner.

"An *illuminated* monarch," Cagliostro added.

He really pours on the oil, Casanova thought.

"What is the news from Bavaria?" Philippe asked, changing the subject.

"Things are the same as ever," Zoesser said glumly. "We are, as always, more priest-ridden than the Papal States or even

the benighted kingdom of Napoli. We have one new recruit, however, who fills me with admiration, and I expect
great things from him. He is a Jesuit named Father Weishaupt."

"We have too many Jesuits already," Casanova said, somewhat hotly. "We might end up someday with *them* running
international Masonry."

"Or," Cagliostro said smoothly, "we may end up someday
with *us* running the Society of Jesus. It depends on who has
studied Machiavelli more assiduously."

"Weishaupt has a plan," Zoesser said, "to form a secret
society within the Jesuit order and another within Bavarian
Masonry and create a union that neither side fully
understands—"

"When the tail wags," Casanova interjected ironically, "how
will we know which is the tail and which is the dog?"

"Weishaupt will be between the tail and the dog," Zoesser
said, a bit excitedly.

Everybody laughed.

"Excuse us," Cagliostro said, recovering first. "That was an
extraordinary metaphor. It seems to situate Father Weishaupt
in the vicinity of the dog's arse."

"The time will come," Zoesser said, "when none of you will
laugh at Adam Weishaupt."

Maybe, Casanova thought. But it will be a long time before I
hear that name without thinking of a dog's rump—such is the
power of metaphor.

The subject of Father Weishaupt was soon dropped and
plans for the Masonic order were discussed at length. Somehow, they all arrived at the conclusion that it should have the
name proposed by Count Cagliostro: the Grand Orient Lodge
of Egyptian Freemasonry.

When the meeting finally adjourned, Casanova returned to
his hotel wondering a great deal about Count Cagliostro.

Nobody had heard of him a year ago, and now he was already in the highest ranks of French Masonry. That the man was not a count was obvious, and Casanova was no more deceived on that point than one cardsharp by another. Cagliostro had the complexion and the accent of the Sicilian peasantry, even if he had acquired the outer trappings of the French aristocracy.

Casanova had the eerie feeling that he had seen this man a long time ago, in Italy. Somehow, he knew that was a false memory. He had some link with Cagliostro somewhere, but he could not quite remember it. Maybe I met his father, he thought, or his brother . . .

One thing was obvious: Cagliostro, whomever and whatever he was, knew as much about magnetism as Mesmer. He already had Philippe under his influence, and Philippe did not even remember the times he had stared into a candle or counted backward or obeyed whatever technique Cagliostro had used. Casanova had learned to recognize the state: Philippe was under mental suggestion, and the memory of the process had been erased.

The man who would be king, Casanova thought, under the control of a Sicilian adventurer. Cute as a grave robber's grin.

The Grand Orient Lodge would have a lively career, he thought.

This Cagliostro obviously came out of one of the more occult and witchy Italian lodges. Perhaps, Casanova thought, he had even been involved with the *strege* once; maybe that's where he learned magnetism.

But, damn it, why do I feel I've seen those violet Sicilian eyes somewhere before?

▲

Sigismundo Celine was blocked; the sonata was just not coming to the right conclusion. Usually he knew what the end would be like long before he arrived there—the end was always implicit in the beginning, in a certain sense—but this time he had gotten himself lost in a forest of counterpoint and elaboration.

Patience, he told himself; sometimes the creative process has to be allowed to happen of its own nature. Trying to force it can just lead to frustration.

It was night, and the whole house was asleep.

Sigismundo suddenly knew what was going to happen. After getting out of the *maison* in Paris without the pox, he had sternly avoided brothels and remained true to the ideal of Maria in his mind, but he had discovered that it was necessary, *absolutely* necessary, to relieve the tension occasionally. Have to get into my nightshirt, he thought. It isn't harmful except in excess. And I am most careful, almost ascetic: I do it only when absolutely necessary.

With his eyes closed, Maria became more real, she was as solid as the four angels Abraham invoked, and then it was like music, carrying him out of himself, going deeper and deeper and deeper into visions of beauty, and the whole Tempio Malatesta came back to him, and then he saw Ixotta degli Atti and all the gold and jeweled mosaics, as he walked through the *tempio* while the great music of Telemann and Scarlatti and J. C. Bach and J.S. Bach were being played; it was like floating above Napoli, during his first initiation; and Maria became shameless and wanton, urging him on, telling him She loved him. He was all over Her, every part of Her, kissing eyes and nipples and belly, cunt and toes and all of Her, all of Her, throat and thighs and knees, and all of Her, all of Her. Going deeper and deeper into the music, thinking that this was just what he felt when a composition began to take form, the same intense centering on one act, the same joy. The Dominicans were crazy; he was sure of it. This was like art and the fourth soul and creativity and all he dreamed of and longed for.

He stopped and got a handkerchief. The Church said that the first entry of sin into the soul came with a plausible lie. It was no lie that this was like art and initiation and the fourth soul. If this was sin, all art and beauty was sin, too. No: the Church was crazy. He went on and on, circling back, pausing, waiting, building the suspense, just as in a sonata, reaching further and further toward the essence of joy and beauty; and Maria encouraged him and inspired him.

He was panting and his heart was beating wildly at the climax. He lay back on the bed, exhausted, thinking that the letter *ship* was like a pyramid, Ψ, and soon he would understand the symbolism of the pyramid, *ship* transformed *JHVH* into *JVShVH*, divinity into flesh . . . And the conclusion of the sonata came to him in a flash.

He wrote the last bars in a flush of excitement.

Strange that the "sin" (as the Church called it) had unleashed his creativity. He would have to think about that. Now, however, with the music finished, he would definitely try to sleep.

Suddenly he understood the Masonic pyramid, because he was within the pyramid.

An idea that had almost been clear to him in England four years ago now came back with a second flush of creative excitement. He sketched it quickly.

And by the next day, he had finished drawings of his machine to show everybody at the university. It would move from place to place, unlike the machines that stood in factories to do their work; you could actually use this to travel in. It had a steam engine based on that of James Watt, and it had three wheels (since three points determine a plane), and he called it an *autokinoton*, from the Greek roots for *self* and *mover*.

Father Pacelli, Sigismundo's professor of calculus, was most impressed, although also very dubious.

"You really think people could travel in this, without being made ill by the motion?"

"Undoubtedly," Sigismundo said. "It could travel just like a horse-drawn coach, but faster. People could cross Europe in hours instead of days."

"If it works," Father Pacelli said.

The student body as a whole was less tolerant. Sigismundo was teased and ridiculed for days, and finally a satire on his device appeared on the bulletin board. The parody machine was called an *ipsemobile*—the Latin equivalent of *autokinoton*. It had five wheels instead of three and ran on moonbeams.

Sigismundo was by then convinced the construction of his device was possible and, with advances in chemistry and mechanics, someday inevitable. He took the sketches to Father Ratti's friend, Father Marconani, of the Department of Natural Philosophy.

Old Marconani studied the sketches with considerable bemusement.

"No horses," he muttered, comparing the side and top views. "Runs by itself. Autokinoton, you say? Very ingenious. Yes, upon my word."

Sigismundo waited.

"As this is designed," Marconani said finally, "it would require a quite large waterfall to power it, and I do not see how you could transport the waterfall around with you."

Sigismundo explained: With the proper chemical reactions, you could get the same power effect as you could get from a waterfall.

"Yes, yes, indeed," the old priest said. "Most clever. Do you have any idea of what chemical reactions you would need to produce that result?"

"Well," Sigismundo said, "I'm still working on that . . ."

The old man looked at him somberly for a moment. "They tell me you are a musician," he said.

"That is a minority opinion," Sigismundo replied. "I write music. Much music. But people say it is strange and unmelodic. I sometimes fear that it is a crazy hobby and not my true talent at all, but I do not know what my true talent is."

"Well, as for that," Marconani said, "you have a true scientific aptitude. If you keep working along these lines, something practical will emerge eventually, perhaps as a side product. This . . . contraption . . . may be a hundred years ahead of its time, but it certainly shows an ingenious mechanical mind."

▲

The day Maria Maldonado married Sir John Babcock, Sigismundo Celine went out and got roaring drunk; but Maria did not know about that at the time. Even if she had known, she would not have considered it a serious matter; she was too happy to believe there were any serious problems anywhere.

Maria had fallen in love with Sir John gradually, not at all in the manner of the passionate heroines of novels. She realized that he was likable, intelligent, and different from most other men in some way she could not define, except that he had a rare understanding of her feminine view of the world.

Sir John did not consider it odd that she had intellectual interests. "I could not be in love with someone who did not share my concern with such matters," he said once.

That he had some terrible tragedy in his past Maria became sure of as she knew him better. This was not (as she first suspected) something she was imagining because heroes of novels always had such melodramatic secrets; she could read it in his occasional flashes of bitterness and cynicism and in the sorrow that came over his face sometimes when he looked at young boys. He was remembering something that had happened when he was a boy, Maria knew.

Thinking about being married to him—thinking about kissing and caressing him and, of course, about the sexual act—she began to realize, more and more, how such images could excite her as well as frighten her. Well, that was what Mother Ursula had told her: women can feel such passions as intensely as men. The belief that nice girls did not feel such things was a myth created by Dominicans and other ignorant males.

"What is it really like?" Maria had dared to ask the abbess once.

"At its best," Mother Ursula said, "it can be almost as wonderful as prayer."

Maria knew that the abbess was not talking about ordinary prayer, the way most people mumbled Pater Nosters and Ave Marias. Mother Ursula meant the special kind of focus, the special concentration on God, which brought the healing power into her hands, for instance, and perhaps gave her other qualities that were not so spectacular but were equally unusual —such as her unfailing good humor and optimism in a world where most people were worried and anxious or full of anger at least half of their waking hours. Maria was capable of that kind of prayer, but only rarely; Mother Ursula lived in that illuminated focus as a normal state.

Mother Ursula also said that to think about sexual things was perfectly normal as you approached the marrying age. The doctrine that such thoughts were sinful, she said, resulted from the ignorance of certain theologians. Jesus had made a joke about that once, she explained, but theologians could not imagine that He had a sense of humor, so they took Him literally.

So the more Maria saw of Sir John, the more she found herself unwillingly and then half-willingly fantasizing about kissing and caressing and doing *the other* with him; and she was always a little bit worried about such fantasies because—despite Mother Ursula—the rest of the Church taught that such thoughts were decidedly sinful; and in the conflict between sensuality and guilt, she began to realize that her attraction to him was not merely sexual but affectionate and not merely affectionate but passionate. She was in love.

And being in love was just as wonderful as the novels said: they had not exaggerated that at all. It was *just like* the first time she had felt the power in her hands and healed the peasant. It was as if the whole orchestra from the Teatro San Carlo were following her around and playing the "Hallelujah" Chorus continually. It was so wonderful that at times she even felt out of touch with ordinary life and seemed to be walking around in a trance; she began to understand that loopy Celine fellow and—for the first time—felt a little sorry for him.

In ordinary life, when somebody walked into a room, you were either mildly happy (if you liked them) or mildly annoyed (if you didn't like them). Being in love was hardly noticing when somebody came into the room, even if they were riding a giraffe and singing *basso profundo*—*unless* it was Sir John; and then, if it was Sir John, Maria would still hardly notice the giraffe. More and more often, the mere sight of Sir John would excite her; Maria would feel a heat and a pleasure in the place she had learned never to touch, the place where birth happened, and she would even have wild thoughts about escaping from the chaperones and giving herself to him at once, without waiting for marriage or even for a proposal of marriage. Being in love was listening intently to everything he said, wanting passionately to share all of his thoughts on every possible subject. And it was also telling him everything, holding nothing back, even talking about the healing power that she dared not discuss with any Neapolitan lest word get back to the Inquisition; telling him all she thought, all she hoped, all she feared; and, best of all, it was never worrying that this stream of confidences would bore him or embarrass him, because he was in love with her, too.

Sir John was not astonished or incredulous about the healing power. "There is a man in France now," he said, "who is trying to educate the doctors about this. Franz Anton Mesmer, he's called. I have never in my life heard so many charges of quackery and charlatanism directed against one lone individual, nor have I ever heard such intemperate and bigoted language from men who are allegedly trying to be objective scientists.

The fact remains, despite all the denunciations, that Mesmer has performed many remarkable cures witnessed by persons of high repute."

"Mesmer is just in the wrong place," Maria said. "The French are all atheists these days." She said it sadly, as if pronouncing that the whole nation had leprosy.

"Mesmer does not claim that his power comes from God directly," Sir John said cautiously. "He claims it is a magnetism between living beings, like the magnetism between metals."

"Then Mesmer is a fool, too," Maria said. "The power works only when you go away and let God come into you."

Sir John paused a moment. "That is the way it works for you," he said finally. "I have an uncle who has seen similar things in India. The *yogins*, which is the name for men who can do such things, say the power is in the spinal column of everybody. They assert that if you do the proper contortions, the power will come up the spine into the brain. They call it *kundalini*. Perhaps it works the same whether we think of it theologically, like you, or anatomically, like the *yogins*, or magnetically, like Mesmer."

"You are not sure what you believe," Maria said sadly. Such uncertainty seemed to her perilously close to French atheism.

"Yes," Sir John said wearily, with a strange, crooked grin. "I do not know what to believe. I have read too much and traveled too far. Certitude belongs to those who have only lived in a place where everybody believes the same things."

Sir John then started reminiscing about some of the strange things he had seen in his travels. In North Africa, he said, there were groups called *Sufis*—a word that meant nothing in Arabic or in any other known tongue. They could stab themselves with swords without bleeding—he had seen it; and he had heard even stranger tales about them from men of good repute. The *Sufis* attributed their gifts to a power they called *baraka*, which they said permeates the whole universe, even the parts we call empty space. In France, he had seen a mountebank who called himself Count Cagliostro, and this man was at least three-quarters pure humbug, but he could make people see and hear astounding things, as if they were traveling to other worlds. In Hamburg, he had seen a man claiming to be the legendary Frankenstein, who could seemingly read minds—a short, squat, blond man, he was, totally unimpressive to look at, but he could tell you things about yourself you thought nobody knew.

"There was another man who claimed to be Frankenstein," Maria said, puzzled, "who came to Napoli a few years ago. I didn't see him, but everybody was talking about him for months and months. But he wasn't short and blond; he was tall and dark."

"That is why I make a principle of uncertainty," Sir John said, smiling. "One never knows, in this wicked world, what is real and what is somebody's masquerade."

It was only after two months of chaperonage that they were occasionally left alone for intervals of up to ten minutes, and it was at such times that these mystifying subjects were discussed.

It was only after two more months that they were left alone long enough for Sir John to take the risk of putting his arms around her.

"One kiss," he said, looking deep into her eyes. "Just one."

Maria could not help smiling. "I thought you'd never ask," she said gaily.

The kiss lasted a great deal longer than she had expected, and she knew that she was encouraging him to continue. It was, perhaps, not quite as wonderful as that special kind of prayer that brought the healing power, but it was at least as wonderful as Mr. Handel's "hallelujahs." Then she felt his penis becoming hard. My God, she thought, that's what novelists mean when they write, "She felt his masculinity hard against her." Why can't they tell us in plain words so we know what to expect?

She pulled away, suddenly nervous. They stared at each other like two strangers meeting in an empty castle at midnight. She knew she was blushing, and Sir John seemed pale.

"I love you," he said with a strange emphasis, as if he could hardly believe it himself. "Maria," he said. "I—I—"

"What is it?" she exclaimed.

"I want to marry you," he said. "I—I—"

And then he was weeping.

Maria believed that Englishmen never wept, just as elephants never fly and Sicilians never forgive an insult. But Sir John had not only forgotten to kneel in the ritual manner when proposing; he was so overcome that he was crying like a child.

Maria threw herself into his arms again. She didn't understand this at all, but she knew he needed to be held. She noticed that his penis was no longer hard: that had vanished in the explosion of emotion. She kissed the tears on his cheeks, murmuring endearments.

He held her fiercely, almost frantically. "I love you," he repeated. "I want to marry you. I have been alone so long."

This had something to do with the tragedy he never discussed; she could guess that much.

"What is it?" she asked gently. "You can tell me, *caro mio.*"

Sir John laughed and groaned at once. They had been speaking English ever since he first said, "I love you" in that language. "*Caro mio,*" he repeated. "That is far lovelier than any endearment in my language. You must always call me that."

He removed her arms and began pacing. "I want to marry you," he repeated. "Am I acceptable?"

"*Si.* Yes. *Caro mio.* Darling."

"I was in love once before," he said, avoiding her eyes. "The ɔer——, the woman died tragically. I felt nothing at the time. I ɔidn't realize that was shock. I thought I was an emotionless monster. I hated myself. Then, when the grief came finally, ɔomething had changed in me. I have never been in love since ɔhen. Let me finish."

Maria, who had been about to interrupt, nodded.

"I have told you that my father was a judge. He had a ɔassion for the law—for justice, I should say. That has been ɔny passion, too; he taught it to me. It is my intent to enter ɔarliament, to work for the causes I believe in. It was conveyed ɔo me, by men in important places, that a family man is much ɔnore acceptable to the electors than a bookish and somewhat ɔeclusive bachelor. I have been searching for two years, ɔaccording to my own notions of honor, to find some woman ɔwise enough and tolerant enough to live with an odd duck like ɔne. I expected an ordinary marriage of convenience. I did not ɔexpect to fall in love again."

He stopped. For a moment she thought he was on the edge of tears again.

"I have to tell you these things," he went on. "I do not fall in love easily. I think I am, perhaps, more passionate about ideas and ideals than about human beings. I want you, Maria, but I must warn you against myself. I do not know what I am."

"You are a good man," she said at once. "An intelligent man. You should not have such doubts about yourself."

He looked at her queerly. "Have you ever seen a man cry before?"

"Yes. When Mama died, Papa cried."

"I have believed that nobody could respect a man who showed such weakness."

"You are human. That is a weakness?"

Sir John sighed. "It is so bleeding *complicated*," he said vaguely. "I would rather blow my brains out with a pistol than think I am going to ruin your life."

"You are not as eccentric as you think," Maria said firmly. "You have been alone too long, that's all. You are kind and often very funny. And I love you."

Count Maldonado received the news the following morning with evident pleasure. He enthusiastically hugged Sir John and kissed Maria.

They had to shout because the count was having breakfast in the garden and Carlo was engaging in his daily target practice at the other end of the grounds.

"There is one problem," the count shouted. "Are you willing to convert to Catholicism?" *Bang!* went a pistol.

"If it were necessary to win Maria," Sir John shouted, "I would convert to Mohammedanism."

"That is most romantic," the count shouted, "but it is not the proper attitude to express when we talk to the bishop. However, considering the political situation in England, I suggest that you get married again, in the Anglican communion, when you return there. Otherwise, you will eventually be accused of being a Jacobite, and your career will be ruined."

Bang! Carlo fired again.

"I will not convert to this Anglicanism," Maria shouted fiercely.

"That will not be necessary," Count Maldonado shouted. "It is still possible for an English statesman to have a Catholic wife, is it not, Sir John?"

Bang!

"Most certainly," Sir John shouted. "Everybody knows Edmund Burke's wife is a Catholic. The Tories bring that up at every election. But the electors continue to return him to parliament."

"So then," the count shouted. "As a minimum courtesy to our respective realms, two weddings are advisable. But after that you can certainly remain Catholic, Maria, and you can remain Anglican, Sir John. Some fanatics of both sects will not like it, but most people will be mollified."

The count smiled. "And I hope I will have a grandson by this time next year," he shouted. "And, to please an old man, I hope you will spend part of each year here in Napoli. Especially when my grandson is young?"

Sir John smiled in turn. "You are giving me your greatest treasure," he shouted. "When my political career allows it, Maria and I will spend one or two months here every year."

"Go away, the two of you," the count shouted. "Before I cry."

Bang! Carlo fired again.

The next days went by like a dream for Maria. The banns were published by the cathedral; Papa was in conference continually with the bishop about the details of the Mass and reception; everybody of status in Napoli was dropping by the villa to congratulate the family—and to look over Sir John.

Sir John remained polite and unruffled under all the scrutiny. He was taking lessons in Catholicism from Father Ratti of Sacred Heart College—Maria had the feeling he and the priest had met before—and both of them seemed aware that Sir John was not going to become an orthodox Roman Catholic and had not been an orthodox Anglican Catholic for many years, but that he would go through the forms with due solemnity.

Sir John rebelled against Neapolitan protocol only once, when the doctor came to examine Maria.

"That practice is barbaric," he told Count Maldonado heatedly.

"It is worse. It is hypocritical," the old man said calmly. "Doctors are notoriously easy to bribe on matters of this sort."

"Well, then," Sir John exclaimed, "why not just ignore the whole hideous business?"

"Because," the Count said, "it would be known. Believe me, I know Napoli. People would talk for years to come about how I swindled the naive Englishman and sold him damaged goods. That would be cruel to Maria and eventually to your children."

"Arrrgh," Sir John said, making a noise of revulsion. "It is *gross.*"

But when this was reported to Maria, she decreed that normal Neapolitan practice would be followed. Doctor Massini had examined her twice before, on occasions when premenstrual tension had caused her worry. She had learned to relax and not be nervous during Massini's myopic probings.

And so Sir John received a signed document testifying that his bride-to-be was *intatta.*

As soon as the doctor left, Sir John managed to have a few moments alone with Maria in the garden. He showed her the certificate and then placed it in the trash-bin and burned it.

"I loathe having you treated as merchandise," he said hotly. "You should not be stamped and approved by government inspectors."

How very English, Maria thought.

"It was necessary," she said simply. "Like your lessons in the faith from Father Ratti."

"Being forced to submit to such a thing was an offense against you. Don't you realize that?"

"*Caro mio,*" Maria said. "I am too happy these days to notice offenses."

Sir John smiled. "When you call me that, I do not notice offenses either. Say it again."

"*Caro mio!*"

And so that matter was passed over. But Maria later found herself thinking that nobody had asked for Sir John's virginity to be attested. Aside from the fact that it was physically impossible in the case of the male, it would be regarded as damned impudent. Mother Ursula was right: to a great extent, marriage was a property relationship, with the woman as the property.

But in this case such social rules did not apply. Sir John's sense of justice extended even to women—and black people (he was against slavery). He would not treat her like property. He worried—for some strange reason—that *he* might be inadequate. He was that sort of man: always making more demands on himself than on others.

Many Englishmen—especially the wealthy ones, if they were Whigs—were like that. Sir John had told her once that it was a mental set created by schools like Eton. The training device, he said, was an ordinary walking stick or cane. That was why, he explained, you will never hear one upper-class Englishman overtly insult another. "An insult, when necessary, is delivered," he said, "as an innocuous remark about the furniture, say, and is always accompanied by a bland smile. The man insulted always replies with an equally bland smile and an equally quiet remark about, perhaps, the latest Irish rebellion. Another Englishman can understand exactly what is being conveyed, but it is most confusing to foreigners. You will live among us for some years before you can decipher such conversations. The first man is really saying, 'I see no new furniture, and I deduce that your business is not doing too well since everybody discovered you are a scoundrel,' and the second man is replying, 'And you may be in debtor's prison soon, if the Irish burn down the rest of your estates.' You see, *cara mia*, the difference between self-discipline, self-restraint, and sheer hypocrisy is always in danger of being blurred among us. The happy result is that there are few liars among us, since lying is scarcely necessary where no conversation means what it seems to say."

Maria realized that she had considered English novels dull because she had never understood the nuances of well-bred

English speech. Those novels might be what she had been told they were—very witty, once you comprehended that the characters were never saying what they really meant.

But Sir John, alone in his room one night, stared at himself in the mirror for a long time. It doesn't show in my face, he thought; that is just superstition. And I have stopped (almost stopped) for nearly two years (with only a few relapses). I can stop entirely. I can. I *can*.

He took out his journal and began writing, deliberately adopting the style of his favorite French aphorist, trying to detach and observed his own mental state:

> The lonely man, mistrustful of himself, can find solace in taking sides *against* himself. To think that the world is right and I am wrong: that is the courage of solitary doubt. And yet it is also the way to one's true self, the essence that can be found only when vanity is rejected as the shabby, flattering beggar it is.
>
> There is something for which we do not have a name, something that will not allow us to lie to it: it instantly punishes every evasion, every weakness. It will not allow us to escape our burdens because it wishes to make us stronger, for greater burdens. Being haunted by this demon is the situation of the "initiate," the elect.
>
> Only inner warfare of this sort causes us to descend to the bottom of things and put away all easy answers, even "philosophy," even "profundity." Then, at the bottom of the pit that has no bottom, we may look the Tyrant in the eye and know who he is, who Destiny is, and what he wants of us. This does not make us "better" at all. It makes us twin brothers to necessity.

Sir John stopped writing and slumped back in his chair. Words, words, words, as Hamlet said. Analysis is an even better disguise than cheerfulness.

He remembered the nickname "Better Logic Babcock" from the years at Eton. Can you tell us the exact time, *t*, they used to ask him, when A becomes not-A? Oh, I could tell you a great deal about that, he answered them in retrospect. I look at Maria, and I am A, as I was with Bertha in Heidelberg; then a boy with a certain brutal beauty passes on the street, and I am not-A again; and yes, I can even tell you the exact instant, t.

Which was more true—time or numbers? The boys had been casual, clandestine, hidden; the affairs with women had lasted longer, because he had not had to sneak and hide then. So: In terms of time, he was about fifty percent A and fifty percent not-A, and in terms of actual partners, less than twenty percent A and more than eighty percent not-A. Either way, a pretty problem for the strict Aristotelians. I am the intermediate term, he thought: more of an affront to logic than to Christian theology.

But there would be no more boys. He was determined. The Tyrant, who might be Destiny, had taught him that it was not important to have what you want; it is essential to want what you have. There was the House of Commons first; the House of Lords later, as a possibility. There would be a happy marriage, and no more whores of either sex. He had almost thought he was in love with Bertha in Heidelberg; he knew he was in love with Maria. There would be no more boys, no risk of scandal.

And yet, and yet . . . he knew he was anxious. He was avoiding the one thought that could seriously undermine his rationally planned decisions.

Suppose you can't turn off one faucet without turning off the other?

That would be a malign joke on the part of God or Nature. Besides, he was sure it was not true; he was worrying himself unnecessarily. After all, he had gone months and months without boys, during the affair with Bertha, and turning off one faucet had not turned off the other.

But for years and years?

I know why they invented Sin and why they have Obscenity Laws, he thought bitterly. It is so that we do not experiment enough and inquire enough to understand ourselves fully. So that we all live with doubts and misgivings. That is the edge they use to govern us. They *literally* have us by the balls.

I love her. It will work. I must not worry about such nonsense.

Being haunted by this demon, he thought, is like being midway between a god and a dumb, sacrificial animal.

He blew out the candle and tried to sleep.

And so Maria was innocently happy, and Sir John was guardedly happy, and the wedding day finally arrived; and when Sir John stood in the great cathedral with the organ music swelling all around him, echoing from all the walls, he looked at Maria coming down the aisle on Count Maldonado's arm, with the five children in white carrying her train behind her, and he knew he would love her devoutly all his life. He was sure of it. At this moment, he loved her more than he had ever loved anyone, more than Geoffrey who had drowned.

Pietro Malatesta was a guest at the wedding, cementing again in public the new friendship between himself and Count Maldonado, the end of the 150-year-old Malatesta-Maldonado feud. At one point, Pietro glanced around and saw his nephew, Sigismundo Celine, standing in the back, in the shadows, trying to be unseen by anyone.

The look on Sigismundo's face was unnerving: it reminded Pietro of the boy's true father, of Peppino Balsamo. Then Sigismundo turned abruptly and left.

He'll probably get drunk and be himself again in the morning, Pietro thought. This is a happy day; I shouldn't ruin it with worry.

And then the vows were taken and the bishop said that Sir John could kiss Maria, and the organ music began to rise again. Maria was in his arms, and he suddenly felt that inexplicable

rising of tears again. As they kissed he was thinking: It is done, I
am no longer alone. I will deserve her love and trust. I will.

When they broke from the kiss, he almost laughed, because
he had a slight erection. Well, he thought, it isn't all that
conspicuous, and the bishop has probably seen it before at
other weddings. It's the organ music that does it, even more
than the kiss. It's a crazy religion that uses the most erotic of all
musical instruments at its sacred feasts, even while preaching
against eroticism.

Then Count Maldonado was kissing him on both cheeks,
and a dozen men were shaking his hand, and then the organ
was more erotic than ever (he could imagine what the
Methodists would say of such a ceremony: pure paganism
disguised as Christianity), and then he and Maria were walking
down the aisle to the nave, and there was the whole damned
banquet and reception to get through. All he could think of
was getting Maria's clothes off, initiating her into the sacrament
of pleasure, rewarding her in every one of the dozen ways he
knew, adoring her for taking away his loneliness.

Sir John and Lady Babcock, he thought: we are now legally
one person.

The afternoon was interminable. Everybody had brought
their huge families to the banquet, of course, and several
children soon gorged themselves on the delicacies, becoming
ill. Vomiting children do not create a passionate, romantic
atmosphere, Sir John thought wryly, although they were
perhaps a warning of what marriage was actually like. He and
Maria could hardly exchange two words; if somebody wasn't
telling him what a lucky man he was and banging him heartily
on the back, some woman was hugging Maria and weeping.
Pietro Malatesta, usually the coolest of men, got drunk and
began doing what he considered a hilarious imitation of the
bishop, although nobody else found it amusing until the
climax, when he suddenly fell over with a crash right out of one

of Walpole's Gothic castles. It took five men to carry him to the well and revive him.

And then somehow, finally, all that was over and Sir John and Maria were in the carriage, on their way to the count's country villa outside Marrechiaro, where they would spend their honeymoon.

"Are you very tired, *cara mia?*" he asked.

"*Di tanto in tanto,*" she said. "But very happy. Oh, I love you, love you!"

They kissed again, with total abandon this time. It went on and on, and Maria felt as if she were bursting into a hundred pieces, like one of the fireworks on a saint's day. Sir John tentatively moved his hand into her lap. Without raising her skirt, through the fabric, very gently, he caressed her.

"That's nice," Maria said softly. "Don't stop." It was as if the whole world were being transformed, as if she herself were being transformed in a fire that was not painful but increasing steadily, inexorably. "Oh, God, don't stop," she repeated. His face was magnified in every detail, as if she had put belladonna in her eyes for the opera. It was more real than flesh, solid as a statue, masklike. "Don't stop."

"Yes, darling, darling," he murmured. He kissed her neck, her ears. Gradually, with the left hand, he raised her skirt. As he got his right hand into her pantaloons, she felt as if the stars were descending into the coach, as if all life was light. "Oh, my God, my God," she said. He knew what he was doing: he had found the exact place. She twisted her head, kissing him passionately on the lips, moaning. There were two fingers inside her now, then three. She could not hold the kiss; she was breathing spasmodically. "God, God, God," she cried out. "*God!*" The whole world went away; she was lost in endless luminous waters, undulating through wave after wave of dilation.

"Did you . . .?" he asked, kissing her cheeks.

"Yes, yes! Oh, *caro mio*, am I terrible? Do you think the coachman heard me?"

"It wouldn't be the first honeymoon coach in which he's heard that kind of invocation of the deity," Sir John said, smiling.

She laughed nervously. "I've disgraced myself. I couldn't even wait until we got to the villa."

"Coachmen must hear such things all the time—if they hear anything above the noise of the horses' hooves."

Maria kissed him again. "Now you know it's true, what they say about passionate Southern women."

"You do think you're wicked, don't you?"

"Not really. But we are trained always to be ashamed, to be afraid. It is hard to believe I am married and it is not a sin."

"Silly."

They kissed. She moved her hand into his lap.

"No," he whispered.

"*You* are afraid of shocking the coachman now? If he heard my moans, he can listen to yours. Darling."

"No, it's different for a man. I am burning, too, but . . . the result . . . if you continue . . . it will be very visible to the servants when we meet them in the front hall of the villa."

"Oh, you poor darling."

"I have found," Sir John said, "that reciting the multiplication table can calm me down until relief is in sight."

"Two times two is four . . ."

"Two times three is six . . ."

They recited the multiplication table for a while. Passing by a *palazzo*, Maria suddenly saw Sigismundo Celine out the window, weaving around in a drunken stupor, being held up by an old man. He shouted something she couldn't hear.

Despicable man, she thought. He haunts me even on the happiest day of my life.

She started kissing Sir John again and, gradually, nerved

herself to move his hand back into her lap. "If it won't get you too excited," she whispered.

"It won't. I love you so much."

"After a few minutes, she said, "Darling, it's even better than the first time. Slower, please, darling. Slow. Slow. Kiss me."

After a while she remembered to repeat, "Don't get too excited." Then she said, "God," and "*Caro mio*," and then she was limp in his arms again, lost in undulating light.

They decided to recite the multiplication table some more.

Then Maria said, "No wonder poets call it the 'little death.' I really felt myself going somewhere the second time, just as death must feel. But so sweet, so sweet. Darling, what is the name for it?"

"'Spending' in proper speech. The lower classes say 'coming.'"

"Oh, when we get to the villa we will spend and spend like millionaires."

"Men are different that way. I will not spend as much as you."

"How many women have you—no, forget that. I don't want to know. I will be jealous of them."

"You're the one I married. You're the one for the rest of my life."

When they arrived at the villa, there was only one servant —an aged caretaker with a drooping white mustache, who kept grinning and grinning as he carried in their luggage. Nobody grins more than a happy Neapolitan, Sir John thought, just as nobody is sadder than a melancholy Neapolitan and nobody is more furious than an angry Neapolitan. We English must seem like automatons to them.

When they were alone in their room, Maria immediately began fondling Sir John. "Darling," he said. "Wait. Darling. Just. Wait. Darling. Oh, God. Darling. Just let me get my trousers off."

"You gave me such pleasure in the carriage."

"Darling. Just let me . . ."

He got his trousers off, clumsily.

"*Caro mio*," she said, kissing his neck. "I hope this makes you feel the way I felt in the coach."

"Oh, God, yes."

"Darling. *Caro mio*. Sweet man."

"Jesus. Look in my eyes. See what you are doing to me."

She looked into his eyes and watched them grow more and more glazed. At the final moment, he involuntarily closed them, and then she felt the warm stickiness on her hand.

"Darling," she said.

"Let me sit down."

They sat on the bed and kissed.

"What a lovely place," Sir John said looking out the window at the trees' black silhouettes in the dark. "I could stay here forever. We have enough money. Stay here and spend and spend like millionaires, as you said. Never go back out into that crazy, violent world. God, I'm happy."

"I think I enjoyed making you spend as much as I enjoyed spending myself," Maria whispered.

They kissed again.

"Listen," he said softly. "I have not been entirely chaste. But the . . . others . . . that was just necessity. God made men that way. He did not invent celibacy; the churches did. It is impossible to be a male and not spend occasionally. If you resist it, it happens anyway, in your sleep."

"I know, *caro mio*. It happened to me once in a dream."

"It happens to women, too?"

"It only happened *once*." Maria was becoming embarrassed; she did not want to remember that she had been dreaming of Sigismundo Celine at the time.

"It can happen to a young man as often as once a week," Sir John said. "If he tries to be chaste, as the churches call it. The whole Christian world is a conspiracy to keep us from understanding that aspect of ourselves and of one another. *We must break the conspiracy*," he said fiercely. "We must be able to understand each other in that aspect, too." He remembered the tombstone that boasted of serving liberty. Swift had done that by speaking *honestly*, despite prudes and censors.

"Yes. What is it called, what you did to me in the carriage and I just did to you?"

"Masturpation. If I were to do it to myself, that would be masturbation."

"Those are the terms of doctors. What do ordinary people say?"

"Frigging."

"I've heard that word, but I never knew what it meant. Some girls did it to each other at school."

"When girls do it together," Sir John said carefully, "it is called tribadism. When boys do it together, it is called sodomy. Both are considered terrible vices, and one should not even admit in public that one knows such practices exist."

"Boys do it with *each other*?" Maria laughed. "That must look funny."

"I would imagine that it does," Sir John said, remembering not to stare too fixedly into her eyes: that was the sign of an amateur liar.

"What is the name for the consummation? People do not say 'sexual intercourse' in private, I'm sure."

"It is called 'fucking' in my language."

"That is a lovely word. I will enjoy fucking with you, my darling. Even more than I enjoyed frigging you and being frigged by you."

"Now you are showing off your boldness."

"I beg your pardon, sir. I will enjoy having sexual intercourse with you."

"I like the other word better."

"You like to hear me say 'fucking'?"

"Very much."

"Somehow I knew you would like that," Maria kissed him again. "You will be very gentle the first time, because of the membrane?"

"I will have to be," Sir John said, smiling. "Men do not recover from spending as rapidly as women do."

"Oh? How long will it be before we can fuck?"

"That depends. Before we experiment upon my rate of recovery, I suggest that we share a warm bath. That is most relaxing and often stimulating."

"Did you learn that from all those other women? I bet you learned it from some shameless Frenchwoman."

"Actually," he said, "bathing is the national obsession of my country. We believe in taking a bath before any activity, and usually afterward, too."

"You didn't answer my question."

"You do not really want me to talk about other women."

"No. Not really. I was teasing."

They kissed again.

"Well," he said, "into the tub."

"Shall we be naked with the lights on?"

"We can bathe in the dark, if you are shy about that."

"I *am* shy," Maria said. "But it is exciting, too. Remind me that we are married."

"We are very very very married, *cara mia*."

"We will leave the candles on."

"Even when we fuck?"

"Yes, darling. Even when we fuck."

"You may go behind the screen to disrobe," he said. "And I will heat the water."

"No," Maria said boldly. "I would like you to undress me."

"Darling."

Sir John had the usual problems with buttons and hooks, but eventually Maria was nude.

"You are as lovely as a painting by Titian," he said.

"And you, I think, are recovering."

"Yes," he said. "Obvious, isn't it?"

"What is it called?"

"My cock."

"Oh, how nice." She took it in her hand again. "Babcock's lovely cock," she said.

"Oh, God," he said. "Say that again."

"Babcock's lovely cock."

"Christ," he said, "I feel as randy as a stallion."

"And what is this called?"

"Your cooney."

"It is almost Italian or Latin. Oh, let us heat the tub quickly."

"Wait," Sir John said. He knelt and kissed her bush.

"Oh, God," she said, embarrassed. "That is better than your hand. But please stop. It cannot be *nice* . . . for you."

"It is very nice."

"Please stop. It is wonderful, but it must be a terrible sin."

"Not for married people." But he stopped. "I love you," he said, standing to look into her eyes. "It's just another way of saying I love you."

"Make the tub." She was flushed and confused.

Sir John heated the water and poured it into the iron tub. "Could you stand some more champagne after this afternoon?" he asked.

"I could drink a gallon."

"You only think you could." He poured two glasses. "Let us take them into the tub."

Maria was pouring perfumes and bubbling agents into the tub. Bending forward, she reminded him of a Greek statue of Aphrodite he had once seen.

They climbed into the tub. "To eternal love," Sir John said, raising his glass.

"To eternal love," Maria answered. They clinked their glasses and drank.

"I wish," Sir John said, "that we had brought along a string quartet, riding on top of the carriage. We could have them playing outside the window. Vivaldi, I should think."

"We don't need them," Maria said. "The music is in my heart."

"Darling."

"*Caro mio.*" They kissed, almost spilling their glasses.

"If we had that *r* in English," Sir John said thoughtfully, "we'd have better poets."

"It is like prayer," Maria said. "Mother Ursula told me that once, and now I understand."

"What is that?"

"It is my hand."

"Much as I suspected. And what are you doing?"

"I am frigging you. Frigging your lovely cock."

"I surmised that something of the sort was transpiring. You are shameless."

"Yes. And you are enjoying it."

"Very much. But I must warn you, darling, about the male anatomy. I should not spend again. Otherwise, we will perhaps not be able to consummate tonight at all."

"So? We can fuck tomorrow night. Or tomorrow morning. Would that not be heavenly—to fuck in the dawn, when the birds start to sing?"

"Can you wait that long?"

"You seem to know many other amusements, my love."

"I was so worried," Sir John said. "I have never made love with a virgin before."

"As for that," Maria said. "I am still a virgin. Is that not remarkable after all the pleasures we have had already?"

"Oh, God," he gasped.

"Are you . . .?"

"Very close."

"Good."

"In India," Sir John said. "I had an uncle. Who served there. Sometimes they do not consummate. For a week or more. After the wedding. They just do this. And other pleasures. So the discomfort. Of the membrane. Does not happen. Until the bride knows. All the pleasures. Oh, *God!*"

"Did you spend again?"

"Oh, Jesus Nelly, yes."

"I thought so. You looked like a tortured god. But it was not suffering."

"No, it was not suffering. Let us get into bed with some more champagne."

He poured more champagne. They climbed beneath the warm quilts.

"To eternal love," he said.

"To eternal love," she replied. They drank and put the glasses on the table.

"The whole world," Sir John said, "is mad. Europe is one huge home for the feebleminded, and the Orient is no better, from what I've heard. What fools we all are. Life can be so beautiful, and we make it so wretched for one another."

"We will make a world of our own. And we will always have that, when the outer world becomes too terrible."

"I have been so lonely."

"With all those women?"

"There weren't that many. Really."

They held each other. Sir John began to kiss her right breast.

"Oh heavens," she said after a while. "I can feel that in my . . . cooney."

"I know. Wasn't God clever in the way He designed our bodies?"

"Darling. Put your hand there again."

"I can do better than that." He shifted his mouth southward.

"That is so sweet," she said after a moment. "But . . . not too much . . . I don't want to spend that way."

"I want you to."

"Oh, God, I love it. But . . . I'm still afraid it is not really nice for you."

"It is better than nice. It is like a prayer, as your Mother Ursula would say."

"Oh, *caro mio* . . . oh, I am so ashamed . . . don't stop . . . I, I, I am so ashamed . . . Are you sure you don't mind? . . . Oh, God, I don't care . . . I think I will die of this and I don't care . . . I am afraid to move . . . I am afraid it will be ugly for you."

"It is not ugly. I adore you."

"Oh, God, I am going crazy . . . I am dying . . . Even in the carriage was not like this . . ." She had both hands on his head and was clutching spasmodically. "It is like the healing power all over me . . . oh, God . . . I am so ashamed and I love you so much . . . and I am dying . . . Oh, God . . . *God, God, God!*"

He held her tenderly, feeling entirely safe from the world and its madness.

"I didn't *really* spend before," she said. "I just thought I did." Her head was on his breast and her eyes were closed. "I have never felt so close to God. Is that silly?"

"No, it isn't silly at all."

But then she began to drowse, and in only a few minutes she was sound asleep.

Sir John stared at the ceiling. *"Eternal love,"* he quoted to himself: that's a myth invented by the poets. I will make the myth come true. I will be good enough to deserve her.

And then he realized that he was drowsing, too.

He awoke to the sound of pounding on the door. The

caretaker. What was the matter with the man? You just do not come pounding on the door of a honeymoon couple's room so early in the morning. But then Sir John realized that a great deal of sunlight was pouring through the window. It was not early at all. He and Maria had slept quite late.

"What is it?" he grumbled.

"Please, *signor*. Terrible news."

Sir John got into his robe and, after making sure that Maria was well covered, went to the door. He opened it a small crack.

The caretaker looked like a rat in the middle of the melancholy process of gnawing his own leg off to escape a trap. Nobody looks unhappier than a sad Neapolitan, Sir John remembered thinking the night before.

"What is it?" he asked anxiously.

"I am sorry, *signor*. The count, he wants you both back in Napoli. It is very bad."

Sir John opened the door and stepped out into the hall. "Do we have to tell the *signora*? Is it that bad?"

The old man had eyes like a spaniel mourning its master. He told the story in broken, half-coherent sentences.

"Damn. Is he dead then?"

"Not yet. But it is very grievous, the wound."

"I will break the news to the *signora*. Tell them to get the carriage ready."

Sir John stepped back into the bedroom and looked at Maria's lovely face, calm and serene in her sleep.

There is no safe place where you can wrap yourself in love and get away from the madness of the world, he thought.

He touched her shoulder. "Darling."

Her eyes opened. "*Caro mio*," she said softly. Then she recognized the expression on his face. "What happened?"

He sat down on the bed, held her. "Darling, I have sad news."

"It is serious," she said. "I can tell."

He told her, hating the ugliness of the words coming out of his mouth.

"We will have to go back to Napoli," she said.

"Of course."

Then she began to weep, and he held her for a long time before they got dressed and went down, in grim silence, to the carriage and the long trip back to Napoli. It had started to rain.

▲

When Sigismundo Celine left the Cathedral, he walked through the market, not noticing any of the noise or the bright colors, and walked on down to the waterfront, feeling very little and thinking not at all. When he stood looking at the bay, he thought: I could jump in, end it all at once. Then somebody will rage against me as I raged against Tony that night when I dived for him again and again.

It was not as if three souls were coming apart in civil war, he realized; the Rosicrucians have it a bit too pat there. It is more like gears turning. I call this gear "the vegetative soul" and that gear "the animal soul" and the next gear "the human soul," but it is all just wheels and mechanical reactions. If I am going to jump, it is not that I decide on death but that the machine has been set to plunge into the sea.

"It is terrible, what is happening in my living room," Uncle Pietro had said, when they were torturing Peppino. "This night will curse us all."

The machine did not feel anything. It just walked toward the bay, blindly.

The truth, Sigismundo thought, is that I do not feel anything because I am *afraid* to feel what is happening. That is why the machine walks without knowing where it goes.

"You will come to us in the end," Peppino had said.

Selfishness. Vanity. Jealousy. Rage. Those were the vices that had to be conquered before the fourth soul could crystallize. And so you tried to conquer them, and you might even think you were succeeding—if people were not stabbing your uncle in church, if *Rossi* were not filling you with diabolical drugs, if the world gave you a few years without murder and horror sitting down at the table every time you ate. You could practice the invocation of the four archangels and try to find the balance point, the Inner Sun, from which they were projected, and you could think the fourth soul spoke more and more often, not just in music but everywhere. You could think you were on your way to superhumanity, to the Rose Cross degree. And then, just because a woman loved somebody else, you found that all the animal passions were still there.

Everybody said that Englishmen were the worst lovers in Europe. Imagine Maria married to a cold, stiff, self-righteous, hypocritical Englishman. She was getting just what she deserved, damn her.

Sigismundo was back in the market.

"Best silk you ever saw, right from Constantinople—"

"Lowest prices you ever heard of—"

That was strange: he did not remember walking away from the bay. This was what happened when your rage was so intense that you could not allow yourself to feel it.

He had been working on his *autokinoton* again, the last month. Great things were being done in chemistry, especially by the Englishman Priestley. Sigismundo was convinced that there was a way to power the *autokinoton*, when the right chemicals were found.

That is probably as crazy as my music.

He entered the Osteria Pompeii. The reason God made grapes was so that men could discover wine and escape from the misery of being human for a while. The reason mules are so sad is that they have never found a way to escape from the misery of being mules.

See, he thought, I have already found one way in which I am better off than a mule.

After the third glass of burgundy, he began to cheer up some more. It was quite funny, actually: pour in certain chemicals, and the machine begins to malfunction. But the malfunction is amusing. I can pound on the table and tell everybody what donkeys and cattle they all are, and the bartender will just stop serving me; they will not hold it against me, because I am drunk. Glorious freedom.

He drank some more wine, and finally he was able to feel something again. He would like to kill her. He imagined himself standing on the Cathedral steps, rushing forward suddenly in the crowd, jabbing the dagger into her again and again. Blood on the white gown. Horror on every face. "Who did it?" "Sigismundo Celine, the one who wrote the crazy music." It would be the one act that would truly, radically make a difference. It would declare his allegiance to his true father, Peppino the Revengeful, and to Peppino's god, Lucifer the Rebel.

Lovely. What marvelous fantasies you have, he told himself. You wanted to be a saint of the Rose Cross; now you want to be a devil? Always the extremist, is that it?

Have some more wine, he decided. It will pass. Tomorrow I will do the invocation of the four archangels again, and I will feel the light in the center, the Inner Sun, and I will not be a raging brute then. I will know I was a damned fool today, but what of it? Everybody has the right to be a damned fool for one day, occasionally.

"Bad luck and too much wine" that was what Elpenor had answered when Odysseus asked how he had arrived in Hell so fast. Don't think about that. Today is your day to howl and rage and be an animal. One day only. You have a right to one day.

Was I serious about throwing myself into the bay? I can't remember. I don't know what I was thinking then.

Have some more wine.

Tana before you, Orpheus behind you, Aradia at your right side, Lucifer at your left side.

No, no, no: he would not let Peppino rise from the grave and take over his soul. He would not be drawn into the Satanic web of revenge and black magick.

I think, he decided, the best thing to do is go home and sleep it off, before I get myself into real trouble. I hear the north wind rising; I haven't done anything really stupid in months and months. The goblins are calling me. Yes, definitely; time to go home and sleep it off.

Sigismundo paid his bill, noticing the innkeeper's worried expression. He's afraid I'll collapse on the street and get robbed. Or I'll go to sleep in an alley and wake up with pneumonia. Well, I'm not really that drunk. I hope.

But ever since rising to pay the bill, Sigismundo had felt somewhat dizzy and light-headed. He hadn't noticed those symptoms while he was just sitting and drinking.

He staggered to the door. Damn it, I don't have to lurch about like this. If I concentrate, I can still walk straight. No sense in letting all Napoli know I'm drunk.

He hit both sides of the door frame going through.

Lovely son you have, Mama Celine. Writes the most bizarre music this side of China, invents machines that won't work, and now he's a public drunkard, staggering around like a blind horse. Contemplates suicide and murder in a single afternoon, too. Don't feel bad about it, though: it comes from his father's side of the family.

And then, stumbling into the street, Sigismundo came face to face with Carlo Maldonado.

My sweet Jesus, he thought, they *do* have the biggest noses in Napoli. No wonder the count is nicknamed "Cyrano."

"Hi, there, banana nose," Sigismundo said, smiling happily.

Carlo Maldonado was not exactly sober himself. He had been drinking champagne all afternoon at his sister's wedding reception.

"What did you call me?" he asked.

"You heard me," Sigismundo said with a drunken leer. "If I had a nose like that I'd go around on all fours so people would mistake me for a rhinoceros and not laugh."

Carlo remembered the last time he had almost gotten into a duel with Sigismundo. He had been a child, then; but now he was seventeen. He was not going to get into an unnecessary fight. There were other ways to protect honor.

"You are drunk," Carlo said cheerfully, "and therefore not responsible for your bad manners. Go home and sober up before you make a spectacle of yourself."

He walked past.

"That was smart," one of the Portinari boys said, emerging out of the dusk. "That Celine is a demon with the sword."

"I wasn't afraid," Carlo said quickly. "It is foolish to get into a fight with a drunk."

"Running away, are you?" Sigismundo shouted. "Just what I thought. That isn't the profile of a man. It's the profile of a dog."

Carlo turned. "You are a drunken fool, and I will ignore your childish behavior." He walked on, not too quickly. I will not appear a coward in public, he thought, but I will not let him bait me. I will be aloof and treat him as a child.

Then Sigismundo was beside him again.

"Hey," Sigismundo said, weaving a bit. "The hell you calling a fool? Elephant nose?"

Carlo thought: You must not, ever, appear to be a coward in public; you are ruined if that happens. But it is stupid to get into a fight over nothing. His family has had much misfortune, and he is drunk. He spoke softly, trying not to attract more of a crowd. "There have been great efforts to make peace between our families. Do not ruin it because you drank too much. Go home and sleep it off."

"I knew you were yellow," Sigismundo said.

It is pitiful, Carlo thought; he is so blind drunk that a baby could knock him over with one finger. "You will fall down in the gutter soon," he said. "Go home and sober up, I tell you."

Carlo walked on with dignity. I am handling this very well, he thought. Just don't walk too fast, now. I must not appear to be running away, as he called it.

But a crowd was beginning to follow them; Sigismundo, like all drunks, was noisier than he realized.

"Well, who does want a fight?" Sigismundo roared, looking around blearily.

Old man Orsini emerged out of the dusk. "You are crazy drunk," he said softly, taking Sigismundo's arm. "It is best that you let me take you home. Already, Carlo would be justified in challenging you to a duel."

Sigismundo was confused: he could not attack an old man. He began to realize that he was behaving abominably.

"I drank too much, the wine," he said. "I am not this sort of person."

"Yes, yes," Orsini said kindly. "But now you will come home, please."

"Thank you," Sigismundo said, weaving again. "I am no good. I have a devil in me. And this world is not our home, I think."

And then everybody heard it at once, coming from the distance, moving faster and faster. It wasn't thunder, they all realized suddenly; it was horses galloping. Orsini dragged Sigismundo out of the street, and others scattered into arches and alleys simultaneously. It burst out of the dusk and night dew all at once; an enormous, gold-decorated carriage; and as it passed, all saw the Maldonado coat of arms on the door. Like fading thunder, it disappeared into the twilight as abruptly as it had come. Suddenly there was silence.

Moira: a knot. The Fates, knitting and cackling, knitting and cackling.

"Carlo," Sigismundo screamed into the murk. "There goes your sister. The Englishman will be ramming it into her all night long. He'll shove it up her arse, too. The English love that."

Old man Orsini sighed loudly and began dragging Sigismundo rapidly uphill.

But Carlo appeared beside them, running.

"You wouldn't shut up, would you?" he panted. "You stupid bastard. You—all right. You want a duel. You shall have a duel."

"He is drunk," Orsini started to say.

"You heard what he said," Carlo panted. "Everybody in the God damn *palazzo* heard him. It is my family honor that has been besmirched."

"I'll kill you," Sigismundo said. "It is Destiny. You don't have a chance." Tennone had recently told him that he was now a master of the sword and could learn no more short of real combat.

"You are the one who doesn't have a chance, you foul-mouthed imbecile," Carlo said bitterly. "I am the offended party. *I* choose the weapons."

Sigismundo began to see with a degree of lucidity again. "What weapons?" he asked, knowing the answer.

"Pistols," Carlo said. "In the field behind the botanical gardens. At dawn."

He's the best pistol shot in Napoli, Sigismundo thought, and I'll have a hangover.

Bad luck and too much wine, Elpenor said.

▲

When they arrived at the Celine household, Sigismundo left Orsini at the gate.

358 ROBERT ANTON WILSON

"I can walk to my room unaided," he said with an attempt at dignity.

If the family learned about this business, he knew, the duel could still be avoided. Uncle Pietro, the master of negotiation, would see Count Maldonado. Even in the middle of the night, even with the count himself probably somewhat drunk from the wedding reception, something could be worked out.

It was possible. Only a dozen or so men had been in the *palazzo* and heard the challenge, and—since dueling was illegal—they would not be talking about it. Yet.

So it might be announced that Sigismundo Celine had received an appointment to teach music theory at the University of Paris. With Uncle Pietro's contacts, such an appointment might even be the truth before Sigismundo was further north than Milano. Carlo would eventually agree, if the count insisted on it, that such an exile was sufficient punishment.

Pietro could negotiate something like that.

But the men who had been in the *palazzo* would know, and eventually they would talk.

"That Celine fellow, who wrote the terrible music, remember? I know why he really left town."

"I was there when it happened. He was as foulmouthed as a Corsican."

"Yes; and when he forced Carlo Maldonado to challenge him, what did he do? Turned tail and ran like a coward."

Sigismundo collapsed on his bed, exhausted and already beginning to feel the hangover.

"They say he's still hiding out in Paris. Afraid to come back."

"Well, how can he come back? A man who's marked as a coward . . ."

The duel could be negotiated away; Uncle Pietro was the man who could sell mud during a rainstorm. But the rumors afterward: they were nonnegotiable. Nothing would stop the rumors.

"Turned tail and ran like a coward."

Christ, Sigismundo thought, it feels as if my head had the drum section of the *teatro* rehearsing inside it.

Everybody has the right to be a damned fool for one day, I told myself. But I forgot that the consequences can last for more than one day—can last for the rest of your life.

Why not let Uncle Pietro negotiate the duel away? Start a whole new life in Paris (or Oxford, or wherever they send the cases too crazy for Napoli)? Does it matter what people in Napoli say, if I am not in Napoli? Does it really make sense to go out there in the dawn, with my head splitting and my hand unsteady, and get myself killed?

There was no use thinking that way; it carried no conviction.

Because I was a Neapolitan before I was a Mason, before I was a musician even, before *anything*; and a Neapolitan does not run away from a fight. That is because we have been conquered so often, Uncle Pietro says. A conquered people develops its own kind of pride.

Sigismundo suddenly wanted water. He wanted to drink a gallon of it and pour another gallon over his head. But he remained on the bed. He would wait a while before attempting to go down the stairs to the well; coming up had been enough of a challenge.

He wondered how many duels had been fought by drunken participants. A great many, probably. Outside the "damnable books of Romance," sober men do not get themselves into this kind of mess. As a matter of fact, Carlo seemed a bit unsteady himself; he had probably been drinking at the wedding reception.

Glorious: the dawn rising on the beautiful botanical garden, and two drunks staggering around, trying to see clearly enough to shoot each other. This is a comedy, Sigismundo decided. Except that one of us or maybe both of us will be dead when it is over.

And I never learned anything about guns, because I dislike them. There is a lesson there: When you hate something, study it, don't ignore it, because it might come into your life anyway.

"Bad luck and too much wine." Even Homer knew that was the quickest way to Hell. And this is the third time: like my initiations. First a joke, then a horror, then the moment of truth.

Sigismundo finally managed to navigate the staircase back to the garden.

I am not so drunk anymore, he thought. I was never once in danger of missing a step and falling. I just have to do everything very slowly for a while.

Once is chance, he thought; twice is coincidence; three times is Destiny. Which is just another name for our bad habits, Uncle Pietro says.

He hauled up a bucket from the well and poured it over his head.

Christ. That was a shock.

But it was necessary. He hauled another bucket and poured it on himself, remembering his baptism, his Masonic raising, his vision of death by water on the English Channel. Three-three-three. *Terza rima.* I'm an extra Canto tacked onto the *Inferno* four centuries late.

He hauled up a third bucket and drank a great deal, then went to the jakes to urinate.

"Nobody buys wine; they just rent it." That was one of Uncle Pietro's favorite jokes.

"This night will curse us all."

He slipped once going back up the stairs.

Let that be a warning. You are going to have to work on

sobering yourself. It will be up and down the stairs for a long time, drinking and urinating, until you are purged.

Sigismundo sat on the bed, looking at his *clavicembalo*, his books, his familiar room that he might never see again if he died at dawn. I don't want to kill him. I don't want to kill anybody. How do we get ourselves into such messes?

Sigismundo breathed deeply. There was only one course of action now. He would have to use everything he had learned of the Craft, to activate the fourth soul and rise above this idiocy that the animal soul had landed him in.

Following Abraham Orfali's instructions, Sigismundo concentrated on his feet, imagining each muscle relaxing, visualizing white light. Gradually, he moved the relaxing light into his calves, his knees, his thighs, into the belly and chest, up from the hands through the arms to the shoulders, into the head. Step by step he tried to relax each face muscle. He was then seeing himself, not as a physical body, but as a lattice of pure light.

Then he began all over. "It never works the first time," Abraham said. "There is always more tension. Start over and do each step a second time."

Sigismundo worked his way up from his feet to his head again. He held the vision of pure light for nearly a minute, remembering the arm movements of his first degree initiation: LVX. Light was the secret, the first matter of the alchemists. God's first commandment was not "Let there be matter," but "Let there be Light."

He was still hung over but definitely feeling better. Time for another perilous voyage on the spiral staircase.

He did not slip or stagger once as he found the well and drank, found the jakes and urinated, ascended the stairs once more.

He sat on the bed, closed his eyes, and relaxed each muscle again, working upward from the feet to the head. When he was feeling himself as weightless light again, he summoned the four archangels. Soon he had them before him in full, vivid detail—Rapha-El in his blue robes, Micha-El in his red, Gabri-El in gold, Auri-El in green. Now the hard part began. Without concentrating on the four guardians, he tried to keep them still present, and he began the Middle Pillar meditation.

The first step was to visualize a white light, about the size of a large melon, floating in the air above his head. Everything else had to be ignored, including the fact that he might be dead in the morning. The white light had to be in perfect focus, until consciousness moved from the pillar of luminosity that had been his body to the sphere of luminosity above it.

Sigismundo then chanted aloud, "AHIH AHIH AHIH." Then he continued the chant, silently, in his mind only. The problem was to keep the sphere of light in focus, remember the four angels at the four quarters, and still sink almost totally into the chant of "AHIH." That meant "I AM" and was the most secret name of God, revealed to Moses.

After several minutes Sigismundo was exhausted and had not even achieved as much success as he had in his first attempts three years ago.

"There is no substitute for hard work, every day," Abraham said. "Or if there is, let me know as soon as you discover it." Sigismundo had not worked hard on this exercise, every day, as he should have. Music and mathematics were more immediately rewarding.

He went back down the stairs and drank more water.

When he returned to the bed, he began again.

He was a pillar of light.

The angels were in focus.

The light above his head was brighter and brighter and brighter . . .

"AHIH AHIH AHIH."

Sigismundo's scalp began to tingle; that was a symptom of success, Abraham said. He concentrated and relaxed at once, trying not to try, trying to let it happen.

There was another tingling in his spine. The light descended, a thousand times brighter than when he had raised it.

He was hardly there at all; the symptoms of hangover were gone.

Now the problem was to hold onto that state and not relapse.

Next, very carefully, the light was centered in the heart; it had to be golden light, not white, in this stage.

The golden light in the chest and the white light above his head interacted. Energy pulsed through him, up and down, up and down. Sigismundo chanted, "IAO IAO IAO," a name of God so secret it wasn't even in the Bible and was known only to the FRC.

After fifteen minutes, Sigismundo's chest was warm and tingling, he felt that the plants in the garden were enjoying this and wanted him to continue, and he was aware that space was not really Euclidean.

Everything went out of focus, and Sigismundo was exhausted.

He lay back on the bed and rested. Then, gradually, he relaxed his feet again, his legs, his torso, his arms, his face. And then he began with the lights above his head and brought himself back to the point where he had failed.

Sigismundo kept the white light in focus above his head and the gold light in his heart and added a pink light around his genitalia. He chanted, "ARARITA ARARITA ARARITA," a word of power created by taking the initials of a Hebrew sentence that meant, "One in His origin, One in His permutations, One in His essence."

"ARARITA ARARITA ARARITA."

I deserve to die in this duel: I brought it on myself.

The lights went out, and Sigismundo sank back on the bed again, exhausted.

"This night will curse us all."

Sigismundo walked carefully down the stairs to the jakes and urinated. He didn't need any more water, he decided. The purgation was proceeding well enough.

Sigismundo relaxed and started all over, one more time.

Relax the feet. The legs. The belly . . .

The light above the head: "AHIH AHIH AHIH . . ."

The golden light in the heart: "IAO IAO IAO . . ."

The pink erotic light: "ARARITA ARARITA ARA-RITA . . .",

The theory was that if you could keep all three light glowing simultaneously, the Rose Cross would form, Dante's "Love that moves the sun and other stars," and the center of consciousness would shift entirely out of the vegetative reflexes, entirely out of the animal emotion, entirely out of human conceptualizing, into the fourth soul, the I AM, the only Mind in the universe.

But Peppino had believed that there was another Mind, an opposing Mind, one that wanted to remake the universe, turn it into something better. Lucifer, the Light Bringer, the Rebel.

That other, opposing Mind was the Devil, the church taught.

It was not the Devil, the Rose Cross Order taught. It did not exist at all. It was an illusion. There was only one Mind.

The three lights were in perfect focus.

Nothing else existed.

The lights united. Sigismundo was aware of himself breathing slowly and easily, in his bedroom, in the Celine villa, high on a hill in Napoli, on the continent of Europe, on the planet earth, in the system of nine planets circling the Inner Sun, in a vast turning spiral, in the womb, in the pink erotic waters, midway between existence and nonexistence.

In vast labyrinthine silence.

▲

The light was far, far away at first, but it approached at a dazzling speed. He remembered canto one of the *Purgatorio*, when Dante first sees that kind of light: *Kneel, kneel*, Virgil had cried, *it is an angel of the Lord.*

The light overwhelmed him. He had an instant of pure horror, thinking it would destroy him, then he didn't care if it destroyed him. He came apart as if his body was indeed made of the atoms of Epicurus and every atom was hurtling away from every other atom.

There was no center, no One Mind, no Sigismundo. There were a million Sigismundos, going in a million directions, living in all parts of space and time.

All of Napoli flowed through Sigismundo; he flowed through all of Napoli. He was beyond Napoli, beyond the world, and it all came together. Quite suddenly, it was unity in infinite diversity: the One Mind, the fourth soul, the I AM. Infinite space. Infinite stars. Infinite play.

Everything was wax and melting in the eternal fire that was not Hell but Paradise. Animals, fish, plants, stars, lattices, energies; melting, flaming.

In vast labyrinthine silence.

▲

He was remembering being a snake, an insect, a tree. It was all going by too fast, and he had to find "his" body again.

▲

He was back in the body of Sigismundo Celine, a male body, twenty years old, in the year 1770, in Europe.

The fact is, he decided, I never went "out" of the body and I never came "back into it." Space and time have nothing to do with this at all. There are no words for what really happens. I was never "in" the body anymore than a sonata is "in" the instrument.

"The Spirit of God moved upon the face of the waters and gave them form."

I am the Spirit of God who moves upon the waters, the fiery flux, and makes all the forms.

I don't know what I'm thinking.

The light was not a blinding flash any longer; that had been some sort of explosion or spasm in his brain. It was the part of Chaos that the brain experienced when losing one set of circuits and reorganizing itself upon a new set of circuits. The light was a simple lucidity now; nothing was overwhelmed by it, but everything was seen more clearly in this illumination.

It was indeed I AM because it was nothing more complicated than his own mind purged of the habits and limits of a lifetime. Purged, too, of desire and fear, of vanity and shame; more like a mirror than a sun: reflective.

And so he waited then, without anxiety and without impatience, listening to his soft breathing, lost in the vast labyrinthine silence, knowing his invulnerability. Having died a million times, he knew that death didn't change anything; the universe had died a million times in those few minutes, and it was back again, too.

The habit of seeing everything but his thoughts as "outside" was only a mind construct, as Hume would say. He could see everything was inside or as outside or as both. It was most amusing, he decided, to hold the double perspective and see everything as both inside and outside simultaneously.

A bird began to sing.

The sound was louder than thunder; he realized that he had never completely heard a birdsong before, because he had never been in the vast labyrinthine silence before.

He listened, enthralled.

The bird sang on, and he became the song. He flowed into the bird, the bird flowed into him. They were singing: they were not singing: there was only the song. More birds joined in. It seemed as if he could hear each one of them, all the way down the hill, all across Napoli, flowing into the worms, into the living earth itself. There was no Sigismundo again.

He came back slowly, not rushing it this time, to the single focus. The sun was beginning to bleed into the darkness, and the sky was turning pink, light like a rose opening. Brother Sun, Sister Moon, he thought: San Francesco was not being fanciful when he wrote that.

Sigismundo took off his damp clothes, washed quickly, and dressed in his best outfit.

By the time the sky was fully aglow, he was standing outside the gate on the street, waiting.

And when the seconds arrived, he greeted them quietly, knowing his infinity, and smiled slightly, not bravely or boldly as he had imagined himself smiling, but simply seeing it all with great amusement, since he had never seen clearly before, still lost in the vast silence like an empty cathedral at midnight: everything left an echo.

And as they walked toward the botanical garden Sigismundo looked about him with awe, as Adam must have looked at Eden on the first morning, seeing every bush, every flower, every petal with that new vision, knowing his invulnerability. He could walk away from it all; he didn't even have to leave Napoli. He could stay right here, with the whole town calling him coward, and that would not matter, since he was no longer Sigismundo Celine but the one Mind, the only Mind, temporarily playing at being Sigismundo Celine. On the other hand, this duel was his destiny, and it did not really matter one way or the other. It was enough just to smell the dawn, the freshness of everything waking after night, and to notice the dew clinging to a rose petal.

In the vast labyrinthine silence, knowing his invulnerability, he did not care that Sigismundo Celine was a damned fool a great deal of the time and might die for his latest foolishness. He did not care that Sigismundo Celine was a very bright fellow at times and might make important contributions to music or to mechanics (the *autokinoton* was possible, somehow), or to some field or other, if he ever got his head straightened out and decided what his real talent was. It was funny, in a sad way, that Sigismundo Celine got drunk and acted like a brute and an idiot because he thought one woman was more important than the rest of the world; but that was the kind of idiocy to which Sigismundo Celine was prone, like many other young males.

He wondered what Maria was actually like. The phantom in his mind, the goddess he had created, was just the fifth soul trying to wake the fourth soul: Shechinah, the embodied glory of God, which always takes a female form, as Abraham had taught him. Who was the actual Maria, the woman he had confused with this eternal presence? He knew less about her than about the continent of Antarctica.

In a sense, he thought, I am still Sigismundo Celine; I have to live out his life. That was sad and funny, since he knew Sigismundo Celine was no more solid than a sonata. Being all mindforms, he could adopt that form, the Sigismundo form, again; but he could also walk away from it any time and watch it. The fourth soul is like being an actor on the stage, he thought, and also like being in the audience watching the whole drama, and being the author Himself.

And now they were crossing the botanical garden and entering the field.

Carlo and his seconds were waiting.

Sigismundo suddenly felt a vast, unexpected wave of compassion. Carlo looked very nervous, even though he was the best pistol shot in Napoli. The poor boy, Sigismundo thought;

he imagines that if "Carlo Maldonado" dies, he will cease to
exist.

The four seconds were conferring. They tossed a coin three
times. It was decided that Portinari, the barber-surgeon, would
give the shout of "Fire" at the appropriate time.

Carlo was formally asked, as the offended party, if he would
accept an apology; if he agreed, Sigismundo would then be
asked to offer the apology.

"No," Carlo said, white-lipped. "You all heard what he said
about my sister."

Another bird began to sing. Just one bird this time
—Sigismundo did not recognize its call: perhaps some voyager
from the north on its way to Africa for the winter—and he was
at one with it, as he was at one with all things, having become
the Inner Sun, the single star, the source of every permutation
of consciousness. He smiled again, knowing his invulnerability.

So when the pistol in the velvet-lined dueling case was
handed to him, he took it without any emotion and examined it
carefully. It required none of the art of the sword. You merely
had to point correctly and fire quickly, and Newton's laws
would do the rest.

I will aim for the shoulder, Sigismundo decided; he is
nervous and I am not, so I can shoot first. Then all this
damned-fool honor business will be satisfied. Old Portinari will
have the bullet out of him in ten minutes, before blood
poisoning or anything like that can happen.

He walked his ten paces with the serenity of a monk telling
his beads on a rosary and turned, cocking the hammer, waiting.
Even at twenty paces, he could see the sweat on Carlo's face.

The strange northern bird sang again—one moment of
pure music, like a trill by Scarlatti, suspended in eternity.

"*Fire!*" shouted Portinari.

▲

The knocking was interminable, like some idiot child who

has just found a drum and pounds and bangs on it until you think you will go deaf. It went on and on, gradually dragging Pietro Malatesta out of his sleep.

"The servants," he muttered. "God blast. Why hasn't one of the servants answered it?"

But then he realized that the knocking had stopped—one of the servants *had* answered it—and now there were thudding steps on the stairway.

I am an old man, he thought. I have had enough troubles to fill three novels and a grand opera. Let me sleep.

But no; the steps had come to the bedroom door, and now there was a gentle rapping.

"What is it?" he growled. I will absolutely and positively not get out of bed for anything less than a summons from the palace, he thought, and I will politely tell them to wait until morning. I will not get dressed and go out unless it's the Second Coming of Christ accompanied by angels with trumpets.

"Pardon, *signor*. Very bad news."

I sell the damned stuff and know what it does to my customers; you would think I'd have enough sense, at my age, not to drink it myself. Oh, God. I think my head is full of goblins with meat cleavers.

Pietro shuffled to the door.

It was Paolo, the gardener. Naturally: his house was nearest the gate; he would be the first one wakened.

"Pardon, *signor*. It is Signor Orsini. He must speak with you. Your nephew Sigismundo is fighting a duel in a few hours."

"I'll be right down," Pietro said.

He groped his way to the washstand and poured the pitcher of water over his head. Sigismundo is special, he told himself. It is not his fault, the damned fool things he does. The power drives us mad until we learn to control it. I was a fool at his age, too. I must be calm. I must not rush at once to his house and kick his arse from here to Baghdad and back.

"What?" Violetta mumbled, almost sitting up. "Is?"

"Nothing," he said, "Sleep, beautiful woman."

"Um," she said, settling back.

I wonder if she really is still beautiful at her age, Pietro mused as he dressed. Or is that just one of the delusions I prefer not to get rid of?

Of course I have to stop this idiot duel. At my age. In the middle of the night.

I'll be sixty next December.

Maybe the stars are right: maybe Sigismundo is under protection until his destiny is achieved. Then I can just go back to bed and wait for the elephants in my head to stop dancing.

No. That is a delusion I cannot afford.

But by the time he had his boots on, he was thinking clearly again. Just another merry day with those fun-loving Malatestas, some casual slaughter before breakfast. At least the boy knows how to use a sword, thank God.

When Pietro arrived in the living room, Orsini looked ghastly. Of course, Pietro thought; he's been up half the night worrying if it was proper to intervene.

"Thank you for coming here," Pietro said at once, making a mental note to send the Orsinis a case of wine the next day. (Always reward the bringers of information, whether the news is good or bad: that was one of his basic rules. It guaranteed that he would know more news faster than anybody else in Napoli.) "Tell me whom my idiot nephew is planning to murder."

"Carlo Maldonado," Orsini said unhappily. "But it is your nephew who is in danger."

"Oh?" Pietro realized what that meant. "Carlo was the offended party and picked the weapons?"

"Yes."

"Pistols, of course."

"I am sorry to tell you this."

"Damn." Pietro grimaced. He's been fencing for ten years now, so naturally he gets himself into a duel with pistols. Against a fellow who is said to be able to shoot the hind leg off a crab louse at twenty yards, riding backward. "Where?"

"Behind the botanical garden. At dawn."

Pietro glanced at the clock on the mantel. Twenty-three minutes after five.

At this time of year, dawn was about a half hour away.

Pietro seized Orsini's hand. "Your kindness will be remembered," he said warmly. "The Malatestas will always be your friends." He was already moving Orsini toward the door, grabbing his own cloak as he went.

No time to get to see Count Maldonado, he was thinking. No time for anything but a mad dash to the botanical garden.

No time for diplomacy or negotiations, no time for wheeling and dealing, no time for any of my tricks. All I can do is try to be there before the shooting stars. And then? Then I improvise.

He thanked Orsini several times more before they parted.

Then, he did not attempt to run. With a few gallons of champagne aboard and fifty-nine years of tiredness in his bones, he knew he would just collapse of exhaustion. He walked rapidly, not letting his heart overtax itself, slowing once or twice when he heard himself panting; he kept a good pace, constantly scanning the east, watching for the first streaks of sunrise; he was doing the relaxing breath and visualizing the Inner Sun.

There is no sense planning anything, since it all depends on when I arrive. I will just have to trust my instincts. There is only one Mind; if I am empty enough, that Mind will act through me. I may not have the power Abraham has, but I have over thirty years of practice by now. Relax, be alert, and remember the eight invisible aides. My habits will carry me through.

Ex Deo nascimur: in Jesu morimur: per Spiritum Sanctum reviviscimus.

And then he saw a streak of rose on the horizon.

Don't run. You are almost there.

·But the rose was turning into a huge fireball of orange.

"He hath given me power to run through a troop and leap over a wall," the Psalmist said. He, the fourth soul, does not know space, time, or limits.

Pietro Malatesta ran. Like a boy of nineteen, as if forty years were removed in the twinkling of an eye, the Psalmist's words repeating again and again in his head, he ran; ran through the gate of the botanical garden, seeing the whole sky eaten by tangerine fire; ran among the lilies and roses and cosmos and daffodils; ran toward the field where he could now see the small group standing about; ran faster as he recognized Sigismundo pacing out his ten feet in one direction and Carlo Maldonado pacing in the other direction; ran and ran and ran, repeating, "He hath given me power to run through a troop and leap over a wall."

He appeared racing across the field with the speed of a deer just as Portinari shouted, "Fire!"

"*Stop!*" screamed Pietro.

Everybody jumped as two shots rang out.

▲

Sigismundo heard the shout of "*Stop!*" and recognized the voice even before he involuntarily turned toward the source of that voice and he jerked the trigger automatically and then the whole universe exploded. He was thinking that the gun had a terrible kick to it before realizing, admitting, that he was hit, that the world was not being destroyed by fire but that it was only his own body contorting with pain: there seemed to be millions and millions of suns (just as Bruno said), and each sun was going out, one by one, as the cosmos plunged into deathly darkness and chaos. But that was only his body; it wasn't really the whole universe. It was like crossing the English Channel on that boat, the waters all cold and choppy, and he was falling off the boat into the cold waters, his whole body freezing, teeth chattering like the night he dived again and again for Antonio. And he was going down, down, down and then coming up, up, up as he realized that Portinari was probing his shoulder with a hot knife.

Water and fire are one.

"Damn," Portinari said. "It went right through you. Jesus, somebody check Pietro."

"My God, he's hit, too," a voice shouted.

"I thought he just fainted from the exertion of running like that," Portinari's voice said, going away. "Hell, it must have been the bullet that went through Sigismundo."

Everybody has a right to be a damned fool for one day, Sigismundo thought. That's what I told myself, and now my uncle may be dying because of it.

He didn't even think of Carlo yet.

He was lying on his back in the field, in Napoli, not watching whole solar systems explode and die.

He sat up.

"Hey, you, don't try to move," Portinari's voice shouted.

Sigismundo got to his feet. The field immediately tilted crazily to the left and the sky started spinning, but he was able to stay erect. He felt like an afterbirth when the midwife wraps it in old rags and buries it in the backyard: but he stayed on his feet.

Portinari was crouching over Uncle Pietro's body, about fifty feet away. "Stay down," he shouted back at Sigismundo. "I can't take care of two of you at once."

Sigismundo took a step and stumbled.

Toward the One, the perfection of love, harmony, and beauty . . .

He fell, and the pain exploded all over him again. He was diving again, but there was no bottom to the bay and Antonio was nowhere in the inky blackness. His teeth chattered, and sweat stung his eyes. Chills and fever: I'm dying, maybe.

One of Carlo's seconds was leaning over him. "You'll start the bleeding again, you damned fool. I'll check your uncle for you. Stay down."

"It's my fault," Sigismundo said. "I am a devil."

Toward the One, the perfection of love, harmony, and beauty, the only Being, united with all those illuminated souls . . .

He lurched to his feet again and promptly puked down the front of his shirt. He went on retching for what seemed like a long time while the grass and sky kept whirling around and around him. *I am not here; remember that. I am the fourth soul, outside of all this, looking in. We do not stand on our legs but on our Will.*

He staggered forward, toward Uncle Pietro.

"Hold that idiot down," somebody yelled.

This night will curse us all.

I will return as millions.

Moira: a knot.

Sigismundo fell again; but he was closer to Uncle Pietro now. Rest a minute, he thought. Try to stop the chattering of the teeth, so that I don't bite my tongue off. Visualize the light. Breathe.

Now. Try again.

"Sit on him," a voice shouted. "He'll kill himself if he gets up again."

He was sitting, not quite able to stand again quite yet. One of the seconds was looking down at him.

"How's Carlo?" he asked.

"Not good. You shot him in the groin."

"Jesus," Sigismundo said. "I aimed for his shoulder."

He was on his feet again. Pain is nothing, he told himself. Only cowards stop when they feel pain.

Take me there, he prayed. I can't do it alone.

He walked, lurching wildly in all directions, stumbling toward the place where Portinari was working over Uncle Pietro. The smell of his own vomit on his shirt made him nauseated again, and the sky kept spinning in circles.

Toward the One, the perfection of love, harmony, and beauty, the only Being, united with all those illuminated souls who form the embodiment of the Teacher, the spirit of guidance. Take me there. There is only You. I am You, the flowers are You, Carlo is You. Take me there.

He fell again, and the waves washed over him, taking him down, down, down into the well, into the cold waters.

He was crawling over the red-hot coals of Hell. The Dominicans were right, after all; he would spend infinite hours and infinite days in infinite torment for all his sins. He crawled onward, blinded by his sweat, seeking to regain his unity with the One Mind, and the red-hot coals became sweet green grass again.

Uncle Pietro turned his head and looked at him.

"At last," Pietro said.

"What?"

"At last . . . free . . . damnable books . . ."

Then Pietro's eyes glazed and the waves came up again and Sigismundo went into freezing blackness.

▲

"What a mess," Count Maldonado said. "What a perfect, classic Neapolitan mess."

Sir John and the count were sitting in the garden, and neither of them were quite ready to accept the relief that the doctor's words had brought.

"Your son will live," Sir John said. "Just remember that."

"I know. I can hardly believe it. The way my Carlo looked

when they brought him home . . . I thought he was a dead man."

"Maria was praying all the way back here in the coach."

"She is a good girl, and her prayers have power."

"We should all be grateful to Pietro Malatesta," Sir John said. "If he hadn't shouted when he did, one of the bullets might have been fatal. He made them both jump, I gather."

"Pietro is the cleverest man in Napoli," the Count said. "I suppose, yesterday, he realized that it was too late for cleverness, so he just made noise. Well, it was good enough. It saved my son's life, perhaps. Still, the nature of the wound—I can never forgive that."

"The doctor said he couldn't be sure," Sir John said. "The bullet entered nearly an inch above the . . . generative organ. Carlo is in no sense a eunuch."

"I know," the count said. "Some men have been wounded there and still fathered children. But the doctor could not say for sure which tubes and arteries were destroyed. It is *God-awful*. Imagine yourself Carlo's age and imagine going to bed with a woman and wondering if you can still perform. It is *unspeakable*."

I'd better not say, "He can always become a monk," Sir John thought.

"Just be glad your son is alive," he repeated gently.

The count sighed, looking out over the hedges and flower beds. "Such a beautiful day," he said. "And I don't know if my son is a rooster or a capon."

"How long should I leave Maria with Carlo?" Sir John asked.

"As long as she wants to stay by the bed. Her prayers are powerful, and I have seen men die of complications after the doctors said they were recovering."

"Very well. In that case," Sir John said, "I think I shall stroll over to Via Capodimonte and pay respects to Pietro Malatesta."

"Yes. Both as a brother Mason and a relative stranger, you are the perfect negotiator at this point. That idiot boy, Sigismundo, must leave Napoli. That is the condition. If this ever got to court, exile would be the *least* punishment. But assure Pietro of my continued esteem for him personally."

"Of course." Sir John stood. "And if Maria does come down, tell her I'll be back in an hour."

But midway on his walk the depression came over him. I must not be superstitious, he thought. It is nonsense to regard this imbecile duel as an omen or anything of that sort. She loves me and I love her; we can find that happy, safe space again. When we return to England, all this will be forgotten. I must not let myself think that the marriage coach has somehow turned into a hearse.

Then he admitted that it was not the duel that was oppressing him. Three wounded, but none dead: it was almost a happy ending to what could have been tragedy.

His dark mood was caused by something he did not want to notice: a boy walking ahead of him on the street, a boy he did not want to stare at, a boy with the grace of an Athenian statue.

▲

After three days, the doctor said Sigismundo could take a walk anytime he wished, as long as he didn't go too far or overexert himself.

Sigismundo went straight to the ghetto and found Dr. Orfali's shop.

As usual, the bell rang and old Abraham came from behind the curtain. Sigismundo again thought of a cuckoo clock.

"You do not look bad for a boy with a hole through his shoulder," Abraham said.

"It's healing. I even played the *clavicembalo* this morning. A little."

"Come in the back, where we can sit," Abraham said.

Sigismundo remembered his first visit to that room and the first glimpse of the four guardian angels.

"So," Abraham said, sitting comfortably. "You have come here to be denounced, no? Hasn't Pietro chewed you out enough already? You need more?"

Sigismundo waited.

"It isn't that," Abraham said. "Oh, how stupid of me. You have found the fourth soul."

"You can tell just by looking at me?"

"How big is it?"

Sigismundo smiled.

"How old is it?"

Sigismundo laughed.

"So. You went all the way. What do you want from me then?"

"It wasn't the way it's supposed to be. I had to get drunk and make a fool of myself and shout obscenities in public. I almost killed Carlo. I almost got my uncle killed, too, for that matter. I am a beautiful example of everything a Mason should not be. I do not *deserve* the fourth soul."

"Never say that," Abraham said, suddenly angry. "*Everybody* deserves it. You know that when you are in your right mind."

"I have been a bigger fool than ever and have disgraced my family. And now I have to go into exile like a common criminal."

"And you have lost the fourth soul already—I can see that, too. Don't worry. Once you have been there, you can always find your way back. It is easier the second time."

"I may have emasculated Carlo," Sigismundo cried. "That puts me in some elite corps with Aunt Gina. We should change the company sign—Malatesta and Celine, Fine Wines and Gelding. We could get an exclusive contract, providing *castrati* for the Vatican choir. If we get any better, we could supply the guards for the Arab hareems, too."

"You *did* come here to be denounced."

"No. All I have to do is think of Carlo's eyes, looking at me. That will denounce me for a lifetime."

"Listen. To find the fourth soul requires forgiveness. How many times have you heard me say that? That means forgiving yourself, too, even though that is hardest of all and takes longest of all."

"My ordinary mind," Sigismundo said wearily, "is so stupid."

"So is mine. And the minds of the rats and fish and trees. Only the one Mind is lucid."

"I know, I know," Sigismundo said tiredly. "But—"

"You think you are a disgrace to the Craft. You think others are more worthy. You think it isn't fair that you have attained illumination and more worthy men haven't. Forget all that. Remember the widow's son."

"It can happen even to fools like me," Sigismundo said. "Because God's ways are inscrutable. Is that what you mean?"

Abraham laughed. "It only happens to fools like you," he said. "Or me," he added mischievously.

And looking into the old man's eyes, Sigismundo suddenly saw a youth much like himself, sixty years ago, getting into all sorts of follies.

▲

Sir John and Lady Babcock sailed for England on July 23, 1770.

Sigismundo was inconspicuously lurking near the dock when the ship sailed. He had no illusions about Maria anymore: she was a total stranger. Whether they would have been compatible at all, if matters had worked out differently, was just another unsolved question. Whoever and whatever she was, he wished her well; Babcock was a true Mason and a true lover of liberty. He wished them both well. Seeing her depart was just a ritual act, completing his cure from the delusions he had had about her.

Sigismundo himself left Napoli the following week. There were no legal problems; Count Maldonado and Uncle Pietro had paid the right bribes to the right people, and even though half of Napoli knew there had been another illegal duel behind the botanical garden, the police (officially) did not know it. Sigismundo was eager to start over, somewhere else, and the University of Paris was said to have one of the best Natural Philosophy departments in the world. Electricity, on which the faculty there were particularly keen, might be part of the answer to some of his problems with the autokinoton.

Uncle Pietro was uncharacteristically brief in his words of advice on parting. "Get yourself a mistress," he said bluntly. "Otherwise, you'll end up haunting those *maisons* and acquire a classic case of the French pox. Don't borrow from professional moneylenders; write to me if you're short. And for God Almighty's sake, *never* play cards with a Corsican."

▲

Once, on the coach, Sigismundo woke from an erotic dream. Nobody was staring at him—the other passengers were all dozing—so he hadn't talked in his sleep, fortunately.

Still: it was odd to be dreaming about Maria again; he had put that folly firmly behind him. Besides, she was the wife of a brother Mason now, and however many kinds of fool and scoundrel Sigismundo might be at times, he would certainly never break the Masonic trust by seducing a brother's wife. And she probably hated him for shooting her brother. And she was in another country. The dream was an obvious absurdity: he would never see Maria again.

He was sure of it.

▲

When classes began at the University of Paris in the autumn of 1770, Sigismundo had found comfortable lodgings in the Rive Gauche and was enrolled in chemistry, music theory, advanced calculus, and physics.

He had begun to discover a Paris that he had not explored on his first brief visit. Whenever he walked about in search of the mistress he knew he really needed in order to avoid the *maisons*, he noticed how filthy the streets were. The worst parts of Napoli were small in comparison to the whole; the worst parts of Paris were most of Paris. Women, he learned, did not get out of coaches at all if they could avoid it; the streets were so dirty that their skirts would be ruined in half a block.

The newspapers printed every detail about the growing unrest in the British colonies of North America, so that everybody who could read knew that a mob had attacked British soldiers in New York City in January and another mob had attacked another British platoon in Boston in March. It is as if, Sigismundo thought, they want everybody to know how a revolution starts, as if they look on what is taking place in America as a rehearsal.

At the university, egalitarianism was not regarded as a radical notion by either students or professors; it was an inevitability, and the only question was, *How soon?* If I told them I am half-peasant, Sigismundo thought, they would take me on tour, as an exhibit proving that all men are born equal and only society determines their differences.

And then on December 17, sitting in an outdoor café, Sigismundo saw the Bavarian lawyer he had met in Abbeville at the time of the La Barre atrocity. "Herr Zoesser," he called out at once.

The obese Bavarian stopped and stared. "Signor Celine, *n'estce pas?*" he asked hesitantly. "Of course! It's been years."

"Have a seat," Sigismundo said. "How long will you be staying?"

Zoesser was as bland as ever. "I am now permanently in Paris," he said. "The Bavarian climate became, um, a bit uncomfortable for me."

That was not a slip, Sigismundo realized.

"It is good to see you again," he said, holding out his hand. Their fingers probed and formed the grip.

Sigismundo was not surprised. Zoesser's opinions would draw him to Masonry eventually; maybe he had been a Fellow of the Craft as far back as their meeting in Abbeville.

"I am more or less permanently in Paris myself," Sigismundo said. "At least, until I have learned what I want to learn at the university."

"How long have you been here?" Zoesser asked cordially.

"More than three months."

Zoesser lowered his voice. "Have you contacted a lodge yet?"

"No. There are so many rival lodges in France these days, I'm not sure which one is closest to what we consider the true Craft in Napoli." Sigismundo added pointedly, "I don't want to get associated with a gang of atheists."

Zoesser nodded. "Atheism is a bit extreme," he said carefully. "Still, it's inevitable—for a while. An absolute church eventually produces an absolute opposition . . . But I think I know what would suit your principles. The Grand Orient Lodge of Egyptian Freemasonry."

"Is its goal the same as that of the Neapolitan lodges?"

"I have never been in Napoli," Zoesser said, "but I have met other Neapolitan Masons, and I think I understand your principles. The Egyptian lodge will be most compatible. They, too, aim at expanding the mind to form higher selves."

"How do I contact them?"

"I will be glad to take you to a meeting. Actually, I have joined several lodges, since I still travel a great deal. I think the conflicts that are developing among rival factions are dreadful, and, in my small way, I hope to be a force for mediation between them."

"*There are no accidents*," Sigismundo said. "It is providential that we met today."

"Greetings on *all three points of the triangle*," Zoesser quoted.

They smiled.

"Well," Sigismundo said. "Tell me more about the Egyptian lodge."

"The grand master is Philippe, duc de Chartres. If succession falls the right way, he may be the next king. Or the one after next. Can you imagine an illuminated monarch? It would be Plato's dream fulfilled—"

"Who else?"

"I can assure you, most of the leading minds of the country, um, aside from the totally fanatic revolutionaries. We have one man who holds the thirty-second degree, just below Chartres himself, called Count Cagliostro. He is the greatest healer I have ever encountered. Some say he performs actual miracles. Just sit with him five minutes and look into his strange violet eyes and you will feel as if you have left this planet entirely and visited other worlds."

"Cagliostro?" Sigismundo exclaimed. "He is Italian, too?"

"Yes. Now that I think of it, he even looks a bit like you. Around the eyes."

You will visit many lands and cross the ocean, but in the end you will come to us . . .

"I will be most interested to meet this Count Cagliostro," Sigismundo said.

It began to snow, just a few lonely flakes at first, then a flurry. Sigismundo and Zoesser moved their cups to an indoor table and watched as the white crystals took on the obvious character of an oncoming storm. The flakes came faster and thicker, and soon the street and the neighboring rooftops lay under a coating of purest white: the color of purity, Sigismundo thought, in both Catholicism and Masonry; the color that was all colors and yet no color really. Under the oncoming winds Paris seemed to crouch, waiting.

ABOUT THE AUTHOR

Robert Anton Wilson, in addition to being the author of more than fifteen books, including *Sex and Drugs*, *A Journey Beyond Limits*, *The Illuminatus Trilogy*, *The Schrodinger's Cat Trilogy*, and *Prometheus Rising*, is a former *Playboy* editor, a philosopher, and a well-known iconoclast.

Watch for

THE WIDOW'S SON

Volume II of the Historical
Illuminatus Chronicles

coming in December from Lynx!